The story of Jesus has been told from many points of view and from many sources, and there is always need for fresh inspiration in interpreting the life which is the subject of the Gospels. In this long, panoramic novel, Robert Payne has recreated the life of the shepherd Yeshua of Nazareth, from his childhood as the son of the carpenter Joseph to the time of his baptism in the Jordan by his cousin Yona. The author's aim, which has been achieved with a brilliant intensity of vision, is to tell a credible story of the growth of the young Jewish prophet at the time when the Jewish people daily awaited the coming of the Messiah and to set it against the turbulent history and the harsh, yet beautiful, landscape of ancient Palestine.

Vividly written, this important religious novel combines a free treatment of description and emotion with reverence for the great central character. A portrait emerges of a man who believed very early in life that he was the Messiah and who tested that belief in the fires of his soul; who saw bloodshed and murder from the hills of Nazareth; who travelled widely and spoke many languages and was aware of the cultures of Egypt and Greece while retaining, until he could retain it no more, a belief in the Hebrew tradition: a man possessed of inner violence and quiet fearlessness, living at a time of upheaval astonishingly like our own.

For the sources of his story Mr. Payne has ranged wide, and much that might seem invented has, in fact, authority behind it. He makes use of the long-continuing Eastern tradition that the Virgin was born in Sep-

The Shepherd

BOOKS BY ROBERT PAYNE

FICTION

Singapore River

David and Anna

Love and Peace

The Chinese Soldier

The Lion Roars

A Bear Coughs at the North Pole

The Blue Nigger and other Stories

The Lord Comes

The Great Mogul

The Lovers

The Chieftain

Red Lion Inn

The Emperor

Harvest

The Shepherd

POETRY

Songs

The Granite Island

BIOGRAPHY

Mao Tse-tung

The Great God Pan

General Marshall

The Fathers of the Western Church

The Gold of Troy

TRAVEL

China Awake

Journey to Red China

Journey to Persia

Forever China

GENERAL

Fabulous America

Zero

The Revolt of Asia

The Wanton Nymph

BY
ROBERT PAYNE

HORIZON PRESS   NEW YORK   1959

THE
SHEPHERD

Contents

ישעיהו

Overleaf: An Aramaic inscription found on a piece of pottery dating from the time of Jesus

The Valley

All winter the earth lay white and cracked beneath the hills while the snow fell and the small gullies bled the snows along the slopes, yet the sound of these rippling waters did not disturb the silence of the hidden valley. Ghostly and quiet the valley nestled there, and sometimes even on the coldest days there would come inexplicable warm winds tumbling over the high hills. On such days soft footfalls echoed in the streets, while houses shone in saffron sunlight under the immense blue of the sky, dripping with icicles; and on these days the dying cactuses were eaten at the roots and the moss crumbled to powder. No flowers grew beneath the winter sun, but the frost sparkled on the roofs and, if you stood on the slopes among the pomegranates and the lemon trees, you would see the flaring of frost like a glitter of swords in the sun, there in the little nest of clustered houses in the hollow. And sometimes, and especially at night, the black panthers came down from the hills, and always there were small white carrion eagles circling the heavens.

Those winters, when the sound of a smithy or of a woman washing at the well or a girl singing came sharp as ice upon the snowy silence of the place, were not forbidding. The winds driving across the Plain of Esdraelon rarely dipped into the hollow cup among the mountains; and while the gales blew overhead, the mulberry trees and cypresses in the valley remained stiff, un-changing and somehow solemn, and so it was with the people of the town, who aged slowly and seemed remote from the changing of the seasons. Winter left them untouched and gave them seclu-sion, concealed them from the great highways which led to Idu-mea in the south and all the coastal ports of the west; a retinue of Arab princes or a Roman legion with glittering pikes might pass within three miles of the town and still no one would know of their coming. So in this hidden valley, where the snow-white houses clung to the slopes, men lived in quietness and peace.

Then when the first rains fell and the snows melted on the plain, the cracked gullies opened wide, the small green lizards crept from their hiding places in the rocks and you heard the water roaring deep in the wells. Quite suddenly in the space of two or three days the valley changed from white to green, and the snow vanished from the sky. The roots of things creaked and pushed up through the frozen earth; and there came to your nostrils the sharp fermenting smell of the warm and buried loam. Where previously there were only a few stunted thorn-bushes on the crests, and the stiff cypresses and mulberries on the slopes, now the whole valley turned green, with here and there sheets of scarlet anemones glowing like burnished metal. Even the gnarled black olive trees turned green, and so did the pomegranates and quinces. Then the blue rain-heads came, and all the valley was silver with rain, and the wells flooded over; but the rain-heads passed, and soon there were only warm winds tasting of the snows.

They used to say of Nazareth that nothing had ever happened there: that in this protected hollow no history had ever penetrated. But it was not so. Men hid there whenever the armies fought across the Plain of Esdraelon: there were caves in the hills and underground passages carved out of the limestone rocks. It was a place of refuge in defeat and a place to sally from when the enemy passed unsuspecting across the Plain.

The people of the valley rarely journeyed abroad. They clung to this little hollow cup and the crests of the low hills. From these crests you could look out upon the whole world. You could see the blue Mediterranean in the west with the ships riding at anchor in the bay of Ptolemais and follow the grain fleets of Egypt and Phoenician merchantmen from Tyre and Sidon as they plied up and down the coast. You could look out upon the heights of

Ephraim and the green hills of Gilead and the endless desert
stretching to the east, and far in the north the snow gleamed on
Mount Hermon, and close at hand lay Mount Tabor with its oaken
groves, and still closer lay the city of Sepphoris with its high
walls. And then, having looked, you could dip down into the valley
again, the world forgotten, and the fierce sea winds roaring harm-
lessly overhead.

In spring the people of Nazareth came to life. If you threw
your arms around an almond tree, you could hear the sap racing
up the green stems. It was the same with the people. The drowsy
calm of winter gave place to vigorous excitement. You saw it in
the glistening eyes of the men and the way the women carried
themselves, the way the young girls danced on the threshing floor.
On these spring days the scents of jonquils, lilies and roses came
to sting the nostrils; the valley became a basket of flowers, with
flaming marigolds and wild pinks and clusters of cyclamen and
bee-orchis growing in all the clefts of the hills; and the crags were
thick with scrub and ilex.

On these spring days when the air smelled like wine, the people
of Nazareth walked knee-deep among lilies, and the sound of their
singing could be heard on the high road to Damascus four miles
away. Pale after winter, the women's cheeks took on color, and
the men sauntered gaily, as though they thought they would live
forever. Mostly they were thickset and handsome, with deep blue
eyes and reddish hair. An unusual number of them limped, and
many had eyelids which looked swollen. Certainly there was no
other town in the neighborhood where the eyelids were so heavy
or so thickly veined.

With summer came the locusts of noon and the scorched winds
from the hills of Samaria. The corn turned bronze in the uplands,
the anemones shriveled, the dust settled on the white-washed
houses, and for a few weeks the women appeared veiled. Soon the
air grew heavy and still, weighed down with the heat of summer,
and the dust lying on the floors would suddenly wheel into inexplicable devils' tails. On these days the women huddled in their
homes, filled with a strange dread. Afterwards, when they saw
that the corn was still ripening, and the water still oozed from
the rocks, and the mulberry trees had not perished, they grew
accustomed to the heat as they grew accustomed to the winter
cold. Summer and winter were the time of solitudes. A boy might

spend a summer day examining the shape of a crack in the wall, while a girl might feast upon the shape of a single square of embroidery. And still they walked with calm and leisurely pace, and only the sheep on the uplands moved quickly, making a sound like a hailstorm when a multitude of sharp hooves broke on the stony path.

Then in the early autumn the hot summer dust vanished, and coolness descended again. One day all the roof-tops and roads were thick with a scale of reddish dust, the next day it had been swept away by the first breath of the autumn winds. Then the rains fell and the berries began to drop of themselves, and once again the air was sweet with the smell of ripeness. The quince trees turned silver in the rain; only the cypresses on the hills remained dark, smoking and glistening. It was the time when everyone gathered sticks to beat the olive trees. The work went on hastily from dawn to dark. Then the late corn was harvested, and when the last olives were gathered the work of the year was done.

At the first footfalls of winter the women looked secretly at one another, knowing that the children conceived in spring would be born at the end of the year. The faces of the girls were red and shining after harvest. The faces of the men were the color of dark mountain honey. Soon the women withdrew into themselves, preparing for childbirth and the crisp and pure winter, the blue skies, the icicles in the wells and the frost in the uplands. All through the winter the earth lay hushed and silent beneath the hills.

The Wine-Jar

When in April the ears of the wheat and barley have formed, and the flower of the lentil has fallen, and the harvest draws near, then everyone in Nazareth, even the old and the infirm, prepare to leave

their houses and live in the open fields. The rabbi blesses the
coming harvest in the synagogue, and riding on his ass he leads the
procession to the barley fields, as later he will lead the procession
to the wheat fields. Then little tents of colored cloth are set up
under the olive trees, so that the borders of the fields resemble a
Jacob's quilt, and all day the work of the harvest goes on. The men
wear hats of plaited straw to keep the sun from their eyes, but the
women continue to wear their veils. And every field has its great
red earthenware jar of cool wine, to quench the thirst of the
harvesters.

Yeshua was six years old when he was given the task of serving
the wine. He was tall and straight, with long auburn hair reaching
to his shoulders, deepset eyes, a square forehead, a heavy upper lip
and a full rounded chin. His eyes were enormous, dark blue and
flecked with hazel, so that sometimes people said they were brown.
He wore palm-leaf plaited sandals on his bare sunburned feet, a
blue- and yellow-striped kerchief round his head and a linen shirt
reaching to his knees with a leather girdle. Along the hem of the
shirt his mother had woven in red wool one of the Psalms of David.

On those hot harvest days the sun came out of the sky like a
sword, and the bronze barley fields shone like hammered metal.
In the shade of an olive tree the boy watched the reapers as they
came through the lanes of barley, the flash of the sickle, then the
sharp hissing sound as the sickle sliced through the heavy stalks,
then the slow stoop of the reaper as he crooked his left arm to
receive the bearded grains and, when he had gathered as many
as he could carry, he paused and waited for the binder to tie a
straw round them; then the little heap of golden grain would lie
where it fell. And all morning and all afternoon the work went on,
the flash and hiss of the sickle, and the queer slow bobbing movement of the reapers as they marched through the bronze field,
hungry and drenched with sweat, the men very solemn in their
pride, the wives and children following them.

In the bluish haze, the sun overhead, the boy watched them with
an overwhelming sense of wonder. How beautiful they were, as
they came through the waist-high barley! How proudly they
carried themselves, the dark faces glistening, the muscles rippling
under the skin, the great curving hairy chests and the small brown
bellies of the men, their cloaks looped over their leather girdles
and falling around their legs! They seemed to dance as they came

through the high field—a slow, effortless and silent dance, the only
sound coming from the crackling of the stalks and the rustling of
the grains and the splash of the little bound sheaves as they fell.
And so they came, very slow and intent, grave-faced, smelling of
earth, with grains of barley sticking to their skin, and some had
wreaths of barley in their hair, and they looked like patriarchs,
were huge and elemental like patriarchs, as they came swinging
through the golden fields.

Only a few days before these fields were softly green; now they
were bursting with ripeness. The ears were heavy and scented,
and glistened in the sun, and when the wind blew softly over the
field, the barley turned silver. At such times the silken grains flung
a flash of silver on the faces of the reapers as they bent down and
with a deft thrust of the sickle separated the root from the stem;
and there was something in the motions of these men, as they thrust
down and then rose to their full height, which made them one with
the fields they reaped, so that every man seemed to have belonged
there for generations. They plowed the earth and sowed the seed
and reaped the harvest; knew birth and generation and death; felt
the wind on their faces and were burned by the sun; lived fully and
richly, and died peacefully. And they thought it right that they
should be followed by women in brightly colored raiment, like
King Solomon attended by his handmaidens.

The boy watched them and sometimes, when the glitter of the
fields became unbearable, he turned away to stare at the dark
shadows of the hills or the white roofs of Nazareth nestling below.
Sometimes a flock of white-breasted barley birds, after dipping and
skimming across the field, would settle on the olive boughs above
his head. He had no desire to destroy them, though when they
were fat with grain, they could be clubbed easily; and indeed, at
this time of the year, the fields and pathways were littered with
dead birds swarming with maggots, food for the rats and crows,
plucked out of the air by any child who could wield a stick. He did
not destroy them because he was content to watch the reapers,
because it was hot and because the fumes of the wine hung in the
air around him. And these fumes, pale blue, dancing and quivering,
made him drunk with pleasure, and he would go off into a long
sleepy contemplation of the shining field and all the glistening god-
like people who walked across the field, until suddenly, from out of
nowhere, a swarthy peasant, bearded and naked to the waist,

sweating and panting with thirst, came marching up to him, a man as huge as an oak tree, and then the boy would throw him a rag to wipe the sweat away and dip the long-handled ladle into the wine-jar and then reach out so that the little ladle touched the man's lips. Then the dulled eyes of the reaper would fill with light as he drank the wine, and there would be drops of the purple wine on his beard, as he laughed and shouted for more, and when more wine was given to him, he would murmur: "Praised be the name of the Lord!" before turning away to join the other reapers. And then mechanically, dazed by the heat, the boy would say: "The Lord's name be praised!"

So the long morning passed, and at noon the reapers ceased their work, the men resting in the shade of the olive trees, the women taking themselves to the gaily decorated tents, into a quiet seclusion of their own, away from the men. A donkey, laden with baskets of wheat-cakes, each wrapped in a cup of moss, came up from Nazareth. Two or three wheat-cakes, a little wine, a little honey, perhaps some cheese or some olives—that was enough. Less than an hour later they were at work again, the men striding through the waving grain, dipping, curving their shoulders down as the sickles sliced through the barley-stems, and then always the gentle sideways movement as they slipped the grain into the crook of the left arm, and the binders hurrying after them, until the whole field was barren, with only the little gold spikes of inch-long stubble left and the dark inert bundles of cut grain lying where they had fallen.

In the afternoon a fuming blue haze lay over the barley field: the heat roared out of the sky. The afternoon was worse than the morning, for the earth smoked with heat, a shameless heat which searched out their secrets and made them cry out. But the work went on, though more slowly and with more visits to the wine-jar. In the morning they drank the cool wine quickly. Now because there was so little left, they sipped the wine and let it melt on their tongues and tasted it all over their mouths. While the heat pelted them, they grew more loquacious, with an edge of complaint in their voices, cursing the barley-birds and the carrion eagles slowly circling in the intense chalk-blue sky. And because of the heat, the reapers fell into short, bitter arguments. The boy shrank from arguments. It was strange to him that out of those full red mouths there should come sounds like the snarling of dogs.

Early in the afternoon the boy tilted the wine-jar and looked
down in its depths. A sweet musty smell clung to it, and faintly
perceptible blue fumes came from it. Outside, the wine-jar was
painted crimson, inside it was black, profound, with walls that
bellied out; and if you shouted into the wine-jar, mysterious
prolonged echoes came from it. But today he was not amusing
himself by shouting into the jar. Down there, deep, deep down, a
little below the level of the dark red wine, he saw the perfect
image of the sun, a gleaming gold circle, very small and remote,
very pure. And this image of the sun floating in the wine was not so
bright that you could not look at it. It floated there, and every
ripple of the wine shook the sun a little. Looking over the edge of
the tilted jar, inhaling the fumes, he was drunk with joy to see the
small golden sun lying there within reach. Reeling a little, because
he was drunk with the fumes, he began singing:

> The Sun is dancing in the wine;
> Praised be the name of the Lord.
>
> I sing the song of the Sun
> Shining down below.
>
> The black arms of the wine-jar
> Enclose the dancer!
>
> Ho! the gold Sun is dancing
> On a lake of blood!
>
> As long as there is wine,
> The Sun dances in the shadows.
>
> Shake the jar, you will see
> Many suns dancing.
>
> Praised be the name of the Lord,
> For the Sun dances in the wine.

When he had finished singing this simple song, he tilted the
wine-jar again, to see that the sun was still there, and it was. It was
brilliantly clear and small, no bigger than your hand, and it was
dancing there very mysteriously and quietly. It did not occur to
him that the wine reflected the sun like a mirror; for him it was
pure mystery.

He was still gazing at the sun in the wine when he felt a blow on the nape of his neck. It was a light blow, but it affected him strangely. He wheeled round, to face whoever it was who hit him. His father was standing over him, big blue veins standing out on the old sunburned face, both hands raised, hands like the roots of ancient olive trees. The boy shrank back. His father was tall and of commanding presence, eagle-nosed, with a bristling orange beard only a little touched with gray. He was just over sixty, but he enjoyed ferocious good health. He was stripped to the waist, gleaming with sweat, and he wore a knotted kerchief of some striped material on his head. Because he was drunk with the fumes of wine and angered by the blow, the boy held on to the rim of the wine-jar.

"I was singing my song," the boy said, his voice quavering. He was shivering with exultant joy, because he knew the song was good, and seeing his father standing over him, his heart knew a real fear.

"What song?"

"The song of the Sun," the boy answered, and he began to pipe the song again in a thin voice, a queer look on his face, exultant and fearful.

He reached the end of the fourth verse and then broke down altogether.

"Poor boy, you have gone mad!" his father said, and again there was that terrible shrinking look on the boy's face. It was worse than if he had received another blow. " 'The gold sun is dancing on a lake of blood!' What kind of madness is that?"

"It is in the song—" the boy began hesitantly, and he tried to complete the song, but his voice failed him.

"No, you have been drinking the wine," his father said. "I can see that by the wine-drops on your chin!"

He strode up to the boy and shook him, big powerful hands gripping the small shoulders.

He bent down and glared into the boy's face.

"You were drinking the wine, and you know I have forbidden it!"

The face was very close, terrible with the swelling veins. The sun roared in the boy's ears. The golden world of harvest was like the sun at the bottom of the wine-jar, shivering and trembling far away. He was sick with apprehension and fear. It was all black. The sun had vanished: it was hidden at the bottom of the wine-jar. There came from his father the smell of sweat and of the barley straws which stuck to his skin. And always there was the weather-beaten sunburned face of his father glaring at him.

"Tell me, did you drink the wine?" his father said suddenly.

"No, I was singing to it. Just singing."

The boy's face had turned bright red, and the eyes seemed to have been splintered like glass. He was cowering beside the jar, trying to hide.

"The eyes of the Lord God are upon you," his father went on in the same threatening voice, leaning over, coming closer and closer.

With a terrible effort the boy forced himself to speak, his lips trembling. He pointed to the wine-jar and said: "The sun is down there!"

"Then you are truly mad! The sun is in the heavens, where the Lord God has placed it. Look up there, Yeshua!"

The boy refused to look. He had never before disobeyed his father, but he dared not look. His mouth was working. He was trying to say something. Though old, his father could pounce as lithe as a panther, and with a single bound he fell on the boy, quickly swooping down and lifting him in his arms and then wheeling round to face the sun.

"My son, my son, look! The sun is up there in the heavens, where God put it."

"Yes, it smells of wine," the boy said, stuttering a little, staring at the sun, and then suddenly he was very limp in his father's arms, and sweat was pouring in streams down his pale face.

His father laid him on the ground, in the pool of purple shadow by the immense earthenware wine-jar. The reapers came hurrying up. They all knew about the boy Yeshua's fainting spells, and they knew that Yusuf could make nothing of the boy. So Yusuf stood there, very tall and straight, looking down at the boy, sick with fear, the blue veins standing out like iron on his forehead; and thinking the boy might be dying (for his words were strange like the words of the dying), Yusuf suddenly fell to his knees, turned in the direction of Jerusalem, flung his hands above his head and groaned: "Have mercy upon me, O Lord! Have mercy upon my bowels, O Lord! Grant to this little one to lie in the shadow of Thy wings—"

And he would have gone on praying interminably if his young wife, who had been working in another part of the field, had not come hurrying up at this moment. Meriam was fifteen when

Yeshua was born, and now that she was twenty-one she still looked like a girl in her long blue gown and blue kerchief of spun goat's wool. She was dark-haired, with thick dark eyebrows and long black glistening eyelashes; she had bright red lips and a full pale moon face touched with dusky red, like almond blossom at the setting of the sun. There was always something terribly reserved and quiet about her: she seemed to live a mysterious and reckless inner life of her own, moving swiftly and silently, rarely raising her voice, and always there was a smile hovering at the corners of her lips. She was the daughter of a rabbi of Sepphoris, and Yeshua was her only son.

Without a word to anyone, she fell down beside the boy and took him in her arms. With the hem of her blue gown she wiped the thick sweat away, smiling tenderly: a strange secret smile. No one spoke. No one went to assist her. There was a ring of quietness around her, everyone staring silent and open-mouthed: and this was not because she was Meriam, the young wife of Yusuf, but simply because she was beautiful as she knelt there. The boy's kerchief had fallen off. Her long fingers wandered through his damp reddish-gold hair, comforting him, bringing him back to life, not troubling to say anything, for it was enough that she was there. And all the time the heat rained down, the damp sodden heat of afternoon, the earth creaking, the carrion-eagles circling lazily overhead.

It was unutterably still: not a stalk moved on the hot, windless field; and no one spoke. It was enough to watch her: the small moon face, the eyes fully round, the nose so clear and straight, and the shadows of the fumes from the wine-jar playing about her cheeks. As so often before, she had entered that world apart where she continued her mysterious existence, a world where no thought of her husband ever entered, where she was supremely alone, even when she was with her son. Everyone knew that Meriam was touched with a heavenly grace. It was even whispered by the maidens of Nazareth that her son would be the Messiah, the King-Priest, according to the prophecy of Hasmonai, for Yusuf was of royal descent, of the house of David, and she was a Levite, of the house of Aaron, and long ago it had been said that a child would be born of the houses of David and Aaron, and he would be the Messiah. But could this six-year-old boy, sickly yellow, moaning and sometimes pushing out his hands and feet in curious spasmodic

movements—could he be the long-hoped-for Messiah? He was
very quiet, very ill, as he nestled there in her arms, uncomplaining.
And they knew something mysterious was happening. They knew
that Meriam, by simply holding the boy was giving him her
strength, her abundant health. They knew he had grown too
quickly. They knew he had a curious stuttering in his voice, and
sometimes his young body, his face, his eyes, were caught up in the
flames of a wild, inexplicable excitement. They did not know how
long they stood there, watching her: it may have been twenty
minutes, or perhaps half an hour, but for them it was like a moment
of eternity, for she was no longer flesh and blood, she was like a
statue, and the only movement came from the soft, blue fumes
from the wine-jar, pouring all round her.

Suddenly from the little throng gathered around Meriam and
Yeshua in this corner of the barley field there came a little cry, a
pure startled cry of pleasure. It came from Anna, the youngest of
Yusuf's children by his first wife, who lay buried now in a cave
above Nazareth. Anna wore a short embroidered blue gown like
her stepmother. She was barefoot, and her red hair was stringy
and damp with sweat, and half covered her face. They said of Anna
that she was a little like Yeshua: the same quick bird-gaze, the
same excitement in her face. And now Anna flung herself beside
Meriam, and made curious little moaning noises of pure pleasure,
looking up at her stepmother, smiling, so full of a sudden joy that
she could not contain herself. She fondled Yeshua. She ran her
hands along the bare legs which were streaked with sweat, and all
the time she was babbling in a happy delirium of love and worship
for her brother; and when Yeshua began to look about him, opening his enormous eyes, she gave such a screech of excitement that
Meriam lifted a warning hand and said: "Would you send him to
sleep again?"

Anna was transfigured. She laid her head beside Yeshua's and
stroked his damp hair and murmured in his ear: "You see, it was
all right, dear one. Little lamb, you are well now. See, you can
even stand up." And it angered her a little that Yeshua was looking
only at his mother, smiling his strange smile, unconscious of the
presence of the reapers crowded round the wine-jar, seeing only
his mother, like someone in the dark fields of night gazing entranced at the moon, the pure beneficent face shining lonely in the
heavens.

But now that Yeshua was awake, Anna recovered quickly, her eyes alight with quiet mischief. She swung between mother and son, caught Yeshua up in her arms and announced that she would take him home. No one protested. Only Yeshua made a little gesture, a curious reaching out of his hand in the direction of his mother, wanting to be with her; but Anna alone saw the gesture, and it was her triumph that Yeshua was now in her hands.

The sun-soaked earth was sparkling, the heat haze hung over the hills, the slow hot winds rippled the scarlet anemones. But Yeshua was aware only of the sun glinting on his sister's red hair, and the smell of the hair which was like warm fur: she had hoisted him on her back and was carrying him along the dusty roads to her father's house. And when they were in the house, in the cool darkness of the inner room where Yeshua slept each night, she laid him on a pallet, nursed him, tended him, hovered over him, brought him some salted olives to eat and then some water, and would not leave him alone.

"You are all right now, little lamb. It was just sunstroke—you were too long in the sun."

"The sun," he murmured, and immediately the whole room seemed to smell of wine.

The Blessing

Occasionally men came riding on donkeys and asses through the streets of Nazareth on those hot harvest days, but always in spring and summer the town seemed to be deserted until the blue shadows swept down from the hills. The sawmills belonging to Yusuf were silent; the synagogue was deserted; few maidens came to fetch water from the well. Sometimes a boy on a donkey would come riding through the hot, vacant streets, selling the blue turquoise beads which come from Persia, or a merchant would ride through, his embroidered saddlebags bulging with mirrors and glassware from the coast. Mostly they came at evening when the harvesters descended for a few hours from the hills.

At harvesting, they used to say that Nazareth took to the hills, there was no Nazareth, only the empty shell: but it was not so. Often the mothers took their babes to the barley fields, hiding the little blue cribs in the tents bordering the fields, but just as often the babes would be left behind in the house in charge of some old servant too weak and too bent to do her proper share of work in the fields; and women approaching childbirth would be left behind, because they were thought to be an unclean influence: and some old men loitered in those stone houses like ghosts already accustomed to their tombs. A few old servants, a few puppies and scavenger dogs wandered the deserted streets in the hot sun.

As he lay on the pallet bed in a high fever, Yeshua heard an old servant coughing in a distant courtyard, and somewhere a cock crowed. He heard the low murmur of fountains playing lower down in the town, and someone planing wood—perhaps for a coffin, since there was little carpentry otherwise during the harvest. He heard water dripping in a water-clock and the fluttering of sparrows. Strange that the silence should be so full of sounds!

Anna was with him. He would see her bright blue gown flashing in some distant corner of the dark room, where the only sunlight came through a small loophole in the stone wall. It was cold in the room. He shivered, and turned his face to the wall. "Drink," Anna was saying. He hated turning away from her, but he knew Anna could not put an end to the fever. He had had sunstroke before: once when he was allowed to spend a whole week with a shepherd in the hills, and again when he had stood on the great threshing floor and seen the great golden cloud of chaff burning in the sun. And he knew what had to be done. He must hold himself very still, facing the wall, saying nothing, not even allowing himself to tremble.

It was evening when his mother returned. She came with a little flickering oil-lamp and pushed the wisps of damp hair away from his forehead and knelt beside him. There was no Anna, no Yusuf: only his mother.

This was the blessedness: to be in a fever, in a small room, and his mother rubbing some creamy white ointment into his forehead

and saying it was good for him, and sometimes as she knelt there
she would hide the flickering flame of the oil-lamp and at other
times the flame ran up the whole length of her blue gown and
settled on her pure brooding face as she gazed at him. Time ceased.
The shadows raced. The blue flame of the oil-lamp grew small and
then flared again. When his mother came, she filled the room; and
when she was absent, the memory of her presence also filled the
room. She poured water in a bronze basin and the sound of the
water trickling in the basin was like someone singing, only because
it was being poured by her; and having poured the water, she
would dip a sponge in it and touch him with the sponge at the nape
of the neck, so that he cried out with unbearable relief and flung
his arms around her. If he asked: "Who am I?" she would gaze at
him steadily, the ends of her lips curling into a smile, saying:
"Thou art like unto a dove on the throne of Solomon."

"And where am I?"

"Thou art in my arms, sweetest name in my mouth."

All that night she remained close to him. He would sleep, and
when he awoke, she was there, and if she was gone, then he knew
she would return soon.

Towards midnight, when the fever was at its height, he began to
rave. She rocked him in her arms, as though he were a babe, and
sang him to sleep.

For three days the fever raged. Then he lay limp and quiet,
while she read to him, telling him stories from the *Book of Kings*
and of her husband's namesake Yusuf who had gone down into
Egypt and dreamed long dreams, and from Yusuf she went on to
talk of Sepphoris, the great city no more than an hour's walk away
where her own mother and father lived, not a stone's throw away
from the summer palace of Herod Antipas. He had never been
there, though he had seen the city from the hills.

"Shall we go there?" he asked anxiously. "Shall we go there
together?"

"Aye, when thou art better," she answered gravely.

"Then I am better already," he cried, and clung to her, begging
her to take him to Sepphoris this very moment.

And then seeing he was determined to go there, she said:
"What shalt thou do there?"

"I shall bless thy house, the place whence thou comest, and thy
father and mother."

He went on to ask all about Meriam's father and mother: what
they looked like, the color of their hair, and what language they
spoke, because every village and every town possessed a dialect of
its own.

Meriam laughed, and said: "They speak as thou speakest,
Yeshua, neither more nor less."

"Are they very old?"

"Nay, for I am young."

"Are they older than my father?"

"Nay, they are even younger."

Yeshua's clear brow was shadowed by wrinkles. He had never
thought before that his grandparents might be younger than his
father.

"Then how is it," he asked, "that my grandfather Yoachim is
younger than my father? And where is my father's father?"

There was no end to these questions, and Meriam explained as
well as she could that she had married Yusuf when she was no
more than a slip of a girl and he was already aged, and she had
herself never set eyes on her father-in-law; and she talked of her
own father, who had been a farmer and was now a rabbi, having
lived in Sepphoris all the years of his life.

"Then you shall take me to him," Yeshua said exultantly, "and
soon," he went on, shouting the words in a pure delirium of
happiness, so that Meriam shook her head, wondering what
strength had come to him and why he had this sudden desire to
look upon his forebears.

"Aye, and thou shalt stay with me all night," he commanded,
"and tell me stories about them to make me glad."

But she shook her head and said there would be no more stories
until the fever had left him, and besides it was time for him to
sleep.

A week later, when there was no more fever, Meriam took
Yeshua to Sepphoris.

It was one of those hot windless days when the black cypresses
stand motionless as ghosts and the perfume of the almond blossoms
is like a fuming radiance, every branch and leaf-tip glowing in the
sun. At first Meriam had thought of riding up the mountain on a
donkey, but remembering his recent sunstroke, she decided to
make the journey in a covered litter, one of those litters which lay
hidden among the carts in the servants' quarters, rarely used, for

they had long ago passed out of fashion in Nazareth. It smelt of barley, and the curtains were torn, and the cushions had fallen to pieces, but it served its purpose well enough; and when the servants went swinging up the mountain pathway, Yeshua sat inside on his mother's knee, every once in a while throwing his arms round her neck, saying: "When shall we get there? Are we there already?"

He had always been close to her, but he had never known such abundant love for her. The sun sparkled. They were climbing high, and he saw the white roofs of Nazareth disappearing below, all flashing in the sun. They were above the barley and the wheat fields, and were come to the small orchards near the crest, and soon he saw the shepherds on the hills not as he saw them from the valley, dim shapes outlined against the sky, but close at hand, wearing their long sheepskin cloaks with their pronged acacia staffs in their hands, bearded men, sunburned, quiet and content among their flocks. He waved to them, and they waved back, and all the air smelt of honeysuckle and the small rambler roses which clung to the heights.

It delighted him beyond measure that his mother was there with him in the litter, close to him, and the sunlight falling through the tattered curtains shone on her face. She wore a blue hood and a blue gown, and there were small thin coins dangling from the hood over her brow. Throughout the journey these little golden coins swung and tinkled. He would put his hand up to stay them, but they tinkled and swung gently and would not be stilled.

Suddenly he glanced at her and saw that she was asleep. He was awestricken. He had never seen her sleeping before, the heavy lids motionless, enclosing the eyes, and her lips were pursed in a way he had never seen before.

He wanted to shout: "Wake up! Wake up! The sun is alight!" Instead he gazed at her open-mouthed, feasting on her beauty, disturbed when a shadow fell on her face, on the soft curve of her cheek. He marveled and let her sleep and wondered what he would say to her when she awoke; but her waking was like her falling asleep; he was not aware of it. One moment he was gazing at her face, blank like the moon: the next moment he saw her enormous dark eyes upon him, and she was saying: "Where wast thou, my son, while I slept?"

They had breasted the hills and were out on the open plain,

immense stretches of bronze wheat reaching to the horizon. The wide paved road led straight to Sepphoris. Suddenly the whole town rose in view, the biscuit-colored crenelated walls rising from the crests of a low dun-colored hill. Along the road came streams of donkeys groaning under heaped panniers. There were also merchants from Jerusalem making their way on camels to Damascus. Some Roman soldiers wearing casques of reddish-bronze and bronze cuirasses came riding past on ponies. Phoenician noblemen, oiled and ringleted, their long beards dyed purple, lay at their ease on immense litters carried on the shoulders of their barefoot slaves. The road was alive with people coming and going. Women rode on asses and donkeys, wearing straw hats against the sun: from the rim of the hats descended long floating veils. There were two-wheeled chariots and farm-carts, and so much dust that all these travelers seemed to move in a perpetual golden haze.

"The noise!" Yeshua shouted, and clapped his hands over his ears.

The noise was worse when they entered the gates of Sepphoris, for this year Herod Antipas had moved his summer court from Tiberias earlier than usual and was in residence in the palace, and the market-place was astir with merchants who hoped to take advantage of the presence of so many retainers of the royal court. Beyond the market-place, beyond the gardens and the fountains, Yeshua caught a glimpse of the royal palace with its snow-white marble columns and stone steps flanked by gilded lions. There were food-booths everywhere. A blind beggar was running beside the litter, clinging to it, screaming abuse because Meriam would not toss him a coin. Banners fluttered. Bare-legged boys darted in and out among the crowds, and there was something on their faces which suggested they had never worked in the fields, never tended the wine-jars, never reaped the barley. It was a world so far removed from Nazareth that Yeshua could hardly believe what he saw. There was no peace, no quiet. A white bull with gilded horns was being dragged unwillingly through the streets. A hundred people were pushing and urging the bull in the direction of the royal palace, laughing frenziedly.

Yeshua turned to Meriam in anguish.

"So thou wast come from here?" he said accusingly, feeling a terrible distaste for this city where the crowds were so thick you could not throw a spear without killing three or four, or perhaps

more, and there was so much noise you had to keep your hands
close to your ears or else be frightened by trumpet-blasts.

Meriam was smiling. She was very quiet, not in the least
confused by the uproar all round her.

"But I came to Nazareth for its peacefulness," she said softly, and
threw her arms round Yeshua and held him close.

The palaces and gardens and painted pavilions fell away; they
left the market-place behind and came to a quieter part of the city.
No parades of Roman soldiers or of Herod's blue-caped mer-
cenaries; no bawling merchants; no jugglers and blind beggars.
No more flashing marble columns and low temples surrounded
with dark groves, whence issued the songs of the priestesses of
Astarte. In Sepphoris there are two towns: the town of the royal
court, and the merchants, theaters, temples, hippodromes; and the
other town, hidden among groves of pepper-trees in the north
where the Jews lived out their lives in quietness and peace. Suddenly the litter, which had been bobbing up and down along dusty
roads shaded by cypresses, turned sharply into a courtyard full of
hanging plants, with a small fountain trickling from a marble basin.
This courtyard lay off the main highway and lay close to a synagogue. It was very drowsy there, very quiet, the only sound coming
from the trickle of water in the fountain. The servants put the litter
down gently. The sun flashed through the hanging plants. And
soon an old man with tired gray eyes, wearing a long cotton *kaftan*,
his beard and finger-nails dyed brilliant red with henna, appeared
from the shadows and ceremonially prostrated himself, murmuring
endearments all the time. It was the old family retainer. Meriam
rose from the litter, smiled, lifted the old man up and taking
Yeshua by the hand, the old man following, she walked into the
house.

In this rich and well-appointed house, with the carpets on the
stone-flagged floor and the delicately carved chests, time seemed to
have stood still. A bronze mirror hung on the wall. A vast cabinet,
inlaid with ivory, stood half-open, revealing an immense quantity
of scrolls all carefully labeled, every scroll tied with blue and red
ribbons. Meriam was smiling to herself. She had not announced
her coming beforehand. She went round the room, solemnly touching the vases and hangings, the little clay ornaments shaped like
ducks and geese in the niches, all those things she associated with
her youth. A door opened silently. A man entered noiselessly. He

looked in some indefinable way as though he might be Meriam's brother. He wore a skull-cap and a long flowing robe and a prayer-shawl with tattered fringes. He did not look like a rabbi. He came straight up to Yeshua, and placed his hands on the boy's shoulders. Immediately Yeshua put his hand to his own forehead and then to his lips and then over his heart, the usual sign of greeting. The man smiled. Yeshua was aware of two eyes flashing down on him, very dark with a glimmer of red. The eyebrows were very bushy and the eyes were sunk deep in the sockets, so deep that the thick curling eyebrows somehow suggested birds' nests. The eyes held him. The soft black beard was silky, but it was not the beard of an old man.

"Yeshua," the man said, and the rich voice coming from deep down in the throat was like a benediction.

Yeshua jumped up and threw his arms round his grandfather's neck. His heart was fluttering in the sleek skin of his chest. His grandfather held him close to his chest, covering his face with kisses, and all the time Meriam was watching, smiling as she stood by the wall.

"Yoachim!" Yeshua said, and the words so suddenly spoken were like an exploration—an exploration of immense territories hitherto unknown to him. Simply to speak his grandfather's name was to receive a blessing.

Soon a woman wearing a long red gown, heavily embroidered in blue, entered the room. If Meriam resembled her own father, she resembled her mother still more: they might have been sisters. Yeshua's grandmother had the same full moon face, the same brilliant dark eyes, the same languid grace, the same quietness. There was about her an astonishing gentleness: an uncouth word uttered in her presence would have meant nothing at all, for she would not have allowed it to have any meaning. She had been in some distant part of the house when she was told that Meriam had come from Nazareth. Now seeing Yeshua, she hurried forward, arms outstretched, crying his name, and her voice was Meriam's. And it was strange to be there in the cool room, seeing Meriam twice over. He burst out laughing.

"Hannah! Hannah!" Yoachim exclaimed. "Thou seest they are worn out by the journey! So let them eat—enough of embracing!"

His grandmother was weeping with joy.

"So tall! So tall!" she kept on saying, kissing Yeshua's hair, his cheeks, his neck, his hands which were damp because it was so hot on the journey. "He is Meriam all over!" she went on, wiping her tears away.

She had fallen to her knees to hug him better, and he towered over her.

"He is strong, the Lord's name be praised!" Yoachim said. "I would say his body is as taut as a bow-string pulled by a strong arm! Let him be, Hannah!"

The old family retainer with beard and finger-nails dyed red with henna came in with a silver tray piled high with apples and honey-scented pomegranates and little cups of red wine to celebrate the journey. When after deliberating Yeshua chose a red apple and bit into it with strong teeth, Yoachim said: "Beloved, remember that of all things in creation the apple is sweetest." Yeshua could not have said why the words affected him so strangely. He paused, with the apple at his mouth, and looked deep in his grandfather's eyes, which were alight with amusement. And somehow it seemed that their approving smiles and the sweet taste of the apple were inextricably confused; and in the sweetness of the apple there was the counterpart to all the love he felt for them.

And he felt something of the same curious illumination a little later when Yoachim, seeing his eyes feasting on the scrolls in the ivory-inlaid cabinet, led him to them, allowing him to unroll and finger them. They were written on the finest and softest parchment, wrapped in silk, with little silver bells hanging like tassels from the wooden rollers. These scrolls were superbly fashioned and far costlier than those used by old Rabbi Eleazar in the synagogue at Nazareth. Even Yeshua could see that the silk was of the finest thread and the creamy parchment was of the rarest kind. And seeing Yeshua's pleasure in these things, Yoachim said: "Unto the Lord God is due all that is most precious of the work of men's hands. Everything thy hands do, let it be done in the Lord's name!" Again it was not what he said, but the way he spoke the words, his hands resting lightly on the scrolls.

For two weeks Meriam and Yeshua stayed in Sepphoris. Together they wandered through the town. Marble glinted: processions passed through the streets: everywhere, even in the Jewish quarter, there were banners to celebrate the birthday of the King. They went to the great open-air amphitheater outside the eastern gate, where Greek plays were staged. For the first time Yeshua

saw young Jews wearing Greek costume, not wrapped in striped
shawls but in softly flowing linen, their hair bound in fillets, wearing sandals of gilded leather, their young beards curled and
trimmed. In one street of Sepphoris there was more wealth than
in all of Nazareth.

On the last evening before returning to Nazareth, Yeshua found
himself alone with Yoachim. Yeshua was curled up on some
cushions, reading from the sacred scrolls. Yoachim entered silently
and watched the boy from an alcove: the calm face, the pursed
lips, the enormous eyes. Then he moved stealthily until he was
standing just above Yeshua, motionless, unwilling to disturb him,
afraid to break the thread of concentration. Then very softly
Yoachim said: "Read to me, Yeshua."

Yeshua began to read in a gentle sing-song voice:

> *Thus hath the Lord God showed unto me: and behold a
> basket of summer fruit.*
> *And he said, Amos, what seest thou? And I said, A basket
> of summer fruit. Then said the Lord unto me, The end is
> come upon my people of Israel: I will not again pass by them
> any more.*
> *And the songs of the temple shall be howlings in that day,
> saith the Lord God: there shall be many dead bodies in every
> place: they shall cast them forth with silence.*

Yeshua read on, but soon he paused, returning to the opening
lines, his forehead wrinkled with a frown.

"The summer fruit," he murmured, and then was silent for a
while. "What means the summer fruit?"

"The summer fruit is a glory—like the apple," Yoachim answered.

"Then is it glory that the feast be turned into mourning and the
songs into lamentation?"

"Yea, that too."

"And that there will be many dead bodies in the Temple—is that
a glory?"

"Yea, it must be, since it is written there," Yoachim said, and his
voice was steady.

"How is it a glory?" Yeshua said like someone thunderstruck.

"Then I shall tell thee," Yoachim said patiently, and he went on
to explain how in the time of Amos the Children of Israel were

threatening to turn their faces away from the God of their fathers, and their punishment was a glory.

"For the Lord our God is a hard and jealous God," Yoachim said, "and brooks no other worship than the worship of Himself. Should we turn away from Him, He will destroy us utterly. None can change the ways of the Lord. Amos was only a shepherd, but he saw the coming wrath of God, and therefore he warned the Children of Israel—"

"And shall I be a shepherd?"

"Yea, that too—and many other things, Yeshua, for I see thou hast in thee the power to become whatsoever thou desirest. I hear thou hast learned works of Greek while wandering in Sepphoris. Truly thou art wise above thy years and thou shalt become a shepherd of men like Amos of Tekloa, should it please thee. Wouldst thou be a shepherd?"

"And be so lowly?"

"Nay, there is no lowliness in a shepherd's life—no lowliness in any life when God has blessed it. What wouldst thou become?"

"A rabbi like thee and spend my days reading books," Yeshua laughed, and he touched the scroll as he had seen Yoachim touch it. It was a touch like the hovering of wings.

"Nay, nay, thou must wait a while," Yoachim said. "When thou hast reached the age of twelve years and become *bentorah,* then— only then—shalt thou decide upon thy life. Thou art young still, and thy mother needs thee."

And saying this, Yoachim made the sign of blessing over Yeshua's head and cupped the boy's face in his hands and peered for a long while into the boy's eyes, but he saw in them only what he expected to see.

All the next day Yeshua was in a fever: another fever. As he nestled against his mother in the litter he kept murmuring: "I shall become a shepherd like Amos," and when he reached the House of the Oil Press he kept repeating the same words, until Meriam burst out laughing and said: "Thou art no shepherd, but the son of a rich man—thou shalt look after thy sawmills all the days of thy life!"

She spoke in this way to taunt him and to see what he really believed.

He curled up to her, smiling. It was evening, and he was back in his own house, and the oil-lamps hanging overhead were swinging in the wind from the hills.

"All my days I shall be a shepherd like Amos of Tekloa," he said, as they sat over the evening meal.

Meriam thought at first he intended to join the shepherds in the hills immediately, for he was disposed to do things suddenly. She held him tight in her arms.

"For the sake of the glory?" she asked, and her lips opened in a bright smile.

"Yea, for the sake of the glory," he answered, "and for the sake of my mother Meriam. Has not my grandfather Yoachim blessed me?"

"Truly he has blessed thee," Meriam said, fondling him.

"Truly," Yeshua said, "but thy blessing is sweeter. I need only thy blessing—thine alone. Shalt thou give me thy blessing?"

"Yea, and it shall be a blessing given for always, for nothing except blessing shall ever lie between thee and me."

Then they were quiet, watching the lamps swinging in the wind from the hills.

The next day Yeshua forgot his desire to be a shepherd: he worked in the fields beside his father, wielding the reaping-hook, assisting the gleaners, hurrying on errands at all times of the day. Soon he forgot Sepphoris, which lay beyond the hills, infinitely distant and desirable, yet close at hand, almost within reach. And though he almost never thought of Sepphoris, he dreamed about the place and standing alone in a field under a fig tree, he would find himself engaging in long, earnest conversations with Yoachim. Once, sitting at table, he announced in a loud voice: "Yoachim is my father!" then he blushed and turned his head away. No one paid much attention to this disturbance. Only Meriam, watching him and understanding why he said these words, gave a little sob and brushed the tears away.

The Old Shepherd

There were many courtyards in Yusuf's house; there was a courtyard for Meriam, and another for the unmarried son Shimon, and
another for Yusuf. The house was built of stone cut from the
surrounding hills. Standing half-way up the hillside, it resembled
like so many of the Nazareth houses a small fortress, white and
gleaming, with a lane of black cedars guarding the approaches.
They called it the House of the Oil Press, but only because Yusuf
owned most of the olive trees in Nazareth. Some called it the
Carpenter's house, because Yusuf was a builder, and employed the
carpenters of Nazareth as well as the stonemasons. There were
delicate tiles in the courtyards and fountains sprang from marble
basins. Beneath the house lay a labyrinth of cellars, vaults and
store-rooms, and though Yeshua knew nearly every corner of the
house, there were store-rooms he had never visited.

Wealth flowed through the house, a quiet wealth without
ostentation. Yusuf took part in the harvesting, but he did so only
because it was the traditional custom for everyone in Nazareth to
partake in this feast: for the same reason he was always planting
trees on the hillslopes. Pomegranates, vines and fig trees grew
around the House of the Oil Press. Yusuf had four sons and two
daughters by his first wife: all had shared the work of harvest,
planted trees and tended the dove-cotes.

In the House of the Oil Press set in the hidden valley, they lived
out their lives ceremonially, according to the holy feasts and
according to the seasons. All life was a festival, every Sabbath a
day of adoration. In Nazareth men walked in holy peace all the
days of their life. The unchanging rhythm of the sacred holidays
was the pulse by which men lived. The year was a great wreath
encircling the sun, changing as the seasons changed, the colors
deepening and fading, the sound of fountains and blue winds
repeating the names of summer, winter, autumn and spring: and
there was no time in the year when you could say the wreath was

best, but in the spring it was richest. Then the fields were floods of scarlet and purple flowers, the delicate ears of barley turned to tawny gold, the fig trees put on their sober green leaves and the pomegranates were flames of scarlet. Spring was the time when all the sky of Nazareth was filled with the soft moaning of doves.

For Yeshua in those days all things were miracles, but most miraculous of all were the holy feasts. He delighted in the Feast of the Tabernacles when sheds made of myrtle and olive branches were erected in the courtyards, and there were great feasts presided over by the children of the house, thick bunches of grapes hanging from the walls of the sheds. He delighted in the Feast of the Lights when Yusuf lit the seven-branched candlestick and read the blessing and praised God for "the deliverance, the miracles and the wonders." But if he had been asked which feast he loved most, he would have said it was the Sabbath, for this was the day he spent almost entirely with Meriam. "None shall come between me and thee," he said once, "though the world perish."

So the months passed, and he grew strong, his chest filling out, his cheeks ruddy. In those days he was excited by everything, and most of all he was excited by tilth and harvest.

And there was no end to harvesting: all the year was a harvest except those strange dead days of winter or those other days when the heavens opened and the flood waters cascaded down the hill-slopes. In spring they harvested the barley and wheat. In July the grapes were gathered, green and succulent, from the sunny slopes. In August the blue grapes were swelling, and still in September they were being harvested, big and purple, not white like the grapes of Lebanon, and giving a thick purple wine. Then in September the bare-legged boys clambered over the fig trees, and shortly before the Feast of the Tabernacles came the olive harvest, when immense straw baskets were heaped up below the olive trees and there were huge fences of matting erected to prevent the wind blowing the bitter olive leaves among the fruit of the presses. If the grape-harvest produced a fiery excitement, the olive-harvest produced a joyous serenity. Those gray and ancient trees, sapless in winter, ghostly in spring, motionless in the hot summer winds, miraculously produced berries the size of plums; and these fat olives were so rich in golden juice that people said in the south: "Have you eaten olives of Nazareth?" when they meant: "Have you been eating well?" And at the time of the olive-harvest, donkeys laden with groaning panniers brimming with silvery-black olives made their way up the steep streets to the House of the Oil Press. Yusuf owned only two barley fields, but nearly all the olive trees of Nazareth belonged to him. They were his chief source of wealth; the richest and the sweetest oils were sealed in special jars and sent to the high priests in the Temple in Jerusalem. From Nazareth had come the oil of consecration of the ancient Jewish Kings.

Long ago Yeshua had outgrown "the service of the wine-jar." Only very young children were employed in this menial duty on the edge of the fields. Now he was apprenticed to the carpenters' lodge, and so he was called "Yeshua the carpenter" as his step-brother Shimon was called "Shimon the iron-smith." Being an apprentice, his task was to see that all the carpenters' tools were ready for their use. He must oil the saw, sharpen the adze, be sure the blade of a plane was at the proper slant. The glue-pot and the boxes of nails, carefully arranged according to size, were in his charge. Yet he was restless in the carpenters' lodge and often absented himself, to wander in the fields and in the foothills.

One day he slipped away from the lodge and climbed the hills. It was one of those pale and misty blue mornings when the gentle south-west wind blew from Mount Carmel. He went past the fig trees and the pomegranates and the last barley fields clinging to the high slopes, along the mule-tracks, up towards the Mountain of the Horns, where thistles grew and the wind-blown anemones stirred in scarlet patches like smears of fresh blood. He went on and on, upwards, past the tombs and the little shelves in the rocks where peasant girls left offerings of honeycombs because they believed a god of love lived deep in the mountain and the honeycombs would summon him to their assistance, then past the dry pools and hollows of deep grass, up until he was close to the top of one of the great horns of the Mountain of the Horns which rises above Nazareth, the only high place overlooking the plain, on and on, until Nazareth was only a faint gleam of white polished roofs in the distance.

All was peaceful here. From far below came voices, sounds of women beating clothes at the well, dogs barking, asses braying, carts creaking. These sounds were like a profanation on the silence of the mountainside.

He looked around on all sides. Far away he could see the little splashes of white where the shepherds stood among their sheep.

Some had wandered far off, others clung to the rim above Nazareth. And now as he looked around, he saw the snow-ribbed summit of Mount Hermon gleaming silvery in the north, to the south lay the great wheat fields of Esdraelon spreading to the horizon and to the west lay the blue sea stretching into the haze of the dark blue horizon, with a few yellow-sailed sailing boats making for the harbors.

Standing there, leaning against the wind, clinging to briars and brambles, his hair flying, he surveyed the world and was delighted with it. He had never wandered so far alone. The silence was deepening. He could feel the sun penetrating his bones, enveloping him, the soft yellow flames of the sun lapping him. The anemones and the white flax were unutterably still. It seemed to him that no voice of man had ever broken this silence. A lark about to break into song seemed aware that the silence must not be disturbed, and its notes were hushed. High up in the mountain air, it seemed to him that the earth had never known such a silence since the first days of Paradise.

He thought he was close to the top of the mountain, but a protruding bluff of yellow rock concealed the top, and so he fought his way up the steep slope, clinging to the stunted dwarf oaks and pines. Then when he was close to the top, he gave a shout. On the very top, on a rounded space no more than fifteen yards wide, a shepherd stood with his flock. It was a small flock of no more than ten or eleven sheep, and the old sunburned shepherd was the one known in the town of Nazareth as "the mad one," for he had no name and people had long ago forgotten his parentage.

The old shepherd resembled a gnarled olive branch, his skin nearly black. Though bent, he held himself well; he had a long gray beard and eyes glittering hard and cold like those of a lion. He wore no knotted kerchief over his head, but allowed his gray locks to fall to his shoulders. He wore the usual linen gown with a leather belt round the waist: the whole gown had once been embroidered with prayers, but now the woolen embroidery had lost all color and the gown itself had assumed the texture of old leather and was patched in many places. Year after year the old shepherd must have lived and slept in this gown which had never been taken off.

"The mad one," Yeshua whispered under his breath, and afterwards was sorry.

"So thou hast come at last?" the old man said, making a salute, a gentle lifting of bony hands such as men make after they have been kept waiting and now are anxious to put the expected guest at his ease.

In the dark leathery face the eyes were terrible, resembling broken pieces of yellow glass. Some disease had afflicted them, or else he had looked too long in the sun. He carried himself with authority: in his weary presence and breaking voice lay a curious strength. He spoke in a thin and distant voice, and leaned forward a little to see Yeshua better.

"Yea, I have come," Yeshua said, smiling. "Peace be unto thee!"

"Aye, peace to thee also," the old man said. "Hast thou come to see my sheep?"

"Nay, but to see thee," Yeshua answered quickly, and he pressed closer among the sheep.

The yellow gaze fell on Yeshua. The eyes were empty and yet penetrating.

"And what shalt thou find in me, who am old and faded like the grass made ready for the oven? Shalt thou learn from me?"

"Nay, old man, I have come for the pleasure of thee."

The answer must have pleased the old shepherd, who permitted himself a small smile.

"And what pleasure shalt thou find in me? Wouldst thou be a shepherd?"

"Yea, if thou wouldst teach me."

"But thou art called Yeshua the carpenter—"

"Nay, 'tis but a name. I have other names. Yeshua the reaper, Yeshua the sprinkler-of-salt-on-olives, and many more."

Yeshua was surprised that the old man knew his name: he must have shown his surprise, for a moment later the old man was saying:

"Ha, thou talkest well! I see thee clearly now! Thou art the son of Yusuf Ben-Yacob, surely! Thou hast red hair reaching below thy shoulders and bright sea-blue eyes, and the same chin and lips as thy mother Meriam. And thou art young, no more than eight or nine years, as I see thee! And knowest thou how I know these things about thee?"

"Yeshua is my name," Yeshua answered a little impudently. "I am not Elisha and cannot see from Mount Carmel, like the Prophet, to the windows of Shechem!"

"Thou speakest well, but with some impudence, my son. Dost thou wear thy impudence like a garment?"

"Nay, I wear it like my side curls," Yeshua answered, meaning that he did not conceal himself behind his impudence, only he liked to flaunt his impudence a little.

The old shepherd thought for a moment, leaning his head on the long acacia staff. Then he said: "I know more things about thee than thou knowest. I know where thou wert yesterday—and the days before to the number of all the days of thy youth."

"Thou knowest these things?"

"Yea, truly. All things that happen on this earth are said by the women scrubbing clothes near the fountain, and canst thou not hear them?"

Yeshua listened in the welling silence which lay on the mountain top, but he heard no more voices from below.

"Ha, but I hear them!" the old man went on. "Even now they speak of thee. They say thou hast gone into the hills, they say thou wast last seen climbing the Mountain of the Horns—nothing is secret in Nazareth, as thou well knowest! I, who stand here, listen to their voices all day and all night, not a word escapes me! Canst thou not hear their whisperings?"

At first Yeshua thought the old shepherd was laying claim to miraculous powers, for the women at the well were far away and there was only the faintest murmur of voices coming from below.

"I hear them not!" Yeshua said.

"Then listen more closely! Hold thy breath and listen!"

Yeshua listened. He still heard nothing.

"They are saying thou shalt be food for the black panthers or the gray wolves," the old man cackled.

"And what else?"

"Is that not enough? I will tell thee. They say thou hast climbed the precipitous slope like a kid which knows not which way it goes, when behind thee was an easier path." Saying this, the old man pointed to the rocky slope behind him, far less precipitous than the slope he had ascended. "They say thou art foolhardy and bright-hearted, and perhaps the Lord God shall protect thy foolhardiness!" Afterwards the old shepherd went on to say many other things about the maids in the market-place: he knew them well by their voices, could even describe them minutely, though it was years since he had been in the town. Wine, olives and bread were brought to him. Long ago he had set his face against living in a town.

"Shall I live in a box?" he exclaimed, when Yeshua asked why he did not descend to the town. "Shall I have four walls about me, when I have the fiery firmament as my roof and the winds as my walls? I bless the Lord God who made the sky, but it was some evil spirits surely who made the houses of men! Thou lightest the lamps in the synagogues, but I have the sun as my lamp, and should I ask better? I tell thee, there is such pure air on the mountain-tops a man would be a fool to live in the valley. Thou art not so ignorant as I thought. I see thee shaking thy head approvingly. Wouldst thou live in the high mountains?"

"And be lonely?"

"Nay, how shall I be lonely with the sheep around me?" the old shepherd said, and he lifted one of the sheep in his arms and ran his bony hands through the thick fur caressingly, and then pressed it upon Yeshua.

"See, he is good to thee, and loves thee, and does not bleat against thee," the old man went on. "Thou has the broad hands of a shepherd, too."

Yeshua had held lambs in his arms before, but never before had he felt any closeness to them.

"And is it comfort to be alone in the mountains?" Yeshua asked.

"Aye, the sweetest."

"And to spend one's whole life with sheep?"

"Aye, the sweetest yet," the old shepherd answered, and he took away the sheep Yeshua was holding, as though unsure whether he dared make so great a gift to one unprepared for it.

Yeshua asked for it back.

"Wouldst thou care for it well? Wouldst thou lay down thy life to protect it from the horned serpents? Wouldst thou search all night when there is no moon, if by chance it were lost? Wouldst thou live alone, with only a staff and a cudgel and a small satchel of food, of bread and olives maybe, and be quiet unto thyself, and learn what goes on in the hearts of thy lambs, who are humble and happy beyond any creatures? Wouldst thou do all this for no reward?"

"Yea," Yeshua answered, and he was fondling the sheep like a shepherd born.

"Then I will tell thee what must be known, and for the rest thou must learn for thyself," the old man said, and he began to talk in a low voice, speaking very rapidly and sometimes pausing for a long while before continuing, explaining all that needed to be explained, though leaving much unsaid, and when he had finished, he lifted his pipe to his lips and began to play for the sheep, which began to frolic and dance there, high up on the Mountain of the Horns, while the wind blew from the sea.

"See, in the heart of man there is a burning," the old shepherd said. "Only in thy lambs is there peace."

The Black Panther

Over the ages the shepherds of Nazareth have acquired a strange power over their sheep. They know them intimately. They know that sheep behave very much as human beings behave: and their rumbling and bleating is a form of speech. Each sheep has a name, and each can be summoned with a low whistling call. The shepherds know how to keep the sheep away from the open patches of wheat and barley. They know how to build quickly the impregnable thorn-fences which guard the folds and caves where the sheep bed down at night. They know what simples to administer in sickness, and all the distracting complications which attend lambing time. They know how to warn the sheep of the presence of horned snakes and carrion eagles which swoop down on stray lambs and kids. They know how to keep the sheep content in the parching drought by day and the frost by night. On their slender reed pipes they converse with the sheep and with all the other shepherds on the hills. All through the hours of waking, and at intervals during the night, they fill the air with the murmur of pipes as they call to one another across the hills.

Yeshua learned all this during the spring and summer from the old shepherd. He learned what rushes to strew on the floors of caves when the sheep bedded on windy nights. He learned how to weave deftly the thorn-fences, and how to light fires, and what berries he could eat, and what berries must be left alone. He learned what hollows provide the best shelter and what grasses are most succulent. He learned that when the red dawn came over the Arabian hills, terrible as an army with banners, there were storms in prospect. He learned to fear the blustery south-east wind which sometimes rolls across the Plain of Esdraelon for eight or nine days without ceasing, an ice-cold wind, giving chills and fevers to lambs and withering up the leaves before their time. And he came to know every whisper of the gentle south-west wind, blowing from the direction of Mount Carmel, herald of warm rains, called "the wind of the sheep," because the sheep delighted in it and frisked about more often when this wind was blowing than at any other time.

He never came to know the name of the old shepherd, or where he was born, or why he had taken the resolve to spend his whole life in the hills. They said he was born somewhere in the north and had come to Nazareth as a child. He was of the house of Benjamin, had never married and was somewhat over seventy years old: this was all that was known. The deep-wrinkled sunburned face, the eyes with their curious yellow gaze, the beard and hair white as bleached wool, all this gave him the appearance of a patriarch. It was said of him that he loved Isaiah and Amos, and regretted that Moses had led the Children of Israel to the land of Canaan, saying they would have become stronger if they had remained in the Mountains of Moab. But to Yeshua he rarely spoke of the Book. Watchful, eyes half-closed, he contented himself teaching Yeshua to be a shepherd.

So from the old nameless shepherd Yeshua learned to play grace notes on the pipe and how to press the lips together so that the sound would carry far. He learned how each ram and ewe has its own particular tune, with which it must be addressed. He learned how to defend himself with knife or cudgel or pronged acacia staff against the marauding wild beasts: wolves, foxes, panthers, mountain lions and snakes. He learned to taste the grass before letting the sheep graze on it: there was good grass and bad grass. He learned to recognize the symptoms of disease and how to care for the sheep when they panted atrociously in the hot summer, panting so that their little sides were like bellows. He learned too, how to carry them gently, and how the young lambs liked to ride on the shepherd's shoulders or in the pouch formed by the loose shepherd's gown above the leather belt. He would stay three or four days with the old shepherd before returning to the House of the Oil Press. And Meriam watched his goings sorrowfully and his comings joyfully.

Whenever he returned from the hills, he talked to her about the old shepherd. As usual she said little, gazing at him in quiet absorption. His cheeks had turned vermilion from being so long in the sun; he was rudely healthy, strong and filling out. His legs had been thin: now they acquired muscle from the constant journeying up the steep slopes. The old shepherd had set him to making ring-fences of thorn-bushes. His hands were red with thorns. And because he insisted upon staying with the old shepherd at night, she made him a cape of thick blue wool, a great woolen square with a hole in the middle just large enough for his head. On the cape she embroidered the words of *Isaiah: He shall feed his flock like a shepherd, he shall gather the lambs with his arm, and carry them in his bosom and shall gently lead them that are with young.*

It was summer before he asked to be allowed to lead his own flock.

"And thou art so young?" Meriam complained, but she knew she could not fight against him.

In the summer the sheep were driven half-way down the hills, where they could pasture in the shade. Her son would not be far from her. Every Sabbath he came back to Nazareth.

One day she asked fearfully: "Shalt thou wander with thy sheep in winter, too?"

"It must be," he answered, while she wondered, almost sadly why he looked so much older than his years.

"Shalt thou go from me then?" she asked, perplexed.

He only laughed and put his hands to her cheeks, caressingly.

"Thou knowest I am with thee always," he said. "There is no hour in the mountains when I do not praise thee, and no hour shall ever come when I have no thoughts of thee. And if thou callest me, then I shall hear thee."

Then he told her how in the mountains you can often hear the voices of people far below, distinguishing each word, each person.

So in the winter he went up to the mountains: not high up, but near the crests, living alone with his sheep. The winter was nearly over when the old shepherd died, killed by a pack of jackals who tore his body to pieces and dragged it into a ravine. The shepherds said he must have been attacked while sleeping, for he was well able to defend himself. They buried him high up in the Mountain of the Horns.

For weeks the shepherds shivered with fear. Every night they retreated with their flocks to the caves and built fires at the cave entrances to ward off wild beasts. Soon the fear lifted, and they began to build the sheep folds in the open again. Only Yeshua still herded his sheep every night in a cave.

He lay at the mouth of the cave, playing softly on his reed pipe, watching the night, how the darkness wheeled round him, for the stars were unaccountably faint. It was one of those nights late in spring, after lambing time, when the stars are snuffed out by mists, and the Nazarenes said of these nights that "their eyelids are closed." There was no moon yet, and no horn lamps shone on the great gates of Sepphoris, and there were no travelers along the road, such as he had sometimes seen, riding on camels with lanterns swinging from their necks in the depth of night. There was only a great wave of darkness, the great cave of the sky, and a strange silence.

As he lay there, the silence did not disturb him. It happened three or four times every night that the laboring earth grew inexplicably hushed: the cicadas ceased their triumphant song, and the little ringing of the sheep-bells ceased, and there was no sound of the trickle of water. It was as though in some strange way the deep heart of the night was yearning to fulfill itself, was preparing itself for some fierce and final knowledge of itself: the silent crouch of the lion before the spring. And there was only this silence, unchanging and unwavering, a thing that would last forever, high up in the dark hushed world of the hills.

Yeshua played so softly on his pipe that no one could hear him unless he was a yard or two away from him. The sheep did not hear him. Untroubled, they were asleep behind the thick thorn-fence he had built across the mouth of the cave. This cave was closed so completely that no marauding bear or lion would ever be able to enter it, yet it could be opened easily by a touch of the fingers, since it swung from a single heavy oak pillar deep-planted at the side of the cave. The making of the thorn-fence had occupied

many days and cost him many wounds from the thorns, but now it
was impregnable and beautiful. When the moon rose, it would
glint fiercely, every thorn gleaming milk-white and silky, so that
it looked very delicate, almost diaphanous. The mouth of the cave
was about eight feet high and the thorn-fence was only half this
height, but no wild beast would ever dare to clamber over it.

The winter was late this year, and the cold winds still played
above Nazareth. The boy lay huddled in sheepskins, a heavy
sheepskin cloak over his shoulders, another shaped like a bag
around his feet. Beside him lay a white acacia staff with a sharp
iron hook at one end, a leather sling, a satchel filled with small
loaves of bread and a wine bottle. For the rest, during those long
days in the hills, he lived on herbs and roots and fruit off the trees.

Lying on the ground and staring up at the sky, he waited for
moonrise, when all the dark plain below would turn into molten
silver, every dark bush becoming a silver tree, all the tilted roofs
of Sepphoris seen in the distance shining in the blaze of moonlight.
Then the sheep would awaken, for the light penetrated deep into
the cave, and then from all the hills around the shepherds in chorus
would pipe a song to the risen moon. And how mysterious it was,
that ghostly moment when there would appear on the horizon a
single silver drop of hissing fire, rising so slowly and effortlessly to
roll back the darkness of the sky.

"It will come soon," he whispered, and he played the opening
notes of the hymn celebrating the rising of the moon. Then he
paused. He thought he heard a jackal's cry, but it came from a
long way away, and it might have been a dog barking in Nazareth.
It would be another hour before moonrise. Then silence again:
silence so complete that it was like a great throbbing. He put the
thin reed pipe away and slipped his hand into the leather satchel to
take out one of those small loaves of bread wrapped in moss to keep
them sweet. While he was eating, he heard from somewhere close
at hand a wildcat's scream. He was sure it was a wildcat, and he
was almost certain it had been caught in one of the traps left by the
shepherds—a thin scream, which died in the night. He could
imagine what had happened. The trap had sprung and done no
more harm than nip the wildcat's feet: it was not the scream that
accompanies death. He knew them all: the long low howling of
the wolf, the fox's bark, the hyena's yell, the black panther's

rumbling growl. He knew the sounds of wild beasts as he knew the songs of birds, knew every intonation, every raucous shout and whispered grunt. He knew what cries the wild beasts made when wounded, and when in heat, and at the hunt, and when they were being hunted; could tell how far away they were, and at what age, and whether they were being gripped by the terror that comes out of the night, for at night all wild beasts are afraid. He knew these things effortlessly, and in fact he was no longer listening to the voices of the night: these sounds came to him unbidden, and were stored in his mind, so that as the night lengthened he came to know the position of all the wild beasts who paced the lonely hills. He knew, too, where all the other shepherds were, and at times of danger he would pipe a warning.

The mist was lifting. A few pale stars shone through the murk of mist. In the light of the stars he could make out a flowering sweetbriar hard by the mouth of the cave, fragrant with the scent of honey and roses: the secret water of an underground spring made it fresh. In the starlight the ghostly glimmer of the thorn-fence was like a veil which seemed to wave in the wind.

He was shaking with excitement. Every night when it was dark before moonrise was like the first day of Creation. Soon all the shapeless dark would acquire form and substance. When the moon rose, all the hills and valleys would rise to shout hosannas to the Creator, and the wild beasts would roar their greeting to the risen moon. "Blessed is the moon" he whispered, and he was still gazing at the little patch of darkness where the moon would rise.

He had finished the bread and now from the bottom of the satchel he took some cheese and olives. The wind rippling on the grasses grew stronger and the smell of the sweetbriar almost choked him with its fragrance. He rose, and began to walk slowly in front of the cave, taking care not to catch his sheepskin cloak on the tangled thorns. He peered inside. The sheep were sleeping peacefully. Then he turned. He heard something moving lower down the hillside. It was moving slowly and deliberately, padding over loose stones, but so carefully that only a few were slipping down the slope from under its paws. At first he could not recognize the beast: it might be a fox, but would a fox move so stealthily? He gripped his acacia staff and made sure that the broad-bladed knife at his waist was secure in the leather scabbard. The wind was rising and roaring in his ears, and high above him he heard the whistle of

wind in a hawk's wings, like a long low cry. He thought of running down the hill, to frighten the beast away, but then he
decided to stay where he was. The hawk was circling lower. The
sheep must have scented the beast, for they awoke with a sudden
ringing of bells and a patter of hard feet on the floor of the cave.
And while he listened to their baa-ing, sweat pricked on his face
and he looked despairingly towards the place where the moon
would rise, as though he thought he could summon it to rise
quicker.

At all other times he might have known what beast it was, but
the wind was flowing downhill and except for the low rumbling
noise there was no other indication of its presence, and soon even
this sound ceased; only he was aware that some dark shape was
coming towards him out of the night. It was not some familiar
beast of darkness—not jackal or fox or wildcat, which could be
sent on its way with a shout or even a sharp note played on the
pipe. It lurked there in the dark, just out of range, silent and
watchful, terrible in its power. It was like a great black shoulder
rising out of the earth, waiting to crush him. It came padding
closer, ever closer, very soft and feline, very sure of itself, and he
thought it was a huge mountain lion until he saw the green eyes
gleaming from the darkness not more than twenty yards away.

The first little blade of moonlight rose above the horizon. On
the hillcrest of Sepphoris the white houses and temples shone like
faint silver threads. There was no more than a little scattering of
milky light across the low rolling hills of the plain which stretched
to Mount Hermon, but though the moonlight was faint, it had the
effect of blinding him. High above him the shreds of mist were
melting away in the warm rays of the moon.

At the moment when he caught sight of the black panther, alert
and motionless, crouching there below, he was aware of a terrible
fear, a terrible weakness. The weakness did not come from himself,
but from the knowledge that the sheep were panicking in the cave.
He could not tell himself why he was so disturbed by their fear, for
he knew they were securely protected. But they kept on bleating
piteously and scampering up to the thorn-fence, looking out and
then dashing madly back again, making a deafening sound with
the click of their hooves on the hard floor of the cave, all their bells
ringing. In the moonlight every sharp spike of the thorn-fence
glinted a pure and poisonous white.

The black panther was a huge male, with heavy shoulders and quivering haunches, the longest and largest panther he had ever seen. It crouched there, very low to the earth, showing its pointed teeth and black lips, which were pink inside, the head lolling on the fore-paws which were placed closely together. It snarled, opening its mouth wide, not pink any more, but scarlet and black, deep-shadowed. The black fur shone silver where the bones of haunches and shoulders pushed up through the skin. There came from its hot, oven-like throat the smell of carrion. The black belly rumbled, and the long black silky tail lifted and swung fiercely in the air, making a sound like the whistle of a scythe as it falls, but the most extraordinary thing of all was the curious sobbing noise which came from the back of its throat as it expelled gulps of air and drew the air in again. It was not at all a rhythmical sound. What was dreadful was that it would stop and then go on again, and you never knew when it would stop. It was as though something had gone wrong, as though this sleekly powerful, beautiful and terrible machine had suddenly and unexpectedly forgotten how to breathe, and at the same time it was a little like a child's sobbing, with those terrible pauses when there seems to be no more air left in its lungs. And standing there, looking down in the mysterious moonlight at the panther crouching below, the boy became aware that its muscles were growing hard and tense, and there was no more crisping of the long curled white claws on the rock.

Yet the black panther was taking its time. It was not ready to spring. The rumbling of the belly grew louder, and the silky black head of the beast jerked up a little, as though it had observed something a little above the place where Yeshua was standing. Darkly malevolent, all black, with black gleaming muzzle, thick black tail, black haunches, it was waiting until the fierce fires of its rage exploded within it. It was purely destructive. It was possessed of a terrible black destructive rage for death. It would have swallowed the whole earth if it could, but was forced to be content with gorging itself on stray sheep and goats, ripping them open with stabbing claws, folding the skin back as it sank its muzzle into the still warm and living meat, gorging itself until there was nothing left except the empty sheepskin and the small rattling hooves. And then, still gorged, it would go on to kill another sheep, another goat, killing for the sake of killing, and so powerful that it could carry a kill for miles without leaving a drag mark. These black panthers of the hills around Nazareth were keen of sight and hearing, and could smell sheep from half a mile away, especially in spring, just after lambing time, when the ewes give off a rich milky smell and the young lambs too have a curious rough sweet smell of their own.

So the black panther lay quiet on the ledge of rock under the cave, while the smooth fur and bristles rippled and the unblinking green eyes gazed straight at Yeshua. The panther knew what it wanted. It wanted to riot among the sheep. It could smell their flesh and their fear. It was perfectly aware that Yeshua stood in its path. It did not understand the white glimmering fence which protected the sheep, but it understood that the sheep were behind it and there was a gap of darkness above the top of the fence through which it could spring. It saw the wicked broad-bladed knife in the boy's hand and the gleam of the hammered iron prong at the end of the acacia staff, and it understood what these things portended, and it discounted them, just as it discounted the hawk screaming overhead and the bark of a fox somewhere in the wheat fields far below.

The panther gave a great heave of its shoulders, threw its weight back on its haunches, quivered and sprang.

With three immense bounds, like a bolt of silver and black lightning, it swallowed up the distance which separated it from Yeshua, hurling itself through the air as though it were simply leaping over level ground, landing easily and gracefully on its soft black pads. There had been no time to sound the alarm on the reed pipe. He had been watching it for perhaps a whole minute, watching every ripple of black fur, every changing glint in the enormous green eyes, every sweep of the threshing tail; and just to watch it, to gauge its strength, to guess the direction it would leap had drained him of nearly all his energy. Ice-cold sweat trickled down the nape of his neck. The black panther was almost on top of him, lifting itself on its hind legs in order to strike, the huge black muzzle with a dribble of saliva escaping from the leathery lips. The boy could see into its throat, and the scarlet tongue, all wet and rough, like a huge scarlet sponge. He could see deep down into the hollow of the throat, where the obscene scarlet changed to black, and the curving ribbed roof of the mouth, and the teeth like huge thorns, not white but a sickly yellow. He staggered back in the direction of the thorn-fence, but the panther came after him. There was no way in which he could wield the heavy acacia staff, and it was in his way. He let it fall, and lifted his right arm with the broad-bladed knife, and when the panther was about to bring his heavy paws down, Yeshua leaped up and with all his force struck the knife into the soft fleshy part of the muzzle, close to the eyes.

He was aware of a noise like the roaring of a furnace, a great shaking sound from somewhere in the pit of the panther's throat. He had intended to stab the eye, to drive the knife through the eye into the brain. He had failed, and the panther reared again on its hind legs, black and glistening, blood trickling from the wound in its cheek where the knife was still embedded, only the haft showing, and then there came a muffled bellow of rage as the panther smelt its own blood and licked the blood flowing in its mouth. It began to shake its head in an effort to rid itself of the broad-bladed knife which hurt fearfully and threw a dark shadow over an eye which had never known a shadow so close before. And because it could not rid itself of the knife or the shadow, and because it could not associate the sharp pain with the presence of the boy standing there, white sheepskin against a screen of white thorns, it began to paw the ground, belly sinking low, becoming suddenly quite small so that Yeshua no longer feared it with the dreadful passionate fear he had felt for it before.

And because he was no longer afraid, he reached out for the haft of the knife, hoping to pull it from the wound and then to strike the panther again. This time he would strike deep in the eye, until all the fluid rushed out, until the point of the knife was cutting through all the roots of the panther's brain. He would strike surely and certainly, with no trembling of the hand, no remorse. He would kill the panther as he had killed rabbits for food, striking them on the head with a sharp stone from his leather sling. So he leaned forward, arching his body, leaning with the wind which poured round him and rippled the panther's black fur, and all the time he was holding his body a little sideways, ready to leap; but the knife was too deeply embedded in the thick coarse flesh to be extracted easily, and the moment he gripped the haft, the panther snarled, bellowed, the huge mouth opened and it sprang again, pouncing on him, rolling him in the grass, the claws tearing at the

sheepskin cloak while it bit and gnawed at the soft wool, and
Yeshua would have been killed if he had not succeeded in slipping
out of the cloak. His long undershirt was torn. There was a great
jagged wound in his left shoulder and another in his right thigh,
where three long strips of skin hung down and the blood was
pouring down to his ankle.

He was sick with despair and fear, with the knowledge that he
was defenseless. Dragging his right foot, he slithered along the
grass and hurled himself upon the acacia staff which lay there, a
white rod of moonlight, not five yards away. Then he sighed with
relief, no longer defenseless, though he could hardly stand and his
strength was ebbing away.

For some reason the panther had picked up the white sheepskin cloak in its teeth and was shaking it grotesquely, exactly as a
dog will shake an old worn sandal between its teeth. Still dragging
his right leg, and sick with weariness and loss of blood, the boy
hopped up to the panther, holding the acacia staff so that the sharp
hammered iron prong hung high in the air. He brought the prong
down on the panther's head, and it must have cracked the skull,
because the panther gave a high piercing yell of pain, let go the
sheepskin and began to stumble and go in queer crazy shuffling
strides in circles round its own tail, which was lifted straight up in
the air like a cat's.

But though the prong must have cracked the black skull, there
was still life and strength in the panther. If Yeshua had struck a
little harder, he might have killed it, but the pointed end of the
prong did not penetrate the brain and left only a small wound. For
perhaps half a minute the panther was dazed. In that time Yeshua
twice attempted to draw near, swinging the acacia staff again, but
each time the panther gave a little spring and warded off the blow.
Blood trickled from the wound in the skull and blood flowed in its
mouth, turning the teeth red.

Now the moonlight lit the vast plain, and everything gleamed
blinding silver. To the north the white walls of Sepphoris gleamed
like a ring of white-hot metal, and beyond Sepphoris, half-hidden
in the steaming mists of cloud that always crowned its summit in
spring, lay the snowy peak of Mount Hermon. The dark hills ran
with wind and moonlight, and every tree and bush thrust like a
white candle toward the serene heavens. But in all this whiteness
there was no sign of any other man. Close at hand, behind the

thorn-fence, the sheep were silent as they cowered in the deep extremity of the cave where the thick beams of moonlight could not penetrate. More dreadful than anything else was the unremitting silence of his sheep.

The panther sprang. For a long time it had been preparing for the spring, calculating the exact distance which separated it from this boy who smelt of warm blood and whose sweat glistened like honey in the moonlight. Yeshua fell over, the panther on top of him, its hot breath on his face. He clung to it by wrapping his arms round it, his head against the warm fur of the panther's neck. There, in the dark, underneath the panther, he was no longer afraid of the panther's powerful jaws; he was afraid only of the terrible sharp claws. And when the panther fell on its side, trying to shake him off, trying to curl its great claws into the boy's flesh, Yeshua was aware for the first time that he had the panther at his mercy. He had only to choke it, to pound the soft belly with his knees, to bind it in his embrace. So he pressed himself hard against it, against the rough fur which was not sleek when seen at close quarters, but coarse and matted, smelling of carrion and offal, a thing which was no longer beautiful as he wrestled with it and heard the awful sobbing noise, not as it came from the panther's mouth, but as it poured with hollow reverberations through its skin. The fur was wet and oily with sweat, as his own skin was wet and oily. He could hear the pumping of the panther's heart and the warmth of the blood underneath the fur. His big hands were still groping for the panther's throat, for the small bones hidden beneath the thin fur at the neck. And because he could not reach these bones, he was full of despair, exactly as the panther was full of despair, because it could not understand what was happening to it; it could not reach out with its claws or its splendid sharp teeth at this thing which was clinging to it. The panther rolled over and over, and still this thing clung to it. It smelled of sheep, and was not sheep. It gripped and pulled at fur, and was painful, and the panther hated it, hating it with a terrible unrelenting hatred. It snapped its jaws open, it bounded in the air, it rolled over quickly, attempting to crush the boy under its weight, and the boy was still there. The panther swung its tail, swung it in great arcs, and the tail cracked like a whip; but the tail could not remove the boy who clung to the coarse warm fur as though he had long ago become a living part of the black beast.

So they wrestled together, and at last the panther lay on its side, feebly waving its paws, and the boy pounced upon the thin bones at the neck and pressed down with all his small strength until he felt them giving way; and he gave a little shout of triumph as he heard the bones cracking under his thumbs. There was a sharp whistling sound, as the windpipe broke. Then Yeshua was no longer afraid. He heard the grunting and coughing of the choked panther, but there was still one more task to be performed. He must lean up and pull the panther's head back until the neck broke, and this he did, with his big hands gripping the slack jaw. He pulled, and there was a final cracking of bones as the neck snapped.

When Yeshua fell off the panther, he had no strength to stand. He simply lay there, looking up at the white glow of the sky, taking deep slow breaths. His shirt was torn to shreds, and it was cold in the uplands, but he was not aware of the cold; he was aware only that the last vestige of his strength had been taken from him and there was not even enough strength to praise God for His great mercy.

Flooded with moonlight the dead panther turned silver. It lay there as though it were resting after having gorged itself on a heavy meal.

Yeshua waited. An hour later his strength came back and he began to look for the reed pipe, so that he could summon the shepherds to view the dead panther, which was still warm and looked, even though it had been choked to death, as if it might spring into life. But though his strength returned, he could not stand: a tendon in his right thigh had been torn by the panther and the leg kept jerking and would not keep still, and yet he could not touch the ground with it. It was terrible, the black surging pain that twisted his thigh, so that he almost howled with the pain, with the scorching and the burning. The pain was like a dark tunnel of flame, and the flames roared in his ears, and burrowed deep in the marrow of his bones. And it was the same in his shoulder, where the panther's claws had torn him: pain welling out and flooding him: and yet he was beyond pain, and indeed he was laughing. There were pools of warm moonlight laughing deep in his throat. He crawled up to the panther, embraced it once more and whispered a name for it over and over again; and then he began to sing:

The black panther shall come out of the dark:
He shall leap: he shall moan:
He shall come with the shadows and the moonlight,
And his claws shall rend me.
O, the black panther, he shall leap and moan,
He shall come silently out of the dark,
His strength shall be as the strength of ten men,
But I shall thoroughly overwhelm him.
The multitude shall see me.
I shall stand upon the living panther,
I shall shout his praises, I shall crown him.
I shall place a wreath of thorns upon his brows,
I shall divest him of his royal power.
The sun and the moon shall look down on me,
And the Lord God shall bless me!

The black panther is the angel of darkness:
Out of his green eyes comes the flame of darkness:
But he is beautiful.
His mouth is scarlet like apples,
His teeth are white like hawthorn flowers.
Only in the deep of his throat lies the darkness.
Sweetly we have wrestled together.

I am the lord of the black panther, the conqueror.
I am his shepherd, and he shall follow me.
Tenderly he crouches before me.
He shall obey me wheresoever I command him.
We shall wander together through all the pathways,
And now no more shall he rend the sheep in the fold:
For the Lord God has given me strength and power
To hold the black panther in my arms as I would a lamb.
Behold, I am the lord of the black panther,
And he lieth in my arms.

The black panther shall come out of the dark:
He shall leap: he shall moan:
All of him is sweet, his fur and his entrails,
The soft fur of the belly, and the thick bristles,
And the tail which is like a whip flaying the darkness.
The hands of men and the mouths of women shall know him,
And he shall skip down the mountain like a lamb!

Behold, I am the conqueror, I stand upon him,
And the Lord God looks down upon me.
Blessed be the Lord God who has shown me these mercies,
And may his name be magnified for ever and ever.

When he had finished singing, there was silence; and he looked
out over all the plain, which was like a blinding silver bowl.
Crouching beside the panther he was warm, for there was still
warmth in the beast, though he could feel it ebbing away. "Too
soon, too soon," he murmured, as he felt the slow hardening of the
panther's skin, so rigid now, no longer rippling with boneless
grace, no longer beautiful in the moonlight. He crouched beside
it for a few minutes more, then feeling hungry, he began to crawl
over the pool of moonlight on hands and knees in search of his
satchel and wine bottle. He drank a little wine and then broke
some bread, and then hearing the bleating of the sheep and the
ringing of their bells, he leaped up, forgetting his wounds. He told
himself he had been selfish: he had wrestled with the panther: he
had hurled all his strength at the panther and rejoiced in the
combat, and not for a moment had he thought about the sheep. He
was their shepherd and he must comfort them. This was the law of
the hills. So he went hopping towards them, dazzled by the moonlight, and fell with a crash against the thorn-fence.

The Wounds

At first when the shepherds failed to hear the sound of Yeshua's
reed pipe in the morning, they imagined he was sleeping, or he
had taken his sheep to one of those hollows whence sound travels
with difficulty. Every morning they greeted the sun with a furious
burst of piping, all the hills echoing with a fierce, ecstatic anthem
of praise to the risen sun. It did not disturb them at first to hear no
answering piping from Yeshua. He might be drowsy with wine.
He might have been summoned to Nazareth. It might be that the
sound of his piping was lost in the great morning chorus when the
air was filled with the song of the larks and the thin silver notes of
the pipes.

An hour after sunrise they began to be perturbed. Everyone had spoken: only Yeshua was silent. Soon all the pipes were saying: "Where is Yeshua Ben-Yusuf? Tell me, where is Yeshua?" Even then no one felt any particular fear for his safety. Someone called out that he was sleeping in a cave known as the Cave of the Acanthus, though no acanthus grew there. It was only much later in the morning, after they had called to him repeatedly, that one of the shepherds decided to make the journey across the crest of the hills to the cave. The shepherd went off half-heartedly. A thin, wiry man with lantern jaw, sunken cheeks and watery eyes, he was dumbfounded when he saw Yeshua hanging on the thorns. He thought it was an apparition. On the little shelf of rock near the cave lay a satchel, an acacia staff, a broad-bladed knife. The air was black with the wings of hawks and vultures, and in the midst of them, not yet touched by their beaks, lay a huge black panther, ten feet from muzzle to tip of tail, and heavy, so heavy that it would need ten men to carry it down the mountain.

"And why is he hanging there?" the shepherd asked himself, turning to the boy on the thorn-fence. "Did he turn and run to his sheep? Come, boy! Come off the thorns! And not dead yet—"

The old shepherd shook his head, clapped his hands together because a cold wind was whistling down the mountain, and tenderly lifted the boy off the fence. Then he summoned more shepherds on his reed pipe and bathed the wounds, and they carried Yeshua to Nazareth.

In the House of the Oil Press Meriam was the first to see him. It was a clear day, unusually cold for spring, with the hawthorn in flower and the barley-harvest coming in. On such a day you would hear the iron-smiths forging sickles and the scream of the sharpened blades drawn over whetstones. A thousand larks were singing, while the shepherds came down the mountain, playing mournfully on their pipes, carrying on their shoulders a kind of stretcher of woven wattles. The iron-smiths were silent, and all Nazareth lay hushed and silent, watching the small procession of men in rough sheepskin cloaks.

So they went on piping mournfully, thinking he was dead, laying him down in the courtyard, watching one another, very quiet and tense: and Meriam, coming out into the courtyard to attend to the oil press, which was used at this time of the year to crush spring blossoms, caught sight of the boy lying on the wattle stretcher and

threw herself upon him, crying out in a loud voice: "Oh my son—
my son!" She lay there with her face against his bleeding face,
sobbing to herself. Her sobbing brought Yusuf hurrying down
from the upper room. He stared at the boy and the stretcher and
his young wife lying there, and he could not speak or make any
movement at all.

On Yeshua's pale white body were a thousand starry wounds,
and all were bleeding, and some thorns were still attached to his
flesh. He lay there, barely breathing. He was naked except for the
bearskin which a young shepherd had thrown loosely over him.
All over the tiled floor of the courtyard were heaps of spring
flowers ready for the press.

Meriam lay there, covering his face with her tears. She did not
see the second stretcher which was brought into the courtyard,
though Yusuf saw it. On this stretcher lay the black panther; there
came from it the terrible sour odor of death. The panther was set
beside the sleeping boy.

For three weeks Yeshua lay in an inner room, white and fragile,
hovering between life and death. There were times, especially in
the evenings, when he would awake and sing in a thin quavering
voice "The Song of the Black Panther," singing the words dis-
jointedly, tunelessly. Doctors were summoned, but they failed to
heal the deep claw-wounds on shoulder and thigh. He took
nourishment. He slept most of the day and night. Meriam and
Anna attended him, keeping watch. The thousands of little
suppurating wounds from the thorn-fence healed slowly, leaving
multitudes of scars. And Meriam broke down completely when
she learned that as a result of the claw-wound in the thigh one of
Yeshua's legs would always be shorter than the other. And all day,
tears streaming down her face, she wandered blindly through the
sunlit courts, repeating the words: "Shall he be lame?"

Yusuf attempted to comfort her, but she was past curing or
comforting. She would sit very still on a chair or in a heap of
cushions, looking towards the hills where Yeshua had tended his
sheep. Yeshua was so beautifully made, and now he was lame!
She had never wanted him to tend the sheep, never wanted him to
leave the House of the Oil Press! So sitting quietly, her hands
folded in her lap, tears streaming down her face, looking neither to
left nor right, she stared up at the hills as though expecting him to
descend from them, untouched and beautiful, as when she had

seem him last coming down from the hills. And sometimes she mourned him as though he were already dead.

Until this time Yusuf had never felt any deep or abiding affection for his youngest son. Now affection overwhelmed him. He accused himself bitterly of negligence. Yeshua was too young, too delicate, to have been left alone in charge of his sheep: there should have been some rough shepherd boy with him. He sent out all over Galilee for herbs and simples and medicaments, and hearing of a learned doctor in Ptolemais, a Greek famous for many cures, he begged the doctor to attend his son. The doctor came, but the great claw-wounds remained unhealed. In despair Yusuf bound phylacteries containing sacred texts on the wounds, but Yeshua only clawed them away in his ravings.

One day the rabbi was permitted to enter the room where Yeshua lay sleeping. The bandages were unwound, and in the light of an oil-lamp the rabbi was allowed to peer at them. He was seen to be muttering to himself and his eyes were staring like those of a madman. Later he said that the two wounds were shaped like the letters *aleph* and *tav*, the first and last letters of the alphabet. The ruby-red wounds were very fresh and glistening. To himself he said: "Surely this is a sign of heaven, for the seal of the Holy One, blessed be He, is written there." To Yusuf he said: "I know by the shape of these wounds that he will be made whole."

It was not the rabbi, but Anna, who helped most to cure him. She slipped into the dark room one afternoon and gazed at him as he lay on the low bed against the wall. She was smiling.

"Why art thou smiling?" Yeshua said angrily. "Because I am ill, because a thousand thorns have poisoned me? Hadst thou fallen into a bed of thorns thou wouldst not—"

Anna was still smiling, shaking her head from side to side. She stood at the door, her young body shaped like a vase, blocking out the sunlight, so that only a little narrow wavering slit of yellow light fell on the bed.

"Art thou smiling at me?" he began again, the voice hot and sharp.

He leaned up, his face swimming with sweat and pus, his mouth quivering in agony. The wounds left by the thorns in his face were like a thousand little red roses glued there.

"Yes, I am smiling," Anna said, and she came to kneel beside him. "I smile at thee in love, Yeshua, and I shall smile at thee many times hereafter."

He hated her. He wanted to raise his hand against her, to blot her out. He clung desperately to himself, uncertain of himself, not knowing where he was, seeing her through mists of anger and despair; and suddenly the anger passed, for all these waves of hatred had exhausted themselves, and there was only his beloved half-sister standing beside his bed, leaning up and running her hands through his hair. He loved her then, for the little gesture of running her hands through his hair.

"For love," she murmured. "For love thou didst kill the panther."

"Yes," he whispered, and unable to bear the warm tenderness that flowed from her he turned his face to the wall.

Already Anna had the appearance of a woman. She was Meriam's favorite among the children of Yusuf's first wife. Her eyes were gray, very warm and steady, and at the least shock, the least excitement there was a delightful flush on her cheeks. She wore a gown of blue cotton, and her veil was tossed over her shoulder, so that the young face was framed with it. Her breasts heaved under the blue gown, and she smiled her warm sidelong smile, waiting for him to return and face her.

"They say there was no weapon in thy hands when the panther came to thee," Anna went on. "Didst thou throw the weapon away?"

He nodded.

"And in the dark?"

"Nay, it was not dark, for the moon came up."

There was a long silence. He felt an extraordinary gratitude towards her. No one had talked of the fight by the cave mouth: it was as though this was a forbidden subject. Instead, they spoke of his wounds, sorrowed over them, wept and prayed, prepared simples, uttered spells, tied phylacteries to him with thin strips of leather, and Yusuf had stood at the end of the bed reciting the Psalms, then kneeling with his arms stretched up above his head the old man had invoked the special blessings of the Lord God: "Thou who hast cherished for so long Thy beloved House of David." But only Anna had smiled childishly and consolingly.

Yeshua was the first to break the silence.

"There was such joy in the fight it was beyond speaking," he said. "We wrestled for an hour, and it was playful—"

"As one plays with a kitten?"

"Yes, as one plays with a kitten, and yet I knew one of us must kill the other."

Anna sucked in her lips and made a low whistling sound. Her long ear-rings trembled.

"Was the panther sent by God?" she asked, as one might ask whether a basket of corn had been sent safely.

"Yes, I am sure of it," Yeshua answered. "But he did not come to tempt me—he came so that I might try my strength, and it was for the glory of God. And sometimes, Anna—come closer, so I can whisper it—I think there was God within the panther! For he came with terrible power, and silently, and if it pleased him, he could have stricken me with a single blow of his mighty paws, but he did not. Oh, there was God in the baring of the fangs! I know it! And so we fought, and God said: 'I shall enlarge his heart and magnify this shepherd, and he shall serve me.' I felt all that at the time, but now I am not sure."

Anna said nothing, only inclining her head a little.

"Thou shalt tell no one," Yeshua said urgently.

"No one," Anna whispered.

"And it shall be a confidence between us?"

"Forever it shall be a sweet confidence between us," Anna whispered, and then she leaned forward and kissed his wounds, and there was a look of triumph on her young face.

Soon afterwards she left the inner room, only to return a little later with a bunch of anemones, which she left beside him, for she thought he was sleeping. But the moment she slipped away again he took the anemones, scarlet and pale yellow, and wet with dew, and he held the petals to his cheeks, gazing for a long time at the wheeling shadows in the room.

He recovered slowly. When he was well enough to walk, Yusuf set him to working at easy tasks in the carpenters' lodge at the other end of the town. He said: "Thou hast one foot shorter than another, but it will not prevent thee from being a carpenter. Thou canst not be a shepherd, and lame!" Sometimes Yeshua disobeyed his father. He slipped away from the carpenters' lodge and made his way up the hills, walking in an ungainly manner, looking like a scarecrow. Only in the hills, with the wind blowing in his face, the lambs bleating, the shepherds playing on their reed pipes, the warm earthy smell coming from the sheep, was he at home. In the hills no one feared him. In Nazareth they made the sign against the evil eye when he passed, saying there was a devil in him, for how otherwise could a boy of tender years have fought the panther which had been exhibited, stretched out on a wooden frame, in the market-place? "He even sings about it," they said, shuddering. "The devil is surely in him when he sings." It was not that they objected to anyone celebrating his own prowess: they objected to the peculiar tone of his triumph, the half-crazy look in his eyes, the terrible spider-like limping walk.

Anna comforted him. Every day there were long earnest discussions between them. On Anna's face there was the fullness of maturity and in her watchful eyes there was determination. Alone, if possible, she would heal his wounds.

One evening—it was the day some small boys in Nazareth had thrown stones at Yeshua, and one of these stones had opened the claw-wound at the shoulders—Anna said: "It is a sign that God has chosen thee."

"None are chosen except the prophets," Yeshua answered gravely, and he put aside the heavy scrolls he had been reading. "I am not chosen," he went on, and a little later: "Would to God I were not chosen!"

"Then thou knowest," Anna said gently. "Thou knowest that thou art chosen?"

"I know I am chosen," Yeshua answered, "but what I am chosen for I do not know. I know only that my wounds burn me. I know I shall be a cripple always. But it is good to be a cripple, for then I shall spend my days praising the God of Abraham."

Saying this, he shut his eyes, squeezing the eyelids tight, seeing himself when he grew up as one of those crippled beggars with white sores on their faces, wearing sackcloth, who sometimes wandered through Nazareth and received the bounty given to all wandering beggars: old men with crazy eyes, hollow cheeks and running sores: and especially one blind beggar who wandered through Nazareth wearing a cloak made of the skins of gray rats and carried the little white glistening skull of a rat in his hands, proclaiming that this little skull partook of God's mercy.

"And be blind, too—" he went on, with despair in his eyes. A little later he said: "The sun is in the wine-jar, remember?"

Then he was quiet, leaning back, a mysterious smile hovering at the corners of his lips.

Anna was close to him, closer even than Meriam. It was Anna who bathed his wounds and rubbed ointment on them and covered them with bandages and, when the pain became intense, she held his hands. She was very quick to detect pain, her eyes glowing with the excitement of womanhood. Sometimes she would curl up on some matting beside his bed, sleeping there on the long nights when the wounds bled.

"Let me be!" he would say urgently, turning his face to the wall. "Don't touch me! Let me be! Let me fight these devils in my own way!"

But he always allowed her to remain near him, and was grateful to her, and when his hands tried to tear the bandages away and she prevented him, he would gaze at her with a curious look of longing and affection, saying her name over and over again. Anna means "the grace of God," and simply by whispering this name he was aware of God's mercy.

The wounds continued to bleed, staining the bed. For weeks the smell of blood filled the inner room. Then when the wounds healed and he felt strong enough to appear again in the town, the people still jeered at him. They gave him a new name. They called him "Ben-Panthera," the son of the panther, and when they whispered the name, they added a prayer against the evil eye.

Rebellion

On this dark night he was lying on the roof, listening to the sound of a water-clock. The water dripped out drop by drop, and always at some hour before dawn the wheel whirled back with a clatter which awoke him from sleep. *Drip-drip* came the noise of the water-clock, and he smiled patiently, hearing the water-clock above the noise of the cicadas, lying there on a bed made of plaited palm leaves, very warm, looking up at the sky, where only a few stars were shining through the night haze. There was no moon, and there was no one else except an old servant in the House of the Oil Press. It was one of those hot nights in summer when the people of Nazareth, after harvesting in the fields, slept in the little colored tents under the olive trees bordering the fields.

Two months had passed since the fight with the panther, and he was still weak: the leg did not heal, the claw marks in his shoulder were still raw. For a few days he had walked about Nazareth, limping, singing the Song of the Black Panther in a strange cracked voice, but the wounds opened and he was forced to spend the day in bed. Usually he lay in one of the inner rooms, where it was dark, but tonight he had climbed up on the roof and spread out the palm-leaf matting. He slept fitfully. Sometimes the pain of the open wounds made him clench his teeth; and then very tense, his cheek muscles quivering, he would wait until the pain passed away, as a rock which has fallen into a stream is swept away by the weight of water. At such times he prayed, fervently and with terrible earnestness, not for himself, but for all those who have been clawed by panthers and mountain lions.

The moon rose, hot and bright above the limestone cliffs, and all the white roofs of Nazareth resembled golden stepping stones in the orange moonlight; and every leaf of every tree turned the color of bronze. In the moonlight, with the tufts of night haze still clinging to the sky, everything looked mysterious, strangely metallic. The larks, thinking the moon was the sun, rose into the empty metallic sky and shrilled, but only for a few moments. Baffled by the strangeness of the moonlight, they returned to the comfort of their nests, where there was no strangeness: only warmth and intimacy and silence.

And strangely, with the huge orange moon climbing the sky, like a metal drum, the night seemed barren, terrible, unfulfilled: it was as though quite suddenly, with the appearance of the moon, the emptiness of Nazareth proclaimed itself. It was all hollow, for all except the sick were out in the fields; and though the metallic moonlight splashed on the houses, which were like squares set on the hillslopes, yet in some strange way the moon seemed to give no light.

"The sun, not the moon," he said, and turned his face away from the great orange thing that flashed down at him through the oleanders planted on the roof. "And where now?" he went on. "Shall I stay here and be burned to a cinder by the moon?"

From the bright moon he recoiled in terror as he had never recoiled from the noonday sun. There was no friendliness in it, no blessing. The moon did not help to heal him, but on the contrary made his wounds ache more atrociously. And the anguish of the pain made him try to bury himself deep in the palm-leaf matting, losing himself among the crackling fibres, pressing his face against it. Then he was quiet again, holding his breath, without pain, like some naked dark child sprawled on the roof-top, but he could not stay with his head buried in the matting for long, and when he turned, he wanted to flee in horror from the moonlight. He could not explain these fears even to himself. He remembered once how a bucket, half-way down the well and full of water, spun on the rope, went mad, banged from one side of the well to the other, the rope caught somewhere; and this mad bucket made a terrible clatter deep down in the well. So it was now: deep inside him there was a mad bucket swinging aimlessly from one side to another. He tried to prevent himself from screaming by sheer force of will, and there came from him a long low gasp of horror. It seemed to him, on this night when Nazareth was drowned in orange metal, that evil came out of the moon, but he could put no name to this evil. It was not death: it was something far more terrible.

He lay there gasping, waiting for the strength to return to him, sick with the heat which still hung over Nazareth, and then unable to endure the sight of the moon any longer, he began to climb slowly down the steps which led from the roof to the courtyard. When he reached the courtyard he decided to look at the panther skin, which lay in the inner room where he had spent the first weeks of his recovery. Limping, he lit an oil-lamp and made his way into that remote and silent room which lay beyond the oil press on the far side of the courtyard. The earthenware lamp jerked in his hands and threw strange shadows on the wall. Fear came to him again. It was a blind gush of white-hot fear, deep down, sickening. He trembled. He wore only a loose gown like a

night-shirt. The sweat flowed out of him, gluey, ice-cold, so that
the gown stuck to his skin. He heard his own footsteps on the bare
stone floor. He knew that the evil thing he was searching for was
somewhere in his own room. It was dark, terrible, welling out of
the air. It was merciless and cruel, possessed of a fierce and unrelenting strength. Holding the lamp at full length, he stood in the
middle of the small room. He could see everything clearly: a
cedarwood chest, some prayer-beads, the little white cap he wore
when he attended the synagogue, his prayer-shawl with the
fringed hems, an earthenware jar, nothing else. He was about to
go, thinking he was suffering from hallucinations when he saw the
great panther skin nailed on the wall. Suddenly his heart began to
lurch, and the hot sweat of fear trickled down his skin. He raised
the lamp, to see the panther better, and then he reeled, clutching
at the air, shouting hoarsely, and the lamp smashed into a hundred fragments on the floor at his feet.

His heart leaped with the horror of the dark, the presence of
the panther. He was melting, growing weaker and weaker. The
bronze moonlight filled the courtyard, but the darkness welled up
in the little room. Blind fear worked on him: the blind fear that a
man has when he lets his will escape from him and then seeks to
defend himself. He could feel the core of himself running loose.
With a supreme effort he limped blindly in the dark to where the
panther skin was hanging and tore it from the wall, and then he
trampled it furiously, trampling it into the stone floor.

"It was not God, but the Devil who came to me at the cave-
mouth," he whispered hoarsely. "See, I trample thee down! Thou
shalt not tempt me! I have fought thee once, and shall fight thee
again!"

Then, choking with sobs of rage, he threw himself down helplessly on the bed.

He had sobbed himself to sleep when he was awakened by
voices coming from a distant courtyard, perhaps from some other
house on the hill-slope. These voices surprised him, for he thought
all the people of Nazareth were in the fields. There were many
voices, and there was something curiously intimidating about
them, as though they were all uttering threats to one another; and
sometimes there would come a sound like a low moan.

For a long while he listened intently. It occurred to him that
perhaps the old servant in the house was talking to himself, and

somehow the old man's voice was reverberating against the stone
walls, but he could distinguish different voices—one sharp and
shrill, another very low, others ringing like metal. He got up from
the bed and went to the door. The voices were louder. The courtyard with its cherry trees lay like a pool of bronze in the moonlight. There was no other sound except the *drip-drip* from the
water-clock. He stood close to the wall, watching, waiting, drained
of energy, not knowing what to expect, his wounds aching.

Beyond the oil press lay a small passageway leading to the servants' courtyard, where the corn and barley were stored and there
were stables for the asses belonging to the family. The voices came
from this courtyard, or somewhere very close to the courtyard. He
braced himself, kept to the shadows and made his way towards
the passageway, taking care to muffle the sounds of his footsteps.
He was sure they were thieves, for it often happened that thieves
entered the towns at harvest time. There was a stone stairway
leading from the lower courtyard to the higher courtyard where
the servants lived. Great wine-jars, sealed and sweet-smelling,
lined the passageway, so that it was always difficult to walk
through. The voices grew louder. If they were thieves, it was
astonishing that they should dare to talk so loudly.

He was in shadow, but all round him the bronze moonlight
glittered from the courtyard walls.

He moved stealthily, taking care not to knock against the wine-
jars, his heart thumping. For a long time he dared not go on, but
remained standing with his back pressed into the wall of the
passageway.

Then he realized that the voices were coming from an upper
room in the servants' quarters, above the stables. There were the
usual stone steps along the wall. He climbed the steps slowly.
When he reached the top, he saw a door half-open and a lamp
burning, and all round the lamp men were gathered with strange
settled expressions on their faces. Peering in, Yeshua recognized
his half-brother Shimon and many of the young sons of landown-
ers; there were shepherds and farmers, too. But the man who attracted Yeshua's attention was a heavy-set man with black eyes,
a great barrel chest and thin legs, wearing a sweat-stained white
gown belted at the waist. In the light of the oil-lamp the man's
face was the color of cedarwood, scarlet, and he had a heavy
dark-pointed beard. Vigor flowed from him, from the burning eyes

and the lean lantern jaw which thrust up below the beard. Many strangers came to Nazareth, but this man was more strange than most, for he carried a curved dagger in his belt and spoke with an air of authority such as no one possessed in the town.

This room above the stables was used by the servants, but it was also a storage place for pelts: the skins of foxes, lynxes, even an old tawny lion skin. The sour smell of pelts fought with the sour smell of the decaying straws strewn over the floor.

Yeshua hovered by the half-open door, faint with weakness. The heavy-set, barrel-chested man was speaking. At first, because the man's face was so sunburned, Yeshua thought he must be a Negro from Africa, but it was not so: his voice was the voice of a Galilean.

"The Lord God of Hosts shall guide us!" the barrel-chested man was saying. "Let the Lord have mercy on us! Are we not the children of Abraham and of Isaac, and shall we be in bondage all the days of our life? I tell you this: the sins of Herod cry out from the depths of the wounds he has inflicted upon us! And the sins of the Romans, which are worse and yet more easily borne—I say there is no end to the sins they commit, the crimes of their heart. Have you not heard the Roman eagle in bronze stands over the gate of the Temple in Jerusalem! And the eagle shall perish!"

There was a murmur of applause, sharp faces peering towards the livid, scowling face of the young rebel with the black-pointed beard, who paused dramatically, lifted his hand high above his head, as though he wanted to see whether it was running with blood, and then seeing no blood there, he smiled, showing a row of dazzling white teeth, and went on to talk of the villainy of the Romans "who marked out my father for the slaughter, and mark out all who are of our faith, and despoil us, and lead us like lambs to the sacrifice." And still there was the terrible silence of the people who attended the secret meeting: they were not yet convinced: they watched with strained eyes, leaning forward, while the pelts gleamed in the light of the solitary oil-lamp and the straw crackled under their feet.

Near the door, just inside, crouched two men wearing white sweat-spotted robes. Their task was to face outward, to see that no one came near the room—no Jew informer in the pay of the Romans. Thinking they were young farmers, Yeshua whispered: "Who is he?"

Startled, the two men jumped to their feet and drew their curved daggers from their belts, pointing them at Yeshua, who smiled and backed away, not knowing why there was so much guilt on their faces.

One of these guards, well-built, with long side-curls, shouted hoarsely: "A stranger!" and would have plunged his dagger into Yeshua if there had not been a sharp cry from Shimon, who suddenly recognized his half-brother. With the cry, the guard's dagger fell slowly back to its place in the belt. Shimon ran up to Yeshua, his long white gown crackling.

"We thought you were sleeping on the roof," Shimon said, and as always there was a faint contempt in his voice. "We are all men here. Go back to sleep."

The man with the barrel chest said in a strained voice: "Who is he? Is he lame?"

It was the voice of a man speaking on the very edge of exhaustion, and there was even a trace of fear in it.

"He is my brother Yeshua," Shimon said, standing at his full height and turning to the speaker.

"Where? Where? Let me see him," the man said, holding the oil-lamp on a level with his own face, so that the bright flames lit his forehead strangely. "I see he is young. And lame, too. I have read that the Messiah shall be lame, and a hunchback. Is he a hunchback?"

"No, he is straight," Shimon said, and he whispered to Yeshua: "He is Yudah ha Neheba." The words meant "Yudah who lives among the animals," an outlaw with a price on his head. "Yudah Ben-Ezekiah. Hast thou heard of him?" Shimon whispered, and for the first time there was a hint of tenderness in his manner to his half-brother. "I see thou hast not heard of him," Shimon went on, "and perhaps that is for the best. All that thou hearest and seest here is secret to the last drop of blood. Dost thou hear me?"

"I hear thee," Yeshua said, trembling, looking up at his brother.

"Then remember," Shimon said, as he was about to make Yeshua sit beside him when the man called Yudah Ben-Ezekiah made his way through the throng and came straight up to where Yeshua was standing. The man came so quickly, thrusting his way through the small crowd, that Yeshua was alarmed and shrank back. There was a terrible glitter in the eyes of this man whose beard, seen at close quarters, resembled a thick tuft of black wire.

"Let me look at him," Yudah said, breathing heavily and peering into the boy's face. "I see he is about twelve years old."

"No, he is eight," Shimon said, and once again there was a note of apology in his voice.

"Then he is well-formed for a child of eight. Was he lame from birth?"

"No, he was a shepherd and killed a panther, but was wounded by the panther's claws."

Yudah smiled and nodded. He understood it all perfectly: no doubt the boy had beaten off a fox or some other small animal of the hills, and the boy's relatives were pleased to call it a panther.

"Did you say a panther?" Yudah said, still smiling. "A small one, eh?"

"Nay, a big one," Shimon answered proudly. "The biggest we have ever seen—it was twice the size of the boy when stretched out. I shall show it to thee."

"No," said Yeshua. "Thou shalt not show it, for I have killed it again."

"He is ill in the head," Shimon whispered. "When he was a small child, he saw the sun in a wine-jar and screamed that the sun had disappeared from the sky."

"I am not ill," Yeshua said, for Shimon had not taken care to speak softly enough.

Up to this moment Yudah had been addressing Shimon. Now he turned his full attention upon Yeshua. His fingers were twitching. He began to run his hands over Yeshua's forehead and down the cheeks, and then over the lips and chin, drawing the boy towards him. The fingers were very hot, and square at the ends, and they did not cease twitching. Though he could see perfectly, Yudah was like a blind man tracing the features of someone who puzzled him, who was a stranger to him, and yet not a stranger, for he felt drawn to the boy and was aware of the suffering in the boy's eyes.

"And so thou didst kill the panther?" Yudah said gently, and he gripped the boy's arms. "With those hands?"

Yeshua nodded.

"Thou didst this thing alone?"

"Nay, with the help of the Lord God of Abraham did I kill it."

Yudah turned to Shimon and the others who were growling their assent to the boy's words.

"He did well," Yudah said. "And speaks well, too. And has the fear of Almighty God in him, and yet no fear of the wild beasts of the field."

It was a taunt, and all except Yeshua were aware that they had been taunted.

"Then let him come close by me, for he is fearless," Yudah said, leading the boy back through the throng to where he had been standing under some nailed fox skins.

Yeshua was sick with fear. His hands leaped to his face, to hide his eyes. He had hoped not to be limping when he walked beside Yudah, but he limped atrociously, and felt all eyes upon him. He was shamed, deep inside. He wanted to turn away to the wall, but knew what he would find there.

The shame was like an embrace: it was as though he was being stripped one by one of his clothes, and his obscene wounds were being shown to these people in the upper room, who were all gazing at him, all wondering at the strange, taut, anguished expression in his eyes. His wounds had opened. He could feel blood trickling down shoulders and thighs, staining his gown. And so he stood there beside Yudah, who was an outlaw and whose hand was forever drawn to the dagger at his waist: this fleshy, barrel-chested man with the twitching hands, the huge chest and the powerful shoulders.

"I am weak," Yeshua murmured, "but this man—he is so strong no one could kill him."

Yudah was talking of how the Roman legionaries could be defeated.

"In the hills and the caves we have our hiding places, away from the roads where the Romans march, far from the eyes of Herod Antipas. The fox knows not our cunning. We shall hide our weapons under the straw. Each farmer shall provide for two of our soldiers. Every town shall be ringed round by men who have pledged their lives to us. We shall slaughter the legionaries in the Antonia Tower and lay their bodies in the Court of Sacrifice and cast them upon the pyre! And there shall be a day of thanksgiving when all the Jews shall feast!

"Not for my dead father's sake do I say these things! I say them because too many Jews have been ground down by the enemy! Let Cæsar perish! Let his body be despoiled, and let the worms feed on the Emperor, and let us have an Emperor of our own! For surely the Messiah cometh!

"I say there will come out of the House of David a Messiah who will lead us against the Roman eagles! The archangel Michael shall go before him, and Rafael and Gabriel shall walk by his side, and Phanuel shall stand behind him, waving a winnowing fan; and so it shall be in the time of shuddering, when the three floods of the last days fall upon us! Behold, the time of the Messiah is at hand!

"There shall come an Emperor to abolish all Emperors, and he shall sit upon the throne of David!

"There shall be no more rulers over the earth, only the angels: but our Emperor shall be worshiped by men in the courts of the Temple! And all who are chosen shall be changed into angels by him!

"But first the ungodly shall be put down, the sinners of the flesh and those who have lusted for power over us! Let there be no truce with evil! Let the sin and the shame be wiped out, abolished, annihilated! Let the sin be like the chaff which is tossed away by the winnowing fan, and let the shame be like the shadow which vanishes at sunrise! Behold, the Son of Man shall come girt with strength, and he shall utterly destroy the unrighteous! He shall come with banners and on his lips there shall be a sign! And everyone will recognize him at the appointed hour!

"I see you murmur and cast down your eyes. You say to yourselves: 'We have made our peace with the Romans and with Herod Antipas. We have paid tribute, we are pleased there are Roman legionaries in our midst. We pay out taxes, and therefore life is very pleasant under the sun. Sepphoris, Nazareth, Cana—all these are sweet cities. Then why should we trouble ourselves over our persecutors, who are so kind and good to us?'

"Listen, the Romans sleep! Yea, even the eagles sleep sometimes! They are fat with the wealth of our land: their heads and their necks are bowed down to their chests: they are slack with the slackness of sleep. And what shall come, shall come! While they are sleeping, they shall be utterly destroyed!

"We shall be like thieves in the night, entering unannounced in their secret places. We shall have armies in the north, in the south, in the east, in the west. And who shall prevent us?

"We are swift, we are silent, we are few—this is our strength! There is not one of us who has not killed a Roman or one of those who defend the Romans, but this was in vengeance, for they killed

my father. Now they shall die in vengeance for the sins they have
committed upon Israel!"

There was a gasp from the people in the upper room, for no
one had expected him to say he had killed for private vengeance.
When Yudah said he had killed those who defend the Romans,
they shuddered, for many Jews had died mysteriously and now
they knew who was responsible. Shimon was staring at his half-
brother. He was wondering how old Yudah was. There were some
who said he was no more than twenty-two, and yet a hundred
people had died at his hands! Truly he was Yudah the Hunted, the
outlaw, the one who lived among animals!

"Read the prophets," Yudah was saying, "for many are the
prophets who have spoken of the coming of the Messiah. It is said
in *The Ascent of Moses* that when he comes the earth shall tremble, and the horns of the sun shall be turned into darkness, and the
stars shall be splintered. The sea shall retire into the depths, and
the moon shall not give forth light, and there shall be no more
fountains, and the rivers shall dry up. For Almighty God shall
arise, the Eternal, and He shall punish the Gentiles and throw
down their idols. Then thou, O Israel, thou shalt rejoice and shalt
mount upon the neck and wings of the eagle, and the eagle shall
die, and God shall exalt thee! And then thou shalt look down from
some high place and see thine enemies in Gehenna, and thou shalt
rejoice and give thanks to thy Creator!"

All the time Yeshua was gazing at Yudah. He could not take his
eyes away from the man, the lantern jaw, the barrel chest, the
small black beard. Suddenly the solitary oil-lamp jerked and sent
a great flash of yellow light up Yudah's face, and in this light
Yudah looked more exhausted than ever, drained of all energy, no
longer a man but a mask. It was as though all the life had gone
from him, and there was only the shell of it, the small husk in the
light of the oil-lamp, the little yellow face with the two hollow
circles for eyes and the sweat streaking down the hollowed-out
cheeks.

There was a long silence. They hardly breathed, and there was
no shuffling of feet, no coughing, no arranging of clothes: only that
deep welling silence, and the strange cracked look on their faces.
They had seen the vision, and they rejoiced, and now they were
returning to earth, and there was no vision: there was only Yudah

Ben-Ezekiah with his lantern jaws, staring into space, his lips parted.

The wind came and lifted the side-curls of the young rebel, and at that moment Yeshua murmured: "There is the mark of death on him. Those who talk of destruction desire their own death." He was sorry for Yudah and wanted to step out before all the others and proclaim that he had no faith in Yudah's desire to make war on the Romans. He wanted to say: "He will die, and lead others to their deaths. We are too weak to fight. We can fight panthers, but who among us dare fight the Romans?" He had never in his whole life seen any Romans, for they rarely passed through Nazareth, but he knew they had conquered Palestine with their short stabbing swords and he had read the histories of their conquest. And he had no faith in Yudah. He felt nothing but a quiet fury and contempt for the lantern-jawed man who wanted everyone in Nazareth to flock to his standard, even though he pretended he wanted only assistance: food, weapons, treasure. And there was weariness in Yudah's voice, the weariness of a man who sees his death coming and makes no effort to leap to one side. Because his father had been crucified by the Romans, the son was determined to avenge his death, even if it meant dragging thousands of young Jews to their deaths.

"And shall you come with me, and lift the standards of the Lord upon the Holy Mountain of Zion?" Yudah was saying, not to anyone in particular, but to the whole congregation in the upper room.

His strength had revived. For a while he had been absorbed and silent, withdrawn into himself, into the little husk of himself, but now renewed strength was pouring into him and there was an uncanny flashing of his eyes. And seeing the reborn strength in him, they all wavered and were no longer set against him. Yeshua was standing close to him. Suddenly he felt a great paw resting on his shoulder, and he was being pulled closer and closer to Yudah, until he stood directly in front of the young revolutionary, who towered over him, the heavy veined hands resting on the boy's shoulders.

"For the sake of our sons, and the sons of our sons, and all the generations which come after them," Yudah began, and he went on to talk in curious clipped words, heavy with hoarseness, of the coming time when the power of Rome would be extinguished and the Messiah would appear in the land, when the grapes would flourish all the year round and the fig trees would never stop growing. "And no one shall deny that our sons shall inherit Zion, and the great fruitfulness which God has promised us. Your own rabbi says that one grape will be a load for a wagon and we shall be able to draw wine from it as if it were a cask. And a single grain of wheat will be as large as the kidney of an ox. And is it a small thing to shed a little blood for the sake of the fruitfulness the Lord has promised us?

"I see you are wavering and have little faith, and yet there is faith in you. The Messiah is living. He is here among us. And if you ask me how I know, I say it was promised to us. Does it not say in the Scroll of Daniel:

The God of Heaven shall set up a Kingdom,
Which shall never be destroyed,
Nor shall the sovereignty thereof be left to another people.

"And further in the same Scroll you can read:

The Kingdom and the dominion,
And the greatness of the Kingdoms under the whole heaven,
Shall be given to the people of the Saints of the Most High:
His Kingdom is an everlasting Kingdom,
And all dominions shall serve and obey Him.

"Therefore the spirit of God enjoins us to fight, and to die fighting! Are we not the sons of the Maccabeans? Let us be like Yeshua, who hurled himself upon a panther! Let us imitate him! You are children of light, who have remained too long in darkness! Shall we be weak-willed because the enemy is strong? But the strength of the enemy is no more than weakness compared with our own! And now I summon you to chant with me the Psalm of the Warrior David."

And saying this, Yudah forgot he had assembled a secret meeting and he began to thunder the words of the Psalm which invokes the Lord God of Hosts:

Blessed be the Lord my strength, which teacheth my hands to war,
*   and my fingers to fight;*
My goodness and my fortress, my high tower, and my deliverer,
*   my shield, and he in whom I trust.*

Bow thy heavens, O Lord, and come down: touch the mountains,
and they shall smoke.
Cast forth lightning and scatter them: shoot out thine arrows, and
destroy them.
Rid me, and deliver me out of great waters, from the hand of
strange children,
Whose mouths speak vanity, and their hand is falsehood;
That our sons may be as plants grown up in their youth, and our
daughters may be shining columns in the palaces,
That our garners may be full, and our sheep may bring forth thou-
sands and ten thousands . . .

When Yudah finished singing, there was a terrible silence. Only
a few quavering voices had joined him. The people were frightened, looking towards the door. They had debated with themselves, quietly and interminably, withdrawn in a debate which
was like an assault against the senses, but now at last, listening to
the hoarse triumphant thundering voice, with its note of tragic
pride, they realized that nothing would be gained by armed rebellion. They knew this as they knew their own strength, their weak-
nesses, as they knew the barley stored in the barns and the feel of
the earth under their bare feet. And Yudah must have known it,
for he looked at them for a long time in silence, his mouth wide
open in horror and bafflement and despair, and then bracing himself a little, he pushed Yeshua roughly aside, so that the boy fell
on the floor, sprawling there with his lame leg twisted underneath
him, and then Yudah vanished through the open door. They heard
him running down the stone stairs, muttering curses. And later,
when they ran outside, thinking to call him back, they saw only a
slight movement among the fruit trees, a shiver, a trembling, as
though a ghost had passed.

The bronze moon still shone on Nazareth. Wisps of smoky mist
hovered at the base of the bronze cliffs, and far away they could
see the painted tents in the olive fields.

The Rabbi

The summer passed, and then it was early autumn, with the cooling winds and the afternoons of winnowing, the golden chaff leaping in the air. All over the tawny hillsides the little tongues of flame were glowing over the stubble, and soon the hill-slopes were the color of a piebald mare, and the air was sweet with the smell of field smoke. Very mysterious at night were the little scarlet rivers of flame gnawing at the stubble, flickering and dying and leaping to life again.

All through the autumn the young men spoke in whispers about Yudah Ben-Ezekiah. They heard he had attacked camel trains on the Damascus road. There were rumors that he had gathered weapons and treasure, and buried them in a cave on Mount Hermon. And then more rumors: he had been seen near Jerusalem, he had been captured by legionaries, he had escaped. Some said he was living at Beth Hepher and had been observed in Sepphoris, disguised as a blind beggar, and then again that he had entered Tiberias disguised as a muleteer. He was everywhere and nowhere. He had captured Roman soldiers and held them for ransom. It was believed that he could creep into any town of Palestine unobserved. There were so many rumors that the old rabbi Eleazar mentioned the name of Yudah Ben-Ezekiah in his prayers in the synagogue, saying: "Must we all tremble before his name?"

All over Galilee the name was feared and the memory of the dark-faced man with the hollow cheeks, the lantern jaws and the thick, small beard was preserved in Samaria. He was like lightning, or a twitching nerve. He had two hundred, or two thousand followers—no one knew how many—and no one ever saw him by day: he appeared mysteriously at night; with the first light of dawn he had vanished, always spending the day in some remote cave or in a tomb. And when the rumors that he was killed were followed by a brazen attack by his followers on a camel train just outside the gates of Damascus, they said he had come back from the grave. Some of the young men who had attended the meeting in the upper room in the House of the Oil Press began to waver. "Perhaps after all he is the Messiah," they told one another. "Perhaps he is the arm of vengeance promised by Isaiah."

But no one really knew where he was, or whether he really intended to attack Jerusalem. All through the summer Herod Antipas remained in his summer court at Sepphoris, heavily guarded. He posted sentinels at the gates, gave them great bronze bells and instructed them to beat on the bells with their swords at the first sign of the young rebel chieftain, and in every town and remote village were posted orders for his arrest, accompanied by a description of a man with burning eyes, a thick, short beard and a barrel chest. But no one came close enough to arrest him, and when autumn came only a few rumors trickled down to Nazareth. They said he had been seen in Hebron, far in the south, disguised as a rabbi making a pilgrimage to the Cave of Machpelah, where the bones of Abraham and Isaac and Rachel lay. They said he had thrown himself upon the tomb of Abraham, demanding a sign, and immediately afterwards a tongue of blue flame had risen from the closely guarded tomb, but people only half believed these stories. They dreaded Yudah, and loved him, and secretly hoped he would be arrested, for they feared reprisals. And by the time the olives had ripened, he was almost forgotten.

Yeshua recovered slowly. Because he could no longer climb the hills and watch his sheep, he worked in the carpenters' lodge. He sawed timbers into rough lengths, fashioned door frames and roof beams, and shaped the handles of the fine, thin threshing flails. He liked the yellow of pine, the blood-red of cedar, the sweet pale whiteness of sapling oak. With the help of Shimon, his half-brother, he learned to choose seasoned wood in place of green timber. He learned to carve a well-shaped yoke by running his strong hands gently over the shoulders of oxen until he knew the place of every smooth muscle, the molding of every bone, and where the yoke would rub. "His yoke lies easy," the herdmen said, and they recognized his handiwork by the soft white finish. He fashioned a cedarwood chest for the Holy of Holies in the synagogue, but he preferred to make plows. "A plow is a gate to God," he said. "If I spend my time making cunning chests for the Holy of Holies, how shall I avoid being proud? So let me make plows for the gentle plowmen."

His hands, always large, grew powerful and muscular. They had known frost and sunburn when he tended the sheep: now in the workshop they knew the punishment which comes to the hands of all carpenters. They were bruised and hurt and broken by the roughness of wood. Many nails tore at his hands. He was a careful workman, but fell into fits of dreaming. Once when he was working on a yoke, he caught his thumb in a vice. Blood spurted, and he stared like someone lost in dreams at the scarlet blood falling among yellow shavings.

"So thou art wrestling with panthers again?" Shimon said, with a short dry laugh.

Yeshua flushed crimson.

"Not panthers!" he exclaimed. "I wrestle not with the living, but with a dead tree."

"And shalt thou spend a whole morning staring at a wounded thumb?"

Yeshua continued to stare at the spurting blood, making no effort to heal the wound.

Shimon reported the boy's behavior to his father.

"But he works well?" Yusuf said.

"Aye, too well. He laughs over his work, father. He laughs in his throat. It is written that pride goeth before destruction, and an haughty man before a fall. He is proud and willful, and takes no thought of what others say. He says a plow is a gate to God, and more nonsense of a like kind."

"I will talk with the rabbi," Yusuf answered, and there was a look of despair in his eyes.

Shimon lost control of himself, his face reddened and he said savagely: "Then talk with him quickly! The boy carries the stench of his wounds with him! And look what he does! When he cuts himself, he simply puts straw on the wound! And when he works, the wounds on his shoulder open. If he would see a doctor and let them be bandaged, I would have more love for him!"

"Then have you no love for him?" Yusuf said, alarmed by Shimon's bitter tone.

"More than he deserves!" Shimon answered. "If I ask him to do something, he simply stares at me like a fool who comprehends nothing, and goes about his own business. I have seen him staring at a knot of wood until his eyes burned in little hot cinders, and other things — He asks more questions than any other apprentices.

Always questions — 'Which wood is better?' he asks, and he shows
you two pieces of wood he always carries. He asks for the sake of
asking, and there is no peace in him. Sometimes I think he is mad!"

Yusuf drew back in terror. It was a long time since he had
thought his son was mad. After dismissing Shimon, he brooded.
He remembered many things: from the very beginning there had
been a strangeness about Yeshua, an apartness, a curious vivid
flame which refused to be quenched, though sometimes the light
in the boy's beautiful deep blue eyes seemed to go out. Looking
at Yeshua at table, there were moments when he felt a breath of
shivering terror: most terrible of all was the sound of the cracked
voice singing the Song of the Panther.

A few days later Yusuf decided to confide his fears in the old
rabbi. The old man lived in the House of the Pomegranate overlooking the arched well and the synagogue. He was a man with a
heavy nose and a sparse thinning beard, grey hairs curling over
the dark mouth, sunken cheeks wrinkled like old leather and eyes
as bright as the eyes of a fox.

"I have a strange son," Yusuf complained. "I am blessed among
men, for the Lord has given me four sons and two daughters, and
they have grown up straight as the columns of a palace. But by
my wife Meriam I have only one son, who is crooked and ill-tem-
pered, and refuses to obey his brother. My son Yeshua has eyes like
the windows of a house that has been burned, dreadful eyes
like those of someone possessed, and he walks lamely and sings in
a cracked voice. Is it some curse upon me? I am of the House of
David, and his mother is of the House of Aaron—so? Would to
God there had been no panther on the night my son stood near
the cave!"

The fingers of the rabbi were like the roots of ancient olive
trees, and now they clutched at the tasseled fringes of his prayer-
shawl.

The old man sat with his head bent a little to one side. He had
expected this visit from Yusuf for a long time.

"Once my son's mouth was full of laughter," Yusuf went on.
"Once his mouth was sweet with song, but now the song is like the
sound of flood water in spate, and truly I believe the proud waters
have gone over his soul. I do not ask thee for the name of some
punishment for my son, but for myself—for myself I ask punishment, and who shall give it to me?"

"God shall give it to thee," the rabbi said softly, plucking at his beard.

Through the open door a square of brilliant sunshine shone on the tiles, and from somewhere there came the smell of pomegranate wine. Tears were trickling down Yusuf's beard and his whole body was shaking.

For a long time Yusuf had hidden this thing from himself. He had talked about Yeshua with his other sons as though nothing had happened: the panther had leaped out of the dark, the boy had killed it, had recovered from his wounds, and they had all celebrated his recovery and blessed the name of the Lord God. And now the strangeness, the hurt in the eyes, the pucker in the lips. . . . Strange how the boy, who had never been close to him, had become so distant.

"My poor son," he said again, his voice hoarse and thin as the crackling of dry grass in the hot east wind.

Then he stumbled out of the House of the Pomegranate, blinded by tears, not knowing where he was going, whispering the terrible word over and over again.

The rabbi let him go. He told himself the old man's wounds would heal, and there would come a time when Yeshua would limp no more, and no more would there be that strange brazen light on the boy's face. And that evening the rabbi took down from a high shelf some old scrolls covered with dust, among them *The Book of Enoch,* and read:

> *His eyes were beautiful, and when he opened his eyes he lighted up the whole house like a sun, and the whole house was ablaze with light.*
>
> *And his father was afraid of him and said: "I have a strange son, who is not like unto men, but resembles what the Sons of God must be like; and his nature is different, and he is not like us, and his eyes are as the rays of the sun, and his countenance is glorious. And it seems to me that he is not sprung from me but from the angels, and I fear that in his days a wonder may be wrought in the earth."*

And having read as far as this, the rabbi closed the scroll and went off in search of Yeshua.

Yeshua was squatting on the stone floor of the lodge, the

wounded leg thrust out in front of him. It was dark. Oil-lamps were burning. None of the other workmen were about. The boy was making the smooth-handled shaft which would be inserted into the two curved prongs of the plow and fitted with an iron tip. The boy's head was bent, the reddish hair glinting in the light of the oil-lamps. The only sound came from the rasping of the chisel on the yellow wood.

The rabbi entered silently, a small bowed figure looking lost and lonely as he stood by the open door. The wind scattered some shavings over his feet, and for some reason the rabbi bent down, gathered some shavings in his bony hands, lifted them to his face and inhaled their scent. And then for a long while he gazed upon Yeshua, the golden head bent a little forward, the sleeves of the boy's gown rolled up to the shoulders, the muscles rippling, the broad shoulders and the powerful big hands. The rabbi studied every movement the boy made, every expression as it passed fleeting over the long face cloudy with concentration: the lips pressed together, the jutting chin, the curious eagerness in every movement. It was a frightening concentration, so deep that only a thunderburst would awaken him out of it; and when the rabbi coughed, Yeshua was unaware of his presence.

"Where art thou?" the rabbi said gently, coming to squat beside the boy, who was surrounded with a small mountain of shavings.

"I am in the wood," Yeshua answered, and looked up, smiling.

"And where is that?" the rabbi went on, speaking as one would speak to a child, very slowly and carefully.

"The wood is in God, and of God," the boy said, and he was still smiling and looking up, but the work of his hands went on.

"And so you have come here to work for the sake of God?" the rabbi said, still patronizing a little, though some frightful emotion was playing in his soul. "Is it because God is present in the wood?" the rabbi went on.

"And in the panther, too," Yeshua answered, and after a pause: "And in my sheep."

"Then He is everywhere?"

"So I am told, but there are places where it is hard to find Him. If you make a plow-handle badly, is He there?"

Because the rabbi knew little about the making of plow-handles, Yeshua explained how it must be fitted and joined with wooden wedges to the prongs of the shaft: it must be light and strong and provide a firm grip for the hand, and it must stand the shock when the iron share strikes a rock hidden in the earth, and if the tugging oxen suddenly plunge forward and wrench the handle out of the plowman's grasp, when the share is dug deep in the earth, it could break easily.

When Yeshua had completed his lecture on the making of plow-handles, the rabbi said: "Then it is because a good plow-handle is designed with enduring love that it partakes of God, and if it is badly designed—that is to say, if it is made without love—then it partakes, I suppose, of the Devil?"

Yeshua nodded.

"Oh, but it is much more than that," the boy went on a moment later. "I believe God has a special affection for wood, and there are even some woods He loves more than others, but it is all mystery. I have looked at a knot in wood until my eyes bleed, and I have not come to the heart of the mystery."

Then he held up the plow-handle. It was beautifully polished, glowing in the flickering oil-lamps, very smooth. Held there, it gave an impression of thrust and power.

"And your leg—your poor leg?" the rabbi went on, for he had a curious feeling that the plow-handle, which Yeshua gripped in his two powerful hands, might suddenly, like Aaron's rod, change into serpents; and he was therefore anxious to change the subject. "Is your leg better?"

"Better," Yeshua answered. "But I believe God has a special affection for wounds, and so I do not know whether to think the healing is good in His sight or whether it would be better if it never healed. When I look at the scars I see God's face."

The rabbi was deeply shocked, more shocked by this than by anything else he had heard. He said sharply: "Do you mean we see the face of God in scars and clotted blood?"

"Truly," Yeshua said and smiled again, that quick flashing smile, more of the eyes than of the lips, which so profoundly disturbed the frail old rabbi. "In the claws of a panther, too. In the thunderbolt, too. I have taken a panther in my arms and looked into its throat, and seen God there."

"Poor Yeshua," the rabbi said, "thou hast a belief in 'the God of terrible places.'"

"Yea, for God is like unto a lion and roars dreadfully," Yeshua answered, and once again there was a quick smile.

"And you mean this?"

"Truly. He is lion and lamb together. Does He not send His angels to disturb the waters? He is eagle and dove, but there is more eagle in Him than dove. He is the soft handle of the plow and the sharp share. He is the gentle smoke and the terrible flame."

"He is all that and more," the rabbi said joyfully, and for a brief moment he thought Yeshua had announced no more than ordinary orthodoxies, but then he remembered the queer reference to God in the clotted blood, and said: "Listen to me! Thou hast spoken of God in the plow, and how the plow is well made, and that is a sign of God's handiwork—or at least this is how I understand your words; but you say too that a wound is a sign of God, but I say that God made us whole, without wounds, and so He desires us to be whole, for are we not made in His image? And so I say to you, Yeshua, that if you would be like God then you must let your wound heal—"

Up to this moment the old rabbi was aware that the argument was entirely in the hands of the young carpenter. Now for the first time he felt he was gaining ground. Yeshua's eyes opened wide. A look of extraordinary gratitude appeared on the boy's pale face. He jumped up, threw his arms round the rabbi and shouted: "Yes, yes, it must be so! Oh, you are right! I am sure of it! I had thought wounds were blessed by God, but it is not so!" Then Yeshua went walking round the lodge, limping terribly, grimacing, putting all his strength on the wounded leg, so that he looked like a bird with only one wing, one shoulder lower than the other, grotesque, gleaming with sweat, with a look of triumph in his enormous eyes.

"I shall do as you say," he shouted over his shoulder at the old rabbi. "I shall get well."

"Of course you will get well!"

"I simply hadn't thought about it, but now I am sure," Yeshua answered, breathing heavily, for the agony of walking in this way was almost too much for him. "Yes, yes, you have given me strength. Thank you. Thank you."

He was like a child in his gratitude. He kissed the rabbi's hand. He swore he would do anything the rabbi asked of him. He took the rabbi by the arm and showed him a wooden camel saddle made by one of the apprentices and said: "Look how well it is made. We do God's work well, eh?" Soon he blew out the oil-lamps, and together the boy and the old rabbi walked through the narrow streets.

No lights shone in Nazareth, and there was no moon, but there was enough starlight for them to see by. They walked hand in hand, the rabbi walking with little quick shuffling steps in order to keep up with the boy, whose firm handclasp was so warm and powerful that the rabbi wondered whether his own little bird-bones were strong enough to sustain the pressure. And he was aware of a great warmth streaming down the boy's arm and into the fingers, a terrible warmth, a fire almost. He wanted to say: "I am an old man, Yeshua, and you are a boy of eight, though you have the appearance of one of twelve, and I am close to my Maker, and you are burning me." But instead he said nothing, and he could not remember afterwards whether Yeshua had said anything. Only it seemed to him wonderful beyond words that they should be walking together, and there was not the slightest sign of a limp: the boy walked as he had walked before the famous fight with the panther.

The House of the Pomegranate overlooked the arched well, and he remembered how they had stood together beside the whispering well for a few moments, standing there in silence, looking up at the stars. And soon afterwards the rabbi had gazed round him, and there was no sign of the boy.

That night the old rabbi returned to *The Book of Enoch* and read:

He was chosen and hidden of God before the making of the world;
And he will be with God through all eternity.
He will judge the hidden deeds of men,
And none shall ever be concealed from him.
Yea, before the sun and the signs were created,
And before the stars of heaven were fashioned,
His name was already pronounced by the Lord.
He shall be the staff of the righteous,
And as a light unto the Gentiles,
And the hope of all those who are troubled.
All who dwell on earth shall fall and worship him.

He shall thrust the kings from their thrones:
Their dwelling-place shall be in darkness,
And their marriage-bed shall be with worms.
He shall burn the ungodly as straw in the fire,
And the unrighteous shall disappear as shadows.
For the Chosen One standeth in the place of God,
And his glory shall be for ever lasting.

That night the old rabbi read as he had rarely read before: all through the night he twirled the spindles of the sacred scrolls, searching amid the crackling parchment pages for a sign, while the candles burned low, and he lifted his eyes from the worn pages only long enough to light more candles. He was in a fever of apprehension. Had not Yudah Ben-Ezekiah, and a hundred others, proclaimed or hinted that they were Messiahs? But what if the Messiah was a child? A babe might cry out, and all the kingdoms fall! And while the shadows wheeled in the small cluttered room where he lived alone, and the smell of sheep-fat from the dripping candles inflamed his nostrils and made him gasp for breath, and there was almost no air in the room, he pored like an immense spider over familiar pages which had suddenly become unfamiliar and astonishing.

There were times as he read when he could not prevent himself from crying out in ecstasy. More than ever before, he felt that he was approaching the sacred mysteries. He was like Moses in the hollow of the rock and in the storm of God. He was on Sinai, and the thunder was flashing, and soon God would appear to him: a veil, a presence, a ghostly face upon the darkness. He would see things that men had never dared to see. So he had prayed during the long lonely nights, and always he had been aware of a veil concealing him from the heart of the mystery. But now with trembling fingers on the scrolls, he read the words of Isaiah, and everything seemed clear to him. "Surely He has come! Surely the Messiah sleeps in Nazareth tonight!" And he began to chant in a strange high-pitched voice the words of Isaiah:

Behold, a virgin shall conceive, and bear a son, and shall call his name Immanuel.
For unto us a child is born: and the government shall be upon his shoulder: and his name shall be called Wonderful,

*Counsellor, The mighty God, The everlasting Father, The
Prince of Peace.*

And there shall come forth a rod out of the stem of Jesse.

*With righteousness shall he judge the poor, and reprove
with equity the meek of the earth; and he shall smite the
earth with the rod of his mouth, and with the breath of his
lips shall he slay the wicked. And righteousness shall be the
girdle of his loins, and faithfulness the girdle of his reins. The
wolf also shall dwell with the lamb, and the leopard shall lie
down with the kid; and the calf and the young lion, and the
fatling together; and a little child shall lead them.*

And when he reached these words, standing there with the scroll
lifted above his head, he could not go on. He was so sure that
Yeshua was the Messiah that he wanted only to run out in the
night and awake the sleeping boy and say: "Thou art the Messiah!
Surely this grace has been given thee! Thou wearest the signs of
thy kingship, the *aleph* and the *tav*. Thou art chosen by God! And
I, thy rabbi, I too am chosen, for thou art in some way placed in
my care!" He wanted to say all these things, and he knew they
would never be spoken, because he would never dare to say them.
He was old; he would die soon; and now he praised God because
in his last days he had seen the Chosen One walking through the
streets of Nazareth, limping a little, a strange unruly boy with
reddish-gold hair and piercing blue eyes and a curious composure
on his face. He kissed the scrolls, put them away and went shaking
to his bed. He slept fitfully, and woke up late the next morning.
As soon as he had dressed, he hurried off to the carpenters' shop.

"Where is Yeshua?" he asked, his voice breaking.

Shimon was running a plane over the length of a door-frame:
always that impatient screaming sound of sharp iron against soft
wood.

"You mean the shepherd?" Shimon said calmly, amused because
the rabbi was so nervous and excitable.

"Yes, yes—the shepherd of men, the Chosen One," the rabbi
exclaimed, his voice drowned by the screaming of the plane.

He wondered whether he could bear the excitement any longer.
It seemed to him that every curled shaving in the carpenters' shop
was sacred.

It was some time later before Shimon accompanied the old rabbi to the door and pointed to the hillside.

"The shepherd is with his sheep," Shimon said.

High up on the sloping hillside, playing on his pipe, surrounded by a white flock, the shepherd was making his way to the heights.

The Flaming Heavens

This evening the sunset flare was purple and gold, and all the heavens were aflame. It was spring, and the uplands were alight with purple and scarlet anemones and pink and yellow flags. He had spent the whole winter with his flock. Now, watching the great flames in the heavens, leaning on his shepherd's staff, the sheep around him, he was grateful for the cool spring winds and for the sky, which was infinitely high and filled with immense golden feathers and leaping dragons.

"Surely the sky in flames is the glory of God," he murmured, but soon, seeing all that golden radiance in the sky, as though the very heavens were burning, he shivered at the thought of how everything in the universe seemed to be on fire: the Plain of Esdraelon, Sepphoris, Cana, even Mount Hermon in the distance, all were touched with the sunset flames. God had but to lift a finger, and He could burn all things to ashes! God blessed every blade of grass and every living thing! He shaped the summer clouds and filled the earth with a riot of color and painted each shadow as it fell! There was no end to God's mercy—no end to the singing of birds and the skipping of lambs! And then he smiled, no longer afraid, to see the lambs near him. Were they not the gayest of God's creatures? The horns of the rams glinted in the sunset as though made of gold; the thick woolly fleeces were turned to bronze.

He adored the sheep, and every night he knelt and prayed that no harm would come to them.

Sepphoris lay below, a heap of jewels in the sunset glow, the great walls with their towers turning the color of honey. To the north, just outside the walls, he could see the vast bowl of the theatre filling with purple shadows, and beyond this a grove of cedars, and beyond the cedars lay the immense plain stretching towards snow-white Hermon. He could see the gardens of the King's summer palace and the painted pavilions, and they seemed no more than a stone's throw away, for the evening light brought everything closer. And now already Nazareth was deep in shadow, but here on the uplands the sun-drenched plains of waving corn shone like hammered bronze, and the wind whistled, making a sharp hissing noise.

"How sweet and fresh is the wind!" he said, and he wanted to cry out a psalm of praise to God for having made the wind so beautiful, but at that moment he heard the bleating of a ewe and he turned quickly to see the heaviest of the ewes shaking with the pangs of labor.

He had known it would come soon, but not so quickly. He ran to her and knelt beside her, and all the time he kept a watching eye on the other ewes, for there were fourteen or fifteen in his flock. His sheep had names, and she was "the gray-eared one." She was very heavy and swollen, and her enormous eyes were bulging out of their sockets, and she kept bleating plaintively, not an open-mouthed bleat, but more like a low rumble deep in the throat, and one of her forelegs was jerking. She was so soft and white and warm, and her smooth bony head was so still, that he felt a desperate tug of affection for her. He laid his head against the swelling flank, the thick curling wool smelling of wood-smoke, and he heard the lamb moving there: a sudden jolt, and then a breathless quiet, all the muscles relaxed, and then the jolt came again, very sharp: and then again the deep rumbling in the ewe's throat: and he knew it would be a difficult labor.

In his leather satchel there was a small bottle of wine and another of olive oil. He poured a trickle of wine over his hands, and then splashed them with oil, rubbing his hands briskly. He was ready for her now, and all the time he was murmuring endearments.

"Come, come," he murmured. "Come, little gray-eared one!

Come, little princess! Thou hast another gray-eared one in thy belly! Ah, let her drop easily! Let her drop smoothly! She shall be a princess as sweet as the balm of Gilead, as lovely as the cedars of Sepphoris!"

It was growing dark now, and the sheep were nuzzling round him, bleating shrilly. He was ready for her: ready for all the blood and phlegm, all the horrible jellies which accompany birth, waiting for the little orange-colored thing which would come lurching into the world. And he could feel it coming. The ewe was straining and rumbling. She cocked her head to one side, as though addressing a prayer to heaven. She dug her hooves into the grass, and strained terribly, and suddenly the heavy brown water-bag was expelled: it broke and splashed on the grass and a sour smell came from it, but this was only the beginning.

"*Tabitha,* little one, come sweetly, come sweetly," he murmured, praying there would be no broken limbs, pressing his face against the soft warm wool, whispering endearments across the crusts of flesh.

He was prepared for anything, and ready to feel his way in the dark contracting walls of the womb, as he had done many times before, hands straining to seize the little damp head lying between its front feet, but now he knew there would be no need. She was fat—too fat. When they became fat, they were always long in delivering. He would have to wait. He hoped the lamb would come palpitating with life: he dreaded the occasions when he tried to revive half-dead lambs by blowing into their nostrils. And now it was coming. Invisible hands were pushing the little lamb down the long funnel to birth, and it was coming sweetly, not lurching any more, but with a strange slow pressure from above, and it did not take so long as he feared.

A baby is born head-first, but a lamb comes with his little damp feet first, and then the head lying smooth against the feet, and the rest of the body twists a little and curls round and jumps down; and it is nearly always easy if the feet and the head come first.

He could feel it coming simply by laying his cheek against the ewe's swollen flanks. The shadows were lengthening, and now he hoped it would be light when the little crumpled orange thing appeared. His hands were waiting for it. The legs were coming out, and he pulled at them a little, to make the coming easier. And then suddenly, as though there had been a convulsion, the little head came out, dangling there, looking quiet and surprised, not caring very much whether it was born or not, and completely soundless. Then the whole lamb fell into his hands: there had been no need to pull it out: it came of itself: and the lamb was a bright splash of orange, nearly scarlet, lying there, trying to get to its feet.

The sun was sinking, but there was enough light to see by; and the little lamb was aware of the light as it struggled to its feet, its bones pushing up through the skin, breathing deeply, so that there seemed to be nothing inside it except air: a little scarlet balloon supported on four ungainly legs. It sucked at his fingers dipped in wine and strained away, so that the cord broke, and kept sucking at his fingers until Yeshua pushed it against the ewe's dugs. It was nursing within five minutes of being born. Strength poured into it. At first it could hardly stand upright, but the legs grew visibly stronger with every intake of milk; and now together with the smell of wool, and the sweet smell of the young lamb, and the sour smell of the afterbirth, there was the heady smell of milk.

All the time, as the sky darkened, Yeshua watched the lamb closely. He knew that those early minutes were the most important. He was watching for signs of weakness. The ewe was running her tongue over the parts of the lamb she could reach, licking up the orange color, and soon the brightness faded to a dusty brown. Yeshua began to sing a song:

> Thou hast sucked the wine from my fingers,
> Thou hast come out from the darkness,
> Thou hast looked around
> And seen that everything is good.
> *Tabitha*, little one, feed well, feed well!
>
> Thou hast come scarlet from the womb,
> And all the scarlet has been washed from thee.
> Thou standest upright
> And thy legs like columns support thee.
> Feed well, *Tabitha!* Little one, feed well!
>
> Thou art sweet as wine in thy coming,
> And thou shalt graze in ripe pastures.
> Milk shall flow to thee,
> And thou shalt grow strong as the lion of Bashan.
> Feed well, my little one!

Yea, thou art a lion, my little one!
Thou shalt skip, thou shalt roar!
Ha, thou shalt roar like the lion of Bashan!
All the sheep shall bow before thee,
And the serpents shall fear thee.
Go thy way, little one! Feed well, feed well!

When he had finished the song, he grew quiet, gazing in wonder
at the small lamb as it butted the ewe's udder, bleating pitiably,
because its soft mouth could no longer find the teat. And yet what
strength there was in the little lamb! Within a day it would be
skipping wildly across the pasture! For a year or two years a babe
crawls, unable to stand on its own feet, but lambs are born with an
unerring strength! "Praised be Thy name, O Lord, who makest the
lambs to stand and the ewes to give suck!" So he prayed, and made
a sign over the new-born lamb, and helped it to find the teat, and
soon, seeing another ewe about to give birth, he hurried to her,
and afterwards because they were still out in the open, he led his
flock to a stone fence shaped in a great square, the stone walls
topped with thorn branches—it had taken him a month to build
this fold from heavy stones gathered in the hills—and then he lay
down at the fence gate, watchful for the faintest noise indicating
that one of the ewes was about to give birth.

The sun had set: there were no more sparkling feathers in the
sky, no more leaping dragons. The furious sunset clouds were
no more than faint icy tracing in the dark blue heavens. There
was no moon: only the darkness, and the ghostly whiteness of
the sheep in the fold. Far, far away he heard a jackal howling.

There were long intervals at night when he slept, but his
sleeping was like his waking. Even in sleep he was aware of the
presence of the sheep. A bleat, a cough, a rumble: he was instantly
awake. But tonight the sheep slept contentedly, very quiet. He
had been asleep for three hours when he was awakened by a sound
coming from far away.

At first he thought it was a distant thunderclap, perhaps in the
north, but afterwards it occurred to him it was unlike any night
noises he had heard before. It was not a rumble from a wild beast,
nor the sudden sharp hissing sound which comes with a gust of
wind striking the waving grasses in the uplands. No, it was very
heavy and very pervasive, a sound that somehow filled the air even
when it was no longer heard. He was wide-awake. He lifted

himself up until his head was above the rim of the stone fence
crowned with thorns, and the sheep must have been disturbed by
the sound, for they too were awake. It was not at all the sound a
panther made. He gazed at the hills and at the great black well of
Nazareth below: nothing had changed; all was still. There was no
moon yet. There were blots of cloud in the heavens, and shadows
on the earth, but there was nothing at all unusual in these shadows.
Silence and the trembling darkness of the night!

He was afraid, but he could not tell why he was afraid. Sweat
dripped into his eyes, making them smart. Here and there the
starlight made the tips of grasses gleam silver, and there was
enough light for him to be aware of the shape and presence of all
the sheep in the fold. And waiting there, ears cocked for the
slightest sound, turning slowly in all directions, knowing there was
danger but not knowing whence the danger came, his hand went to
his dagger. He thought of calling upon the other shepherds with
his pipe, and it surprised him that they were not aware of danger.
It was the dead of night, the hour when dangers are most intently
felt.

All the time he felt the danger coming closer, impalpable,
inexplicable and obscene. It was like the terror of the moon or the
sudden roar of sunset, only it was a thing that came soft-footed, as
though some vast animal, all fur, had taken up its abode in the hills
and was watching stealthily. There came to him the knowledge of
some terrible tragedy forever inexpiable. Blood would be spilt;
all these hills would be drenched in blood; and the raw wounds
would bleed forever.

He caught his breath and hung upon the walls of the stone fence.
Terror overwhelmed him. His mouth opened wide. The terror
was drawing near: no panther, but more terrible than panther;
and it was not coming from the sky. It was something that was
fashioned by the hands of men. It had no name. It would not
speak. And at every moment this terror was coming closer until
he almost screamed for mercy, almost shouted at the top of his
lungs to awake the people of Nazareth, to warn them of this terrible thing which was approaching faster than any charioteer.

The wind came from the west, and now it turned a little, and
he heard a sound like crackling, but this too came from a long way
away. Then he heard shouts, the clanging of weapons, terrible
groans; and all of them were very soft, almost beyond the range of

hearing. They were like the sounds one hears in nightmares. He heard hoofs thundering in the night and the creaking of doors and whispers uttered in urgent voices, and perhaps these whispers were in fact sounds bellowed at the top of men's voices, but they seemed like whispers.

He could not understand even now where the sound was coming from: metal striking on metal, sudden cries, the groans of the dying, the tumult in the night. The sheep were rumbling. Now the air was filled with the piping of the shepherds on the hills, as each shepherd called for some explanation of these strange and distant noises; and the sound of the piping drowned the terrible uproar coming out of the dark.

Even now, when the uproar was growing louder, when it rose above the thin flute-like song of the shepherds, he could not tell where the sound was coming from. All the Plain of Esdraelon was in deep shadow. The steel-bright stars were glinting. The wind had died. He strained and looked into every dark shadow, and saw nothing moving: only the faint patches of whiteness where the shepherds stood by the sheep-folds, only the faint glitter of the grasses in moonlight.

These strange sounds had been going on for half an hour when suddenly a great pillar of liquid-gold flame rose out of Sepphoris. In the light of the flame he saw the palaces and the gardens like blazing honeycombs. Never had he seen such a tower of flame against the heavens. He shuddered and threw his hands up to his eyes. He thought of Yoachim and Hannah, his grandparents, and of his mother Meriam, who had spent all her childhood in Sepphoris. He looked again, because he thought he was dreaming the flame. This leaping flame sank low, and rose again, and was never still: it was of a brightness the eye can perceive: if it had been a little brighter he thought he would have been blinded. The flame shone on the fields outside Sepphoris: every palm tree was black against this flame: and it was so bright he thought he could discern the little clumps of oleander beside the gates. And now there was no end to the piping of the shepherds, for all had seen the flame and they were all summoning one another to witness what every one of them had already seen.

The flame was so bright that the fleece of the sheep turned a tawny gold in the unearthly light. He saw some Roman soldiers— he knew they were Romans by the gleam of their helmets—as they

rode pell-mell out of the western gate, making perhaps for Nazareth. Flames seemed to be rushing from one end of the sky to
another. There came shouts and the beating of gongs and the
blowing of trumpets, piercing-sweet, and then again confused
sounds of fighting, sounds like those the wind makes before a
storm, mingled with screams and hideous cries. Then the flame
died down, sucked back into the dark, until there was only the
glow of embers, a sprinkling of rubies, to show where the flame
had been. And then a long silence broken only by the hoofbeats of
the Romans, who were not riding towards Nazareth, but were making straight from the summer capital of Herod Antipas to the coast.

Sweat poured down Yeshua's cheeks. His voice shook as he
prayed. "The flames, the flames," he moaned, and sank his head
against the thorns ringing the stone fence, not caring whether they
broke his skin. Suddenly all the shepherds' pipes except one were
stilled, and this one was spelling out a long message to all the
shepherds on the hills, saying that every shepherd must give aid to
Yudah of Galilee, who had broken into the arsenal at Sepphoris,
had captured weapons and was raising the standard of revolt.

"All must help, all must help to the uttermost," the thin wailing
pipe was saying.

A black cloud of smoke hung over Sepphoris. Lights appeared
on the outskirts of the walled city. The sound of sobbing came on
the wind, and this sound was more terrible than any of the sounds
he had heard previously.

Yeshua froze with fear. He knew now what had happened.
Secretly, in the dead of night, Yeshua's strange enemy, Yudah of
Galilee, had entered Sepphoris with an armed band, attacked the
arsenal and then fired it, either because the Roman guards were at
his throat and the firing of the arsenal provided a diversion, or
because he hoped the pillar of fire by night would be as a sign for
all the Jews to come out in open revolt. Most ominous of all was
that small detachment of Roman cavalry which had ridden off by
the western gate in the direction of Ptolemais. There had been
fighting in the city—there was fighting even while the Roman
soldiers galloped away—but these soldiers had not stopped to
fight. There could be only one reason for their sudden flight.
They were escaping in the direction of the great Roman garrison
at Ptolemais to seek for reinforcements.

All night the black cloud hung over Sepphoris, drifting over

Nazareth in the early morning. When dawn came, the walls of Sepphoris glinted pure and untouched in the sun, but in the center of the city behind the royal palace, where the royal flags still fluttered in the wind and the royal guards still paraded in the courts, lay the gaping black ruins of the arsenal. The solitary shepherd's pipe was saying: "All must help, all must help to the uttermost."

"And where shall help come?" Yeshua asked himself, and he knew in his heart no help would be given. Somewhere in the north Yudah of Galilee, armed with the weapons captured in the arsenal of Sepphoris, would soon be assembling his forces. From vineyards and wheat fields, from olive groves and sheep-folds, hot-blooded youths were gathering to join Yudah in his mountain caves; though none came from Nazareth. At night, along hidden mule tracks in the mountains, they came like shadows, men from Nain and Endor and places far south up to the borders of Samaria; the shepherds gave them wine and bread and sent them on. All the time Yeshua waited with fear clutching at his throat for the expected explosion.

All that day, and all the next day, the country lay peaceful. Camels rode up to Sepphoris, people gathered in the market-place, that market-place surrounded by marble buildings which could be seen so clearly from the heights of Nazareth, and it was as though no liquid-gold flame had issued out of the heart of the city, as though there had been no fighting and no screams in the night. An immense building, once filled with helmets and spears, breast-plates, swords sharpened to a razor edge, had burnt to the ground: nothing more.

Four days later a Roman army two miles long marched to the city of Sepphoris from Ptolemais.

They came with trumpets and with heavy rumbling carts, and at the head of every column went the standards and the golden eagles. The silken banners shone red and yellow and green through the curling golden dust-clouds above their heads. Sunburned Gauls with long flaxen hair and heavy shoulders and steely blue eyes came marching and singing gay songs oddly at variance with their heavy tread. These soldiers camped outside Sepphoris, while their general, the lean and slender Publius Quintilius Varus, took up residence in the royal palace. A week passed. It seemed that Sepphoris was at peace with itself, quietly maintaining its existence with a Roman army camped outside its walls, while a smaller

Roman army occupied Magdala on the shores of Lake Galilee. "A
show of force," some said. "A threat—no more than a threat."
Yudah Ben-Ezekiah had vanished. There was no trace of him in the
mountains in the north, and some said he had reached the desolate
swamps around Lake Merom, where the silence in the evening was
broken by the clamor of a million birds. Yudah was a ghost. He
had vanished so completely that not even the shepherds knew
where he was hiding with his men.

At night the camp fires of the Romans twinkled outside the gates
of Sepphoris. All was quiet except for the blare of the Roman
trumpets at dawn and dusk. Suddenly more armies came to assem-
ble before the gates. They came from Berytus, from Arabia Petraea
and from remote Roman outposts in the north, until Sepphoris was
surrounded with a ring of bronze cuirasses. And then one day the
Romans heard that young Yudah Ben-Ezekiah, with the barrel
chest and the thick pointed beard, was marching on Tiberias, and
on that same day the Romans discovered that in Sepphoris itself,
hidden in underground apartments, in lofts, in synagogues, even
in the sewers, were young Jews who had thrown in their lot with
Yudah. Varus arrested them on the spot and ordered them to be
crucified. The first crucifixes were put up outside the northern
gate. Then he gave orders to the armies to march to the north.

It was strange how quiet and composed everything had been:
nearly ten days had passed since the arsenal was put to the flames.
Armies had gathered. Thirty young Jews were crucified. The
work of the fields went on, and the camp fires twinkled, and sometimes Varus himself, riding on a horse with a gilded saddlecloth,
an immense red cloak around his shoulders, was seen going among
his troops. And that was all: and in Sepphoris people went about
their business exactly as they had on all the other days, except that
now they were immensely richer, since the Romans paid in coin
for everything they purchased.

On the afternoon when the armies under Varus set out for
Tiberias, Yeshua watched them from the hills. All morning he had
wandered among the sheep walks in search of a drinking place for
the sheep. Two more ewes had given birth to lambs, and there was
trouble with a wolf which circled around his flock at a distance,
sending the sheep wild with fright. Afterwards he remembered it
as a day of many difficulties. A little copper-colored snake, hiding
in a mole-hole, had bitten a sheep in the nose, and its bleating as

it lay dying had nearly broken his heart. Never before had any
sheep under his care suffered from a snake bite. It was a day of
omens, a day of tribulations, and the vast army marching northward with the shrill trumpets and the clanging of metal drums had
confused and troubled him. He was sorry for Yudah Ben-Ezekiah.
He imagined that in some far distant place in the north or the east
there would be a bloody battle between the Romans and the Jewish Zealots.

"Have mercy upon them, O Lord," he prayed. "Have mercy on
all alike. Let them not suffer grievously. Let the black panther's
claws strike neither the living nor the dead. Let them walk in the
holiness of the sun. Let Thy sheep be fed, O Lord, and let them
come to quiet pastures all the days of their life, for the sake of Thy
glory and for the beauty Thou hast created."

He did not know why he prayed in this way. He knew only that
fear, raw and undisguised, clutched at his throat. It was afternoon
now, and the great clouds of dust thrown up by the Romans were
like yellow flames among the fields of wheat.

And that evening the earth trembled. Once again he knew the
fear he had known on the night when Yudah's men attacked the
arsenal and put it to the flames, but this time there was no warning
shout, no creaking of the grasses, no terrible silence. It was like
every other night, except that you could feel on your face the
beating of the wings of the angel of death. He remembered how he
had done everything in a very normal fashion. Shortly before
sunset he herded the sheep into the stone fence, whispering to
them, telling them everything would be well. In one hand he held
a horn filled with olive oil and in the other a cup of cedar tar, and
he held these things in his hands exactly as he had held them on
every other evening; and when he saw a sheep which had bruised
its knee on the side of some rocks, he would pour oil on the wound,
and if there were sharp scratches from thorns, he would make a
kind of plaster of cedar tar which put an end to bleeding. But the
sheep were restless in the fold. Usually he could quieten them by
singing psalms to them, but they remained restless. And all the
time the angel of death was hovering near.

Never, not even when he was fighting the black panther in the
hills, had he felt so strongly the presence of the angel. Ghostly
and silent the angel took possession of the hills and the plain below.
Her shadow fell on the sea and on the huge shoulder of Mount

Carmel; her darkness filled the valley of Nazareth. As he stood there waiting, he had his hand on his long-bladed knife and clutched it feverishly, till the hot sweat ran in the palm of his hand.

"They will come, they will come," he kept murmuring, while the sweat ran down his face and neck and the hollow of his back.

It was shortly before dawn when he saw the darker shadow moving across the plain.

This shadow was shaped like an arrow, and came very slowly, pushing through the wheat fields. Varus had left a small garrison behind at Sepphoris, camping at the gates, but there was no stir among the tents. And still the black arrow-shaped shadow moved stealthily across the ghostly fields in the starlight, and this black arrow-head, which seemed to have been made of metal, moving so cautiously and resolutely across the night, was more terrible than any black panther. It was like a vast emptiness, an abyss, crawling nearer. He stifled a scream, threw his hands up to his eyes, dug his elbows into his chest and called out for mercy against the terror of the black arrow-head, a mile long, moving straight towards the Roman camp.

A quarter of an hour before dawn, Yudah Ben-Ezekiah sprang out of the wheat fields with his armed men and fell upon the Romans. In less than ten minutes they destroyed every sleeping soldier and every sentinel on guard duty. At the moment when the sun rose, they burst through the gates and took possession of the city, shouting at the top of their voices; and the confused sound of rejoicing, lifted by the wind, echoed against the hills of Nazareth.

All day there was rejoicing. The people of Sepphoris went wild with delight. The thirty crucifixes at the northern gate were taken down; the followers of Yudah Ben-Ezekiah were solemnly buried; from all the towers of Sepphoris the silver trumpets announced the triumph of the Jewish army. Along the roads to the south and west armed bands rode out to bring the news of victory to all the other cities of Galilee. On the golden throne in the palace at Sepphoris, wearing the purple mantle of King Herod Antipas, with a strange bitter smile on his lips, Yudah Ben-Ezekiah sat in splendor. A thin circlet of gold studded with small emeralds crowned his head; his beard was oiled and perfumed; and his hands, studded with rings, kept drumming on the side of the golden throne as he shouted orders to his commanders.

When Varus heard of the destruction of his garrison at Sepphoris, he had already reached the outskirts of Tiberias. Immediately he ordered his army to return to Sepphoris by forced marches. Within eight hours his whole army was outside the north gate, and Varus himself on a white horse hammered at the gate and demanded the surrender of the ring-leaders. Yudah Ben-Ezekiah had posted his men on the battlements. They laughed. All night their laughter and their revelry could be heard, but the Romans remained silent. They lit few watch fires. There was no moon. In complete silence they made their plans. They were in no hurry. A battering-ram was brought up, Varus himself taking charge. The north gate could not be forced, for while the Romans were waiting outside, Yudah Ben-Ezekiah had taken the precaution of shoring up the gate with cedar trees cut down from the great avenue of cedars lining the approaches to the royal palace. Failing to break through, Varus sent the battering-ram to the east gate. Again he failed to break through. And having failed, Varus simply rode back on his white horse to his tent in the middle of the Roman camp.

From the hills of Nazareth all that happened within the walls and outside the walls of Sepphoris could be seen clearly, but no Roman soldiers climbed the hills. All that day, and for three following days, none of the shepherds dared to play on their pipes.

On the third day Varus sent a message to Yudah Ben-Ezekiah in an arrow shot over the walls. In the message he wrote that his patience was exhausted and unless there was immediate surrender he would crucify everyone, even the old men, the women and the children, now hiding behind the walls. "I have plenty of wood," he wrote. And in fact carts laden with wood from Lebanon were streaming into the camp.

There was no reply from Yudah Ben-Ezekiah. That night the fires in the camp burned with unusual brilliance. At the dead of night, at three o'clock in the morning, the Roman soldiers marched round the walls of Sepphoris, while the musicians played a lament. A little later the first flaming arrows were shot over the walls. They came in thousands, every arrow with its little flare of smoking pitch. Some arrows overshot the mark and set fire to the wheat fields. The first arrows that fell in Sepphoris were soon stamped out by the soldiers inside the walls, but they came in such numbers, whistling high, and from so many directions, that the defenders were completely unable to put out the flames. They could be seen racing along the streets, shaking their fists at the descending arrows, cursing, singing hymns, blowing madly on their trumpets, as if they thought they could summon the angels to their assistance. A huge wall of flame rose in the eastern section of the city. The wind sent the flames roaring high above the walls of the city, which stood on the crest of a hill and was therefore windier than the surrounding plain. In the light of these flames the shepherds could see men standing on the flat-roofed houses with their arms outflung as they prayed for mercy and vengeance, their voices drowned by the crackling of the burning wood. Roofs fell in, and showers of sparks rose into the cool night air. And all the while the Romans hurled their flaming arrows without pause, so that these arrows could be seen hurtling through leaping flames.

Before dawn all of Sepphoris was in flames. Where there had been a city, there was a glowing bush of fire, a million red jewels glinting, and here and there little tongues of blue and green flame, where wine casks were burning. The smell of burnt wine and burnt cedarwood was flung against the hills, and the heat of the roaring furnace was felt on the faces of the shepherds, who lifted their arms to shield their eyes from the brightness of the flames. Yudah Ben-Ezekiah himself shepherded those who survived the flames out of the western gate. Once again the Romans were in no hurry. They simply roped the survivors together, then led them away to the center of the Roman camp. More terrible than the raging flames was the quiet, methodical, unhurried behavior of the Romans whose tongues seemed to have vanished from their throats, for no one on the hills heard them uttering orders. But the Jews and the Greeks who streamed out of Sepphoris screamed and wailed, cried out for mercy, hurled themselves on their knees even when they were roped closely together, and they were still lamenting their fate when they were hemmed in by Roman soldiers, lances pointed in their direction, in the middle of the camp.

When the last of the survivors had escaped and all the prisoners were wedged in a small space in the camp, and when their wailing became unendurable to Varus, orders were given for them to be whipped. Then the wailing ceased.

Everything was done by the Romans with silence and despatch. As soon as Yudah Ben-Ezekiah was recognized, a heavy chain was put round his neck and orders were given for him to be taken to Jerusalem in a wood-cart—he would be punished according to the desires of the Roman procurator. For the rest, Varus took com-

plete charge. The Jews were separated from the Greeks; most of
the Greeks were given safe conducts to the coastal ports. All old
Jews were beheaded or stabbed. Maidens and youths were sent
down to Ptolemais to be sold as slaves. The followers of Yudah
Ben-Ezekiah were crucified; and soon there was added to the smell
of burning wood and the smell of burnt wheat and the smell of
burnt wine the sour smell rising from the crucifixes which ringed
all Sepphoris.

For a week of endless nights smoke rose from the burning
embers. The vultures and the eagles gathered. In their vast camp
outside the blackened walls the Roman soldiers went about their
duties as though nothing untoward had happened. Along the road
to Jerusalem, at intervals of about a mile, crucifixes were erected,
and on one of the hills overlooking Nazareth three crucifixes were
set up in full view of all the Nazarenes. Immediately after the
Romans had crucified the three prisoners, they announced in
Nazareth that anyone who attempted to prolong the lives of these
condemned men would be immediately cut down; then the Romans vanished, to return to their camp.

On the hill-top Yeshua wept. Day and night he had looked down
on the scorched and darkening hill, once a teeming city. One day
he approached within twenty yards of the crucifixes. He shivered
with fear. The three men were dead, their bodies had turned a
curious blue and their greenish tongues stuck out. The slime of
excrement gleamed on the cross below the wooden horns which
supported them at the crutch. "Shall the dead return?" he whispered, and then he knelt before the dead prisoners and begged
them for mercy, not knowing what he was doing nor what prayers
he was uttering.

Exactly eight days after the flaming arrows soared over Sepphoris, Varus marched his army to Tiberias.

The Crosses

All over Palestine there was the calm that follows a storm. The rebels nailed to the crucifixes rotted away, their bodies turning purple and then black: sometimes only the nailed hands and feet remained on the cross, for the rest fell away, lying in a little bloody heap at the foot of the cross. And always you knew where the crosses were, from the thick clusters of carrion eagles circling in the heavens.

All that winter the crosses remained above Nazareth, dark and silent warnings above a brooding town, and all day there was the tramp of marching men. A Roman garrison occupied Nazareth. There were garrisons everywhere—in Sepphoris, in Cana, in Gethhepher, in Bethlehem, in all the towns bordering the Lake of Galilee, small garrisons of no more than twenty or thirty legionaries under a captain, but they seemed a multitude. They searched the granaries and the caves for hidden weapons; they were forever scrambling up the cliffs and looking for the hiding places of the rebels. They closed the synagogue, defiled it and then used it as a prison. They examined one by one the young men and maidens, and pushed torches closer and closer to their faces if they refused to answer questions promptly. They threw a chain round the neck of the old rabbi and twisted it until his eyes bulged out and his swollen tongue lolled like a scarlet bobbin between his teeth. These legionaries were dark-faced Libyans, crinkly-haired and bearded, with leathered wrists and bronze cuirasses and short kilts which left their black knees bare. They wore heavy white goatskin cloaks slit down the sides, for easy access to their short stabbing swords. And they marched heavily down the narrow sloping streets, always with a bronze eagle and an embroidered standard flying before them. But they found no hidden weapons or concealed treasure in Nazareth, nothing to suggest that the Nazarenes knew anything about the uprising. So they were sullen and discontented, and received no rewards from their general, who set up his headquarters in a small village to the east of Sepphoris, overlooking the burned town, where only the scorched pillars and colonnades and smoke-blackened outer walls remained.

It was the dead of winter, with a light snow on the ground. Nazareth was like a white bowl, or like a rose, in the hush of winter, very pale, very quiet, waiting for the storm to expend itself. The people went about their business furtively, living within the inner rooms, hardly showing themselves. The blue winds came from the east, and the trickling of the fountains could be heard beneath the earth. From the three crosses on the cliff the smell of death filtered down to Nazareth.

The legionaries took over the carpenters' lodges and the smithies, where the sickles were fashioned; they seized the grain in the barns and carried it off on donkeys, as provision for the Roman garrison in Tiberias. Some children, seeing the black Libyans in the smithy naked to the waist, dark shoulder muscles rippling in the light of the furnace, reported that they had seen the horned devils, and could not sleep at night. Yeshua remained in the inner rooms of the House of the Oil Press. He read the sacred scrolls until his eyes became little red beads in the light of the oil-lamps. Meriam, who had been born in Sepphoris, was strangely calm: her brothers and sisters had been sold into slavery, but no one saw her weeping. She who was always calm seemed to grow still calmer, acquiring from some deep resources in herself the power of a perfect grace and silence. In those months it was observed that she was very close to Yeshua and she would read the scrolls with him silently, and she rose from reading with a quiet joy on her face.

While Meriam stood close to the walls and drew her veil about her face when the Roman legionaries passed, Yusuf gave way to bitter groans. He rolled his eyes, cursed secretly and raged dreadfully. At every meal he spoke a curse upon the oppressors; and he did this not for love of Yudah Ben-Ezekiah, but for hatred of Rome.

One day in winter, near the turn of the year, the people of Nazareth were awakened by trumpet blasts and were ordered to present themselves in the market-place. They were dizzy with fear. They wept and hurled themselves on the ground and tore at their hair, thinking they were to be chained and driven to the coast, to be sold as slaves. The Libyans laughed at them, pummeled them, drove them to the market-place with whips, and then commanded them to kneel, facing the cobbled highway which runs through the market-place. Far away they heard trumpets, the clanging of metal drums, the *clop-clop* of horses, the curious whistling sound made by many men riding in full armor. So they knelt shuddering beside the cobbled road, not far from the arched well and facing the synagogue, where instead of the star of David stood a Roman standard with bells and ribbons hanging down; and the ribbons were stiff with frost.

The morning sparkled: the leaves of the pomegranate trees were silver like ice, the sky a pale blue, with a few clouds drifting lazily overhead. A cold wind came down from the hills: the lips of the dark-faced Libyans were blue with cold. And so the Nazarenes knelt in the soft snow, waiting, and sometimes a bull-hide whip whistled over their heads, while the legionaries taunted them. The sound of kettledrums grew louder; they were deafened by the trumpet-blasts of the approaching army. They were sure a thousand men were riding into Nazareth. Meriam was there, kneeling beside Yusuf, who had turned white to the throat, the big blue veins throbbing at his temples. He looked prematurely old as he knelt there. Yeshua knelt beside Anna, who wept continually, her tears falling down her cheeks like lace.

And then it came: a procession of no more than two or three hundred horsemen in full military array, with lances and shields, belonging to the private guard of Publius Quintilius Varus, Governor of Syria. At the head of the procession rode the youthful Governor himself. He wore a gold helmet with a crest of flame-colored feathers and a scarlet mantle embroidered with a golden sun. He rode as though the whole earth belonged to him. He had a sharp aquiline nose and a smooth chin, and his thin lips were curled in derision as he rode straight forward, followed by his cohort of guards. He looked neither to right nor to left, and his hands in their scarlet gloves lay slack on the bridle. The most extraordinary thing about him was the terrible pallor of his cheeks, which were transparent and the color of snow: he looked more like a ghost than a man. There was nothing human in him. The curl of the lips might have been painted on him. And so he rode, staring straight ahead, in the splendor and insolence of his pride, and it was only when he came near the little knot of people grouped around Yusuf that he turned his head. His eyes met Yeshua's. They blazed for a moment, caught fire, and there was the faintest inclination of his gold-helmeted head.

In that brief moment while their eyes held, the Governor was aware only that a boy huddled in goatskins, kneeling on the edge of the crowd, had gazed at him with a look of worship or of dread. He did not permit himself to look deeply into the boy's eyes, though he remembered there was some strangeness about the eyes that attracted him. He did not allow himself the faintest smile. Having looked at the boy, he immediately turned his attention to the three crosses which hung high on the cliffs above Nazareth, and it pleased him that at this precise moment the first drops of morning snow fell on the snowy ground, and soon the sight of the crosses was obliterated by the softly falling snow. He was weary of the crosses. Strung between Tiberias and Jerusalem there were two thousand of these crosses, every one of them placed in a position where it could be seen by the people of Palestine, where it was impossible for them not to see the crosses. He had given orders for the burning of Sepphoris. Without troubling to consult Augustus Cæsar, he had ordered the Roman legionaries to herd the boys and girls, and men and women, of Sepphoris together and to drive them like cattle over the hills to the sea coast, to be sold as slaves. The sight of the chastised and enslaved Jews did not please him; nor did it offend him. He had put down the rebellion, and he had not himself at any moment of the brief campaign raised his voice. And so smiling to himself, lost in his own magnificence, he rode on towards Ptolemais.

A shiver ran through the crowd of kneeling Jews in the marketplace. They had seen the stern-visaged Governor: the face of iron, the eyes like enormous blue pebbles, the fair hair glinting under the gold helmet with the waving plume of feathers. Power streamed from him. Long after he had passed out of sight the people of Nazareth looked in the direction he had gone, cowed and frightened, not daring to avert their eyes, paying no attention to the guards glittering in bronze armor, their long blue capes blowing in the wind.

Yeshua, too, had been strangely affected by the Governor. The glance they exchanged stung him. At first he reeled back, as though he had received a blow, and then he murmured: "Have mercy upon him, O Lord!" Afterwards he felt only a deep sorrow for the man—the same sorrow he had felt for Yudah. Both wore

the marks of death on their faces. Both wore on their terrible
foreheads the sign that they would be cast into the outermost
darkness. He could not explain why he knew this; only he knew it
was so; and he shuddered, and prayed for all those who live by the
sharpness of their swords. "And let him not be tempted by the
darkness, but let him go from us!"

The great procession of wheeling guardsmen rode through the
market-place with thundering hooves. Snow flew up into the faces
of the kneeling, shivering Jews. Trumpets blared; the bronze
cuirasses rattled with every movement of the horses; the blue capes
billowed in the wind coming down from the hills. These guards
were not Libyans, but men with fresh, red faces, beardless, with
thick necks and heavy jowls. It was said that they came from
Britain, an island in the western seas so far away, so cold, so
clammy that no one in Nazareth knew anyone who had been there;
others said they came from Gaul, which was nearer, and merchants
from Gaul were well-known in the coastal cities of Ptolemais and
Sidon. There was something terrible about these stern, beardless
youths who rode like conquerors, with bare knees and bare arms,
and rosy flesh. Because they belonged to the private guard of
Publius Quintilius Varus, they rode on silken saddle-cloths, but
there was nothing in their manner to suggest luxury. They were
earthy and belonged to the earth, and all their gilded cuirasses and
gilded greaves were no more than trappings. And seeing the last of
them disappear in a great scurry of snow, Yeshua murmured: "Oh
let them be at peace with one another! Let them smile peacefully,
and may they never glare like conquerors!" And he knew it would
never happen as long as the Roman power remained in Palestine,
and he knew too that the Jews would never be able to destroy that
power. Only if the Romans left of their own accord would the
Jews be at peace in their own country.

On the next day the small garrison of Libyans which had
occupied Nazareth for nearly three months marched away. No one
knew where they went. In some distant headquarters, perhaps in
the Tower of Antonia in Jerusalem, a Roman commander had
given the order to transfer the Libyans to the borders of Parthia.
And once more Nazareth was a small secluded valley forgotten by
the outside world.

For a week the people of Nazareth were too dazed to realize

their good fortune. On those hushed winter days they moved about like people in a dream, talking in whispers. They wondered whether a trick was being played on them, and they expected to see the Libyans returning down the long winding road which passes beneath the cliff of Nazareth. A Sabbath passed, and then another, before they dared to enter the synagogue and chant the psalms of freedom.

On that Sabbath all the people of Nazareth crowded into the synagogue which the Romans had defiled, now once more consecrated to the Lord God of Hosts. Wrapped in their most precious praying scarves, threaded with spun gold and silver, they fell to their knees and sobbed over and over again: "Hear Israel, the Lord is God, and God is one." Their tears sprinkled the stone floor like rain, and they could hardly see the old rabbi who threw open the door of the Holy of Holies at the back of the altar and displayed the scrolls of the Law and the Prophets, six enormous doll-like objects enshrouded in heavy silk with lacy tassels. The old rabbi knelt on the floor and kissed the lacy hems, and afterwards there came six elders who each lifted one of the scrolls and carried it in procession around the synagogue, while little bells tinkled and everyone pressed forward to kiss the scrolls, and if they could not come close, they blew kisses at them.

It was a day of thunder, and heavy rains falling in the uplands. Everyone was laughing and sobbing at the same time. The ram's horn was blown three times. The traditional responses were offered, and then the six doll-like shrouded figures in their watery blue silk clothes were laid together, and one by one they were undressed, no longer mysterious. They were seen to be no more than parchment wound on wooden spools. And now as always happened, simply because they were unveiled, because the mysterious wrappings were taken from them, they became in a strange way more potent and more terrible. Through His scribes, the fingers of God had touched these faded parchment scrolls. These words were mouths, and all these mouths were Moses. The sobbing grew fainter when the old rabbi began to twirl the spools as he searched for a psalm to intone, but suddenly he swerved round, lifted the heavy scrolls above his head and without troubling to read the written words, he cried out in a pure voice a psalm of deliverance:

Praise ye the Lord.
Praise ye the Lord from the heavens:
Praise Him in the heights.
Praise ye Him, all His angels:
Praise ye Him, all His hosts.
Praise ye Him, sun and moon.
Praise Him, all ye stars of light.
Praise Him, ye heaven of heavens,
And ye waters that be above the heavens.
Praise the Lord from the earth,
Ye dragons, and all deeps:
Fire and hail, snow and vapors:
Stormy wind, fulfilling His word,
Mountains and all hills, fruitful trees, and all cedars:
Beasts and all cattle; creeping things, and flying fowl:
Kings of the earth, and all ye peoples:
Princes, and all judges of the earth:
Both young men and maidens, old men and children.
Let them praise the name of the Lord—

And then his voice dropped, and the old rabbi could speak no more, and when the congregation had completed the psalm, he turned to them and made a little bow and said: "For the Lord God has been merciful unto us. Amen."

He stood there smiling, while the white tears of joy trickled down his withered cheeks, and he would have stood there for a long time if someone had not brought a blue-bordered Roman standard, left behind by the legionaries, and offered it to him. The rabbi bent over the standard, as if at first his weak eyes had not been able to recognize it; then he took it in his hands, holding it only by the edge, and walked slowly towards the altar where the five-armed Maccabean candlestick with the candles aflame stood below the Ark. The old rabbi held the standard over the flames. A flame the color of brass leapt up, and the square standard with the fringed edges was completely consumed in only two or three seconds. On the stone altar there were only a few charred shreds of silk and some white ashes.

The old rabbi smiled, turned to face the congregation, lifted his hands in blessing. Immediately there occurred something which had never happened in the synagogue before. A roar broke from the congregation, a roar so loud that it was like the explosion of air when a furnace gate is opened. They wept and screamed and laughed and danced and shouted until they were hoarse; and gradually their voices became one voice, intoning the ancient incantation: "Hear Israel, the Lord is God, and God is one." They spoke these words three times, and then fell joyfully in one another's arms.

All through the rejoicing Yeshua was silent. He stood as usual among the men who crowded close to the altar. He was eight, nearly nine, but he carried himself like a child of twelve. His wounds had healed, there was a flush of health on his cheeks and his enormous deep blue eyes watched everything closely, even when he gave the impression of someone dreaming. He saw one of the elders of the synagogue unfolding the standard, and gasped. He had not thought the Libyans had left anything behind, and at first it had seemed a sacrilege to display the standard in a synagogue; and when the standard was solemnly offered to the old rabbi, Yeshua turned his head away, hoping in some way to attract the attention of Meriam, who sat with all the other women of Nazareth in the stone gallery. When he saw the flag suspended over the five-branched Maccabean candlestick, he gave a shout of horror which was drowned in the joyous cries of the congregation. "Must we make war on the Romans? Shall they consume us in their flames?" He shuddered and leaned his head against one of the dark stone pillars supporting the roof. He heard the rain roaring down the gullies and the thunder on the hills. He was sure some terrible punishment was about to fall on the synagogue. He saw the candlelight flickering on their faces and shining teeth: the huge, delirious joy of the people of Nazareth as they saw the hated symbol of Roman power consumed by the little bud-like flames. They cried and shouted and danced and kissed one another, and the old rabbi smiled at them approvingly with his arms uplifted above his head, glowing like Elijah in the light of the flames.

Yeshua remembered the face of the stern Governor, hard, lean, sculptured from stone, with blue pebbles for eyes. He remembered the dark-eyed Libyans who had pushed torches close to the young men and maidens, so that even now many of them were bandaged and others, who wore their burns proudly, were covered with suppurating sores. He remembered the shape of the short swords, the gleaming reddish-blue steel, and he knew a Roman would cut the throat of the old rabbi as easily as he would cut the throat of a lamb. Then why should men dare in Nazareth to defy the Romans? "Oh, let them be at peace! Let them not burn the flags! Let them walk quietly in the ways of the Lord!" And saying this, he wanted to blot out the sight of the people dancing and shouting, and he threw his arms round the dark pillar, pressing his head against it, burying himself in the rock, shuddering, not knowing where to turn, weary of their dangerous excitement, until at last he turned to them and shouted: "Shall ye all be crucified?" In the sudden riot and confusion no one paid attention to the boy who shouted in the synagogue.

Winter was the time of short, sharp thunderstorms and day-long rains. The heavy blue clouds swung over the Plain of Esdraelon, only to be unloosened when they came to the bowl of Nazareth. There were days when bluish flames of lightning flickered all day on the heights, and other days when the water running down the hillslopes came with a sound like thunder, sweeping every unprotected thing from its path, so that the market-place was knee-deep in water, and olive trees, uprooted in the storm, swam in furious circles. Sometimes there were cliff-falls. Sometimes, too, even in a rainstorm, a forest of fruit trees would explode in a great glow of red flame when struck by thunderbolts. Usually in Nazareth, even when it rained, you could see the shapes of the surrounding cliffs, bluish-gray in the surrounding mists.

It was evening and close to sunset when the congregation left the synagogue. The rain no longer fell. There was a curious hush in the air, the sunlight trembling in the moisture-laden air. All Nazareth seemed to have changed, cleansed by the storm, glittering in the rosy sunset. The flat roofs gleamed silver and rose, while the shadows deepened to purple. Afterwards no one remembered who it was who first pointed to the cliff where the three crosses had watched over the town. *The crosses had vanished.*

At first they believed a miracle had occurred, or perhaps the legionaries had themselves removed the crosses, or perhaps the nightmare was over—there had been no crosses, no slaughter, no legionaries had ever occupied the town and no Roman Governor had ridden silently across the market-place. No; it was all a bad dream! They had awakened from their dream! None of the terrible and tiresome things they imagined had happened! And then, even as they stood outside the synagogue, they saw something that none had ever expected to see: they saw the three crosses floating in the market-place, turning in slow circles, in the ebbing floodwater. On one of the crosses was the ravaged body of one of Yudah's young rebels, glistening like a silver-colored serpent, for there was no shape to the body: only a long, thin streak of flesh glued to the cross. And on the others there were only legs and the torn shreds of arms and shapeless hands. Silvery-gray water rats were already swimming across the market-place and attempting to climb on to the floating crosses, which had come with the flood waters down the hillside.

In later years no one spoke of the day when the three crosses came floating into Nazareth. It was something they wanted to forget, and therefore they maintained a conspiracy of silence. Instead, in hushed voices, they spoke of the day "when our rabbi Eleazar burned the Roman standard in the five-branched candlestick," and though it was a day of pure horror they remembered it as a day of rejoicing.

The White Asses

When Yeshua was thirteen years old, he journeyed with Yusuf and Meriam to attend the Passover at Jerusalem.

It was a year of peace, of fat harvests, of cloudless blue skies. In Rome an old and ailing Emperor looked out upon an empire stretching from Britain to Persia, and from Africa to the borders of Scythia, where all men were at peace. Roman ships bulging with corn sailed unhindered from Egypt across the Mediterranean: there were no pirates on the seas and no rebels on land. The temples in Rome groaned under the weight of tribute which came from the furthest reaches of the empire. No one listened to the soothsayers who predicted that the sun of Rome was now at high

noon and soon must fall into a long evening of twilight. That was
the year when the Emperor bade farewell to the lean and slender
Publius Quintilius Varus, summoned from Syria to destroy the
simmering revolt of some obscure German tribesmen. In the following year, at the battle of the Teutoberger Forest, Varus who
destroyed Sepphoris was himself destroyed. For the first time in
living memory there was a breach in the carefully guarded frontiers of the empire.

In Nazareth the burning of Sepphoris was almost forgotten.
How could men remember it when they had only to climb the Nazareth hills and look down upon a new and gleaming city on that
hillcrest where they had seen a single roaring flame leaping to the
heavens? By the order of King Herod Antipas the city was rebuilt.
Within a year a white marble palace replaced the heap of scorched
and broken marble columns which was all that remained after the
fire; within eighteen months there was a thriving city called
Sepphoris-out-of-the-Flames. Money flowed into Nazareth, much
of it passing into the hands of Yusuf, whose sawmills produced the
timbers for the new city. From his wealth Yusuf endowed the new
synagogue in Sepphoris, and there Yeshua was sent to school. For
him Sepphoris was holy ground, for had not Yoachim and Hannah
perished there on the night of conflagration? In the library he
learned Greek and Hebrew. From all the reaches of the Roman
Empire men gathered in Sepphoris. Yeshua picked up a smatter-
ing of Latin, Egyptian, even of Persian. He attended the plays
performed in the great amphitheater outside the walls. For him
it was a new world, remote from the sequestered life of Nazareth.
On all holidays he walked over the nearby hills down into the vale
of Nazareth.

When he was thirteen years old he became in the eyes of the
Judaic law a full-grown man, a son of the law. All the duties men
performed in the synagogue were now performed by him. He was
nearly full-grown, tall, graceful, curiously reserved, always close
to Meriam but always distant from his father, who sometimes
hesitated to talk with him, unable to follow the movements of his
son's mind. There were days in the House of the Oil Press when
Yeshua and Yusuf passed one another in silence, like ghosts.

With Meriam he was aware of a desperate affection, a terrible
love. His spirit burned in him when he set eyes on her. He loved
her to distraction. He told himself that if she died, he would kill

himself instantly. He heaped presents on her—flowers, strange
rings bought in the market-place at Sepphoris, veils of silk, beads
of amber. She had not changed. She was still the young and beautiful woman who had caught him up in her arms on the day when
he saw deep down in a wine-jar on the edge of a barley field the
face of the sun. For him the sun was eternal wine, and his mother
was the morning star. He listened to her as he listened to no
one else.

"Thou shouldst speak more gently with thy father," Meriam
said one day.

"Ha, and spend my time talking about the cost of running a
sawmill," he answered, bridling.

"Nay, be more gentle, my son. Thou art too headstrong—"

"And he is more headstrong still, though I cherish him."

"But he is thy father and must be headstrong for his health's
sake," Meriam smiled.

Then there was peace between Yusuf and his son. But when
Yusuf announced that he intended to take Yeshua to Jerusalem,
he was red of face.

"I would have taken thee before, but thou wast ill or strange,"
Yusuf explained. "There were troubles between us. Had I not
asked thee to work in my sawmill, but thou must become a shepherd and then a student—" It was the old complaint, with a little
whine in the voice. "But I shall not speak of that now. I ask thee
to come to Jerusalem, for thou knowest Sepphoris and Nazareth
no more. My son, they say the road through Samaria is free, and
we shall see no Romans save those who prowl about Jerusalem.
When thou seest them, my son, turn thy head away and say a
prayer that they shall become food for vultures—nay, that the
worms shall burrow into their flesh and eat them living!"

Horror of Rome remained, fierce, unchanging. It spilled into
the vale of Nazareth where a girl looking at the sudden gleam of
sunlight on bronze or the swirl of some colored garment in the
wind would suddenly start screaming, remembering the bronze
cuirasses and capes of the Roman legionaries. And older people
remembered that even now there were survivors of the army of
Yudah of Galilee hidden in the caves and the hills.

"Hast thou heard what I said concerning the Romans?" Yusuf
asked, putting his gnarled hand to the face of the boy whose eyes
were downcast.

"Yea, I heard, my father."

"Then thou shalt do as I am telling thee, for all else is iniquity in the face of the Lord. And in Jerusalem thou shalt attend the Sacrifice with me, for art thou not *benhatthorah*, and worthy to attend? So thou shalt prepare thyself with fasting and with singing the psalms of the ascent, and thou shalt be of good counsel in these following days."

Yusuf was sitting on cushions in the upper room, and the sunlight came flooding through the small loophole on to the old man's face, the beard turning gray, the forehead all wrinkled, as though acids had bitten into it. Four years ago there was still a youthful strength in the old man, but now the strength was going from him, and his voice was quavering. It was spring, and the fields of Nazareth were scarlet with anemones.

Yeshua thought he would go alone with his father to Jerusalem, and was pleased when he learned that his mother was accompanying them. For the eighty-mile journey to Jerusalem they were to ride on the white asses which come from Bithynia, on saddle-cloths encrusted with gold and silver wire. Twenty other families from Nazareth would accompany them.

Ever since the bright sickle of the Passover new moon had appeared in the sky, Nazareth had been in a fever of preparation. There were solemn feasts in honor of the Passover pilgrims, and special prayers were said in the synagogue. The poorer pilgrims were given money and goods to defray the expense of the journey: an expensive journey, with need to give offerings to the Temple, and nearly everyone in Nazareth had relatives who lived in Jerusalem or close by, and for them there were presents. And some went off with heavy hearts, knowing they would be penniless when they returned.

The diamond-bright dawn broke in a sky of the purest blue, the earth dazzling. The asses were combed and shone like snow. In the market-place, at the arched well facing the synagogue, the pilgrims met to fill their waterskins at the fountain and to bind their cooking vessels and hampers of food on the backs of asses, donkeys, mules and dromedaries. There was so much bustling and shouting, cracking of whips, buckling of leather belts round the animals, lighting of fires and cooking of food to prepare the pilgrims for the journey, that hardly anyone observed the coming of Yusuf, Meriam and Yeshua on their snow-white mounts. According to his custom, Yusuf was determined to ride close to the end of the slow-moving caravan, taking his time. He had ridden along that stony winding road built by the Romans so many times that he knew every town, every hill and dale: he could have ridden blindfold. He felt no particular excitement. He was too old to enjoy the wild farewells. As a wealthy landowner, he rode in princely fashion, not troubling to carry food satchels, for he had money enough in his scrip to purchase it on the way. But all the three asses carried waterskins, against the heat of the sun.

The silver mists were striking off the hills when the gaily colored caravan set out along the Roman road, the tall green wheat waving on the Plain of Esdraelon. Soon they were riding through Nain. All the villagers were out in the fields. As they came down the dusty road, under the scarlet pomegranate trees, into a strange, hot emptiness made more desolate by the flashing of the sun on the coarse jets of black basalt overhanging the village, it was very quiet except for the humming of bees. "A poor place," Yusuf said, waving his hand at the empty houses, all quiet as the grave. "You could buy it all, if you had a mind to, for a few shekels."

By midday they were in Shunem, with its yellow walls and ornamented gateways, as full of bustle as Nazareth on a feast-day. There were fruit trees everywhere, and the wheat was silkier than the wheat of Nain. Here the prophet Elisha had lived in a little chamber on the wall presented to him by a good woman, who was rewarded with a son, and when the son died, Elisha breathed upon him and gave him back to her alive. From Shunem, too, had come the fairest of all virgins of Israel to the bed of King David. All those things Yusuf repeated to his son, pointing out the house where Elisha had stayed: though the house looked surprisingly new. You were expected to make offerings in the little white-washed shrine built just outside the house, but Yusuf refused, saying he was sure Elisha had passed through Nazareth, which was therefore equally worthy of charity; but he searched out the house where the Shunemite girl Abishag, "the tender one," was supposed to have been born.

Early in the afternoon, when the pilgrims were resting in the inn, Yeshua wandered out into the hot streets, telling himself he would go outside the town walls and gaze upon the blue ridge of

Carmel, for there was a wonderful view of Carmel from this place. Yeshua had gone only a little way down the dusty street when he saw a girl, no longer a child and not yet a maiden, no more than ten years old, very likely a slave, leaning her face wearily against a well-post, and beside her was an immense earthenware jar. Her body was listless, she was sobbing and her shoulders were shaking. She wore a ragged red gown which reached to her feet and made her look curiously grown-up, and she wore her hair in the manner of someone many years older. Yeshua was touched by her. He knew she was sobbing because her little bird bones were incapable of lifting the immense earthenware jar. So he went up to her, and begged for water and, when she gave him a small cup of water, he offered to lift her jar for her. She wiped her tears away, and stared at him as if he had suddenly become an enemy.

"No," the girl said through her tears. "I gave thee to drink freely for the sake of my mother, who lately died, and for charity, and for love of God."

"And shalt thou not suffer me to lift the jar?"

"Nay, for that would be charity."

The great jar had been filled to the brim.

"Wilt thou let me carry it away a little way?" he said, laughing.

The girl put her hands round the jar, protecting it.

"Nay, I shall not let thee."

"And if I should sing for thee?"

"Nay, thou shalt not—"

He took her hand and smiled at her, feeling the small warmth coming through the tattered dust-stained red gown.

"And shalt thou prevent me?" he asked, taunting.

"I shall," she said, and clapped her hands to her ears, and because her hands were no longer occupied, he swiftly bent down and began to lift the brimming jar.

Then she was confused, the blood rushing to her face, her eyes filling with tears, and to put her at ease he began to sing for her:

> The little one in the red dress
> Weeps by the wellspring.
> Oh, the red flower of the pomegranate!
>
> The little one in the red dress
> Walks beside me.
> Oh, the pure scarlet of the anemone!

The little one in the red dress
Is singing merrily.
Oh, the red dawn in the East.

So they walked down the dusty road, Yeshua with the wine-jar on his shoulder and the girl running at his side, laughing. The hot winds poured through the streets, where a few children played out of doors, and here and there a goat was tethered. It was very quiet as they walked along, accompanied by little ink-black shadows.

And when they came to her master's house with the courtyard of shriveled gray olive trees, he taunted her again, saying: "Shalt thou give me something so that I shall remember thee?"

"Nay, 'tis for charity thou hast done this," she answered, blushing.

"And what is charity?"

"Nay, nay, thou shalt not tie me in words! For charity thou hast done this, surely! Let me be!"

"Dost thou not love me?"

"Nay, but thou hast charity—"

She stood there in the sun-splashed shade of the olive trees, holding her head a little to one side. She was ten years old, but she possessed a woman's wiles, inviting him while pretending to reject him, all her quick changing emotions written clearly on her young face, her wide dark eyes gleaming in her childish pockmarked face where the tears had dried and left a little stain, like the stain left on a stone wall by a snail. And she did not in the least remind him of his sister Anna: there was more depth in her, more curiosity, more of the woman; and as she stood there with the wind flapping her loose red gown, he was aware of her cunning and was delighted with it, and wished he could stay with her, but he remembered that they would be setting out early in the afternoon, and so he said: "Little one, thou shalt weep no more."

"I shall not weep for love of thee," she answered, and she knew by his expression that he was leaving her, and she began to weep again, her small face crumpling.

He left her then after singing another song. A little later, when the caravan set out again, as he was riding on his white ass, he saw her again standing at the well. Once again she was leaning her head wearily by the well-post, while tears trickled down her cheeks. As he passed her, he saw she was trembling, and so he sang softly:

Rise up, my fair one, and come away,
For lo, the winter is past,
The rain is over and gone,
The flowers appear on the earth,
The time of the singing of the birds has come.

Yusuf overheard the song and turned sharply to Yeshua: "Didst thou sing for the little slave?"

"Surely," Yeshua whispered, "but I doubt whether she heard me, for she was weeping."

Yusuf's eyes were blazing with surprise and anger.

"How so—thou singest for a strange maiden?"

"Nay, not strange, for I have spoken with her."

"How—spoken to her?" Yusuf exclaimed. "And didst thou know her before? Did some intermediary bring thee to her? Remember, thou shouldst not look upon strange maidens unless they are in need of help from thee? Knowest thou not the dangers?"

"Yea, father, I know the dangers well," Yeshua said, and he bent his head low. And then for a long time he rode in silence, thinking of the dangers.

All afternoon they rode across the rolling tawny-colored Plain of Esdraelon. The sky was a pure and endless blue, and the larks rose singing. Once Yusuf turned to Yeshua and said: "I see thou lookest strangely upon people now. Thou hast the light of enquiry in thine eyes. But beware of people who are not approached through intermediaries."

"Then shall I not speak to the people on the pilgrimage?" Yeshua asked innocently.

"Better not to speak with them," Yusuf answered. "But in Jerusalem thou shalt speak with thy cousins."

Yeshua was overjoyed. Ever since he could remember he had heard talk of these mysterious cousins who lived far in the south. Yusuf belonged to a large family: there were cousins and uncles in many cities of Palestine. In Hebron lived Yona Ben-Zachariah, the son of the hereditary Sacrificer at the Temple, a boy of his own age, perhaps a few months younger; but Hebron lay far in the south, an unknown place near the Dead Sea. There were other cousins nearer at hand, in Bethphage near Jerusalem, and these too he had never set eyes on, though he had heard they were lately orphaned and lived alone with an old servant on an estate called the House of the Green Figs, and this was within a forty minute walk of Jerusalem! Though he had never seen them, he knew these cousins well, had spoken with them, exchanged greetings with them, having conjured them up in his imagination when he was tending his sheep in the hills. At such times he spoke to them as though they were present in the air around him. He had only to whisper their names—Yona, Eleazar, Maritha, Meriamne— to see them hurrying to his side as he lay in the long grass. But for many months he had forgotten them; and now it pleased him that he would soon see them in the flesh.

"And will they be waiting for us?" he asked, excited, his eyes gleaming.

Yusuf smiled: "It is likely thou shalt see them soon, my son, for I received but a few days ago a letter from your cousin Eleazar, saying that the House of the Green Figs is placed at our disposal. Your cousin Eleazar has the penmanship of a learned man—aye, a better penmanship than any I have seen! So thou shouldst bow the knee before him! As for thee, thou writest as a spider would write, should a spider have a pen in his hands!"

Yeshua was well aware that he deserved the rebuke, but he was too happy with the prospect of meeting his cousins to care. The long blue shadows were falling over the plain. Now the evening lay before them as sweet as ripening fruit, all the mountains misty with sun-veils. It was one of those evenings when every tree seems to have been dipped in crystal, and all the scarlet anemones were glowing like rubies. In the cool greenish light of evening the furrowed earth looked ghostly, softly pale, as though dissolving, and there were no birds singing. It was the ghostliness which comes with the coming of a storm: in the blue heavens were splashes of silvery white.

But though it rained in the evening there was no storm, and it was still daylight when they rode into En-gammin, which means "the fountain of gardens," on the very edge of the Plain of Esdraelon and on the border of Samaria. A torrent, diverted into a hundred rivulets, rushed through the town. The houses rose in tiers on the slopes of one of the innumerable hills that rise at the foot of Mount Gilboa, but you could hardly see the houses for the fruit trees. The air smelled of fruit: quinces, pomegranates, figs, green apples. Even though the air was darkening, children came running out of the houses with baskets of fruit as offering for the

pilgrims. The figs tasted of honey, the pomegranates were almost
sickly sweet and the wine was soft on the tongue, unlike the wine
of Nazareth, which is bitter. Here, listening to the torrent and the
creaking of a watermill, they passed the night. The storm hovered
overhead. By morning it had vanished.

Early the next morning, when they set out along the mountain
road, the sky was a pure blue again, while a following wind
brought the scent of the fruit trees of En-gammin. Now there were
only the rough roads through the hills, the gaunt blue mountains
on either side. By midday they were watering their asses at Jacob's
Well and soon they came to the holy city of Sichem, half-hidden
among palm trees. Here they rested, and in the afternoon pushed
on along the pass between Gerizim and Ebal, while the great caravan of pilgrims went on ahead. Far behind them came the three
white asses on the darkening road.

The Meadow of the Daughters

When evening came they were in a landscape of gaunt hills and
bare scrub, with only a few clumps of palms and pale wheat fields
set among the stony fields. Here and there strange cone-shaped,
blue-ribbed mountains rose above them. The great caravan of pilgrims had gone on ahead, and the road was almost deserted save
for some merchants riding on dromedaries and some beggars wandering barefoot. Blue shadows swept over the plains, and the
white-breasted barley-birds uttered thin screaming notes as they
skimmed low over the fields in search of grain.

As the shadows fell, the three white asses moved more slowly
and seemed lost in that immense landscape. The little collar-bells
on the asses tinkled. As always, there was an entranced expression
on Meriam's face: everything she saw, even the sharp burning

ridges of the mountains, delighted her, but whenever she glanced
at her husband, a strange quietness descended upon her. Lost in
her little cell of quietness, she smiled at the sleek shapely head of
the white ass, and once or twice she turned and glanced at Yeshua.
Only on her husband's face she detected a strange blankness, a
pallor under the eyes, a weariness in the lips, as though the journey had taken too much from him.

Once Yeshua murmured: "Let us stay a while in the shade of
the terebinths, for thou art hungry."

"Aye, and what then?" Yusuf answered. "Shall we sit by the
roadside when Shiloh awaits us?"

It was on the tip of Yeshua's tongue to say: "Why Shiloh? Why
not in one of these farm-houses by the wayside? We shall find no
lodgings at Shiloh, for surely we shall arrive there after nightfall."

But instead of saying this, he said nothing, filled with an inexplicable feeling of grief.

An hour later, when it was already dark, they saw the low
crested hill of Shiloh in the starlight. The walled town stood some
five or six miles off the Roman road to the west. Below the walls
camp-fires were blazing—sign that there were no lodgings left in
the town, and the pilgrims were spending the night in the fields.

Now, because they were the last of the pilgrims on the road,
Yeshua rode on ahead to select a site for the night. Cool winds
fanned the hillslopes, bringing the scent of young vines. The air
along the approaches to Shiloh was bronze with the glow of flame,
and sweet with the smoke of incense. On the sloping fields the
pilgrims jostled one another, sang songs and crowded round the
solitary well which lay just outside the silver-studded gates of
the town. From the terebinth trees on the edge of the sloping field
colored lanterns were hanging. Noise, smoke, playing of flutes,
beating of bronze instruments. With the moon hanging over the
hills, the sloping field resembled a fair-ground.

The color came back to Yusuf's cheeks when Yeshua returned
to say he had staked a place for the night under the terebinth trees.

"A good place," Yeshua said, "and well sheltered from the wind.
Here thou shalt rest, my father, and put off thy sandals and sleep,
and I shall bring thee whatever food thou needest."

"Dost thou know the place?" Yusuf asked, his eyes twinkling.

"Aye, I know it well."

"But the true meaning of the place, dost thou know that?"

For his father's sake Yeshua pretended not to know, or to have
forgotten. The slope outside the gates of Shiloh was the famous
dancing floor of the sons of Benjamin, who made love to the
daughters of Shiloh among the vineyards.

Gleam of gold jewelry, and lanterns; smoke; blaze of cooking-
fires; everyone resting, sprawled out beside the camp-fires; smell
of lentils and corn porridge sweetened with honey. Basking in the
warmth of the cooking-fires, striped cloaks around them, the pilgrims chanted the song of the ascent to Jerusalem. In a cradle of
blue wattles a baby lay, its lips smeared with honey to keep it
quiet; and the flame-light on the smeared face turned it the color
of beaten gold. Some barefoot girls with heavy panniers of fruit
wandered among the pilgrims, shouting their wares.

Yeshua arranged the bedding for Meriam and Yusuf beside the
terebinth trees.

"Dost thou remember the two hundred sons of Benjamin?"
Yusuf was saying.

Yeshua was too busy attending to the small fire he was building
to pay attention to his father.

"Didst thou not hear me?"

"Aye, I heard thee, father."

The fire burned merrily with little puffs of red flame, and a
crackling. When the fire was roaring, he still knelt there, on his
knees, staring at the heart of the flames. From a long way away he
heard his father saying:

"Thou shouldst listen, young one, when I speak of the sacred
places. We came to Shiloh of set purpose, that thou shouldst know
the sanctity of the town. God be praised that we have come where
the two hundred sons of Benjamin hid in the vineyards and waited
there until the daughters of Shiloh came to dance, here, here, in
the Meadow of the Daughters—thou hast only to look around thee!
Aye, and the evil sons took the daughters for themselves after
slipping out of the vineyards, coming upon them as a hawk
pounces on a field mouse, but it was for the sake of the tribe of
Benjamin!"

"The daughters went willingly?" Yeshua asked innocently.

"Aye, it was for the sake of the tribe," Yusuf went on, his eyes
narrowing.

In the light of the fire his long bony face looked hale and swarthy;
and his beard, tinted red by the flames, gave him something of the

appearance he must have possessed when young, only the watery
eyes and the sickly pouches under them giving proof of his age.
As usual, Meriam sat quietly with her hands folded in her lap,
her blue veils floating around her as the wind whistled through
the branches of the terebinths.

Yet it was warm in this corner of the field; warm, and strangely
comforting after the long journey on the flinty roads; warm, and
tender with the tenderness of familiarity again. Yeshua bought
milk and boiled it—milk was the best after journeying. Afterwards
he made a dish of corn porridge sweetened with wild figs and
some small pancakes dotted with raisins. None of the pilgrims
would eat meat until the time of the Passover. And while he ate,
Yusuf questioned his son about his knowledge of Shiloh, which
was also the dwelling place of the Ark of the Covenant, and here
was the first division of land in Canaan, and here the boy Samuel
called three times to the Lord.

"Aye, all that and more," Yeshua said, "for the place was accursed, remember? Did not the prophet Jeremiah put a curse
upon it? 'Go ye now unto my place which was in Shiloh, where I
set my name at first, and see what I did to it for the wickedness of
my people Israel.' The wife of Jeroboam came here from Tirzah
to enquire of the prophet Abijah after her son. And shouldst thou
want more, then I have more—"

"Nay, 'tis enough," Yusuf answered, smiling and warming his
hands by the fire, and then he turned to Meriam and said admir-
ingly: "Hear him, he knows all things! And he cooks well, and has
little lameness now, and is good to his parents: so we shall sleep
well."

But there was little sleep that night. After their long journey
the pilgrims gave themselves to merry-making. Soon the whispers
around the fires and the tinkling bells of donkeys and camels gave
place to other music. Timbrels and cithers were taken out of saddle-bags, and the small painted earthenware drums. At first the
sound of the drums was no more than a soft throbbing in the dark,
a murmuring, but when the moon rose, flutes, cithers, hand-bells
and timbrels suddenly exploded into sounds of rejoicing, and the
men who squatted with little earthenware drums on their laps
began to pound the thin stretched sheepskin across the mouth of
the earthenware. The drums were insistent, heavy like the pulse of
blood, soft sheepskin meeting the soft flesh of men's palms, re-

petitive, swinging out in great encompassing waves until everyone
was caught up in those dark welling pulse beats. Heavy beakers of
wine were passed around. A song rose, and then the voice faltered,
only to be taken up by a clear tremulous voice of piercing sweetness—it was the song known as "Rejoicing over the Terebinths"—
and then everyone was singing it. Now in the Meadow of the
Daughters, in the soft moonlight, a quiver seemed to run through
the pilgrims as they put their cooking-pots away. They sang and
beat drums and gazed at the pure cloudless sky, almost blinded by
the whiteness of the walls of Shiloh; and when a rich landowner
from Cana opened a basket of doves and threw them into the air,
where they tumbled all snowy-white, fluttering from one side of
the sloping meadow to the other, people said they had never
known such delight.

"Look! Look! There is manna falling from heaven!" Meriam
murmured, and tugged at Yusuf's arm, pointing to the wheeling
doves, but the old man was aghast at so many young people enjoying themselves and said: "Shall the sons of Benjamin—" But he
did not go on, and soon he fell into a stern silence, his eyes on
his son.

There was nothing in the least unusual about the merry-making
among the pilgrims. Every night when they were resting after the
long journey, they gave themselves to wine-drinking and singing.
But it often happened, when they were near Jerusalem, that they
decided to forsake festivities, either because they were tired from
traveling or because they were thinking of the solemnity of the
coming sacrifices. And more often than not, on the last stage of
the journey, there was a kind of sullenness about them.

A girl in an apricot-colored dress, with a wreath of anemones
and thorn roses in her hair, leaped out of the throng and began
to dance feverishly, flinging her arms above her head, her dark
eyes glistening strangely. She could not have been more than
eighteen, but she danced with the abandon of a mature woman;
and all the time she was singing. The drum-beats became louder.
The cithers were like a chorus of strident children's voices. Other
young girls joined her, until there was a circle of dancers in the
center of the meadow, their faces alight with the quick red gleams
of the fires, all garlanded. All of them had put off their sandals
before flinging themselves into the dance, and together with the
throbbing of the drums there came the rustling of their bare feet

on the bare earth. Sweat ran off their faces, trickling away in little
silver showers, and there was no pause when the songs finished;
immediately, as though at a given signal, they were off on the
wings of another song. When one of the girls reached up and
pulled a fluttering white dove out of the air, one which was so
blinded and dazzled by the moonlight that it did not know where
it was flying, they stopped the song they were singing and sang
"When a Dove Alights." And there was no end to the mad frolic
of the doves as they wheeled over the meadow, never resting on
the branches of the terebinths. It was as though the doves, too,
were caught up in the madness of the night.

Now in their brilliant red, green and apricot-colored dresses,
the girls took possession of the meadow, and dared the sons of
Benjamin to dance with them. They had danced so lustily that
their dresses clung to them. With faces tilted, and inviting eyes,
they had no need of words and gestures to make the young men
follow them. There was a shout, a tremendous burst of laughter,
a few sheepish looks, and suddenly the ring of dancing girls was
surrounded by another ring of dancing men. The dancers faced
one another. The men had removed their sheepskin cloaks and
danced in their long linen shirts, weaving backwards and forwards, crouching, suddenly springing in the air, while the drums
pounded, a terrible and remorseless pounding that stirred the
blood and inflamed the senses, so that they found themselves
dancing shoulder-dances, the shoulders of the men swinging towards the shoulders of the girls until they touched, their young
bodies glowing in the light of the flames, the girls jumping higher
than the men because this was the only way in which they could
be seen by the pilgrims, tossing their heads so that their long hair
was whirling, black, orange and gold in the light of the flames,
until at last like pomegranate seeds the fever exploded in them,
and the girls burst through the circle of crouching, dancing men,
and imprisoned them, and danced round them, overwhelming
them, leaping higher and higher, while the drums pounded and
the flutes sang, and no one knew what happened within the circle,
for some of the girls were unable to escape and others lay sprawled
on the grass of the meadow and were bruised by the bare feet of
the young men; and then quite suddenly, softly, at that moment
when the dance became most frenzied, when the dancers were
aware only of glistening faces and glinting eyes, of the smell of

sweat like the smell of crushed grapes, of flashing shoulders and shining teeth, the singing and the dancing came to an end, and there was no echo, only silence, the dreadful silence of exhaustion as the dancers crept back to the fires, listless and limp, all the fires of their hot youth drained from them; and then they seemed to be like shadows wandering restlessly in the dark, more ghostly than the doves which now soared high in the air, to vanish in the smoke from the cooking-fires burning to embers.

"Shall the flesh feed on flesh?" Yusuf moaned, and turned his head away in horror and derision, but Yeshua remembered that all the time the dancers were dancing, his father had watched them closely, his eyes narrowed, no more than pinpoints of reddish light in the light of the small flames.

Yusuf was about to draw his blanket over his face when he saw something which struck terror in his soul.

A well-formed girl of about seventeen summers, with flushed cheeks, thick black eyebrows smeared with sweat, and laughing lips, came swiftly across the grass to where Yeshua was tending the fire; and standing over him she gave a little shiver, bent down, swept off the garland of anemones and thorn roses she was wearing crookedly and set it on the boy's head, saying: "Thou shouldst have danced with me!" and when old Yusuf leaned forward, shaking with anger, his whole body quivering, his beard thrust up, too tongue-tied to heap curses upon her, she only laughed at him impudently, and then knelt down with utmost shyness beside Yeshua, taking his hand and kissing him on the cheek.

"Shall a harlot enter my house?" Yusuf roared, for anger had succeeded in putting words between his teeth, and it hurt him that this girl had entered the circle of his possessions. "Let the witch perish! Let her be struck dumb! Let her not enter my house!"

"She does no harm—" Yeshua murmured.

"Aye, she does no harm to thee," Yusuf roared, his face red with passion and his eyes protruding, as though they were being forced out of him by the anguish in his soul. "No harm to thee, thinkest thou, when the touch of her hand is poison!"

Yeshua smiled and lifted her hand to look at it more closely.

"But her hand is pure," he said. "It smells sweet and there is no poison."

Yusuf tried to lift himself up. His dark face was scowling.

"Let her go! Let her go!" he said, in a moaning voice. "What has she done to thee?"

"She has done nothing to me, only shown me her hand and given me a crown of anemones. Her hand is pure and the anemones are sweet-smelling even now. Let her stay, father."

"Nay, let her go—for the last time!" Yusuf exclaimed, staring at his son as if he could no longer recognize the boy, his willfulness, the way he held his head a little to one side, his secret smile; and when Yeshua let the girl's hand fall away, a softness came to his father's eyes, as of pure pleasure.

"Then she shall go," Yeshua said with a half-smile, "but remember that she crowned me, father."

A moment later the girl in her apricot dress was gliding away into the shadows.

In the Meadow of the Daughters the pilgrims slept beside their fires. Some hung up embroidered linen or goatskin on the branches of the trees to protect them from the wind. And not all slept: some kept guard, for robbers knew that pilgrims carried large sums of money, and others whispered. When Yusuf and Meriam were asleep, Yeshua rose and wandered soft-footed across the meadow, where the last embers were dying.

The moon, which had risen silver, turned to gold; all the smoke from the cooking-fires had been winnowed away. There was a blue dimness in the lower air, where the huddled pilgrims lay, but all above their sleeping heads the sky quivered—shimmering moonrings, and the bright stars eternally blessing. Stepping lightly, he paused to look down at the face of a sleeping girl, so calm and blessed in sleep she seemed on the edge of waking in delighted surprise at the world around her; and he waved his hands above her in a blessing, and went on to bless the wrinkled old man, her father, who sprawled beside the white ashes of the fire not far from her. Some white figures flashed among the trees; he blessed them too. So he wandered barefoot over the meadow, more like a ghost than a boy of thirteen on the way to the Passover.

This was his world: the hushed night, the silence, the murmur of the wind and the powerful night enclosing him. He stood quite still and listened to the words the cool wind brought to his ears: the sighs of lovers, prayers, old men muttering. But there were other words which came to him sharply, words that sent his blood racing with excitement to his flushed cheeks. He stood as silent as

a sentinel outside a goatskin tent, listening. There was passion in
the words he heard—not the passion of disputatious men, but the
passion of men who have followed righteousness and know
whither it leads. Half the night he wandered; then thinking he
was unobserved, he crept back to the place where Meriam and
Yusuf were sleeping.

He had hardly put his head down when he heard his father's
urgent whispers.

"Where hast thou been, my son?"

"Among the tents," Yeshua answered simply.

"Aye, and what hast thou done there?"

"Nought that I should not do," Yeshua said, and turned his face
away, for he thought he heard others whispering not far away,
and he wanted to listen.

"Thou shouldst be sleeping," Yusuf went on despairingly. "Thy
mother sleeps."

"As all good people should," Yeshua smiled, but there was no
impudence in his smile.

"Hush! Thou art impudent again! A harlot came here! Thou
wearest still the garland she gave you! Is not that enough? And
yet thou wanderest through the night like a beggar!"

"Nay, not like a beggar."

"Then like a blind owl."

"Nay, not like a blind owl either, for owls see well in the dark,
as thou knowest! I wandered abroad to listen to what men were
saying."

"Ha! And what did they say?"

"They said if we but look carefully, we shall see the Messiah in
Jerusalem! Aye, first Elijah, and then the Messiah! They say we
shall see him with our eyes! They say he will be dressed in a seamless garment, and men shall know him by the brightness of his face
—the light of God! There will be a crowd of people in the Temple,
and there will come a whirlwind and a clap of thunder, and suddenly, where there was no one before, there will be the Messiah
shining in glory!"

"They say this, do they?"

"Truly. He will be standing there—"

"Thou dreamest," Yusuf said, and turned away with a smile.

Then they slept, and in the morning they made their way over
the steep hills to Jerusalem.

The Blood of the Lamb

Four days after leaving Nazareth, towards sunset, coming in a cloud of dust along the winding road, the three white asses reached the House of the Green Figs in Bethphage at the foot of the Mount of Olives on the side away from Jerusalem. Occasionally through the gaps in the hills Yusuf had seen the walls of the holy city, but there was so much dust from the long camel trains and the hosts of pilgrims on the road that it seemed no more than a mirage, something that appeared in the golden haze for a few brief moments and then vanished. Besides, he was weary after the long journey and rarely raised his eyes. When they came to Bethphage the darkness was drawing on, and at first he mistook the road, so that they spent some time trying to find the entrance to the fig tree orchard, and it was only when Meriam pointed to a huge flowering almond tree standing on a little mound that he recognized the place. Beyond the fig trees lay the large white house known as the House of the Green Figs.

Yeshua had half expected his cousins to come running down the long lane between the fig trees, but there was no sign of them. The house was dark, shuttered, the hill rising steeply above it and therefore making it darker. There was something haunted in the place. Bare stone walls, and above the flat roof lay the graves on the hillslope. He shivered in terror, but not for loneliness: there came to him, coming down from above and all round the Mount of Olives, the roaring hum of the pilgrims crowding into Jerusalem, or camping on all the hills facing the holy city.

Suddenly, at the moment when he was sure this lonely house was an abode of ghosts, hardly more than an enormous cavernous tomb at the foot of the hill, and indistinguishable except for size from all the other tombs, he heard a wild shout and twenty lamps burst into flame in front of his eyes. Dazzled, he lifted his hands to his eyes. All round him there seemed to be a multitude of young people of his own age screaming with laughter. A girl of fourteen or fifteen, in a long dress embroidered with green threads, had run up to Meriam and flung her arms round her, shouting at the top of her voice. Another girl was clutching Yusuf's white ass by the head and smiling up into Yusuf's face. A tall youth with a long thin face of remarkable pallor was gazing down at Yeshua and saying over and over again: "I praise the Lord thou hast come! I praise the Lord!" The solemnity of the youth was almost frightening. The multitude of young people had vanished. Yeshua had thought there were so many only because he had been blinded by the heavy lamps which hung suspended across the front of the house.

The girl in the gown embroidered with green threads came running up to Yeshua.

"I am Meriamne," she said breathlessly. "I watched thy coming from the roof. Truly, I watched thee—" And she began to explain even more breathlessly how they had put up the hanging lanterns and joined them all by a waxed string, and set light to it exactly at the moment when the three visitors arrived just outside the door.

"And do not tell me thou wast not frightened!" she exclaimed. "I saw thee, cousin. And now let us take thee to thy chamber, for surely thou art weary."

Her eyes mocked him. She had a small laughing face of great beauty. She wore a long coral necklace, and there was a hood of some green material which covered only the back of her head. She had a wide mouth, and smiled easily.

An old servant—he looked almost as old as the mad shepherd of the hills—hobbled across the courtyard, leading the asses away.

Yusuf asked only to be allowed to sleep, and so Eleazar, the young man who kept saying: "I praise the Lord," led him to an upper room.

When he returned, Yeshua was already drinking from a bowl of goat's milk and his mother was eating some sliced fruit, while Meriamne was explaining how difficult it was to live alone in a large house with only one servant, but she was so healthy, so excited and so delighted to see her relatives that Meriam said: "I *see* it is difficult," and then even Maritha, the youngest of the three children in the House of the Green Figs, broke into a smile.

A few moments before, Yeshua had thought of the house as a tomb; now he wondered whether he had ever been in a house where there were so many lamps, so much rich furniture, so much laughter. The house was violently alive. It was solidly built, more like a castle than a farmhouse. There were colored tiles on the floor, and cabinets of inlaid wood, heavy bronze lamps, soft patterned carpets, embroidered hangings. The children gave the appearance of being perfectly at ease there, and at the same time they did not behave as though they were accustomed to luxury. Meriamne explained that they spent most of their time in the gardens or on the roof. Ever since the death of their father, a distant relative of Yusuf, they had clung together for comfort in this house, which reminded them of their father and was therefore sacred to them. And while Meriamne explained these things, she kept pushing dishes in front of Meriam and Yeshua, saying over and over again how pleased they were to have visitors, and how she hoped they would all go together to the Temple on the following day.

"And if it should be taken from me," Meriamne exclaimed, and suddenly her eyes filled with childish tears. "Oh, we have prayed for it. We sent you messages, too."

"What messages?" Yeshua asked.

"We sent prayers for you on your journey. Eleazar composed special prayers for your safe-keeping. If you like, he will recite them for you."

Eleazar began to recite in a lugubrious voice a long prayer on behalf of all pilgrims, "and especially those pilgrims who are coming from Nazareth." Meriam said she thought them "very well composed." Meriamne wrinkled up her nose, and Maritha said nothing at all, though she watched everything that happened with an expression of fondness and trust.

Soon afterwards Yeshua and Meriam were taken to the rooms prepared for them. Then Yeshua discovered that not all the rooms in the immense house were luxurious. To his delight, his own was almost barren of ornament, a bare bleak cell-like room not unlike his room at Nazareth.

The next morning at the clap of dawn the house awoke. At breakfast Eleazar suggested that they should go to the Temple early, taking the road at the foot of the Mount of Olives.

"If we go early," he explained, "we shall be able to take up good places in the Temple courtyards." And he went on to say that it were better to go on foot, because there was a terrible press of

people on the road, and donkeys and asses would have difficulty
making their way through the crowds.

It had rained a little during the night, no more than a light
spray, leaving the air fresh and pure. Yusuf had enjoyed a good
night's rest and felt stronger. Yeshua had been prepared for everything except the first clean sight of the walls of Jerusalem as they
turned out of a valley and gazed on the holy city gleaming after
rain. He was stupefied by the immensity of towering walls, by the
great thronging crowds making their way towards the gates. Dust
rose. Everyone was babbling excitedly. Yeshua gaped with astonishment at sheer walls like precipices, at battlements and towers.
Meriamne was running a little ahead, until she was almost lost
beneath the legs of camels. When Yusuf called her back, she spun
round, laughing, just in time to avoid the high-stepping camel of a
Syrian nobleman in scarlet and purple, the borders of his tunic embroidered in gold and blue, with heavy gold chains round his
neck, rings on his fingers and bracelets on his wrists, followed by a
retinue of servants on horseback, wearing blue capes and with
turquoises threaded on their bridles. A rich smell of pomades came
from the young nobleman, whose beard glistened with oil.

Meriamne could not be silenced. She laughed at everything, in-
cluding the young nobleman.

"Ha, he smells!" she exclaimed, and put her fingers to her nose;
and when the nobleman allowed his eyes to rest upon her, she
crept close to Yeshua for protection. "Shalt thou smell like that?"
she whispered, when the nobleman and all his retinue were out of
earshot. "All dipped in perfumes, and thou art a man!" she snick-
ered, very bold because he had disappeared from sight, hidden
behind one of the huge boulders which dotted the valley. She
turned to Yeshua. "Nay, thou shalt smell clean as the wind, else I
shall not love thee!"

And then she was running ahead, wanting to have one last look
at the scented nobleman.

So they walked carefree under the huge walls of Jerusalem,
along the broken valley where the weeds grew rank and the
stunted pepper trees flourished beside the tombs. The air smelt of
spring, heavy and resinous. Along the valley came camel trains
laden with spices and donkeys from Galilee with panniers full of
pomegranate wood, to be sold in the Temple, for the lamb of Passover must be turned on a spit of Galilean pomegranate: so it had

been for generations. And now from all directions donkeys, mules, asses and camels converged on the rough pathways of the Valley of Kidron under the cypresses and Aleppo palms amid tangles of wild lavender.

In the clear light of morning Jerusalem wore a new garment and opened wide her gates. On this day the dark cypresses and silver-gray olive-trees were lit with little flames, and the sky was aflame, especially the sky above the Temple, which shimmered with the flashing of reflected marble. And the air was filled with the cooing of the green pigeons from the reed-beds of the river Jordan, which flew over the city battlements and dropped down among the shadows of the Valley of Hinnom.

As usual, Eleazar walked sedately, one hand lifting the skirts of his gown, his eyes half-closed, preoccupied. No current of affection flowed from him to the outside world. Yusuf made excuses for him. "He will be a Scribe, a protector of the Law," Yusuf said, and he made a little scribbling gesture with his hands, while laughing into his beard: Yusuf admired Eleazar, but had no love for him. Also, he detested Meriamne, always running ahead and shouting at the top of her voice, peering into the faces of the pilgrims thronging the dusty road—the dark-faced Babylonians with curling beards and heavy gold rings on their fingers, chattering in an ancient tongue; Tyrians wearing purple; Lebanese Jews in heavily-embroidered costumes; farmers in coarse black goatskins; black Jewesses from Libya and Numidia; wealthy Alexandrians who rode on white horses with orange manes and orange tails and chewed pepper-seeds and left the sweet-sour smell of Egypt behind them; and then the fair-haired youths and maids from the Danube, rosy-cheeked and firm-muscled, their sheepskins painted in bright colors: stout men, thin men, men with hawk-noses and eagle-eyes, smiling Persians and garrulous Greeks, shepherds from Moab and the barren hills of the Dead Sea, plowmen in ragged skins from the desert of Seir, and those who came from Beth-Shemeth in the heart of Egypt and wore the linen costumes of Egyptians, holding themselves stiffly upright in the Egyptian manner. And all carried palm leaves and recited the psalms and rejoiced to be pilgrims; and here and there were men with wild eyes, half-naked fanatics robed in camel skins, muttering shrilly to themselves, staring at the walls of Jerusalem like men afraid of the

city's holiness, forever throwing themselves upon the rocky ground
in prostrations and rubbing the dust over their faces.

"Come, come, walk in holiness and grace," Yusuf said to
Meriamne, when she came running back to say there was a leper
foaming at the mouth being attended in charity by some Syrian
nobleman with greasy ringlets.

"The leper smells, and the Syrian, too," Meriamne announced,
wrinkling her nose again, and she threw a smile at Yeshua, thrusting into his hands a little sprig of lavender.

"Thou thinkest only of smells," Yusuf complained.

"And why not?" Meriamne answered quickly. " 'Tis a feast-day,
but the holy city smells no sweeter."

And that was true: the smell of dead damp, of tombs, of excrement, of jostling sweating people, ten thousand of them milling
in the direction of the carved gate below Mount Ophel, and half
of them lifted herbs to their nostrils. The smell of fever and sickness, smell of sunlight on sunburned rock: flash of crimson garments, of swords, of beaded head-dresses. Now the huge press of
people became greater. It was as though a rock had been overturned and the teeming ants were running out. Shouting, swearing,
singing psalms, the pilgrims were converging on the small gate
guarded by yellow-haired Roman legionaries who glared at them
darkly, overwhelmed by the strange and ragged procession of
fanatical pilgrims. At all the gates, on the towers of the fortress of
Antonia, in the Temple courtyards, these stern-faced Roman
soldiers were stationed, their bronze armor newly polished and
gleaming reddish-gold, their heavy helmets shading their eyes, so
that it was impossible to see the expressions of their faces: and
there was a strangeness and impassivity about them which terrified
the Jews.

Yusuf averted his eyes from them when he passed under the
gate.

"A curse on them!" he muttered, taking care not to be overheard. "May the horned snake strike them! May they—"

Yeshua saw his father's face turn savagely scarlet, and turned
away, sick with a momentary weariness and dread. More and more
he feared the hot gusts of his father's anger, the stern patriarchal
face livid with anger. And there was more anger as they climbed
up the steep and cluttered street where the awnings of the merchants, striped red and white, hid the sun. The street smelled of

damp. On both sides were merchants' booths smelling of fresh
leather and curdled cheese and freshly-killed meat. Here were
shops selling camel saddles and leather water-bottles, bales of
cotton cloth from Egypt, seven-branched candlesticks, jewels,
amulets. Books were on sale; and the crackling of parchment
mingled with the humming of the scribes as they wrote in full view
of the pilgrims—a loud humming, like millions of bees. But the
most terrible sounds came from the merchants who shrieked at
the top of their voices, trying to stem the tide of the pilgrims,
standing in the middle of the street, waving their arms, cursing
those who brushed past them, clutching at passers-by, saying:
"Come, beautiful pilgrims, I make leather goods which are the joy
of the beholder's eye—spare a minute, spare a minute." Women
wailed, men argued fiercely, children screamed. The narrow street
was like an oven. Yeshua hated the merchants, greasy, loud-
mouthed, ringleted, who pushed and pulled, screamed, haggled,
roared abuse at the pilgrims for not buying their wares here in the
lower city. Booths filled with jars of olives, of oil, of raisins,
bread, sticks of incense, thick mounds of sweet-meats—Yeshua
hated it all and gripped Meriamne by the hand, saying over and
over to himself: "Oh, Jerusalem, how thou art fair!" saying this
ironically and bitterly, because everything had changed, there
were no longer clean white walls shining in the misty dawn, there
was only a huddled crowd of people breathlessly attempting to
make their way past the shopkeepers, fighting their way up the
steep road with its trickle of dirty water flowing down the middle,
all of them laughing and shouting and weeping, and some were
screaming, caught up in the hysteria of excitement. Yeshua caught
a glimpse of his mother walking a little behind Yusuf, and it was
extraordinary how the surging crowd made way for her, perhaps
in respect for her beauty, the shining about her, the deep quietness. It was as though she alone of the pilgrims had brought with
her the quietness of her native place.

Earthenware jars were overturned. Horsemen pushed their way
through the crowd with a cracking of whips. Everywhere there
were little groups of people with faces reddened with anger, shouting at the shopkeepers who tried to bar their way. Once Meriamne
turned to Yeshua and was about to say something when she
paused. A cold and sullen anger stood on Yeshua's face, the lips
pursed together, the cool lines of his cheeks hard like marble.

There was no joy on his face, only that terrible quickness of the eyes, the sudden flashing.

It was better, of course, when they came to the top of the hill and had put the streets of the merchants behind them. The roads widened. Here among flowering almond trees were the mansions of the wealthy, and beyond these mansions the Temple could be seen shining like a mountain of snow, tier upon tier of marble columns crowned with carved cedarwood, with the blue smoke of incense climbing lazily in the blue air. The snowy white columns dazzled them, the carved and painted cedarwood glittered in the hot sun. Now there came from the pilgrims a huge roar of praise, as they sang the psalms with full throats and gleaming eyes.

All that had gone before, all the long days of marching across a barren land, all the saving to purchase the means for the journey, all the purifications and nights spent in earnest prayer, the little daily sacrifices, all this was as nothing compared with the great sacrificial feast which awaited them. It was not only that the Temple was the most holy ground in the world and that Herod had decorated it more sumptuously than any other building known to man. More important than any of these things was that here at last, after long wandering, every Jew came face to face with his God, as Moses came face to face with God on Mount Sinai; and where Moses saw God through mists of cloud, the Jews saw God through the mists of incense and the smoke of the holocaust. And as they came surging across the immense bridge which spanned the Tyropaean valley, joining Mount Zion to Mount Moriah, they were aware of the divine power which lay concealed within the Holy of Holies, which could be felt as though it were something physical, as though the great throbbing energy of God had its center here, and the nearer they came to the Holy of Holies the more they were aware of the hidden radiance and the pulsating energy which sprang from the place where ages ago Abraham had led Isaac for the sacrifice. They had come to celebrate the Passover, the night when the angel of the Lord protected the children of Israel and led them out of Egypt, but they were also celebrating Abraham and Isaac, the uplifted knife and the ram caught in a thicket; and for them in some mysterious way the figures of Moses and Abraham were confused and became one figure, for were not both mediators between the Jews and the Lord? As they pushed and fought their way across the Tyropaean Bridge they heard the bleating of the lambs and the bellowing of the bulls, waiting in the Court of the Gentiles for the supreme moment of sacrifice. And the wind coming from the north-east brought to their nostrils the oily reek of blood.

As they pressed through the huge gateway, the bronze doors thrown wide open, they could see in front of them the three great blinding marble terraces which formed the walls of the Court of the Gentiles. So many people were crowded there it was impossible to see the paving stones of colored marble, impossible to go forward or backward. Yusuf, and the small tribe attending him, had come in one of those great waves which periodically hurled themselves upon the Temple, and now was held motionless, struggling in the heat and half blinded by the flashing of the snow-white marble columns, which seemed all the whiter now that they were within the courtyard. Suddenly Yeshua and Meriamne swung away, sucked into another wave which traveled the whole length of the immense court; and Yusuf, seeing them disappearing, called out in an agonized voice: "Be careful, my son, for thou art more precious to me than all—" Yeshua heard no more. He fought his way back to where he thought Yusuf and his mother together with Eleazar and Maritha were standing but, when he reached the place, they had vanished.

The heat, the scent-sprinkled air, the shouting in a hundred tongues, the lowing of calves and bellowing of bulls and bleating of lambs, the cooing of innumerable doves, clink of coins, the huge mutterings of the crowd intoxicated by the near presence of the Holy of Holies, all this affected Yeshua and Meriamne strangely as they wandered hand in hand across the immense courtyard in search of Yusuf. They were alternately deafened and blinded. One moment they were being buffeted towards those cloisters underneath the triple-tiered marble walls where the Temple scribes were at work, or they were suddenly flung towards the tables of the money-lenders. They were like sleep-walkers. They held hands and walked with their eyes half-closed. The golden gates, the balconies, the snowy marble, the shouts, the streams of incense, all this was like a great flashing in their minds. Everyone was streaming with sweat. Everyone was talking and shouting, gesticulating, pointing, and some were weeping with excitement.

"I am dreaming," Meriamne said. "And thou, Yeshua, art thou dreaming also?"

She threw her hands up to her eyes and let them fall away, but the Temple was still there, the white marble was still flashing and the sun was still glittering on the large golden plates let into the walls.

So they wandered in the press of the crowd, until Yusuf found them at noon eating barley cakes at one of the stalls. Soon it was time to choose the lamb for sacrifice, and after pushing past the whining beggars they came to the fenced stalls where the young lambs were gathered together, so many of them that it was like looking down on a sea of white. According to the Law, all the lambs of sacrifice were without blemish, males, not less than eight days old nor more than a year. The supply was constantly being replenished, for already many had been taken into the small court-yard known as the Court of Women. Yusuf asked Yeshua to choose one of the lambs.

"But how shall I?" Yeshua complained. "There are so many, and how shall I choose among them?"

He could not have told why it seemed suddenly important to choose the most beautiful, the one that was softest and whitest and most filled with life. For a long time he gazed at them, going from one stall to the next, unable to decide. He peered intently into their sleek faces. He put his hand in their soft wool, felt the weight of the heavy tails, and he let them nibble his fingers. The sun hurt their eyes. And looking down on the lambs packed so closely together, he was aware of the pure flame of life streaming through them, a quickness, an alertness. How gentle they were! How they frisked their silky ears and contrived to leap and rejoice in life even when they were crushed together! How their heads perked up when he called them in the soft, low rumbling voice of a shepherd calling to his flock! He let his hand fall among them, and they licked the salt off, and leaped towards him. And he could not choose one, and had no desire to choose among them. He looked appealingly at his father and then at the sheep, murmuring: "Let them live! Let them not be sacrificed!"

"Shall there be no Passover?" Yusuf said, smiling. "Wouldst thou take the Passover from us?"

Yusuf knew the affection of a shepherd for his sheep, but he had not expected Yeshua to delay so long. Eleazar had already chosen the lamb he would sacrifice. It was but seven months old, a quiet fearful little thing with a small head and long legs like sticks, which suffered from the heat, panting. There was a rope tied round its neck. Eleazar held the end of the rope and looked at it without feeling, without emotion, as though it were some dead thing, annoyed when it came too close to him, and still more annoyed when Meriamne began to fondle it, kissing the little pointed head, trying to comfort it, even falling to her knees and holding it in her arms.

Yusuf had been watching Yeshua closely, and now he said: "Well then, if thou canst not choose among so many, then let me choose."

"Nay, father, since thou hast given me the choice of the lamb of sacrifice," Yeshua said quickly, "then must I choose the best for the sake of its worthiness before God."

"Then choose one which is fat," Yusuf said tartly, and growled into his beard. "And be quick, my son, for the best will be taken if thou delayest!"

But Yeshua took his time. He searched among them until he found one about ten months old, well-fleshed, with a heavy creamy white tail, a long well-modeled head and delicate legs. Even Yusuf admitted that Yeshua had chosen well, so well indeed that the vendor at first refused to sell, claiming that this sheep had already been bespoken. Yusuf paid for it in coin, and when it was lifted over the fence he admired it and bent over it and stroked it, muttering to himself and nodding his head and motioning to Meriam to come forward and examine it.

"Our son has chosen the best, the very best," he said. "He is a good shepherd, as anyone can see," he went on proudly.

Yeshua lifted the lamb in his arms and carried it across the immense marble courtyard towards the Court of Women, which was a kind of ante-room to the Court of Priests where the sacrifices took place, pausing to glance at the Stone of Forbidding which warned all strangers, all those who were not of the Jewish faith, from passing beyond the gate "under penalty of being the cause of their own deaths." Here, in the Court of Women, were marble benches and galleries and thirteen trumpet-shaped chests into which coins were tossed, and there were chambers in the four corners, made of latticed marble and inhabited by learned rabbis and secretaries of the Temple who watched everything that passed and received tribute and offered advice. Here musicians played on ten-stringed *nebels* and on flutes of oleander wood cut from the banks of the Jordan. Here, too, were great bronze incense-burners shaped like winged lions. And it was strangely quiet here after the turmoil in the outer court. Here people walked sedately, knowing that they were now close to the Holy of Holies, and would soon be closer still, though the women and girls would have to be left behind in the galleries running round the courtyard.

The heat pelted the marble court. The bronze incense-burners gleamed like spurts of flame and the sunlight flashed on the great Nicanor Gate of hammered gold and silver. Yeshua held the spotless lamb tightly against his breast, and when it began to bleat piteously, smelling the dried blood in the further court, he stroked its neck and sang to it:

> Lo, I am with thee, little one.
> Rest in my arms.
> Thou art sweet as blossoms
> That fall from the almond tree.
>
> Nestle there, little one.
> Rest peacefully.
> Thou art whiter than the snows
> That fall on Mount Hermon.
>
> Lo, I am with thee, little one.
> The night shall not fall on thee,
> Nor shall the dew of morning
> Touch thee again.

And when the lamb grew restless, he sang the song again and did not cease from stroking it even when it licked his face. And soon, seeing that it was thirsty, he took it to the well which lay just inside the gate and crouched beside it as it lapped the water. He had known many sheep like this on the hills of Nazareth, but never one which clung to him so affectionately, for as soon as it had lapped a little water it would turn to him and nod in a sort of greeting and then rub its head against his knee. It was as though the lamb knew the fate in store for it. Once, when it looked up at him, he flung his arm over it and buried his face in the soft wool, close to weeping, not daring to look at his father, who hovered over him. Afterwards he ran his hand up and down the long white throat of the lamb, until he could feel the little throat-bones moving under his

finger-tips, and then again he stroked the curly white head. Then it
seemed rested, quiet, strangely subdued, not drinking any more,
and so he sang to it again, but this time in a low rumbling voice
without words, the voice of a shepherd to his sheep, and at the end
he said: "Thou art mine forever, little one. Knowest thou not
thou art mine?"

The smell of blood from the Court of the Priests threw the lambs
into a frenzy of bleating. The bleating grew louder until the whole
courtyard was in an uproar. Some of the worshipers gripped their
lambs about the muzzle, to prevent them crying out. Others, enraged, beat them stealthily, or kicked them, or plucked out their
eyes, so great was their annoyance at this hideous high-pitched
bleating. The nerves of all the worshipers were on edge. Soon,
very soon, they would be in the presence of the Holy of Holies.
Soon they would see the blue-robed priests and watch the clouds of
black smoke rising from the altar of holocausts and partake in the
rewards of the sacrifice. And so they paced nervously, or suddenly
flung themselves down on their knees, praising the Lord God
whose mysterious curtained abode lay so close to them. Sweat
dripped down their faces. Those who were not holding the lambs
to their breasts kept their hands joined in prayer. All the men
wore the *talith*, the long fringed prayer-scarf inscribed with sacred
texts.

A hundred hands pressed against the great shining gates. Suddenly they were flung open, and three blasts from silver trumpets
split the air. There was a moment of intense sorrowing silence,
as though none could believe the time had come for the sacrifice,
as though all the worshipers were frozen into immobility by the
solemnity of the occasion. Then the crowd pressed forward, pushing aside the temple guards, who shouted frenziedly and drove
the worshipers back, allowing only twenty in at a time. Then the
gates were closed, clanging together with a sound like an explosion.

A crash of cymbals, a thin piping of flutes, and then the massed
voices of the white-robed choir at the foot of the altar of holocausts. Groans, sighs, the scamper of feet, and the great chorus of
voices rising from the innermost court.

Yeshua stood before the gold and silver gates with the ten-month
lamb in his arms. He was gazing at the sky, at the blue pigeons
wheeling overhead, at the sharp pointed prongs which rose above

the walls to prevent birds from alighting and defiling the sacred court. The lamb lay very quiet with its head against his breast.

Though he had never before entered the precincts of the Temple, Yeshua knew exactly what happened there. There was no detail he did not know by heart. And as he pressed the lamb tightly to his breast, he shivered in apprehension.

"Let us move closer to the gates," Yusuf was saying. "Let us be the next to offer sacrifice."

"Nay, let us wait," Yeshua answered. "The little one sleeps in my arms, and let him sleep a little longer."

Saying this, he looked about him, hoping to see Meriam, but she had withdrawn already to the shadowy galleries surrounding the courtyard. Eleazar was standing beside him. There was a curious, strained expression on Eleazar's face. He was almost unrecognizable, very pale, his lips twitching and his eyes wide-open and glazed.

"May the Lord be praised!" Eleazar was saying over and over again. "Praise ye the name of the Lord!"

The gates clanged open. Again there was a press of people attempting to make their way past the guards.

"It is time," Yusuf said. "See, they are all entering! Surely thou shalt not be the last to offer sacrifice!"

"Nay, wait but a little while," Yeshua answered, and he closed his eyes and bent his head over the lamb, which was very silent there, nestling against him.

Eleazar's lips curled into the faintest of smiles.

"Shalt thou be the last of all?" Yusuf said impatiently. "Have we made the long journey so that thou shalt come at the tag-end of the worshipers? See, my son, I brought thee here that thou mightest make the sacrifice for me!"

The veins were standing out on Yusuf's forehead. A wild impatience seized him. He had thought Yeshua would behave properly. It was absurd that the boy should be caressing the lamb, his fingers continually running along the soft warm fur while he clasped it to his chest. The blood had drained from his cheeks. He looked like someone who was about to turn and flee, taking the lamb with him.

"Tell me," Yusuf said gently, "is he not the best of the lambs and the most worthy for the sacrifice?"

Yeshua nodded.

"And is it not proper that thou shouldst sacrifice him to the glory of God?"

Yeshua nodded again.

"And is it not meet that thou shouldst do all that is demanded of thee according to the Law?"

"Yea, all that," Yeshua said, "but let him live a little longer."

Yusuf felt frail. The heat, the crowds had affected him, and so he said tenderly: "If thou wouldst sacrifice another, and keep this little one—"

Yeshua said nothing. He bowed his head before his father. He was filled with uneasiness. Above the voices of the choristers he heard the shouts of the priests. Suddenly the doors flew open, and he was caught up in the crowd. In a moment he was swept up the marble steps, his arms wrapped round the little lamb, clinging to it, afraid some harm would come to it. Then for the first time, when he was at the top of the steps, he saw the full extent of the courtyard, with a great marble altar and the marble columns and the huge bronze laver supported on four superb bronze bulls, and at intervals there were iron rings let into the marble floor. Flames and smoke rose above the altar of holocausts, huge black billows of smoke, and the smell of burning fat, and the crackling flames. Already the courtyard was gleaming and slippery with blood, and the skirts of the priests were scarlet with it. Impassive and motionless, the choir chanted at the foot of the altar. The blood-spattered priests were everywhere, dark-faced men with hard mouths and eyes that were lusterless. Through the smoke he saw the High Priest in a blue cope ascending the steps of the altar.

"Fear not, little one," he whispered to the lamb. "Thou art pure and stainless, and I shall not hurt thee."

He was delirious with grief and anxiety. He looked wildly from side to side, seeking a means of escape. Yusuf and Eleazar had fallen to their knees. They bent forward and kissed the blood-stained stones and, when they lifted their heads, there were smears of blood on their forehead and lips, and Yusuf's beard was drenched with blood.

The little lamb was growing restless, jerking in his arms.

"Fear not, for thou art altogether in my arms," Yeshua said, and he knew that he must comfort the lamb and continue to stroke it until the moment came when he would lift the blood-stained knife the priest handed to him.

Eleazar was pushing his lamb forward, pushing it by main force, because it pressed down with its little hooves and refused to move.

The bleating of the lambs rose until it was like a hundred people screaming. The sunlight flashed off the walls, off the marble columns, off the lakes of crimson blood at their feet. Yeshua put his hands over the lamb's eyes, shuddering. He did not know why he was shuddering. He did not know why he had so great an affection for this lamb. He knew only that he was deafened by the choir and the crashing of the cymbals and the piercing notes of the silver trumpets and the bleating, and his eyes were smarting from the black smoke which was now pouring across the courtyard. For a moment he let his mind dwell on the Holy of Holies, where the spirit of God lay in holy quiet in a small curtained room. His lips were twitching as he murmured: "Little lamb, little lamb, thy precious blood shall be an offering to Almighty God!" And still with one hand covering its eyes and stroking it, he let it down to the ground and tied it to one of the iron rings and then very solemnly he turned the lamb in the direction of the Holy of Holies, and then he bent his head in prayer, saying: "Almighty God, receive now this offering."

A priest gave him the knife. It was long and thin, and there was only a small smear of blood on it, for it had been wiped nearly clean on the priest's robes.

Yusuf was trembling.

"Strike well, my son," Yusuf said, and he gave a sound like a small sigh.

Yeshua glanced up to where Eleazar was standing over his seven-month lamb. Eleazar had stabbed its throat four or five times, and still had not killed it. The lamb was bleating piteously.

Employing all his strength, Yeshua drew the knife across the lamb's throat.

The blood spurted. A priest waiting by Yeshua's side caught the blood in a silver bowl and passed it on to another priest, and so it passed along a whole row of priests, till the last took it and dashed the blood of sacrifice at the foot of the altar: then it slithered down a crevice in the hidden rock of sacrifice below.

The lamb fell over, and the blood oozed from the deep wound in its throat. But it was not dead yet. It made strange choking sounds and bubbles of blood were blown out of its mouth and the eyes became bloodshot, and sometimes it jerked its feet. Then suddenly a great convulsive movement shook it, and afterwards it lay still. As it lay there, Yeshua could no longer recognize the lamb he had held so tenderly to his breast.

By this time the entire floor of the Court of Priests had become a vast lake of blood. The priests were splashing in it. The water in the bronze laver, where the sacrificers washed out their gold and silver bowls, was stained bright crimson. There was hardly anyone in the courtyard whose hands and clothes were not stained in blood. And all the time the choir was singing the story of the coming of Israel out of Egypt, their voices rising triumphantly above the music of flutes and *nebels,* and still there came from outside the courtyard the heart-rending bleating of the lambs waiting to be sacrificed.

A heavy-jowled priest, pock-marked, a man with a sad smile and deep-set eyes and a thick wiry beard, bent over the lamb and deftly, expertly skinned it. Then, with the skin still hanging about it, he inserted a spiked hook in its throat, lifted it up and cut open the belly, removing the kidneys and all the surrounding fats, which he scooped into a silver tray. And this tray, like the bowls of blood, was handed along the row of priests until the last received it and sprinkled salt on it, and then tossed it into the fire on the altar of holocausts. Then the lamb was flayed and dressed and wrapped in its own skin, and Yeshua received it back.

Sobbing, blinded by tears, carrying the flayed lamb over his shoulders, he made his way to the Court of Women.

The Passover

Then it was evening, and they were back in the House of the Green Figs. In the clay stove a fire burned merrily. The lamb had been spitted on a sharp spit of pomegranate wood, and the air was full

of the sweetness of roasting meat and the fragrance of pomegranate wood.

Yeshua stood by the slit window, looking out over the Mount of
Olives where the darkness had descended, only here and there a
spray of hawthorn or a gleaming cedar branch catching the fading
light. The curving hill with its caves and outcroppings of white
limestone seemed to be sinking under the weight of shadow.
Yeshua did not once look in the direction of the fire.

In this large upper room the world lay hushed, curiously somber.
Yusuf watched over the roasting of the lamb, Meriam prepared the
table, Eleazar whispered prayers, Maritha helped the old servant
downstairs and Meriamne, though she pretended to be engrossed
in contemplation of her folded hands on her lap, secretly watched
Yeshua. A single painted clay oil-lamp hung from the roof-beams
and threw fierce shadows across the room.

The fat of the lamb bubbled and sang. All that was red in it was
turning a rich brown. The yellow flames exploded when the fat
dropped among them. There came the sound of the crackling of
juices and of the crusts of fat melting into sweetness.

"All this, and more—" Yeshua murmured, gazing out on the
darkening hillside, quiet among the disturbing shadows. The
thistles and the purples had disappeared: gone were the yellow
flax, the scarlet anemones; only the spray of the hawthorn still
glistened mysteriously, there in the dark lake of the night. The
wind shivered the leaves, and the rustling swept down the slope of
the hill, but of the living flowers none remained, they were all
sucked up in darkness and despair.

"All this, and more God has given me," he murmured again, and
held himself very quiet, not daring to let his mind dwell on what he
had seen, Herod's palaces blazing with gold, the poor twisted
sheep hanging on hooks, the blood dashed at the foot of the altar,
and then the blinding whiteness of the marble courts. These things
his mind would fasten on for the fraction of an instant, and then he
would send them away, like someone dismissing an acquaintance
with a gesture of the hand. He shuddered, drew himself to his full
height, pressed himself against the window and stared out into the
patch of blackness beyond, and whispered into the dark: "There
must be an end to sacrifices, and this too is given to me."

He did not know what he was saying. He seemed to himself to

be in some strange way removed from the upper room, the smell of cooking, the soft padding of bare feet in the rushes.

Meriamne came up to him dancing and said in a low voice: "Art thou shivering?"

He nodded.

"For what I have seen," he whispered. "Shall there be an end to Passover?"

"Nay, it shall last as long as the stars," Meriamne answered, her voice low and gentle.

She wore her veil still, and in this light her face beneath the veil looked unaccountably tragic, with two dark pools for eyes. It was a trick of the shadows, for she was smiling at him gently.

"An end to Passover?" she murmured, stepping so close to him that her veil touched his face.

"Not an end," he said, "but a single sacrifice. Isaac did not perish: only a single ram was sacrificed. I have seen today more blood than I ever saw."

Meriamne could make nothing of Yeshua's words. He seemed to be talking as people talk in sleep, not understanding the words they say, and so she whispered: "Because thou art shivering, I shall bring thee a sheepskin cloak to warm thyself."

He said nothing, but stared at her, as though wondering why she had not understood him. When she put the sheepskin cloak round his shoulders, he was hardly aware of her presence. Her black flashing eyes played upon him, but he remained oblivious of her until Meriam rang a little silver bell, sign that the Passover meal was beginning.

He was still in a daze when he sat at the table. He washed his hands, received a cup of wine and listened to Yusuf reciting the prayer: "Be Thou blessed, O Lord our God, eternal King of the World, who hast sanctified us by Thy commandments and hast ordained that we should eat the Passover." Yusuf spoke haltingly, his voice sometimes hoarse, sometimes sweet with passion.

There came to Yeshua the smell of unleavened bread, of the thick red sauce called haroset, which is made of almonds, figs and grapes mashed in vinegar, and of the bitter herbs which commemorate the bitterness of the first Passover. The unleavened bread recalls how they had no time to bake bread in their hasty departure from Egypt. He sat there with his head bent low, trembling, seeing nothing except the red wine in the cup glowing like jewels and

flashing scarlet in the light of the swinging lamp. The blood had
gone from his cheeks. Yusuf watched him carefully and sighed, and
whispered to Meriam that perhaps their son had stood too long in
the sunlight of the marble courts.

He was utterly quiet, utterly removed from them, lost within
the flashing of the cup, pale and drawn, with terrible dark eyes as
deep as pits. The cicadas were chirping on the Mount of Olives
and now the moon had come out, full and glowing, the deepest
orange. The roasted lamb lay on a silver dish, smoking, swimming
in its dark blood, beside the stove, not to be brought on to the table
until Yusuf had pronounced a special blessing over the bitter herbs
which he dipped ceremonially into the bitter sauce, and all had
eaten of the herbs. Then the lamb was brought to the table, so
small and succulent, roasted a tender brown. There it was, a little
shriveled thing compared to the lamb they had led to the sacrifice,
with a skewer of pomegranate wood thrust through its mouth to its
buttocks, and without legs—the legs and entrails were inside it.
It did not look like anything that had lived. The eyes had swollen,
resembled immense blue bubbles. The mouth was open and black,
and the tongue lolled under the skewer, and the teeth glinted
horribly.

Yeshua stared at the lamb like someone possessed, his lips
trembling, his dulled eyes gaping. Steam rose from the lamb. They
were all watching him, waiting for him to recover from that
strange fixity of gaze.

"Drink wine!" Meriamne said, and slipped from her place at the
table to bring her own cup to his lips. His lips moved, he sipped a
little of the wine and then smiled at her, but it was a distant un-
recognizing smile.

"We are waiting for you, my son," Yusuf said, leaning forward
over the table, half his face lit in the orange glow from the clay
stove. "You are the youngest, and we are all waiting for you to ask
the question."

The singing of the cicadas was deafening.

"And what shall I ask?" Yeshua said tonelessly, not looking away
from the roasted lamb, the little bubbles of creamy fat bursting
through the flesh, the oily blood, the smoke rising.

Eleazar made a little gesture of impatience. Maritha smiled
nervously, and suddenly buried her face in her hands. Only Meriamne seemed calm and composed.

"Surely you remember the question?" Yusuf said insistently. "It is not a difficult question. You have attended many Passovers. Eleazar will ask the question for you, if you are unable to remember."

At last, as though with a great effort, Yeshua said: "Why is this night different from all other nights?"

"Then I shall tell you," Yusuf said. "On all other nights we eat leaven and unleavened bread alike, but on this night only unleavened. On all other nights we eat any kind of herb, but this night only bitter herbs. On all other nights we dip our hands in water not at all, but this night we dip our hands twice. Tonight we commemorate the Passover of the Lord God who passed over the houses of the children of Israel in Egypt and smote the first-born of the Egyptians and delivered us from Pharaoh. Tonight Yeshua is celebrating his first Passover in Jerusalem and therefore it is a specially holy occasion, for in this first Passover he has really come to manhood. He was actually permitted to enter the Court of the Priests—a very unusual distinction—and perhaps this is why he quite properly exhibits a sense of awe in front of the Lamb. What we are eating is the food of the spirit, not of the stomach. We eat now to celebrate how we were slaves unto Pharaoh in Egypt, and would still be so, had not the Lord our God brought us out thence with a strong hand and an outstretched arm."

Yusuf said these words about his son because Eleazar was smiling in quick-witted contempt of his cousin's slowness. He was in fact praising Yeshua for his strange behavior at table. All this had come about because, in glancing round the table, he had met the steady and reproachful gaze of Meriamne.

And then Yusuf set to reading from the Book of Exodus how the children of Israel were led by Moses across the Red Sea and over the desert of Sinai to the hills of Moab, and there Moses died, and Joshua took up the leadership of the twelve tribes; and the people crossed over into the land of Canaan. On this very hill where they had attended the afternoon sacrifice in the Court of the Priests, Abraham had performed the sacrifice of the ram, when God spared Isaac.

"This is holy land," Yusuf went on, "and therefore we shall sing in praise of the Lord our God."

At this moment, although Yusuf seemed about to talk at great length about all the reasons which made it necessary for the

children of Israel to sing God's praises, instead he suddenly burst
out singing in a low, quavering voice:

> *Praise ye the Lord.*
> *Praise, O ye servants of the Lord,*
> *Praise the name of the Lord.*
> *Blessed be the name of the Lord.*
> *From this time forth and for evermore.*
> *From the rising of the sun*
> *Unto the going down of the same,*
> *The Lord's name is to be praised.*

They all sang the psalms haltingly, in very low voices, for they
wanted to hear the voice of Yusuf; and after the singing they
dipped their hands again in water and again broke the unleavened
bread. Then the roast lamb was carved up deftly, Yusuf's hand
shaking so much that Yeshua and Eleazar went to his assistance.
Afterwards they sang more psalms, and once more washed their
hands, and once more drank the wine. And they ate all the lamb
except the bones accordingly to the law which demanded that the
lamb be consumed entirely. At the very end, after four cups of
wine had been drunk, they sang the closing psalm, and this time
they heard the voice of Yeshua rising high above the others:

> *I will pay my vows unto the Lord,*
> *Yea, in the presence of all His people,*
> *In the courts of the Lord's house,*
> *In the midst of thee, O Jerusalem,*
> *Praise ye the Lord.*
> *O praise the Lord, all ye nations.*
> *Praise Him, all ye people.*
> *For His merciful kindness is great towards us:*
> *And the truth of the Lord endureth for ever.*
> *Hallelujah!*

So the singing came to an end, and Meriam swept up the silver
tray and the bowls of reddish sauce, to put them away in the cupboard. She would not wash them this evening, for the rest of the
evening should be spent in contemplation of God's mercy towards
the children of Israel. And when everything was put away, Yusuf

said: "Let us now go up the Mount of Olives and feast our eyes on Jerusalem."

It was no more than a short twenty-minute walk from Bethany to the summit of the Mount of Olives, along a ragged footpath winding past the tombs. They walked in silence, taking their time, listening to the murmur of the pilgrims camped in their painted tents on the further side of the mountain facing Jerusalem. Sometimes Yusuf muttered prayers, and he would talk to them about how he had climbed this same hill sixty years ago: he remembered this tomb, this gnarled olive tree, these stone benches which were all worn now, for so many travelers had rested there. Eleazar walked stiffly, unseeing, but Meriamne walked ahead, tossing her long black hair which reached to the middle of her back, sometimes smiling and running back to take Yeshua by the hand and whisper into his ear. Maritha walked sedately, as befitted one who sometimes dreamed she was a great lady in the land. Only Meriam did not accompany them, saying she had many things to prepare for the remaining days of the Passover.

When they had come half-way up the mountain, they saw the moon scudding through the thin clouds: a bronze moon, veined like a leaf, and frightening because it was so enormous against the dark sky. The moon turned the cedars on the crest of the mountain the color of dulled gold. It was strange to be walking there, in the silence of the eastern flank of the mountain, while all before them lay the clamor of multitudes. Twenty thousand people were camped on the western slope. Trumpets blared. There were shouts: prayers were being intoned; the whole westward shore of the hill seethed like an anthill.

And when at last they were standing on the crest, in the shade of the dulled gold cedars, looking out over Jerusalem, they were like people who see a great city for the first time. Tears of pure joy streamed down their faces as they looked upon the battlemented walls, the moonlight flooding the Temple, all white marble and gold, and the long sweep of the valley of Kidron below, where mysterious shadows moved. It was no more than a small craggy valley under the arching walls, but it seemed immense, unbridgeable, a huge chasm dividing them from the glory of the city, where the many-storied roofs gleamed like hammered bronze; and though there was the clamor of the pilgrims all round them, they were aware of a welling silence and a ghostly quiet.

"Is this Heaven?" Yeshua said, and he held back, as though he did not dare to look for long at the gleaming pillars and the marble courts of the Temple, where they had passed the afternoon; and then Meriamne took his hand and pointed to the Court of the Priests in the distance, saying: "Was it there the lamb was sacrificed?"

"Yes, it was there," Yeshua murmured, and he began to look eagerly for the place where he had stood beside his father.

Even now smoke rose from the great marble altar, but the fires must have been banked low, for he could see no flames.

Somewhere close at hand a goatherd played on his reed pipe, surrounded by his small black flock. The fireflies danced, and glowworms lit the stones, and they heard the wind rustling the cedars.

"If thou shalt stay here," Meriamne said, "then every evening we can walk up the footpath and see the city. Shalt thou stay, Yeshua?"

Yeshua said nothing. An awful pity flooded his mind as he gazed upon the loveliness of the city, so near, so far, so beautiful: and he shuddered as he remembered how the Court of the Priests had run with the blood of sacrifice. Far away, on the other side of the city, on a little scarp of rock jutting out in haggard splendor, lay the place where Yudah Ben-Ezekiah had been crucified.

Yona

In those days the Passover pilgrims spent a week in Jerusalem; every day there were ceremonies in the courts of the Temple. On the evening after the Passover lamb was eaten, three men from each family, carrying sickles and reed baskets, made their way to the small fields in the Kidron valley and gathered a sheaf of barley, the first fruits of the harvest to the Lord, which they carried to the Temple. On the following morning the grain was threshed, and

the kernels were slightly roasted and ground with great care; and
when the flour was mixed with oil, the paste was burned on the
altar of holocausts. Then there were more feasts, more celebrations,
more sacrifices. There were pilgrimages to all the sacred places;
and water from the sacred wells was solemnly poured into
earthenware jars and sealed. All through that week there was a
ceaseless traffic of pilgrims through the city, and the sun burned in
a cloudless indigo sky; only at night came the gray clouds to veil
the moon.

In the House of the Green Figs life continued tranquilly. Every
morning Eleazar practiced his penmanship, pale and solemn, with
a load of phylacteries on his arms and forehead, so much older
than his years that Yeshua, gazing upon him, grew afraid that he
would die young. Maritha spent the morning at her embroidery
frame: there was some of her brother's solemnity in her pale face
as she worked the scarlet and green wool, but her pink tongue,
darting between her lips, made her less solemn than her brother
would have liked. Only Meriamne was always gay, always humming or singing under her breath, chattering away, never quiet, to
the despair of the old servant. Yeshua was happy in her company.
Her full mouth, her flashing white teeth, her defiantly blue eyes
overshadowed by long black eyelashes in a face of healthy peach-
bloom, the rainbow-colored shawls she wore, the silver anklets—
all these pleased him, and he watched her with a wondering sense
of delight.

Once, seeing her playing ball in the courtyard, leaping up like
a bird to catch the ball in mid-flight, he murmured: "Too much
life!"

Meriamne turned on him savagely.

"And would you have me less alive?" she said, her face crimson.
"Oh, you are like all the rest! What am I expected to do? Should I
study the ancient texts like Eleazar until my eyes are as small as
spiders' eyes. For Yeshua's sake should I be meek and modest?
And then—have you heard the dry grasses rustling in the tombs,
Yeshua? Eleazar is the withered grass, and I—"

"What are you?" he asked, mocking her.

"See! I am an almond tree!" she exclaimed, and she threw her
arms round the trunk of the almond tree in the garden, shaking it,
so that all the green nuts and wax-white blossoms flashed in the
sun, and it was as though quite suddenly a milky fountain had

sprouted out of the earth. And the shaking of the tree somehow released the ripe fruitful smell of almonds. A moment later, her
black hair swinging out, effortless as a bird, she began to climb
the tree, nestling along the branches, taunting him, smiling down
at him.

"You are like Yona," she said, taunting.

"Yona?" he asked, puzzled.

"What a nincompoop you are!" Meriamne laughed. "I mean
your cousin Yona Ben-Zechariah. He lives at Hebron, but he has
a house too in Ain Karem. He is much more the man of the world
than you are!"

Yeshua was stung to the quick, not because he ever wanted to
be regarded as a man of the world, but because Meriamne was
implying that she loved Yona more than Yeshua. There was something in the way she pronounced the name which suggested she
knew him well, admired him and was always happy with him.

"Then you should meet him," she said, when she had climbed
down the tree. "It is very easy. I will send a note to him. I shall
tell you what to write, and you shall write for me."

Meriamne ruled over her own world and took no pains to hide
her prominent position in the House of the Green Figs. She was
the mistress of the house. Even Eleazar submitted to her judgment. She lowered her eyes and behaved meekly only in the presence of Yusuf and Meriam, and more rarely in the presence of the
old servant.

The letter to Yona was never written, but one day towards the
end of Passover a tall, handsome, raw-boned youth, lean as a yard-
broom, with eyes like twin points of black flame, appeared in the
courtyard. His long gown was thick with dust and clung to him.
He was barefoot, and his feet were covered with small scars,
strangely white: the burning earth had not scorched the brass skin
of his soles nor browned the delicate white skin with the golden
scars. He had thick black curling hair which fell to his shoulders,
and though from a distance you might take him for a nomad, on
closer view you might take him for a prince, perhaps of Idumea,
for he had the high cheekbones of the Idumeans. He had a craggy
brow, a mobile mouth, a pointed chin, a quite extraordinary air of
refinement. The most astonishing thing of all was that he gave the
appearance of rugged strength and a delicate aristocratic melancholy at the same time, as though two entirely different people

were being chained together in an unruly body. Drenched in sunlight, he stood in the courtyard, leaning on his staff, quietly observing the sparrows at their love-play. He had been in the courtyard
for more than an hour when Meriamne observed him from an
upper window, rushed down the steps and threw herself in his
arms. She was so excited by his appearance that she babbled nonsense in his ears for five minutes, asking interminable questions
and not waiting for an answer.

"So you have come, my dearest? I was writing a letter to you—
truly I intended to write to you! Have you been to Hebron? You
never tell me where you go. Of course, everybody knows you like
the country, though why anyone should choose to live there is
beyond me. Do you like my beads?" Saying this, she lifted some
pale turquoise beads, which Yeshua had given to her, and thrust
them within an inch of Yona's eyes. Then she gave a little gasp, for
she noticed that his eyes were bloodshot and the lids fell heavily,
making them appear drowsy. "But you need a rest," she exclaimed.
"Did you walk all the way from Hebron?"

"No, from Ain Karem," he laughed.

Hebron is near the shores of the Dead Sea many miles to the
south. Ain Karem is a small, busy village in a circle of black
cypresses only a few miles away.

Yona asked about Eleazar and Maritha.

"Eleazar is studying for the priesthood and Maritha is studying
to be a housewife."

"And you?"

"I am me!" Meriamne replied at the top of her voice. "I am
Meriamne! I am honey! I am the tender horns of the deer!"

She babbled on, so pleased to be with Yona that she allowed no
door to close on the words which rose unbidden to her lips. She
danced round him, examined him from all angles, said he was
tired and needed to rest, and the next moment suggested they
should climb the Mount of Olives together.

"You are all fire, Meriamne, and you will burn me!" Yona said,
and though there was laughter in his voice there was a sombre
glow in his eyes. And then, because she was so pleased with his
words, he said heartlessly: "The truth is, I haven't come to see you,
Meriamne. I came to see Yeshua of Nazareth."

The effect was instantaneous. Meriamne wheeled round in the
center of the courtyard, put her hand to her face, stared at him,

blushing crimson, her young body quivering under the lash of his
rebuke, for he spoke the words in such a way as to imply that she
talked more nonsense than was good for her. It was like an abrupt
dismissal.

Trembling, she said: "Yes, yes, I know you have come for him,
Yona."

For a few more moments she was aware of fine, pitiless, aristocratic features in the hot sun, a terrible icy smile. Her face was like
glass shivered into a thousand fragments. Her tongue was dry.
Hot waves of anger and compassion were coloring her cheeks.

"Shall we go?" she said, and her voice was torn from her, a
jewel torn from the cup of her throat.

She held his hand and led him into the House of the Green Figs.
It was the time in the afternoon when everyone was sleeping; even
the caged birds were asleep. The soft white puppies were curled
up in the shade. It was unusually hot for Passover, the flowers
wilting, the heat foaming off the stone walls of the house, the indigo blue sky pelting them with heat. Meriamne was subdued,
quiet, listless now: somewhere deep inside blood flowed from a
wound. The shutters were closed, the house airless. They walked
over floors covered with sheepskins until they reached the room
where Yeshua was sleeping. Meriamne did not bother to announce
herself. She simply walked into the room, where purple shadows
swirled and the mistiness of summer hung in the air.

"He is here," she whispered, her voice toneless.

Yeshua was lying on some matting on the floor. In the heat he
had thrown off his gown. He lay there very quiet, asleep, his face
turned away from them. He was naked, but it was too dark to see
clearly and they were still blinded by the hot sunlight outside.

"Where is he?" Yona said, and Meriamne pointed in the direction of the boy sleeping close to the wall.

She was smiling again, but it was a forced smile, the smile of
someone who is still wounded.

Meriamne remained at the door, leaning her face against the
door-post, waiting. There were some rushes on the floor, and as
Yona walked barefoot there came the crackling sound of the
rushes underfoot. By this time Meriamne's eyes were accustomed
to the light. She thought Yeshua was wearing a thin gown, but she
was paying little attention to him. In the dark room Yona seemed
to be immensely tall and powerful as he swung across the floor

and stooped over the boy sleeping there, smiling to himself as he
gazed at the sleeping face, breathing innocently and lightly like
an infant. Sighing, Yeshua awoke. For a moment he gazed steadily
at the tall youth with the thick curls reaching to his shoulders, and
then he said: "Who are you? Have you come from heaven?"

"I am Yona," Yona said gravely, shuddering in the heat. "I come
from Hebron."

Yeshua leaped to his feet.

"Yona!" he exclaimed, and threw his arms round Yona. He was
wide-awake and smiling, all the drowsiness gone from him.

Then he stood back to see Yona better: a long face, a pointed
chin, a dust of freckles, eyes blazing like little flames, a curious
lean strength about him. All the while Yona was examining him,
looking him up and down, as though he were searching for something which was familiar to him and yet barely discernible. At last
he found what he was searching for. The scars left by the panther's
claws had long since healed: in their place were long dints in the
flesh, the barest trace of claws. Yona bent forward and kissed these
faint traces of wounds on shoulder and thigh, saying: "I kiss the
aleph and the *tav.*"

"So you have heard?" Yeshua whispered, and hung his head.

"Everyone has heard," Yona answered.

There was a long silence as they gazed at one another. The
heat was an intoxication. Meriamne had seen everything. At the
moment when Yona kissed the wounds, somehow suggesting a
courtier kissing the hand of his king, she gave a little frightened
sob and buried her face in her hands. Or at least this is what she
had intended to do. In fact, she was peering through her fingers,
unable to take her eyes away from them, and especially unable to
take her eyes away from Yeshua. She had never seen him naked
before. She was confused and overjoyed and close to swooning,
and this happened not because she was seeing someone naked for
the first time, but because she too had heard about the wounds
and dreamed that one day she would be allowed to examine them.
Many times it had been on the tip of her tongue to ask Yeshua to
show them to her. Neither Yeshua nor Yona were aware of her
presence. She belonged to the silence, and was one with the
shadows.

"The *aleph* and the *tav,*" Yeshua said, and in the pure living

silence of the small room the words were as though uttered by
silver trumpets.

Then seeing that he was naked he bent and gathered up the
gown which lay at his feet and wrapped it round his middle, smiling secretively and murmuring: "Yona, Yona, my brother—" It was
a sound like the moaning of doves.

He shivered a little, aware that some terrible thing was happening. This terrible thing, this sudden closeness, the knowledge that
they had come together and would never be separated as long as
they lived, even though their physical bodies might be separated;
the knowledge that they loved one another and would die for one
another; the certainty that this meeting would be repeated many
times, and always it would be as though they had never set eyes
on one another: always a shock, an astonishment, a pure flame—all
this passed through Yeshua's mind in an instant of time. It was as
if he had seen at last the face which confronted him every night
in his dreams.

"Yona!" he said again, and burst out laughing; then he clapped
his hands and danced round the room, paying no attention to
Meriamne, not seeing her, aware of nothing in the world except
the presence of the tall youth who resembled at one and the same
time a prince and a wanderer from the desert.

He took Yona by the arm and said with a dazed smile: "Please
come out in the sun! I must see you in the sunlight! There are a
hundred things to talk about!"

Dazed with happiness, still shouting at the top of his voice,
Yeshua ran out into the courtyard, dragging Yona with him. From
somewhere in the house they heard the sound of sobbing.

Because the house was beginning to awake after the long siesta,
Yona was impatient to pay the proper respects to Yusuf and
Meriam, but Yeshua insisted that they leave the courtyard altogether. He was entirely selfish. He wanted Yona for himself. He
was determined to have his own way and, when Yona demurred,
Yeshua said brutally: "I suppose you prefer the company of girls."
He was blazing with anger. A moment before, standing solemnly
in the room where he had been sleeping, he looked like a man:
now he resembled a spoiled child.

"I suppose you think we both ought to comfort Meriamne because she is sobbing her heart out," he exclaimed. "But if you only
knew, it is good for her."

"Why is it good for her?"

"Because she is completely frivolous, and I am sure she will become nothing better than a dancing girl or a prostitute if she continues to behave like this. She is always giggling and throwing herself about, and when anything very solemn happens she throws laughing fits! Come!"

And saying this, Yeshua pulled Yona by the arm, led him past the fig-trees and the great flowering almond tree, out of the courtyard, past the Prophet's Tomb and along the dusty scented path which led to the Mount of Olives. He still wore his gown wrapped round his waist, but there was nothing unusual in this: in hot weather the shepherd boys did the same, and he could easily be mistaken for a shepherd boy.

They climbed past the empty tombs through a mist of yellow butterflies. The sunlight was blinding, and the tombs glared, blinding white. The hot grasses curled and withered in the heat, and the bright scarlet anemones were fading. They said little. It was enough to be together, flashing quick smiles, holding hands, in the mystery of closeness.

"So many tombs," Yeshua said once, "and all empty! Do you imagine there will be a resurrection, Yona? Will the dust burn in God's flame?"

He smiled his quick mysterious smile.

"Oh, please don't be puzzled," he went on a moment later. "I have slept in the tombs. I know all the caves in Nazareth were tombs once, and I must have slept in all of them when I was a shepherd. Have you ever in your life let the dust of a cave trickle through your fingers and found yourself saying: 'A man was here, and now he is dust.' I have taken the dust from a cave and lifted it to the wind and seen it scatter over Nazareth, and perhaps it was the dust of my ancestors, and sometimes I think the whole world will become dust crumbling in God's fingers."

Yeshua did not know why he talked in this way. Again and again he came back to the visions of Enoch: the place of darkness, the river of gleaming fire, the high mountains which look out upon the treasuries of the stars, and then the abyss, the mountain hollows, the fountains of cooling water. The stars sang, the whole heavens were alive: all the multitudes of creation were praising the Lord. Then why should a priest lift a jeweled knife and slit the throat of a lamb?

They were standing under the ancient cedars on the top of the Mount of Olives. The hillslope was still crowded with a rainbow of tents, and the sun flashed from the gnarled olive trees and the tombs.

"The smoke from the holocaust," Yeshua said quietly. "The smell of blood! I do not believe the courts of the Lord should reek with blood, and do you know anything more beautiful than a lamb? When a lamb skips, he is an angel singing. And when he butts the udder, why, there's such force in him—"

"You are a shepherd in love with your lambs," Yona said, and turned away, disturbed by the passion in Yeshua's face.

"The whole of the Temple reeks with blood!" Yeshua said, astonished by his own fury.

"Because God demanded it," Yona said softly.

"No! He did not, if He loves us. Have you ever been with sheep? Have you ever been with the ewes at lambing time? No, of course, you haven't. But then I suppose your father, who was a high priest in the Temple, took you to see the sacrifices when you were very young and you have become accustomed to them. I have hardly slept for three nights thinking of the slaughter."

"Do you know what you are saying?" Yona asked, and his voice seemed curiously weighted with sorrow.

"Yes, I know."

"You know that what you are saying is a kind of blasphemy?"

"Yes."

"And there are terrible punishments for those who commit blasphemy?"

There was a long silence. It occurred to Yeshua that he was saying things he would never have dared say to anyone else. Neither to Meriamne nor to his mother would he have dared say these things: for had not Moses, and then David and Zadok the Priest blessed these sacrifices, saying they were demanded by God, and was not the Temple the heart of the world?

They walked down the hill in silence. The air was hot with the aromatic odors of mint and poppy, and the heavy sweetness of honeysuckle. The red sun glinted in Yeshua's hair and there was no wind to lift the dark helmet of ink-black hair which fell to Yona's shoulders. Everywhere were tombs, tents, goatherds, half-naked children, women suckling infants, old bearded men sitting in the sun and gazing upon Jerusalem. The slope of the Mount of Olives

was like a fair-ground. Lovers stood there hand in hand, looking
upon the golden city. Above the Temple the black smoke of the
holocaust drifted lazily.

And when they had come down to the Valley of Kidron, they
were still silent, thoughtful, wrapped in one another. At last Yeshua
said: "Are you angry, that you keep silence so long?"

In reply Yona turned sharply and said: "You really believe there
should be an end to sacrifices?"

"Yes, I believe that, truly. I believe there should be silence, not
sacrifices. Did not the prophet Habakkuk say: 'The Lord is in His
holy temple: let the earth keep silence before Him.' I do not
believe God feasts on flashing knives. I believe there is evil in
killing. I have spent many nights poring over the words of the
prophet Habakkuk, and I believe the spirit of God flowed through
him, and everything he says breathes God's voice. It is such a short
book, and there is so much richness in it. He said: 'O Lord my
God, Thou art of purer eyes than to behold evil, and canst not look
upon iniquity.' I believe that, too. I believe that the earth will be
filled with the knowledge of God, as the waters cover the sea: and I
believe this, not only because Habakkuk said so, but because it is
impossible for me to believe anything else. And when Habakkuk
says: 'Art Thou not from everlasting, O Lord my God, mine Holy
One? We shall not die!' then I believe he is saying something of
such great importance that the head spins as you contemplate the
words."

"And do you believe that the Messiah will come in our time?"
Yona asked, thrusting at some green thistles with his staff.

"Yes, yes, I believe He will come," Yeshua said. "Perhaps not in
our time, but very soon. And there, too, I find meaning in the
words of Habakkuk, for he said: 'The vision is for an appointed
time and hastens towards an end and does not tarry. Though it
tarry, wait for it. It will surely come.' And therefore I believe we
shall all recognize the coming time."

"And do you believe He will come in clouds of glory?"

"I believe it."

"Attended by angels?"

"Certainly He will be attended by angels, or perhaps only with
the archangels. Yes, He will come with angels and in glory. The
skies will open, and He will descend to earth at the Temple and
He will show Himself in the Holy of Holies and then everything

we have ever known will come to an end, but before this time there will be wars and pestilences—it is all written in the books, and that is why we must believe it!"

"Then you believe God demands there should be wars and pestilences before the coming of the Messiah?"

"Yes, truly."

"But only a little while ago you said that the pure eyes of God cannot look upon iniquity. Do you mean that God will turn His eyes away?"

Yeshua was watching an old man riding on a donkey along the broken boulder-strewn pathway. The old man's face was the color of black leather, deeply wrinkled, but his beard blazed white. His eyes were closed, his lips murmured and he fingered his prayer-shawl, paying no attention to where the donkey was taking him, deep in his meditations. There was something grotesque in this dark-faced old man, his solemn trust in the donkey picking its way among the boulders. A faint wind was stirring, and it blew the old man's beard under his chin. And seeing the old man, a few bones wrapped in withered flesh, he said: "We can only trust in God's mercy. It is written in the books that there will be wars and pestilences and terrible lightnings. The most awful things will happen—the curtains of the Temple will be rent—oh, there is no end to the dark savage things that will happen—I read somewhere that the whole Valley of Kidron will be piled high with corpses—but perhaps none of these things will happen—perhaps there will be a flash of lightning and the whole sky will be full of the beating of the angels' wings! The more I think of it the more I am sure there will be no need for these terrible things. The grace of God will come upon us. There will be no need for sacrifices. The Lord will be in His holy temple and the earth will be silent before Him and we shall all worship Him. Do you agree?"

"No, I believe there will be wars and pestilences," Yona said abruptly. "And as for the sacrifices in the Temple, I believe they have been ordained by God."

Yeshua was hurt and puzzled. The thought that Yona should disagree with him on any subject whatever alarmed him.

"What you are saying," Yona went on, "is very much what the Essenes are saying. They say it is absurd to offer sacrifices of lambs and goats. They say the only sacrifice pleasing to God is the sacrifice of oneself."

"The Essenes?" Yeshua murmured, puzzled.

"Have you never heard of them?"

"No."

"Then perhaps it is better that you should never hear about them," Yona said, his voice curiously sharp and resonant, and then he turned, his eyes glinting, the twin flames flickering, to look fully at Yeshua's face. "Are you sure you have never heard of them?"

"I am quite sure," Yeshua said, blushing.

"But surely you have heard of Yudah Ben-Ezekiah?"

"Yes. He came to Nazareth. He stayed for a night, I remember, and then vanished."

"Did he come alone?"

"Yes."

"Without guards?" Yona asked insistently.

"Oh, they say there were some guards hidden in the orchard near the house. It would be dangerous to come alone, and so I suppose the guards were there."

"And you are quite sure he was alone?"

"Yes, Yona."

There was a short silence. Yeshua could make nothing of these questions spoken very quickly, almost fiercely. He had the strange feeling that he was being cross-examined by someone who knew a good deal more about Yudah Ben-Ezekiah than he did. He could remember everything that took place in the upper room in the servants' courtyard of his father's house: the yellow light from the oil-lamp streaking across Yudah's face, the pointed beard, the look of agony and despair in the eyes of the young revolutionary when he was rebuffed. He remembered how Yudah had lurched out of the room into the moonlight, and how the whole room froze in silence afterwards, everyone shivering, and how afterwards there was only the sound of the hot wind on the rushes.

"He came to Nazareth?" Yona said, and again there was that strange insistence in his voice, as though he could not believe.

"Yes, I told you. I saw Sepphoris in flames. I know Yudah Ben-Ezekiah has done harm to us. I know we shall never reach our salvation by killing—neither the lambs nor the Romans. The courtyards of the Lord must be kept pure. I know this. No blood, no blood—"

"You are sure?"

"No, I am not sure. It is all in the mercy of God. But I believe God is merciful."

Yona's lips curled, and he repeated the word "mercy."

"The Romans have never shown mercy," he went on, "nor the Jews who work for them. And there is no mercy in Heaven? I do not believe in mercy, nevertheless—"

He did not go on. He seemed sunk in a dream, and sometimes he would turn to stare searchingly at Yeshua.

"And his sons?" Yona said at last, and there seemed to be a taunt in his voice.

It was all mystery and perplexity. Yeshua could not fathom this sudden question. He looked into Yona's eyes, but there was no comfort in them: the eyes had turned steel-black, very cold, mysteriously empty.

"What sons?"

"The sons of Yudah."

"I did not know he had sons."

"Nevertheless he has many sons, Yeshua. They were of his own loins, not brought to him. There is Shimon and Yacob, and perhaps one day you will meet them. They have sworn vengeance on Cæsar and they do not believe in mercy. I tell you, if you see them, you will be like the rest of us, and you will worship them because they are strong. Those sons were his bodyguards when he went about Galilee begging for weapons, and now Shimon and Yacob are continuing the war against the Romans. Even now they are at work, Yeshua—even now!"

Yeshua closed his eyes. When Sepphoris was burned to the ground and the crucifixes were raised along the whole length of the Roman road which leads to Jerusalem, he had prayed that there would be an end to bloodshed. He had thrown himself on the grasses among his lambs, looking up at the stars, praying for peace. Were not the stars peaceful, and the rivers, and the hills? And surely the silence of the world at night was only the presage of peace, and surely the night lay in the protection of the everlasting wings! "Let there be peace," he had whispered, and sometimes it seemed to him that all the earth echoed his voice. And now with drawn face, thinking of the sons of Yudah preparing rebellion, he said shuddering: "They will fail, Yona. Everything in me tells me they will fail."

"And will you pray for them?"

"Yes, I will pray for them, even though they fail."

Then there was quiet between them, and they walked holding hands as though there had been no dispute between them.

All afternoon they wandered around the walls of Jerusalem. Once, when they came to a rocky place near some refuse pits and crumbling graves, Yona began to talk about the black panther, asking Yeshua whether the skin still remained. Yeshua answered that the skin was still in the House of the Oil Press in Nazareth, though he had not set eyes on it for many months; and suddenly, his voice failing, staring around at this barren landscape on the hilly edge of Jerusalem, he said: "There is a secret place where the black panther still waits for me. I know I shall see him again." And saying this in his strangely weak voice, Yeshua felt that the panther was very near, he could feel its humid breath on his face and hear the curious sawing sound it made, like the sound of an iron saw cutting through wood, blade thrust forward and then back again. He must have fainted for a moment, leaning against one of the crumbling graves, for he remembered afterwards how Yona had stared at him wildly, saying: "Little lamb, little lamb, hast thou gone from me already?" And in fact for a few moments Yona had thought he was dying, there on the windy hills to the west of Jerusalem, among the broken potsherds and the skull-shaped rocks. Suddenly all the blood had gone from Yeshua's face. He was drained white, his hollow staring eyes possessed no light, were glazed over, and had the color of ashes. With his red hair matted over his forehead, Yeshua had looked more terrible than the dead. Then he recovered, put his hands to his eyes, said: "I was dreaming," and began to walk slowly, tottering a little, down the rough path bordered by thistles which led to the valley below. Soon Yeshua forgot the incident, and for Yona it was only something that lingered on in dreams or on the frontiers of memory, the face of the boy he called his brother, a beautiful face hollowed out, white as a sepulchre—one of those sepulchres which are newly painted at the time of Passover—a boy who seemed like a ghost with eyes that had turned to ashes.

Towards evening it began to rain: one of those gentle rains which make the air more luminous. In the warm twilight the grasses swayed and the earth gave off a rich sweet smell. The solemn shadows of the city towers were flung down to the bottom of the pool of Gihon and higher up the haunted darkening valley they watched the broken cliffs haggard with riven old olives where the angel of the Lord smote the army of Sennacherib: those cliffs seemed to fall away, to be swallowed up by all the mouths of darkness. Soon all the shadows were hurrying headlong down the hills of Berotha and Zion into the valley of Jehosophat, resting awhile in the bottom of the ravine, then slowly creeping up the Mount of Olives, entering tomb after tomb and cave after cave, touching the feathery olive trees and occasional palms, until at last they settled upon the great cedars which crowned the summit; and all was dark except the cedars silhouetted against the sky.

As darkness fell there was a hush, a growing silence and a sound like weeping as the evening winds poured along the Kidron Valley. Then one by one, from the depths of the valley and along the walls of Jerusalem and over the swelling breast of the Mount of Olives, glimmering oil-lamps appeared. Even half-way up the walls of Jerusalem, two hundred feet high, the gleam of oil-lamps shone mysteriously. There were caravans where every man held an earthenware lamp in his hands. Light shone from caves. And those high up on the Mount of Olives saw Jerusalem below them, agleam with light.

Yeshua and Yona made their way back to Bethphage and the House of the Green Figs, skirting the Mount of Olives, taking the goat paths to avoid the crowds of pilgrims now once again noisily proclaiming their existence as they prepared for the nightly feast. Yeshua was wrapped in silence. Once he said: "I have seen the enemy." And once when Yona talked again of Yudah of Galilee, Yeshua silenced him, saying: "Tell me, does the knife seek the throat of the lamb, or the lamb seek the knife?" When they came to the House of the Green Figs, Meriamne was nowhere to be seen, but they heard Eleazar chanting as he wrote in one of the upper rooms in his impeccable handwriting from the Book of the Psalms.

All that night while the darkness roared outside and the cool wind rustled the fig trees, they talked in the small room where in the morning Yona had found Yeshua sleeping. They opened their hearts to one another. Sometimes in hushed voices they chanted the psalms together. More than once Yeshua spoke of the Temple, washed clean by the rains of God, no longer reeking with blood. And suddenly while they were talking Yeshua remembered something his father had told him during the journey to Jerusalem: how one day Yona would be able to claim the office of Sacrificer in the Temple by right of inheritance.

"And wilt thou claim thine inheritance?" Yeshua asked, and his voice was like that of a man brooding passionately.

He saw Yona robed in blue, crowned with a white mitre, standing among the fumes of the altar of holocausts.

There was no answer from Yona.

"Oh, let there be an end to sacrifices!" Yeshua exlaimed. "Let there be an end, Yona! Thou shalt be the last Sacrificer! Surely thou shalt be the last!"

The silence gathered. Somewhere a green pigeon sang, a long low mellow note, and soon everyone in the House of the Green Figs was asleep.

The Longest Journey

At the end of the Passover, when the last crumbs of unleavened bread had been eaten and the last ceremonies had been attended, Yusuf decided to return to Nazareth. Had he not offered a lamb for a sacrifice in the Court of the Priests, walked around the walls of the holy city, drunk from the waters of Shiloh, and paid the sacred half-shekel to the Temple treasury? Had he not spoken earnestly to Eleazar, offering the boy and his two sisters the hospitality of the home in Nazareth, saying that it was wrong for the three children to live alone, assisted only by an old servant, in the immense house —better that they should have older men and women around them to lead them in the paths of righteousness; but Eleazar had only smiled his tight-lipped superior smile, saying that he regarded himself as the head of the family and how better would he learn to be a Scribe than by consorting with the Scribes in the Temple? And Yona with his long face, so young, so elegant, with a strange jerki-

ness in his movements, always walking hand in hand with Yeshua
—ah, it would be better to leave soon before those two conspirators
became too friendly! Better to return to Nazareth, the quiet valley,
than remain beside the holy mountain! But when Yusuf announced
his intention of returning, Yeshua gasped: "So soon! So soon!" and
there was so much pain in his eyes that Meriam took him by the
arm and said: "Is not thy father's house in Nazareth?"

"Yea, truly," Yeshua answered quietly.

"And is not thy work in Nazareth?"

"Yea, truly."

"And didst thou not say thou wouldst become a shepherd, and
where better shalt thou watch thy sheep than in the hills of
Nazareth?"

Yeshua bowed his head. All this, and more, he assented to, but
he could not prevent the tears springing up. He clutched his
mother's hand.

"Give me one day—just one more day," he begged. "For Yona's
sake—for Yona—"

Meriam smiled, but there was a flame of impatience in her smile.
She knew Yona and Yeshua had spent most of the week together.

"Aye, and one day will become two days, and then three! Thou
hast a way of making the world please thee. I shall speak to thy
father."

"Shalt thou speak for me?"

She smiled again, and he knew he would have his way. He ran
out into the courtyard. Meriamne was playing ball. She wore a
thin embroidered blue veil dotted with flowers, but the veil did not
prevent her from playing vigorously. As soon as she saw Yeshua
emerging from the house, she turned away from him, a quick blind
turning of the shoulders. She had consigned him to blank oblivion,
to nothingness. She was trembling a little, full of a fierce childish
hate. Tears were trickling down her face, and she choked back her
sobs, standing there lonely in the courtyard, shriveling.

Yeshua was perplexed. Even though he was perfectly aware why
she had turned away, he was puzzled by her vehemence, her
violence. He ran up to her and peered into her face. She gave a
little moan, and flung herself away from him, so that he had to run
after her to catch up with her. And then holding her by the
shoulders, while she looked away, he whispered into her ear:
"Shalt thou not speak to me?"

Her eyelids were lowered, and she was shivering.

"Why should I speak to thee?" she said, her voice soft and moaning.

"For the sake of the love I bear thee," he answered quickly.

She turned to face him, her head held high, a smile of derision on her lips.

"Love!" she said derisively. "And what is love to thee? Thou lovest the dead lamb better than thou lovest me!"

She was like a wildcat, her eyes blazing, spitting the words out.

"The dead lamb," he murmured sorrowfully, remembering the white teeth glaring from the skull.

"And thyself, too," she went on, pleased with her triumph, for she saw the pain in his face.

He knew why she was punishing him: because he had spent so much time with Yona and seemed hardly aware of her existence. Her face was flushed, and her eyes blazed. And suddenly, seeing him so downcast, all her anger went from her.

" 'Tis for thy sake I am doing this," she said, and she was still smiling to herself, though her voice was grave.

"How—for my sake?"

"To teach thee!" she replied, and suddenly pushed him away, brutally repulsing him, her little forehead knit with sharp frowns. "To teach thee to behave better, not head-in-air! Thou art all puff-ball," she went on angrily, stamping her feet. "Thou stayest in our house, but who are we to thee? Maritha, hast thou talked to her? And Eleazar, hast thou spoken a word? Nay, not once: or else a little word like a squeak—'May God bless thee!'—but no more than that!"

And saying this, seeing him perturbed, she gave a little cry of triumph which nearly gave her game away, but he was too shocked to understand the sharp hissing cry that came from her lips. He stared at her like someone struck dumb: the small pointed face, the violet eyes, the cheeks of apple blossom, and all on fire. His eyes downcast, he murmured: "Meriamne!" and he was going to beg her pardon when she exclaimed: "Shall I be grateful thou knowest my name?"

"Not grateful," he said, still with lowered lids. "It is a wonder and a glory thou rememberest when so many better things occupy thy mind!" he went on quickly, and another cry of triumph came from her.

He was like wax in her hands, at her mercy. She ran away into the shade of the fig trees, throwing her ball in the air and catching it, but soon she returned to face him. If he had looked her squarely in the face, he would have detected her triumphal smile.

"Then what am I to thee?" Meriamne went on cruelly. "I am a house, a place to rest in! At the end of a long journey thou comest here! Know ye not I am Meriamne?"

"Yea, truly I know."

"Nay, thou knowest not!" she said, and danced away until she had vanished in the shade of the fig trees.

Yeshua was lost in thought, sunk in misery. Everything Meriamne had said was true. He had paid almost no attention to Eleazar or Maritha or Meriamne, while enjoying their hospitality. He had been tongue-tied in front of her, and this was the sign of his guilt. So he gazed at the ground and his head reeled and he wished he was in Nazareth, away from her accusing smile. And Meriamne, hiding among the fig trees, could hardly contain the laughing excitement which bubbled up within her. She had played with him! She had worked on his emotions! She had demonstrated his guilt and brought a crimson blush to his face, and she was therefore delighted with herself and prepared to show him some sympathy. So she emerged from her hiding place, playing with her ball, and said: "I have thought about thee, and have much sorrow for thee, and shall forgive thee!"

His face lit with pleasure. He smiled at her so eagerly that she was dazzled by the smile.

Catching her breath, she said: "Shalt thou stay with us again?"

"Truly," he said, taking her hands and gazing into her eyes. His own eyes were the deep blue of the sea in which men drown. "Yea, truly I shall come, if thou shalt take pleasure in my coming."

Meriamne held her head a little to one side, thinking.

"And when shalt thou come?" she asked.

"At Passover—at every Passover."

"So thou shalt come at Passover," she repeated, mocking him. "Nay, thou shalt come more often—to please me!" And after a pause she said: "Shalt thou miss me in Nazareth?"

"Truly."

"Shalt thou miss me deeply?"

"Truly I shall."

"More than Yona?"

There was a long pause. His face turned crimson again. She had pity for him and said: "I shall come to Nazareth to see whether thou art in need of me. If I come, shalt thou be kind to me?"

He threw up his hands and then kissed her on the cheek, saying: "I shall be as kind to thee as I am with my sheep, for there is no greater kindness."

"Thou swearest it?"

"Truly."

"Thou hast said 'truly' three times," Meriamne exclaimed, and once again there was a note of triumph in her voice. "Hast thou but one word on thy tongue?"

Then he smiled and said "truly" again in a voice so low it was like a caress and she burst into wild cries of merriment and kissed him and then she took his hand and led him down the path between the fig trees, the long dark path, half covered with brambles down which they first saw the House of the Green Figs a week ago.

The sun lay hot on their faces as they wandered in the dust of the small pathways. The fig trees gave deep shade, but they never rested in the shade. She babbled on, talking about her dolls, and all the trouble of managing the large house, and Maritha's eternal sewing and embroidery, and Eleazar's everlasting writing. "Look at him closely, Yeshua! He has a face which becomes every day more like a pen!" She was delighted with herself, delighted with the blue sky which was like a burning blue window, and with the waving fields of bronze-colored barley. Everything was delightful and odd to her: a piebald mare, a Syrian officer puffing in the shade, a procession of Bactrian camels. She made faces. She mimicked everyone. She even mimicked the camels, twisting her lips and frowning while she attempted to walk like a camel. The burnished bronze barley threw off a suffocating heat, but she seemed immune. She forced him to accede to her mood. He became gay. He sang songs to her. All the time he was aware of a wariness, an eager reaching out for something mysteriously hidden from him, and when she laughed, he was aware she was watching him closely, darkly, as though from some secret hiding place.

She asked him where she would live if she came to Nazareth, what room, on what side of the house, and with what furniture. She wanted to know every detail of life there. And when he had told her all he could remember, she said: "Then what art thou but the son of a rich man, full of laziness?"

"Nay, I have worked hard," he answered, with a touch of anger.

"Ha, and is it working hard to be studying at Sepphoris and spending the day reading books and doing whatsoever comes into thy mind?"

"I have been a shepherd—"

"But long ago!"

"And a carpenter—"

She raised her eyebrows.

"But a few months!"

"True, but I could be a carpenter again, if needs be. And I am a shepherd always."

"How so?"

"Because it is bred in me. If you have been a shepherd, then you never cease being a shepherd, Meriamne."

"So," she said, and held her head to one side, examining him. "So thou art a shepherd! I thought they were all old, with gray beards! If thou wert truly a shepherd, thou wouldst have a staff in thy hands!"

There were moments when he was powerless with humiliation and chagrin. She was determined to mock him, to be equal with him. He did not know where she was taking him. The valley fell away: they came to the bare glistening ashen-colored rocks, and beyond this were fields of stunted barley taking a bleak nourishment from the Judæan hills. Here the hillsides were stony. A few goats browsed on them. Along the pathways, beside the dried-up gullies, came women and girls carrying bundles of thorns and faggots on their heads. They walked like angels, proudly, silently, thrusting their bodies a little forward, but this did not prevent Meriamne from mimicking them, marching in front of Yeshua while she pretended to be carrying an impossible tall burden of faggots on her head. And when Yeshua frowned, she said: "Am I not graceful? Am I not beautiful as they are? Thou hast eyes only for them, Yeshua, but for Meriamne thou hast no eyes at all!"

They walked on in silence, staring at the mountains ahead, while the heat pelted them. Long ago Yeshua had removed his sandals, but his feet grew hot and the sweat was glueing his robe to his skin.

Suddenly, where two valleys met, they saw green fields, olive

groves, quiet houses in the shade of fig trees. Birds sang. A stream
bubbled at their feet. Thick clusters of almond and pomegranate
trees crowded the shores of the stream, where the reeds waved in
the soft wind. The spring, the watered gardens, the orchards with
the scarlet blaze of the pomegranate flowers, the small neat barley
fields, all this intoxicated them after the long journey among barren
rocks. In some places the barley had already been reaped, and the
stubble glowed white under the sun. There was the smell of
flowers and wine, and there were only a few workers in the fields.
And standing there on a little stone bridge over the stream, looking
out towards a row of country houses set against the green shadow
of the hills, Meriamne said: "Knowest thou not where we have
come to?"

"I know not," he said, entranced by the quietness and beauty of
the two valleys.

"Then say the name after me—" she began, pursing her lips
together and watching him closely with laughing eyes.

Baffled, he said: "What name?"

There was no answer. He was weary of her mystifications and
said hurriedly: "It must be paradise and we are both dreaming."

"Nay, we dream not."

"Then where are we?"

"In Ain Karem," she answered, her voice low. "Come, I shall
take thee to thy cousin Yona. Truly he shall be pleased to see thee!"

Repeatedly during the journey, and always subtly, she had
shown her dislike for Yona. It was absurd that Meriamne should
be taking him to Yona's house. And yet it was so.

They skirted the edge of a barley field and then walked through
a grove of fig trees where young vines were growing from the
branches. Meriamne ran down the path, her veil fluttering behind
her.

They found Yona chopping wood at the back of the house. He
glanced up as soon as he saw them.

"Have you walked all the way from the House of the Green
Figs?" he shouted.

The sun flashed from the side of the house, a livid white. Above
the orchards the bare white rocks glinted in the hot sun.

"So you have walked all the way," Yona went on, turning to
Yeshua. "Then you must come into the house at once and drink
some cool wine!"

He was all smiles. He towered above Meriamne, and his bare arms (for he had rolled up the sleeves of his gown to chop wood) were running with milky sweat. Yeshua smiled. He was glad to be in Ain Karem, and a little frightened. He had wondered why Yona had never invited him there.

"My mother is ill, so walk quietly," Yona pleaded, leading them into the house, and then turning to Yeshua: "I thought thou wast gone towards Nazareth already, and my heart was sore." He said no more, but led them into the dark quiet house, icy cold, where the shutters were fastened and only the servants moving like shadows in the dark betrayed that the place was inhabited. The house smelt of dried fruit and pepper pods, of medicines and age. "She will want to see you," Yona went on, a finger to his lips, and he led them across the whole length of the house to a small curtained chamber where only a frail silvery light shone from a slit in the wall.

At first Yeshua could not recognize the figure lying on the long bed. It was a woman, but she seemed small like a child, and the face was like a skull topped with a mass of white woolly hair.

"My mother, Elizabeth," Yona whispered, while they tiptoed up to her, holding their breaths.

Elizabeth had been sleeping. Roused by the presence of the children, she opened her cavernous eyes and stared at them penetratingly, lifting her head a little. Yona whispered something in her ear. Something in the way she held herself suggested that she was still young, perhaps no more than forty, but terribly withered by disease. Her face in the silvery light was chalk-white, the skin stretched taut over the bone.

"Come, come," she said, and her voice seemed to rise from deep down in her throat. And then she said softly: "Have no fear."

Holding hands, Yeshua and Meriamne tiptoed to the bed and then knelt. They dared not look at her, the shriveled face, the terrible white hair. There was no strength in her bony hands. She smiled and whispered something they could not understand, and then, her voice growing firmer, she said: "The saints of God, the saints of God—" Then she lay back exhausted, and the bony hands fluttered like butterflies. Tears trickling down their cheeks, Meriamne and Yeshua gazed upon her.

They stayed there for perhaps fifteen minutes, exchanging brief smiles with her, comforting her, then they hurried into the sun-

light. An old servant brought them cool wine, bread, olives, even
some apples stored from the previous year. Yona was delighted
with their coming. At first he could not stop talking. His father,
Zechariah, was dead. Because he belonged to the lineage of Aaron
the Priest and inherited the priestly duty of Sacrificer at the Temple, he should have taken part in the sacrifices, but these duties
by a decree of the High Priest were held in abeyance while he
attended upon his mother's sickness. So he was free, but his freedom irked him.

"Dost thou know why I brought thee here?" Meriamne said
when they were in the sunlight. It was no longer the voice of a
girl, but of a woman.

Yeshua frowned. These sudden changes of mood disconcerted
him.

"For pleasure," he murmured. "And because it is my last day in
Jerusalem before returning to Nazareth."

"Nay," she said darkly. "Not for pleasure, nor for the memory
of Jerusalem. Listen carefully. Thou must make a choice between
us."

"And how shall I make a choice?" he answered miserably. "I
love thee both. How can I choose, when I love thee both?"

"Nevertheless thou shalt choose," she said, and there was no
weakness in her.

Both Yona and Yeshua were sitting on stone benches in the
orchard. Meriamne was standing in front of them, her eyes glistening. She was like steel. He was enraged by her calm determination.

"Hast thou made thy choice?"

"Nay, for thou art stubborn, and how shall one choose between
those one loves equally? There is some demon in thee, Meriamne."

"Not a demon!"

"And more—one cannot choose between men and women. If
thou wert a man—"

"Thou knowest I am not a man! Still, there must be a choice
between us! I brought thee here of set purpose!"

Yeshua clung stubbornly to silence. He refused to say anything
which would console her. Anger spilled over in her, and suddenly
a white lace of tears appeared on her cheeks and she turned her
head away.

"Why cry?" Yona asked gently, going to her. "Thou shouldst not
demand of him what he cannot give thee."

"He can! He can!" Meriamne moaned, burying her head in his shoulder.

Then she was quiet, lost within herself, sometimes staring at Yeshua with an expression of desperate anxiety, as though he had already vanished from her sight and she was surprised to find him there.

They spent the afternoon in the orchard and in the evening dined quietly in the house. Once Yona said: "So thou shalt return to Nazareth tomorrow. I had thought to give thee something, but I could find nothing of sufficient price. I know we shall see each other, for we belong to one another." And Yeshua, thinking how after the death of Elizabeth Yona would be compelled to assume the priestly life as Sacrificer, murmured: "Thou shalt be the Sacrificer and I the sacrifice." When they parted, it was like people parting who see each other every day. One moment they were in the house in Ain Karem, the next moment, accompanied by an old servant with a lantern, Meriamne and Yeshua were making their way along the barren trails to Bethphage. It was a hot moist evening, with a wind from the south-west, and in less than an hour they were in sight of the House of the Green Figs, for the servant knew the way.

Darkness had fallen. In the great house set against the hillside everyone was asleep. Yeshua went to his room and for a long time he stood there silently in the dark, summoning the image of Yona to his imagination. He felt bound to Yona by inflexible bonds. And it mattered nothing that they were separated, since they were bound to one another. A glance, a smile, a shaking of the air around them—these were the signs. It was written in the heavens that they would know one another! So he gazed in the darkness, seeing Yona clearly and whispering to him across the darkness of the night, and he would have communed with the mysterious image of Yona all night if he had not heard Meriamne whispering at the door, begging to be let in.

"Thou shouldst be sleeping, Meriamne," Yeshua said gravely, when she entered, holding an oil-lamp near her face.

And she, just as gravely: "Shalt thou be leaving us on the morrow?"

He nodded, smiled, and took her free hand.

"Can I not show thee my dolls?" she said breathlessly.

"Nay, for I must sleep."

"And what is sleeping, when I have so many things to show thee?"

So he bowed his head and followed her into her own room, the largest in the house, with its huge curtained bed and silver hangings on the wall and great chests of ivory wood. Displayed on one of the chests were her dolls, all splendidly gowned, of painted wood, each one with the appropriate wig. The dolls glittered in the harsh light of the oil-lamps. They were so well appareled, and the faces were so exquisitely painted, that they looked alive. But what was extraordinary was the way they were arranged, all of them kneeling with their hands folded in prayer except one robed in scarlet with a crown of gold on his head, and this robed figure was twice as large as the rest and had evidently been painted and appareled by Meriamne herself, for it had not come from the market-place.

Meriamne's upper lip was trembling. She was still wearing the dust-stained robe she had worn during the journey to Ain Karem.

Gusts of wind entered the room, lifting her veil, and the flames of the oil-lamps grew small and then rose again sharply. Outside, the singing of the cicadas was deafening.

"The Messiah!" Meriamne whispered, indicating the large scarlet-robed figure which towered over all the other dolls.

Yeshua went to examine the figure closely. Though Meriamne had carved it, the figure gave an impression of tremendous power. The cheeks were dead white, the lips were slashes of crimson, and the eyes were no more than black circles painted on the whiteness. On the scarlet gown, on the shoulder and thigh, she had embroidered in gold thread the letters *aleph* and *tav*.

Suddenly she gave a cry, wheeled round and threw herself at his feet. He lifted her up gently. She was weeping and her mouth was formed into a strange square.

"Dearest Meriamne," he whispered. "Why hast thou shown me these things?"

"Because thou art the Messiah," she answered, and went to pick up the scarlet-robed figure and cradled it in her arms. "See, I have thee always in my arms!"

Then she began to sob again, burying her face in the doll and rocking it from side to side.

"I am young," Yeshua said calmly, rebuking her, "and this thing

thou hast made is an old man, with white face and eyes dark with
pain."

"Then how should I have painted him?"

"Make him a shepherd with his staff, and let there be sheep
around him."

"A young shepherd?" Meriamne asked, and there was an expression of craftiness in her lips. "Shall it be a young shepherd,
Yeshua?"

He said nothing, only gazed at her with an astonishing sweet
smile.

"Shall it be a young shepherd from Nazareth?" she repeated.
"Tell me truly."

"It is a secret between us," he said, and put a finger to her lips,
and suddenly she grew quiet, no longer distraught, her head
bowed over the doll in her arms.

Soon he left her, making his way to his own room in the dark.
He could not sleep. He heard her sobbing. For a while he lay
down on the bed, but afterwards he rose and stood silent in the
middle of the room, continuing his meditation. He was alone in
the dark room, and at the same time he was wandering in strange
regions where he had never wandered before. He was standing in
the Temple and slitting the throat of the lamb, he was gazing at the
red doll, he was in the orchard with Yona, he was wrestling with
the black panther, and in some strange way all these things were
happening simultaneously, outside of himself, outside of his will.
The anguish drove deep in him and the sweat poured down his
face. It was as though all the winds of heaven were driving against
him, and he was trying to withstand them. Once he cried out: "If it
be Thy will—" His mouth had fallen open. Most terrible of all was
the red doll, which in his feverish imagination seemed to grow
until it was the size of the house and then it became as high as the
heavens.

Afterwards, when he thought of that dreadful night of meditation, it seemed to him that he was like someone attempting to com-
municate in a language still foreign to him. He was battering
against a wall. He was trying to say: "I am unworthy! I am not the
Messiah! I am not the red doll!" And all the time he was increasingly aware of the secret he shared with Meriamne.

An hour before dawn he slipped out of the House of the Green
Figs and made his way to Jerusalem.

At the moment when the sentinels in the Temple were gazing from the pinnacle, looking out for the first streaks of blue in the night sky, Yeshua was already in the Temple courts. The stalls of the money-changers and the vendors of doves and lambs for sacrifice were still empty. Alone, hovering like a shadow, he crept along the colonnades, silent as a ghost. He saw lights flitting among the archways, robed figures disappearing in shadow. A small procession of Romans in long sweeping purple cloaks marched in torchlight across the marble slabs of the outer court, their bronze helmets glittering. Then suddenly, from the highest place in the Temple, a white-robed priest was heard chanting: "There is red in the sky above Hebron," and a moment later a silver trumpet blew a resounding blast. It was still dark in the courtyard, but imperceptibly the air lightened, the shadows became gray, and the marble columns began to glow.

All morning Yeshua wandered through the courts alone, not speaking to anyone, strangely absorbed in himself. It occurred to him that if he was the Messiah, the Son of God, then he should force his way into the inner precincts and stand in the Holy of Holies, but he dared not. He watched the money-changers at work, their large thickly-veined hands moving unerringly in the baskets of coins. He watched the white doves in their wicker cages, and once when he saw a dove that reminded him of the lamb he had sacrificed—it was the purest white and possessed an appearance of the most perfect purity—he bought it and solemnly let it free, admiring it as it soared over the Temple and laughing softly to himself. And here and there among the small crowds (for after the Passover the Temple was no longer crowded to the full) he listened to the rabbis who gave advice to the pilgrims.

In the Court of Women, in a latticed marble enclosure called the Place of the Leper, he came upon two rabbis discussing the Scriptures in public. Rabbi Meir was an old man with a gnarled walnut-brown face and thin wisps of beard like the froth of milk. His eyes, sunk deep under thick white eyebrows, were sharp and penetrating. With Rabbi Manasseh, a younger man with a long face and a jutting chin and a small mouth like a trap, he was discussing the coming of the Messiah.

Rabbi Meir was saying: "Shall He come upon the clouds of Heaven, as the Prophet Daniel says, or shall He come, as the Prophet Zechariah says, 'riding upon an ass and upon a colt the foal of an ass'? Shall He come as King or as a lamb to the slaughter? And how shall we know Him?" Whereupon Rabbi Manasseh discoursed at length on the two Messiahs, saying it was a mistake to use the words "the Coming of the Messiah," for surely there were two, and perhaps three, and all would be revealed in due time.

Rabbi Meir had been watching Yeshua closely, and suddenly he turned to the boy and said: "I have seen thou hast been following eagerly upon our discussions. What thinkest thou?"

"I think He will come as the summer fruit," Yeshua announced gravely, remembering the text from *Amos*.

"The summer fruit?" Rabbi Meir asked in surprise.

"So Amos says."

"Ah, I remember the passage. 'Then the Lord said, Amos, what seest thou? And I said, A basket of summer fruit. Then said the Lord unto me, The end is come upon my people of Israel: I will not again pass by them any more.' The child has spoken well. Truly the words of Amos are a similitude of the Coming of the Messiah."

"The summer fruit is no more than an extravagance," Rabbi Manasseh interjected. "Of the manner of the Coming of the Messiah everything is made clear according to the accepted interpretations—there shall be the lowly Messiah, and the Messiah in glory, and each will be greeted with a clap of thunder, with choirs of angels and with the presence of Elijah, or as some say with the presence of the Archangel Michael. And truly there is no mystery—"

"He shall come as a red doll," Yeshua murmured softly.

"What sayest thou?" Rabbi Meir asked, for he had heard something he had never expected to hear.

"He shall come as fire," Yeshua murmured. "As a curtain of fire He shall descend upon the earth and utterly consume it!"

"We are speaking of the Messiah," Rabbi Manasseh interrupted. "Fire and fruit are nothing but extravagances. They are to help us to understand the glory, though it is my belief that the words of Amos of Tekoa are not to be interpreted in the light of a prophetic utterance concerning the Coming of the Messiah, but have another application—"

"He shall come as a scorching flame," Yeshua murmured, "and as flame He shall be seen. He hath neither eyes nor lips. For it is written in *Isaiah*: 'The Lord shall kindle a burning like the burning of a fire, and the Light of Israel shall be Himself a Fire, and the Holy One a flame. It shall burn and devour the thorns and briars in one day, and shall consume the glory of the forest and of the fruitful field, both body and soul—' So it is written, rabbi, and shalt thou say nay to what is written by the Prophet?"

"All these are but similitudes," Rabbi Manasseh smiled. "A man in anger has a face aflame, and therefore we say He shall come as a flame. Truly it would be possible to find many, many other similitudes: as lightning, as the first-born, as a plowshare, as the horns of a buffalo. But the truth is that our tongue cannot convey the majesty of His coming, nor do we know precisely how He shall come or whether it will be soon—"

"I pray it will be soon," Rabbi Meir said simply, "so that with my own eyes I shall witness the Coming."

"It will be soon," Yeshua said, and then for a while he said nothing more: for too many people were gathering around, and Rabbi Manasseh was swelling with his own importance.

All that day Yeshua remained within the Temple. It seemed to him that he had been there for many days, and he had long ago forgotten the House of the Green Figs. As he walked around the Temple in the sunlight he recited with bowed head: "Art thou not from everlasting, O Lord my God, mine Holy One?" And at night, when he lay huddled behind the columns he recited: "Arise, O Jerusalem, and shine; for thy light is come, and the glory of the Lord is risen upon thee."

On the morning of the next day, when he was talking about the Last Judgment with the two rabbis, he heard a cry behind him. It came from Meriam, whose cheeks were wet with weeping. Beside her stood Yusuf, the blue veins standing out on his forehead, his fists shaking. He was angry beyond any anger Yeshua had known.

"We searched for thee everywhere!" Yusuf exclaimed. "We asked of everyone where thou mightest be! None answered! Dost thou not think we care for thee?"

"Behold, thy father and mother have sought thee sorrowing," Meriam said.

"Why did ye seek me?" Yeshua answered in a dream. "Did ye not know I must be in my Father's house?"

And he had no desire to leave the Temple behind, saw no reason to follow them to Nazareth. Since the night when he stood alone in the room in the House of the Green Figs, he had known he must haunt the Temple. He had not yet learned the language with which to speak to God. It was a language he would learn, not from the rabbis, but from the Temple itself: for if the Temple were a place of sacrifice, it was also a musical instrument perpetually hymning His praises. Yet, seeing Meriam weeping, he said: "How shall I comfort thee?"

"Thou shalt come with us to Nazareth," she answered, and in a low voice whispered: "For thy father is ailing."

So Yeshua returned to Nazareth on a white ass in the hot spring sunshine. The roads were deserted, for most of the pilgrims at the Passover had returned home. They rode in slow stages, for Yusuf had difficulty in riding, and part of the journey he rode in a litter which they hired at Shechem. When they came in sight of Nazareth, the old man fell to his knees and with tears streaming down his face, with hands uplifted to heaven, he exclaimed: "Merciful art Thou, O God, to let me have sight of my home!"

All through the summer and autumn they thought he was about to die, but it was winter before he was bedridden. On the eve of the New Year he cried out at the top of his voice. Meriam and Anna hurried into the room. He turned stiffly on the bed and stared at them angrily.

"Where is Yeshua?" he asked, and his voice had the tone of a command.

Servants were sent out to find Yeshua. When at last Yeshua entered the room, the old man gave a loud sigh and tried to lift himself up from the pillows, supporting himself on his elbows.

"Come closer, Yeshua," he said. "Thou wert the child of my old age, and therefore dearest to me. Because thou wast weak and puny, I did sometimes belabor thee, but it was to do good to thee."

Then he paused and for a long while said nothing, staring into Yeshua's face as though attempting to read something there. At last he said haltingly: "Hast thou still the marks of the *aleph* and the *tav* on thee? Art thou the Chosen One?"

There was no answer from Yeshua.

"I could have wished thou wert the Chosen One, in my extremity," Yusuf said, his voice failing. "If thou wert the Messiah, thou couldst summon the lightning and the fires of God to bathe and purify me: thou couldst cure me: thou couldst bring the health back to my flesh; thou couldst make me whole again. But I see thou hast no power in thee."

Then he paused and for a long time said nothing, staring into Yeshua's face as though attempting to read something there. At last he said haltingly: "Let thy light shine on the world, Yeshua. I shall leave money for thee. Travel far. Learn—learn—"

Then he gave a loud sigh and fell back on the pillows. Quite suddenly, in the space of a few minutes, his face became waxen yellow and the big veins on his forehead vanished, becoming no more than faint threads.

For two years Yeshua remained in mourning. One day in the early spring, remembering his father's command that he should travel and learn, he rode to the sea coast.

The Temple of Serapis

In those days Ptolemais was the largest town on the coast: a great port, with many government buildings, a library and a theater which lay outside the walls of the city. To the south-east lay the huddled tenement buildings where the Jews lived. Along the teeming streets Greeks, Romans, Egyptians and Jews walked unhindered. And near the port stood the headquarters of the Twenty-third Legion whose officers and soldiers came mostly from Britain and northern Gaul.

One afternoon in summer Yeshua found himself wandering aimlessly along the coast. There had been a small storm in the morning, but the storm had passed, leaving the air fresh and pure. Like many young Jews, even those who lived in the tenement quarter, Yeshua wore a Greek gown folded simply over his body, leaving one shoulder bare. He wore a straw hat and straw sandals and carried a staff.

As he walked, he asked himself for the thousandth time what he was doing in Ptolemais. "Travel far. Learn—learn—" so his father had told him, and he had obeyed, but the learning weighed heavily on him. Soon, turning inland across some fields of sesame, he cried aloud: "How long is the time?" and then shivered, for the words seemed to be spoken by someone else. And then beyond the rows of springing sesame, he saw a small temple facing the sea high up on the cliffs among banks of oleanders, and he thought he would rest there and meditate upon God.

He walked through fields of anemones. It was very quiet, the noises of the city coming from a long way away. He walked jauntily. The rains during the morning had left a glitter on the fields, so that they sparkled and sent up little puffs of steam towards the sun. The air was transparent, very pure and sweet. As he climbed the winding path up the cliff, he could see an ox wagon moving along the sandy road below, and the creaking of the axles of the wagon was as pleasant as the scuttling of the little pink lizards in the grasses. "How cool, calm and beautiful everything is this afternoon," he murmured as he climbed the slope, and because he was sweating he allowed the white gown to fall around his waist, leaving both shoulders bare. When he reached the small temple, he turned towards the sea and blew it a kiss of welcome, so blue it was, so full of sparkling light.

The journey had taken nearly half an hour, and he was glad now to be in the shelter of the temple, for the sun beat pitilessly down. It was not a large temple, though it seemed large, perched on the edge of the cliff. There were marble steps, four columns of honey-colored alabaster and a stone roof. Inside the small *cella*, on a veined column, stood a statue of Serapis in blue basalt with heavy curls and a thick curling beard, the heavily-lidded eyes closed in meditation. Incised into the column were inscriptions in Egyptian. It was such a statue as one might see in a hundred places along the coast, except that there was a rare nobility in this blue carving, a resigned majesty, even a touch of ferocity in the face of this bearded youth, so that people came for many miles around to present offerings of flowers; and the floor of the *cella* was strewn with decaying petals and dried stalks. Usually there was an old priest in attendance, but either he was sleeping or working in the fields.

Yeshua smiled when he set eyes on the statue and pressed his hands together as he bowed in greeting. The blue face seemed

alive, yet he was in no fear of it. He was happy there, on the
heights, listening to the moaning of the bees and the soft rustling of
the waves breaking on the shore. So he stood there on this lonely
eminence above Ptolemais, seeing the smoke from the distant city
drifting out to sea and the blue shadows in the valleys of ripening
wheat, and there came to him a sense of the solemn stillness and
mystery of the place, but it was the sea, so smooth and blue, a
stretch of trembling blue silk ending in the delicate curve of the
horizon which entranced him. High above the maternal sea rose
the bluff of yellow rock and the four columns of the sturdy temple
and the scent of flowers.

Standing there with his back to one of the columns, he felt the
weariness dropping from him, the loneliness vanishing. In some
mysterious way the walk from Ptolemais had showered strength on
him. The wind played on his hair, and he murmured: "I shall go
back soon, for nothing will ever happen to me here, but whether I
remain or whether I wander again, something has happened to me
this afternoon which will never change." He could give no name to
this thing—it was strength, but what kind of strength he did not
know. It seemed to him that this new-found strength came from
the outermost heavens; had come, as he walked through the fields
of anemones, and again as he climbed to the temple of Serapis.

He said, very loud, looking out to sea: "I shall not be lonely."

Time passed. It drifted like the scented wind through the columns of the temple. Once, after having turned his back for a long
while on the blue head of Serapis he turned to study it minutely:
the thick little coils of the beard, the love-lock, the pursed lips
which had never felt the imprint of kisses, the heavily-lidded
eyes which had never looked upon the world: a thing so holy, so
chaste, so cold that it startled him: and as he gazed at the statue
he heard himself saying: "Terrible that a god should be turned to
stone." And gazing at a hawk hovering high above him, he murmured: "Birds are the life of the sky, and when they fly they reveal the thoughts of the sky, as the waves reveal the thoughts of
the sea! And truly we are like the waves of the sea, lifted up for a
brief moment to flash in the sun, then drowning in that blue immensity again!" But even while he was murmuring these words,
somewhere deep down inside him a voice was saying: "How long
is the time?"

Long ago he had told himself he would stay until sunset: perhaps would rest there all night, sleeping on the temple floor. The sun was beginning to climb down the sky when the sound of a lizard scuttling among the decaying petals made him prick up his ears, and then he heard some other sound, as of someone breathing close by. He turned sharply. Standing near the statue of Serapis, watching him, was a beardless youth. At first Yeshua was stunned: he was sure the boy had not been there the last time he entered the temple: he had entered quite mysteriously, having come from nowhere: it was as though he had dropped mysteriously from the sky. What was most puzzling was that the beardless youth looked exactly like himself, bare-chested, with a white cotton gown gathered round his waist, with dark eyebrows and a long mouth and an extraordinarily sweet smile like a smile of recognition.

"Who are you?" Yeshua asked sharply.

There was no answer. It occurred to Yeshua that he had been meditating too long, and now that it was growing dark he was being plagued by ghosts who came unbidden out of shadows; and what if he should come upon the ghost of himself? Worse than the silence of the youth was his expression of devilish effrontery as he smiled there, deep in the shadows.

"I asked you a very simple question," Yeshua went on with a nervous edge to his voice. "Who are you?"

As before, there was no answer: only the quiet searching eyes of the youth, and the lips turned up in a devilish smile. It was growing darker in the temple, the sun descending in a great crimson flare, and still there was that bare-chested boy standing insolently in front of him, legs planted firmly apart, head cocked a little to one side; and now for the first time Yeshua was aware of the musty smell of bird droppings inside the temple.

The boy smiled, his teeth glinting in the darkness like the flash of a sword.

"Oh, you are one of those who ask difficult questions," he said, his voice very low, very musical. "Who am I? If I knew that, Yeshua, I would know the answer to all the questions of philosophy."

Yeshua was not startled to hear his name coming from the lips of the stranger in the shadows. What startled him was that the voice was so low and musical; he had expected a deeper and more vibrant voice.

"So you are a student of philosophy?" Yeshua said calmly.

"I don't know," the boy answered. "What is a student of philosophy? You ask such difficult questions. First, you ask who I am. I
don't even pretend to know who I am, and as for the study of philosophy—what is it? All I know for certain is that you came up
here and meditated half the afternoon, and I had no desire to disturb you, but you seemed to think the place was your own—"

"You mean you were here all the time, watching me?"

"I was here. I wasn't watching you. I have more important
things to do. But the truth is that you were a nuisance." He smiled
deprecatingly. "If you want to go on meditating, no one will prevent you. But you're a strange person—you came up here, but you
never made any offering to Serapis."

"I don't worship Serapis."

"I don't worship him either, but I made an offering. After all, it
is his temple."

After this, the youth came out of the temple shadows for the
first time. He walked like a panther, his face and chest the color
of bronze from the setting sun, and Yeshua saw that he was obvi-
ously a Greek, or at least a youth with Greek blood in his veins,
for he had a rounded forehead and wore his hair down the nape of
his neck and carried himself more elegantly than the Hebrews,
and above all he had a nose which was absolutely straight, coming
clean down from the forehead, and his eyes were a little slanted,
like Greek eyes; and yet at first sight, as he stood in the shadows,
Yeshua could have sworn this was the semblance of himself. As
the boy came past the columns into the open air, walking barefoot, he no longer looked at Yeshua with an expression of effrontery, but instead smiled easily, and in the manner of his salutation
there was only friendliness, and when he went on to say: "Are you
going to stay here through the night?" Yeshua thought there was a
curious hesitancy in his voice: he was like someone apologizing
for having come unbidden upon the meditations of another.

Yeshua paused, stared towards the darkening sea and said: "I
have not thought to stay."

"Well, let us stay here as long as it pleases us, and let us stay
together," the boy said. "My name—at least the name my parents
call me—is Atys."

The sun was sinking into the sea, which was blue beneath the
cliffs and a fiery red along the length of the horizon. The wind
pummeled the boy's gown, pressing it between his legs, and he

shivered a little; and now some chicken-hawks, flying very high, caught in the freshening wind, began to utter their faint cries.

"I am Yeshua from Nazareth," Yeshua said, and then wondered why he had added the name of his village.

They sat down on the steps of the temple, watching the sunset, paying hardly any attention to one another, though they were both conscious of the undeclared war between them, and were wary of one another. The sea was like blood now. Little snakes of red fire curled over the sea's rim. A fresh wind blew in the almond groves. Though the inside of the temple was in darkness now, flames licked the columns as though a great conflagration was taking place nearby. As the sun sank lower the sound of the wind in the dry grasses became deafening, but when the sun sank into the sea at last, the sky and air were stilled.

"On such a night," Atys said softly, "one could believe in any miracles."

It was more like a sigh than words. Yeshua was startled by the solemnity of his tone and turned to watch him, but saw only a dark shape standing there with a tenseness about him like an animal about to spring. A quivering life came from this youth invisible in the dark, allowing the darkness to penetrate him, washing the darkness all over him. It occurred to Yeshua that Atys must have come many times to this rocky cliff to meditate.

"The darkness comes from Serapis, from the dark waters of Serapis," Atys went on softly.

This time Yeshua was outraged. The boy spoke like some old prophet, in a voice like honey dripping in the dark. Yeshua covered his face with his hands. What kind of devil was this who spoke of darkness and Serapis in the same breath?

"Who is Serapis?" Yeshua asked, hoping he would give some easy answer and end the doubts arising in his own mind.

"They say he is water," the boy answered, "but that is the least of the things that he is. After his body is torn to pieces, then he is resurrected in the flesh."

"Then how is it that he is water?" Yeshua heard himself saying, peering into the dark. "Surely water is not flesh? Surely flesh is fire."

There was a long silence.

"There are mysteries in the worship of Serapis," Atys answered. "Certainly he is water, for if you come into this temple in daylight and look carefully, you will see an inscription in Greek, Egyptian and Syrian which says: 'May Serapis bless thee with cool waters.' I see that we talk a different language. Your outermost depths are far from mine."

"What do you mean by outermost depths?"

"I mean that everyone has depths in him. They are like deep wells. But only a few of us drink from heavenly waters. Do you believe that if one possessed divine powers, all the sea could be made to vanish away?"

"I believe it."

"I thought you would. You are willful. You believe in the power of the spirit. You believe that mountains could be moved if one desired, if one prayed hard enough, if the divine spirit was moving in you."

"I believe these things because I am a Jew," Yeshua said simply. "By faith the Jews have parted the seas. As for mountains, I do not believe that anyone has yet moved a mountain by the power of faith, but I believe it is possible."

"By faith you can move mountains?"

"Not I, but some other might. By faith, by prayer, by the divine will."

They could hear the murmuring voice of the sea below; and sometimes a distant sail or the white scut of a wave reflected starlight. There was no moon.

"How strange," said Atys. "You are a Jew, and yet you look like a Greek. You have a curious way of holding your head a little to the left—everyone knows that all affected people do that, because Alexander the Great did it. Then you speak Greek perfectly. I could have sworn you were a Greek when you said that flesh is fire —surely the Jews do not speak like that: or are you a Jew who no longer practices?"

"I am a Jew and I worship the God of the Jews," Yeshua said quietly.

"Yes, I have heard of that God," Atys said, peering into the darkness until he could see the faint outline of Yeshua's face. "I have heard of him, and I confess I do not like him. I prefer Plato's god which 'moves, being motionless, and creates itself, and is exceedingly pure, and is at the heart of all things.' It seems to me that the Jews worship an old prophet called Moses and they have made their god in the shape of Moses. He is a man, and the god of Plato is a splendor and there is nothing more wonderful than Plato's god."

Saying this, Atys went on, as though lost in his own visions, to speak of the god of Plato, from whom all things came and to whom all things returned. There was a god in every wind and leaf, but they were only aspects of the divinity which ruled the universe; our minds could not contemplate the greatness of the god except in mathematics and in the dance and in silent meditations. While he was speaking, the blue flames of summer lightning crackled on the horizon and they heard the booming of distant thunder—it was that harmless thunder which comes only on hot summer nights.

"By Hercules," Atys said, when he had come to the end of his discourse on the attributes of Plato's god, "we are becoming theologians. Let us examine the theology of the thunder. To tell you the truth, I had not thought of this before, but now that I think about it, I am sure I am about to discover some secret, even though it may not be a very great secret. What do the Jews say about the thunder?"

"They say it is a loud noise," Yeshua answered, laughing in the darkness.

By now their eyes were accustomed to the shadows and they could see each other more plainly, almost as plainly as in daylight, though everything about them and behind them remained dark. The eyes of Atys were very bright and shone like cats' eyes. The youths were of the same age, and both were inclined to prolonged meditations, and there was a warmth between them now that they had overcome their early suspicions. And it seemed to both of them that it was good to be there, with the rushing sea below and the floods of stars in the sky. They felt nearer to Heaven, high up on this cliff of limestone rock.

"You are joking, Yeshua," Atys said after a pause, "and these are things we must not joke about. Plato says somewhere that to joke about divine things is to incur the wrath of the gods, and Socrates says the same. Surely the thunder is a sign of divine vengeance, or at least a mark of divine power?"

"Yes, indeed."

"And surely it is a proper thing to send a kiss to the lightning, just as we send a kiss in the morning to the sun?"

"We do not blow a kiss to the sun," Yeshua answered. "We **pray** to God, and our prayers are more than kisses. We believe that God is greater than all the suns."

"Then you are completely stupid. Of course God is greater than the sun, or any suns, but not to throw a kiss to the sun—surely that is impiety! As for prayers, you pray only to your God, while we pray to a thousand gods, and so I believe the worship of the Greeks is better than the worship of the Jews. How absurd it is! Of course there is one God, but there are a thousand manifestations of God."

"There is one God," Yeshua said, "and that is all, and that is enough and more than enough, and He is the Father of all things."

"Wonderfully said! But how austere and virtuous you are! When you said you did not blow a kiss to the sun every morning, you spoke with temper. I can only conclude that you object to blowing kisses."

"We have our ways of worship," Yeshua said. "They are not your ways—that is why there is always an abyss between the Greeks and the Jews."

"But you can build bridges over abysses?"

"No one could ever build a bridge so infinitely big," Yeshua answered with a sigh. "It is beyond the doing of any man, and sometimes I think it is beyond the doing of God. There are laws which we obey, and by obeying these laws, and by the promises contained in the Commandments, we have become the Chosen People; and the Greeks are not chosen."

"And so—?"

"And so, beloved Atys, there is this measureless gap between us."

If Yeshua had turned to watch the face of the Greek youth in the dark, he would have seen a look of horror-stricken incredulity; and this look was immediately exchanged for a grimace, followed by a curious short jabbing gesture with the hand. Yeshua had spoken quietly, but with pride; and Atys, who hated pride above all things, turned quickly and said: "You dare to say these things! It's all nonsense! I've read the Ten Commandments, and you will find them in the Greek books, and for all I know in the Egyptian and Persian books. Do you really believe the Jews are the Chosen People?"

"We obey the law," Yeshu said, and turned his face away, gazing at the dark sea.

"Oh, the law!" Atys said defiantly. "Well, the Greeks obey the laws, but we know all laws are man-made and fraudulent. The laws were made by men who lived long ago. Dead men made them. The dead are beyond reckoning, isn't that so, and what have they to do with us? No, it is better to follow perfect beauty and perfect virtue than the silly laws—it is best to live in the present and celebrate the majesty of man."

"The majesty of man," Yeshua repeated softly, and suddenly his eyes blazed in indignation and he answered: "Man has no majesty except what is given to him by God. As I am here, I am aware of God's infinite grace and majesty streaming through time, always there, always within us. The earth is alive and so are the heavens, and God pours His mercy and majesty upon us, but it is not something 'of the present': it is eternal, as God is eternal."

"Then men are eternal?"

"No, men die."

Yeshua said these words in a voice as soft as an echo. He had been thinking of death for many days with a somber awareness of its presence. He could not tell why he had been meditating on this subject. He was young, vigorous, full of a strange exaltation of tenderness. He had seen men die, but only in Nazareth and along the road to Sepphoris. Then why this strange new obsession which haunted him as he wandered the dusty streets of Ptolemais? He said: "They die because that is God's will, and perhaps we shall never understand it. Plato said, I remember, that if the soul is robed in jewels of truth, nobility and courage, she will go happily on her journey; but he said nothing about the road she would travel on after death, or where she was going. A man dies and that is the end of him! And yet it seems to me that everything depends upon whether we are born again in the flesh, isn't that so? Plato said nothing about death, and the Jews have said little enough, but surely this is the important question. I am certain of God's splendor. I am certain that men shine in the light of God. I know that God's splendor lies within us and outside us—I call it 'the spirit,' but you may call it whatever you please—and if I could know why this spirit encloses us (for sometimes it seems to me that we are enclosed in the holy spirit as in a tent), if I could know this, then I would not need to know anything about the things you spoke of, like perfect beauty and perfect virtue, and indeed these things are very small compared to the holy spirit. And they are smaller still when compared with death."

"You should worship Serapis," Atys suggested. "Serapis came back from the dead."

"But I know enough of Serapis to know that he is simply the Egyptian god of the Nile. Why should I worship him?"

"One must worship something. So you are plagued with death! Well, I know that I am going to die, but I do not believe it. Alexander died. I do not believe it either, and in fact he did not die—he is eternal, even if it means that he remains eternally alive in our memory. We Greeks have a way of dealing with death—we look it in the face and refuse to humble ourselves by asking questions. What happens afterwards does not concern us."

"It concerns me," Yeshua said.

"By the way you say it," Atys laughed, "it would seem to concern you to the exclusion of anything else, and that's a pity. It's foolish to think about, because there is nothing you can possibly do about it. I simply cannot believe that Alexander died, but he did, and the Emperor Augustus opened his tomb, and so did Julius, and they saw him dead. No one else ever left so great a mark upon the world. Oh, Alexander crowned and diademed, why that's the greatest power that ever streamed from one man's hands —and he died, and so there's no help for any of us! We live in the world, but does death belong to the world? No, death is something else, and I have no concern with it."

"Let Plato and Alexander sleep," said Yeshua. "I worship only the God who has power over death."

"And the living?"

"Sometimes I think there is almost no difference between the dead and the living."

"Then you are a fool!" Atys exclaimed. "A poor, bigoted Jewish fool!"

Atys was amazed by his own outburst. The air lay heavy on them now, the wind had dropped, the small enclosure of the temple smelled of musk and dead flowers, and sometimes they heard a lizard scuttling through the dried stalks. Now and then an owl flew noiselessly overhead, to drop noiselessly in the bushes along the steep slopes of the cliff. Atys threw out his hand to ward off the blow, but Yeshua was too quick for him. Barefoot in their white gowns they grappled together, breast to breast. Where

they had been calm and ceremonially polite to one another, now
they were caught up in a frenzy of hatred: the spark of madness
kept them together, as they struggled on the edge of the cliff, the
dark waters wheeling below. They were young, slender and firm-
muscled. They fought vigorously, until the sweat pricked out of
their skin. They pushed up with their knees, pummeled with their
fists, attempted strangle-holds, breathing hard, inching their way
to the cliff-edge and the sand-dunes below. "Pray to Plato and
Serapis!" Atys shouted through clenched teeth, and Yeshua answered hotly: "There is only one God—the Father of us all!" They
hardly knew what they were saying. They fought grimly, bare
hands clutching, knees jerking, and sometimes Yeshua would
catch a faint gleam from the sea, and immediately afterwards he
was aware of the fierce processions of the stars. Once he nearly
lost his foothold and was in danger of falling off the cliff, and only
saved himself by an immense backward leap, which threw Atys
to the ground. Then they were rolling over one another on the
crumbly limestone, not caring where they went so long as they
could pummel one another and draw blood.

"Have you had enough?" Yeshua whispered hoarsely, when they
had somehow rolled inside the temple; and the sound of the dead
leaves and flowers under them was like the crackling of a furnace fire.

"Never—never enough!" Atys answered, and his sweat-glisten-
ing arm fell out of the sky like a battering-ram, once, twice, three
times: it was like an ax splitting against Yeshua's skull.

There was warm blood all over Yeshua's face, and his shoulders
felt as though they had been lacerated. With tremendous effort,
arching his body, he was able to keep Atys away from his throat,
but all the time he could feel the hot breath of the Greek youth on
his face. The worst was when they were locked in one another's
arms, or when they rolled to the edge of the cliff. Faintly, he saw
the glitter of a blood-smear on Atys's face, and smelled the blood.
His head ached. All his nerves were tense and quivering. At first
the sense of danger had been pleasant enough: it was somehow
pleasant to contemplate this remote place, the sheer rock fall, the
huge animal ferocity of Atys. Then very swiftly he realized that it
was more dangerous than anything he had known since the crucifixes were set up on the rim of Nazareth. Now it was as though
terror was springing out of the temple with the honey-colored

columns and the blue god on the plinth. He had never felt death
so close. His fist drove into Atys's soft abdomen, glancing off the
pelvic bone, so that his knuckles cracked; and then Atys gave a
heavy groan, like the groan of an animal in pain, and lay still, but
only for a moment. When Atys returned to the attack, he was
fiercer than ever with a harsh vengefulness which showed itself
in hard slapping. His nose was bleeding, and so he kept his mouth
open; and his breath came in hard agonizing gasps. There was an
almost supernatural strength in Yeshua. He was Jacob wrestling
with the angel, but with this difference—he was alone on the edge
of the cliffs, and Atys was crouching in front of him, and the best
was to keep still, digging in with the feet, with one's back to
the sea.

"You haven't had enough yet, have you?" Atys said, breathing
with difficulty, crouching low, his hands gripped by Yeshua's so
that, if Yeshua fell over the cliff, Atys would be dragged down
with him. "You are proud, eh—prouder than Moses?"

"What has Moses to do with all this?" Yeshua asked, hardly
knowing what he was saying.

"He laid down the laws, and you obey them, and so you have to
be punished," Atys gasped. "By Hercules, have you had enough?"

"Never!" Yeshua answered, throwing himself forward in a sudden lunge which threw Atys to the ground, and then he sprang on
Atys, and they rolled over the temple steps.

Yeshua had a cut lip, one eye was closed, one shoulder was already swelling, and there was blood over his chest, where Atys
had scratched him.

Once Yeshua yelled into the dark: "I am a Jew, and proud of
being a Jew!"

"Then we shall have to fight to the end," Atys muttered, and
once again they were close to the edge of the cliff.

For a long while they fought in silence, calmly, bitterly, their
legs so entangled in the skirts of their gowns that they could fight
only with their arms, their chests and their shoulders, using their
bodies as springs, helpless in their hot rage which subsided a little,
as a flame subsides, only to grow strong again. And so they rolled
towards the sheer, abrupt cliffs, the glistening darkness beyond
the limestone edge, the darkness shining with stars and silver
wave-caps, and both the stars and the wave-caps shone like fishes'
scales. The wind rustled, and their long gowns grew wet with

sweat, and still they clutched at one another, jabbing and pummeling one another, and sometimes there would come a slow moan of pain, but after the pain the violence only increased.

At last, when they had been locked together for some while without moving, their muscles exhausted, their faces grimy with sweat and blood, Atys said: "Enough!"

Immediately Yeshua released his hold, even though he thought of treachery, of some ruse or other. But there was no treachery. Atys was at the end of his strength, and he lay across the stone steps, breathing in long slow breaths, very quiet as he lay there spread-eagled on the stones, his eyes opening only long enough to catch the gleam of hot anger in Yeshua's eyes.

"I didn't think you would have the courage to say 'enough,'" Yeshua said scornfully.

"It wasn't courage," Atys said.

"Then what was it?"

"Something else. I could see no purpose in killing you, and besides, it would have been so easy!"

Saying this, Atys pulled up the damp skirts of his gown to show the knife bound to his inner thigh. The knife had a jeweled haft with many small cornelians embedded in it, and was looped to his thigh with a double thong of pigskin. In the starlight the jewels shone like the embers of a dying fire.

Atys tossed the knife into the air and caught it. Pointing the blade at Yeshua, he said: "You see, I could easily have killed you." Yeshua said nothing, as he nursed his bruised knees on the lower steps of the temple. Suddenly Atys was filled with a sudden sense of remorse. He let the knife fall, threw his arms round Yeshua and said quickly: "When you first meet, it is always good to fight. We would never have known each other otherwise. Are you all right?"

"Yes."

"You are quite sure?"

"Yes, of course."

"Please believe me. We have fought, and that is the end of it, Yeshua. Now we can be brothers."

"And what is it to be brothers?" Yeshua said in a voice so low that Atys hardly heard him.

"All my life, yours. Everything I am. You are mine, and I am yours, and so we are brothers."

Yeshua said nothing. He was still breathing hard. He was sore

and bleeding, and he had no love for Atys. His eyes glittered, and
there came from the broken skin of his face the sweet treacly
smell of fresh blood. Slowly, with immense difficulty, not knowing
what he was doing, like someone drugged with poppies, he rose
to his feet, and he was thinking of wandering away, leaving the
temple and Atys behind, with no thought of ever returning to
them, when Atys said: "If you leave me, Yeshua, I shall hurl myself from the cliff! Let us be brothers!"

For the first time there was something pleading in his tone.
Yeshua looked down and saw the Greek boy lying on the steps at
his feet.

"Where are we?" he said. "Is this some strange magical place
where enemies become friends?"

Atys leapt up from the ground, smiling.

"Yes, indeed," he said quickly. "And now let us seal our friendship."

Once more they stood together, breast against breast, and between them they felt a strange pressure which seemed to come out
of the darkness, as though the wind and the grasses, the flowers
and the columns, the sea and the starlight were all conspiring to
force them together.

"Behold, this is the mystery—the mystery of being brothers,"
Atys murmured, and then moving a little way away and looking
straight into Yeshua's eyes, he went on: "Then we forgive one
another? Surely we must forgive one another! If there is no forgiveness, there is no peace."

"Yes," said Yeshua, and looked away, not knowing why he was
so strangely moved. "In forgiveness is peace. So I forgive you, as
you forgive me."

"Then we are truly brothers," Atys answered. "Everything I
have is yours. If ever you want anything, you have only to ask me.
And now we must bathe our wounds. The god Dionysus was
tested in fire and then cleansed in water, and so it must be with us.
So let us go to the baths and rid ourselves of our wounds and
sleep the night away."

Yeshua nodded, and soon afterwards Atys laid the jeweled
knife and the leather thong on the altar of Serapis as an offering
and then hand in hand they walked down the path cut in the limestone cliff.

At the Baths

As they climbed down the path, they heard the sighing of the night wind and from somewhere afar off the wailing of the *kinnora*, the shepherd's pipe, and from somewhere closer at hand the faint sighs and laughter of the lovers hiding among the tamarisks. There was still no moon, and the flood of stars seemed darker now that they were no longer in sight of the sea.

At night the smell of sesame and the herbs growing on the slopes of the cliff was bewilderingly sharp; all the earth seemed a fragrance. They breathed deeply and walked slowly, listless with weariness, heavy with a curious sense of accomplishment, not knowing where they were going and not caring. A languor had come over them—the languor that follows bitter fighting. Yeshua's eyelids trembled, and he was aware of some deep alteration in himself: his soul was swooning on the edge of some new world, a world where there were no pathways, no roads, no recognizable buildings: everything changed beyond redemption. Strange that his feet had wandered to the temple of Serapis; strange that he should have found Atys there; strangest of all that they should have fought desperately on the edge of the cliff.

"And to what profit?" he asked himself. "Now it is over, is the profit in ourselves, and where shall this profit take us?"

Atys was saying: "The blessing of water heals all wounds."

At first Yeshua thought Atys intended to bathe in the sea, but then he remembered that Atys had spoken of going to the baths, and he fell silent, determined not to break the peace between them. And then a little while later Yeshua heard himself murmuring: "I did not know that Dionysus was cleansed in fire and water. There is so much I do not know. I know that a man dies and is born again, and truly I have learned this again in our fighting."

Crossing the sesame fields, they passed a shuttered farm-house, all dark, in its pool of shadows; and sometimes they came upon a ghostly cock tethered to a wattle roof or an unsaddled ass slumber-

ing in a yard, and always the owls in the sycamores. Soon they
came to the edge of the city, in sight of the harbor walls; here
there were more huts with the glint of fire outside the doors, from
the copper pans filled with incense which burned through the
night. The city slumbered. Sometimes they saw the flash of a
white garment, a girl wandering down an alleyway, a small group
of shrouded figures passing hurriedly from one shadow to the next,
and from the houses they heard, or thought they heard, the same
soft sounds they had heard among the tamarisks. Once Atys drew
back, clutched Yeshua's arm and said: "Be careful, the place is full
of ghosts!" But it was only a black horse whinnying and shaking
its long neck and setting up a quick ringing of bells.

Entering Ptolemais from the north, Yeshua could recognize few
landmarks: the Jewish quarter was in the south-west, away from
the sea. Because it was like entering an unknown city, he fell back
on his own thoughts. He felt as a plant must feel when it grows, a
kind of unfolding of light within him. Something had been stripped
from him as they fought. It had no name. It was beyond him to
understand the change in himself, the sudden surge of vitality, how
everything in some strange way had become clear to him. And
while there came to his nostrils the smells of the dark slumbering
city, the deep purple alleyways, the huge wheeling shadows of the
place and all the familiar smells of the coastal city, Atys gripped
him by the arm and whispered: "By Hercules, you are a man who
loves stumbling in the dark! Beware of the cess-pools, Yeshua!"

They had wandered for half an hour when they came in sight of
the darkened forum, where the empty shop stalls were only
squares of intense dark against the marble porticos. Beyond the
forum lay the palace of the Governor and the barracks of the
guards, and beyond these lay an open space, from where a great
flare of light shot up to the stars, and a huge surge of voices
echoed. This was the place known as the Baths of Dionysus. There
was no roof: only the columns and the immense marble basin open
to the sky. Yeshua had glimpsed these baths before in daylight,
seeing the swimmers and half envying them for their ease and
grace, the whiteness of their bodies, shining against the glitter of
pure blue water which issued from the wells, and the mocking
voices, and the singing, and the crowd of Negro slaves hovering
over the bathers as they clambered up the marble steps with their
hair lying limp over their foreheads—slaves everywhere, and

white-skinned Greek boys, sons of merchants and accountants and bankers, with no dark-skinned Syrians among them, unless some of the slaves were Syrians. Now, as they walked quickly and lightly towards the baths, Atys was explaining how everyone had been talking of putting a roof over the baths, but it was better without, it was good to lie there after the bath on straw matting and look up at the stars.

"And the water has some healing property," he went on. "I remember falling from my horse and being badly bruised, but after being in the water, there was no sign of any bruise."

He laughed softly in the darkness, while Yeshua listened to the voices of the bathers, the splash of water, the strange echoing which all bath-houses set up at night. The place was blinding with light from the torches fixed in iron brackets on the marble columns. These torches, which were set at an angle, gave off sparks and great clouds of black smoke which hung over the bath like a roof. Listening to their shouts and the cavernous echoes, Yeshua thought there must be at least a hundred people there; instead there were about twenty, most of them quite young, their bodies ruddy in the glare of the torches. They were all naked, except for strips of colored cloth they wore round their necks for wiping off the sweat. Some were pouring oil over themselves, others were reclining on benches, a few were playing with a pigskin bladder in the water. To Yeshua, who was not accustomed to seeing so many young Greeks together, they all looked well-formed and so much like one another that they might have been brothers.

As Yeshua and Atys came between the marble columns, the wind changed, and the pall of black smoke which hung high over the water came plunging close to the water. Immediately some Negro slaves came running up with great white sheets, which they began to wave vigorously, to push the smoke away. The slapping sound of the sheets, the cries of the boys in the water, the sound of someone being vigorously slapped and massaged, the feverish smell of burning incense and the great gusts of flame from the flares which turned everyone the color of bronze: all these things affected Yeshua strangely, for his mind was still on the cliff-top, and as for his body, he was hardly aware of it, because it was so dulled with pain.

"Here he is! Here is Agathon!" someone shouted from the water, and then nearly everyone was turning in the direction of Atys as

he leaned negligently against one of the marble columns, shading
his eyes to protect them from the smoke and the bright shining of
the torch above his head.

A youth who was unnaturally thin, unshaved, with a high forehead, very large eyes and a dark quizzical face, with a broad
mouth and a long upper lip, lifted himself out of the water and
came loping up to Atys.

"By heavens, Agathon," he shouted when he was still some distance away, "have you been offered for a sacrifice, or did you fall
among brambles?" And then turning towards Yeshua: "You, too?
What in the world have you been doing? Or didn't you know
there was blood all over your gowns?"

"I know," Atys nodded, and he was still shading his eyes.

"Have you been fighting?" the tall, beetle-browed youth went
on, his teeth glinting red in the light of the torches.

"Yes, we wrestled on the edge of the cliff," Atys answered at
last, but he was not looking at the tall, beetle-browed youth, who
somehow resembled a monkey, for his body was covered with thin
glistening black hairs. He was looking away, across the whole
extent of the baths, into the darkness beyond.

"Yes, we have been wrestling," he said. "No one will believe
that we wrestled as we did—even I cannot believe it! We really
wanted to kill one another! It all happened only a little while ago
high up on the edge of the cliff of Serapis."

"On the very edge?" the monkey asked incredulously.

"Yes, on the very edge," Atys answered. "And now we have
sworn to be brothers. Isn't that strange? We fought like demons.
Do you understand, we might both have been hurled over the
edge of the cliff."

"I suppose the excitement pleased you," the monkey said, grin-
ning and smiling easily at Yeshua, as though he understood everything that happened, "and now of course you are fond of one
another. Well, I congratulate you. There's nothing like friendship
to improve the appetite. But I do not know why I am standing
here talking to you, when you should be bathing your wounds.
Why, it looks as though you have been in the wars, and it is impossible to tell which has been more badly wounded, you, my dear
Agathon, or the young Jew by your side."

And then because he heard the faint note of distaste in the
monkey's voice, Atys said hotly: "For me he is not a Jew but a

Greek; and whether he is a Jew or not, he is my brother. Be careful what you say, Ariston!"

Yeshua could make little of this conversation, and in fact he was not listening to it with any degree of concentration. The Negroes were still waving the white sheets, and some of them were puffing their cheeks and blowing, as though they thought they could blow that heavy black smoke away. Yeshua's attention was concentrated on Atys. Now for the first time he was able to see Atys clearly, the lean face beautifully modeled, the long neck, the pointed chin. In the blinding light of the torches, those great orange-red explosions of light which were reflected in long ripples and bars of scarlet on the surface of the water, Yeshua seemed to be blinded. He was lost in some dream or other, incapable of moving. Everything that took place around him, even the coming of the monkey, seemed in some way fantastic and miraculous. Everyone was treating Atys with great deference. They were waving to him and shouting his name, but they called him "Agathon." There was nothing strange in this: a man might have two names—a Syrian name like Atys, and a Greek name like Agathon. Even those bathers who were still splashing one another had their eyes turned towards Atys. The strangest thing of all was the young girl, no more than fourteen or fifteen, small-breasted and very pale, who suddenly came out of nowhere and began running along the marble colonnade wearing a blue gown which was already wet through, so that it clung to her skin, and suddenly she threw off the gown, stood completely naked on the edge of the bath, put her hands to her face and jumped into the bath, and now she was swimming under the water with her long black hair trailing on the surface behind her. Seeing her, Yeshua had an impulse to run for his life. It was not that he objected to immodesty or nakedness, but all these things were happening so quickly that he was out of his depth; and he would have run into the darkness beyond the colonnades if Atys had not held him back.

"Oh, just look at yourself," Atys said in mock horror, dismissing the monkey with a curt nod of his head. "We stand here when we ought to be bathing and getting the dirt out of our skins."

Yeshua smiled. Somewhere a flautist was playing; and the music of the flute, coming over the water, somehow had the effect of hushing the bathers, so that their voices no longer came loud and clamorous. Now the black smoke no longer hung low over the

water, but seemed to be drifting away high overhead; and the
Negro slaves, after carefully folding the white sheets, resumed
their dice-playing in the shadows.

"Are you ready to wash away your sins?" Atys asked, laughing
and pointing to the caked bloodstains on Yeshua's gown.

"Yes," Yeshua answered, "but first of all, tell me why you are
called Agathon."

"That's easy," Atys answered. "When I am playing in the theater
I am called Agathon, and when I am at home I am called Atys, but
those who love me best call me by whatever name they please."

"So you are an actor?"

"And a very good one, I assure you," Atys laughed. "Why should
you be surprised? It is a very honorable profession, surely, or have
you some special objection to actors?"

In reply Yeshua smiled, and the bright flashing of teeth in the
long oval face delighted Atys so much that he threw his arm over
Yeshua's shoulder and said: "I was afraid you had some objection.
I have never heard of Jews coming to see the plays, and yet they
are the most wonderful things ever composed by the mind of man.
Will you come and see me on the stage?"

"Of course I shall come!"

"Then we are doubly friends," Atys said, and a moment later he
had slipped out of his gown and was looking at his bruised flesh,
the bloodstains and the purple weals, and a moment later, pinch-
ing his nose between thumb and index finger, he jumped straight
into the water, sending up a great splash; and Yeshua, not knowing how to avoid appearing naked in front of the Greek youths,
did the same.

Though the night was warm, the water was icy-cold. He gave a
little scream as he felt the sudden cold invading his flesh but,
when the shock had passed, he found himself swimming leisurely,
his eyes closed, surrendering himself to its coolness, its flow of
strength, conscious of nothing in the world except the flame-lit
water. The girl had risen from the bath, thrown the wet cloak
round her and gone running out into the scented darkness, a flash
of blue like a kingfisher's wing. As for Yeshua, he felt the pressure
of the water like a healing on his flesh, and he was aware of unaccountable strength entering his pores. He was being held up by
the soft hands of the water. The water was a subtle and murmur-
ous presence, whispering in his ears, a soft breath uplifting him,

swift, clear and flame-lit. He swam easily and well, and when he
had reached the end of the bath he paused only for a moment
before striking out towards the other end. He did not know that
all the Greeks were watching him closely, examining his strokes,
the way he swam with great over-arm movements, while keeping
his feet close together.

He had been swimming up and down the length of the bath for
a quarter of an hour when Atys dived under him and then swung
round, treading water, to face him.

"Oh, you have swum enough," Atys exclaimed. "This water—it's
so cold it is even dangerous to swim in it for long."

"I am not in the least cold," Yeshua answered.

"Nevertheless it is still dangerous," Atys went on. "You have to
be terribly careful when bathing here at night."

Seeing the flames lying lightly on the surface of the water,
Yeshua murmured: "Are these the flames of Gehenna?"

"Please don't talk in riddles," Atys said quickly. "There are
enough riddles between us, and we shall never understand one
another, never so completely as I should desire. Don't you feel
now that you have a new body, and you are born again?"

"How many resurrections?" Yeshua exclaimed delightedly.

"We must eat," Atys said soberly, "and that is a resurrection,
and then we must talk and that is another, and then we must sleep
and that is still a third, though I dare say we can do without sleep.
The world is full of resurrections, isn't that so? And where is the
end of it?"

"In love," Yeshua said simply. "All those resurrections you speak
of partake of love."

They were swimming now close to the edge of the bath. Atys's
face was blood-red in the light of the flares. Atys was swimming
on his back, and the strange thing was that his flesh no longer
looked bruised, there were no more wounds and only the faintest
trace of scars. They climbed out of the water, throwing off dazzling
fountains of spray, smiling at one another. Some slaves came
hurrying up, but Atys threw them some coins and barked at them
to leave him in peace. He took Yeshua to a bench, ordered him to
lie down at full length, poured a beaker of oil over him and then
tossed him a scraper. The oil was scented with sweet herbs. Some
of the bathers were lying on towels spread out beneath the braziers. They were nearly all Greeks, but among them were to be

found a few Syrians with dark eyes, oiled ringlets and long, slender, olive-colored bodies, and though they spoke in Greek, they had characteristic Syrian intonations. Mostly they were fair-haired, with bronze skins, square shoulders and the heavily-developed chests of swimmers.

While Yeshua was scraping himself, a heavy-set bearded man who had been sleeping under the braziers suddenly awoke and catching sight of Atys roared at the top of his voice: "Come here, ungrateful one! Come here, Agathon! Lord of Thunders, what moved you to go away from me, eh?"

As soon as he heard the huge voice, which echoed and re-echoed across the baths, Atys turned sharply, clapped his hands and shouted: "Did you think to keep me by your side, old drunkard? Why, I have better things to do than sit and watch the wine trickling down your beard!"

"Ah, you say that, Agathon," the old man said, heaving and wheezing, "but by Bacchus, you shall change your tune!"

Then the old man lifted himself up until he stood majestic under the columns, and still wheezing, he made his way along the side of the bath to where Atys was standing negligently, with one foot on a bench, scraping himself.

"I thought we were to spend the evening together," the old man said. "I should have known the promises of the young are not to be trusted. When I left my house, I expected to find you here; and not finding you, I sent out for wine, which explains the condition I am in! I have slept the evening away, to no profit except the abuse of the common folk, who have thrown me into the pool half a dozen times! Well, thank the gods you are back again! An old man should not spend his evenings alone."

"Then he is out of mischief," Atys said, smiling, but not looking.

"No, he is in worse mischief if he is alone," the old man said sadly. "I suppose you went to some wench and passed the time gazing into her eyes."

"I went to the temple of Serapis."

"Oh, the temple of Serapis, eh? The one on the cliff, where the lovers leave little messages to the blue-faced god? And to what purpose? If you had gone to the temple of Apollo, a divine spark of intelligence might have entered your brain. But no, you must go to Serapis, 'the shredded one'! Heaven knows what you find in those Egyptian gods!" And then with a glance at Yeshua, the huge old man went on: "Unless you are following the Jewish god, who is very jealous, as everyone knows, and not at all the kind of god who is pleasant to a Greek!"

At first Yeshua paid little attention to the old man who came shambling up to Atys, who bellowed and roared and smelled of wine. The man was a head taller than Atys, with a great bull chest and a neck as thick as the stump of a tree. He wore a loose white crumpled gown. He had enormous eyes, heavy eyebrows and a great domed forehead. He had thick sensual lips, and his short gray beard was uncombed, and he carried himself in spite of his drunkenness with amazing dignity, an imposing and forthright air, as though he owned the baths and everything in them, and Yeshua observed there was a look of majesty about the man, a hint that he regarded himself on a level with the gods whose marble statues lay outside the colonnade. He was smiling now, rubbing his hands together, and wheezing, but if he had wanted to, he could have assumed the look of thundering Zeus.

Now nearly all the bathers were listless and ready for sleep. Soon the torches would be dowsed, and soon the young bathers would be lying down on mats at the edge of the bath, waiting for dawn.

"May you come out in boils, Agathon," the old man went on, not angrily, but like someone who throws in a curse for good measure. "There's blood on your gown. So you have been fighting again! And this time you fought a Jew for some reason best known to yourself."

Atys flashed his eyes, and stared angrily, but said nothing until the old man looked Yeshua up and down, his lips curled in insolent distaste.

"I told you we fought together," Atys said, "and now we are friends, and that is good. You are drunk, old man, and had better go back to sleep."

"Shall Geresimos sleep on a night like this?" the old man answered, and Yeshua wondered whether he had heard the name Geresimos before.

Some fat blue pigeons were sleeping on the columns. When the old man spoke in that heavy, resonant, drunken voice, the effect of his words was to startle the pigeons out of their slumbers, so that they all rose from the columns and began to fly backwards and forwards through the veils of smoke over the baths, and the

air was full of the rustling of their wings. The torches shone on
them, the flame-light giving depth and brightness to their blue
wings, so that they shone eerily, now blue, now gold. A sense of
fear of the unknown came to Yeshua as he watched Atys and
Geresimos whispering urgently together; and seeing them with
their heads nodding together, he was content with withdrawal
into an interior, ethereal world of his own, watching the pigeons.
Why had he come to the baths, where Greek and Syrian boys imitated the habits of Athenians and spoke in soft tongues and spoke
with a deftness foreign to the Jews? He smiled as he thought of the
statue of Serapis glowing in the dusky interior of the temple: was
it for cool waters alone that the Greeks and the Egyptians lived?

"They shine like fish and love to lie on the water," he murmured.
"Not for them is the august presence of Moses or the Burning
Bush."

He felt, then, that there was some augury in his presence at the
baths, where the slaves were fanning some of the bathers and
dowsing the torches by tossing wet sponges against the flames.
Atys and Geresimos were still whispering hotly. A slave passed
with a basket of wheat-cakes and a flagon of wine. Without a
word, with a look of astonishing craftiness, Geresimos lifted the
flagon out of the slave's hand and slipped some wheat-cakes out
of the basket into the rumpled folds of his gown. Geresimos was
saying: "Oh, what a little fool you are! There is no hope for him!
A student of philosophy, eh? And what shall we do with students
of philosophy?" All the time Geresimos was looking up through
his bushy eyebrows, intently watching Yeshua, watching every
movement he made.

"I say he *knows*," Atys said. "By Hercules, it is the best opportunity we ever had! It is enough if I say he is good, Geresimos!"

"Are you quite sure?" Geresimos said, and once more there was
that sharp intent look in the direction of Yeshua.

"Of course I am sure! Try him! Let him come down to the
theater."

Yeshua was puzzled and inclined to be angry. He was weary of
their arguments, their whispers, the crafty beady eyes of the old
wine-besotted giant. He said softly: "What theater? What is all
this talk about the theater?"

Atys said: "Well, evidently you don't know there is only one
theater in Ptolemais, and Geresimos is the only actor of any con-

sequence in the city. Oh, you needn't be ashamed to know nothing about it! You come from Nazareth, which is a small village somewhere in Galilee, isn't that so? I was simply asking Geresimos if he would take you as a pupil."

"As a pupil of drama?"

"Of course! What can be more splendid than drama? I truly believe that you have the voice and the presence for it, and I believe Geresimos could lick you into shape. By the way you speak, there is an actor in you!"

Yeshua was alarmed. It was true that he spoke Greek well, but he had no great talent for it: he spoke the gritty language of the seaport more easily than he spoke in the cultured accent of the forum. He had no Greek friends; and though Atys behaved like a Greek, even to the smallest gestures, he was a Syrian. Perplexed, Yeshua simply bided his time, and turned away to watch a dark-skinned slave swimming with the help of a pigskin bladder in the water. It astonished him that a slave would be allowed to bathe there, and he must have been lost in contemplation of the slave, for he remembered afterwards how Atys caught him by the elbow and swung him round to face Geresimos. Atys was saying: "It is a wonderful opportunity, and the best of it is that Geresimos likes you!"

The old actor was twisting his fingers in his beard and smiling the secret smile of all men drunk with wine.

"Then you are asking me to give up everything I am doing and become an actor?"

"That's exactly it, but first of all we will need to see how well you behave on the stage. I have told him you will be wonderful. I thought of this while we were fighting on the cliff. Please be sensible, and above all don't be angry."

It was on Yeshua's tongue to say: "You are being completely ridiculous. What has the stage got to do with me?" Instead he said: "I shall never be an actor."

"You are quite sure?"

Yeshua nodded.

"Well, will you promise at least to see the theater?"

"When?"

"When the sun rises, we can wander down to the theater. Of course you don't have to decide now. Nevertheless, let me tell you it would please me if you joined us, and I am sure you have the talent for it."

To this Yeshua said nothing, only smiling a little at Atys's impulsiveness. Geresimos waved his heavy, thickly-veined hands, as though beating time to music; and a trickle of dark wine, slipping out of the corners of his lips, stained his ragged gray beard. In his great rumbling voice Geresimos said: "Agathon says you have an amazing talent for acting—you can say things which are very light, and other things which are very dark and even dreadful, and whatever you say, you are convincing. I confess—" But Geresimos did not finish the sentence, and instead turned to Atys and said in a petulant voice: "You are always bringing boys from the marketplace and saying they make wonderful actors! Are you quite sure this time?"

Then Geresimos slumped down on a low wooden bench, held his fat cheeks in his hands and stared glumly across the water, heavy with wine and sleep. He rocked slowly from side to side. Sometimes he made little gurgling noises, and slowly the heavy eyelids closed, and soon he was snoring. As he slept, the look of drunkenness wore off, and in its place there was an expression of astonishing calm and power.

"I have never been so sure of anyone," Atys whispered, turning to Yeshua, and because there was a faint note of patronage in the voice, Yeshua trembled. Then he steadied himself, reminding himself that everything that happened here in the baths was artificial, remote from the green and growing world, and it was time he returned to his lodgings, to his loneliness, to his eternal hungering after spiritual truths. Who was Atys? Why should he trouble himself with this boy, whose only virtue was his beauty and openness? They had met by accident: surely it was time they should part! And so he told himself again he had come to Ptolemais to lose himself in his meditations, and not to strut across the stage. Atys must have read his thoughts, for he said: "When you read Sophocles, it is more difficult than Plato, because you have to meditate on every word and every line." And a moment later Atys said: "So it is decided! We shall stay here until the dawn and then go down to the temple."

"What temple?"

"The temple of Dionysus, which is only another way of saying the theater. And surely the theater is sacred and worthy of being regarded as a temple. I see you are shivering, so let us put on our gowns and eat some wheat-cakes and then with the first rays of the sun we shall go to the temple."

Though he had every intention of saying: "No, this is all useless, I have not the least desire to accompany you to the theater," Yeshua heard himself saying: "I shall come because you desire it."

While Geresimos slept, they lay down on mats near the edge of the bath, and soon a slave came and threw some padded cotton quilts over their feet up to the knees. Only a single torch blazed on the dark waters, where there were no ripples—only this dark mirror of glass, and the pigeons on the columns, and the starlight beyond. Soon Atys fell asleep with his face pillowed in his hands; and seeing him lying there, it occurred to Yeshua that he had spent many nights in the same place and seemed to belong there, and perhaps most of the other bathers spent their nights there, and were content to be homeless among the marble columns. Yeshua had no desire to sleep. He stared at the silent water, where the one remaining torch threw on the dark surface the pattern of scarlet snakes. Sometimes, and then only because he was still absorbed in troubled recollections of the struggle on the cliffs, he would look away from the water and steal a glance at the youth by his side, who slept so peacefully and innocently he looked as though he had spent his whole life in preparation for just this sleep, for this simple abandonment of himself beside the sleeping waters.

"And where is the end of it?" Yeshua asked himself. "Shall I slip away now, before they awake, or shall I stay with them until the inevitable time comes when we quarrel and go our own ways?"

A sense of pity for the sleeping youth rose in him. He smiled because it seemed so unexpected a ripeness in himself—this pity, or rather this impulse to pity. There was no love between them, only friendship: and beyond this he would not go. Then why pity? Why this desire to protect? How strange it was, this senseless world of sleep in which men fell at evening! There was no expression on Atys's sleeping face, no laughter, no turmoil, no hint of dreams. "I have nothing to do with Atys, nothing with Geresimos," Yeshua whispered. "Best of all if I left Ptolemais and returned to Nazareth."

The dawn came slowly. Yeshua wrapped himself in the padded cotton quilt, but he could not sleep. A rosiness spread over the high columns and touched the sleeping waters, and then came the first wavering shafts of saffron. At the moment when the sunlight began to warm the columns, the painted doves rose with a fierce whirring of wings and flung themselves towards the sunlight.

The Painted Mask

As they walked to the theater in the early morning the heavens were chalk-blue, the larks were singing and the rock-pigeons were rising from their nests. It was one of those calm mornings when all the earth seems to be dissolving in silver and blue, with a clean wind to quicken the appetite. Atys was all for running ahead, so eager was he to show Yeshua the theater. His face was flushed. He held Yeshua by the hand, and hardly stopped talking, until Geresimos bade him be silent. "The young bull bellows too much, eh, eh?" he said, winking at Yeshua, and then he lowered his voice and said: "For a Hebrew thou talkest our tongue well, if Agathon would give thee leave. So speak up! Speak up! I like thy soft purring. Wert thou a cat in some previous incarnation?"

"Nay, not a cat, a whole dragon," Atys interrupted, throwing back his beautiful dark face and laughing. "He can roar like a dragon, too. Has a dragon's heart, too. Shall we call him 'dragon,' master?"

"A little one?" Geresimos suggested, and his huge black eyebrows went up and down.

The morning had changed Geresimos. Heavy and shambling, with the drunken vapors moiling in his brain, his beard uncombed, his immense eyes hooded, he had rolled about the marble edge of the baths like some droll creature of the woods, smelling of age, which is sour, and wine, which is sweet. He looked swollen in the light of the flares, a sick doddering man. The morning air had revived him. He strode like a conqueror. Because his hands were cold—it had something to do with too much wine-drinking during the night—he looped up the folds of his coarse cotton gown and wrapped his arms in them, to keep them warm. Atys wore sandals, but Geresimos wore expensive high-heeled boots of black leather with crimson laces—it was his only tribute to the actor's profession, for otherwise he could be taken as a sturdy farmer on the way to market, if you saw him from a distance. Close at hand you were aware of the mobility of his face, the heaviness of the white dome with only a fringe of white hair around the ears, the extraordinary mobility of his mouth and the quickness of his enormous eyes, which glinted and absorbed the surrounding light and threw it out again. Yeshua watched him closely. He had the disturbing feeling that he was in the presence of some kind of greatness, even of holiness.

"See him playing Œdipus!" Atys whispered. "Ah, Hercules, there's a player for you! Is it not true, Geresimos, you received the crown thirteen times in Athens, and in Ptolemais more than fifty times?"

Geresimos shrugged his heavy shoulders and made a gesture which suggested that crowns won in Ptolemais were of small account.

"And in Tiberias and Sepphoris, too," Atys went on, lost in dreams of his master's grandeur, darting smiles at Yeshua.

"In Sepphoris?" Yeshua asked, pleased because the memory of the city always pleased him.

"Of course in Sepphoris! Did a mouse squeak? Geresimos says the theater in Sepphoris is the best in Galilee, isn't that so, master?"

Geresimos nodded, stood stock still and turned slowly towards Yeshua, his enormous eyes filling with warmth.

"So you know Sepphoris well?" he asked, and it was as though he were paying a great tribute.

"I was born near there—in Nazareth," Yeshua answered softly.

"Ah, Nazareth, the little place in the hills! I asked Herod—it was the day I performed *Prometheus* in the summer palace, and I remember we put on such a display of lightning and thunder that the court ladies trembled, and even Herod, who does not tremble easily, was hard put to it to keep his seat—it was the summer before the whole city was burned to the ground because some zealot or other stole all the weapons out of the armory and all the gold from the treasury—well, as I was saying, I played the part of

Prometheus, of course, and afterwards Herod took my hand and asked how he could reward me, and I answered that he could best reward me by attending to divine things and by encouraging more attendance at the play, for that in my view is the same thing, but then he laughed and said: 'Come, Geresimos, think of something more practical,' and I think he meant to offer me some pretty Jewesses for my bed, until I said that the greatest of all gifts was peace, and would he out of his kindness show me where I could find it? Have you ever seen him, Yeshua?"

"No, not with my eyes," Yeshua said promptly.

"Then I shall have to tell you about him. He has a long nose like a carpenter's saw and a very small delicate face, but this face is surrounded by a mountain of blubber, and it is very odd—the blubber is a curious purple color, which comes from drinking too much Galilean wine. And so, when I asked him where I could find peace, the delicate little face inside the big face looked at me intently, and then he thought for a while, and then he said in his high-pitched voice: 'Then, Geresimos, if you want peace, you must go to Nazareth, because that is the place where nothing ever happens, whether good or evil,' and then he howled with laughter, and the great mountains of purple blubber went swinging from side to side."

Geresimos paused and blew a kiss to the sun. It was an actor's pause, and Yeshua was curiously impressed by it.

"Ever since then," Geresimos went on, "I have often wondered where Nazareth was. So you say it is near Sepphoris?"

"Very near."

"And how far is that?"

"An hour's walk in the sun."

"Then the next time I perform in Sepphoris, you must take me to Nazareth, my dear boy. Truly I desire to live in a place where nothing ever happens."

Yeshua smiled grimly, his face darkening. There was a rage in him, but he could not tell the cause of the rage. At that moment— they were already out in the open country, beyond the biscuit- colored walls of Ptolemais—a farmer's cart came down the road, and Geresimos hailed the farmer, asking whether he had any honey to spare.

"I have Tryphon's hunger!" he exclaimed, red-faced. "Honey

and bread and olives for a poor actor! Have mercy on the poor
servants of Dionysus!"

The farmer whipped his horse and was going to pass the little
group of actors, when an astonishing transformation took place.
Geresimos hunched his back, hopped about on one foot, threw his
arms out, letting the hands fall loosely, and began to make little
barking noises. In the twinkling of an eye the enormous heavy-
built man had become one of those mangy dogs which haunt the
market-places, cringing in the shadows, quickly racing up to the
stalls when he thinks he is unobserved, whining and pretending
to be lame when the meat-seller threatens him. As he limped and
hopped beside the cart, every movement he made resembled the
queer lurching movement of a whipped scavenger dog. The
farmer, a young man with a lean long sunburned face and a wisp
of reddish beard, looked at the mad hopping creature who imitated a dog to perfection in spite of his billowing gown and the
gleaming black leather boots with crimson laces, and suddenly
burst out laughing.

"Geresimos!" he exclaimed, and jumped off the cart, landing in
the dust beside the old actor.

"The same," said Geresimos. "The very same, I do believe."

For a moment the young farmer simply gazed in bewilderment.
Geresimos was still a dog, low to the earth. He had a dog's face,
there was no doubt about it, and there was even somehow a suggestion of a dog's low dragging tail, and all the pain and horror in
the eyes of one of those famished creatures. But gradually he
straightened himself, the muscles of his face changed, the bared
teeth disappeared, and soon he was towering above the young
farmer, who then hurled himself on Geresimos, embraced him,
kissed him on both cheeks, and began to announce in a thick
nervous farmer's voice a complete list of all the plays he had seen
Geresimos performing in, and this list, uttered so ponderously and
nervously, would be interrupted by Geresimos saying while rolling his eyes: "Ah, my *Suppliants*! Ah, my *Antigone*! Ah, my
Œdipus at Colonus! Ah, my *Ajax*! Blessed be the names of Æschylus and Sophocles for ever and ever!"

The young farmer was still dumbfounded. To put him at his
ease, Geresimos asked him in a lordly manner where he came
from; and learning that he was from Melos and had recently taken
an Idumean bride, said in a preposterously patronizing manner:

"Then, my dear fellow, I shall dedicate a performance to you—to you alone! Anyone who has the courage to marry an Idumean woman deserves a performance of *Hercules in the Poisoned Robe* at least! I promise you an absolutely outstanding performance!"

The young farmer was at once crestfallen and dizzy with pride. He began to kiss the hem of Geresimos's robe, muttering: "I am unworthy! I am only a simple peasant from Melos! Come and stay on my farm, Geresimos! Everything I have is yours!"

Atys was hopping about on one leg, and Yeshua was withdrawn in a happy silence of his own. There were no other carts on the road. It was one of those feast-days when there is very little early morning traffic, for the feast would last through the night and the people of Ptolemais and the surrounding villages therefore rose late. Usually, on this highway which joins Ptolemais to the Jordan, there are teeming caravans, hosts of donkey-carts and laden camels, and usually there are some soldiers on the march. But this morning it was very quiet, and the air was full of shimmering light unusual even in spring, a light that seemed to come in wonderful silvery bursts, never still, as though the whole sky was the reflection of a stream.

"And now, of course," Geresimos said, continuing his lordly tone, "you shall honor us with a little wine and beans and honey and perhaps some bread and olives as well, unless of course you are—as I suspect you are—of such unmitigated poverty that you live on the crusts fed to the swine!"

The young farmer was overjoyed. He kissed Geresimos again on both cheeks and pointed to the cart, which had gone a little way along the road, and said: "It is all yours! I adore you, Geresimos! I say prayers for you every morning, when I address the sun."

"In that case," said Geresimos, "I shall probably accept whatever miserable gifts you offer me."

The young farmer whistled. The horse came back. It so happened that the young farmer, on his way to attend the festival in Ptolemais, had loaded the cart with good things: there were big red jars filled with honey, three *amphoræ* filled with scarlet wine, great loaves of bread kept fresh in moss. There was yellow Syrian cheese, and the heavy black cheese of Melos. There were strings of dried beans which become soft and succulent when dissolved in milk. There were even cakes, still warm from the oven. All these were lifted out of the cart and placed beside the road. There were no cups or beakers, so they had to drink from the huge *amphoræ*. Geresimos sat there, his legs sprawled out in front of him, lifting the absurdly large *amphoræ* above his head, so that the wine splashed purple on his coarse stained gown. He ate ravenously, and when he saw that neither Atys nor Yeshua were eating in the same way, he would say: "He's a miserable rich farmer, perhaps the richest farmer within fifty miles! Eat away!" And all the time the farmer smiled nervously and happily, thinking of the special performance of *Hercules in the Poisoned Robe* to be given in his honor.

When the meal was finished and the empty wine bottles were being loaded on the cart and Geresimos's beard was trickling with honey, Atys laughed: "Now you see what a great actor Geresimos is!"

"You mean," said Yeshua, "he can change his appearance exactly as he pleases?"

"Yes, that is exactly what I mean. Just now he was a peasant pretending to be a rich man, and in a moment he will be a rich man pretending to be a peasant. Have you seen him with wings, when he is one of the Furies? No, of course you haven't, and the truth is he rarely plays such lowly parts. He plays the powerful and terrible parts, and he will tell you that being an actor is truly terrifying. A man who is a good actor can become anything he pleases, he can become a god and possess the powers of a god. He quite seriously believes that a man acting the role of a god can become a god."

Yeshua was still a little enraged with Geresimos. He had the feeling that the whole story of the conversation between Geresimos and King Herod Antipas had been invented. It was simply that Geresimos knew the current saying: 'Nothing good has come out of Nazareth,' that inexplicable saying which made the cheeks of the Nazarenes burn with shame, and then Geresimos had embroidered on it, subtly changing the words and putting them in the King's mouth. And then he saw that Geresimos had only been attempting to please him.

There were affectionate farewells between Geresimos and the young farmer. At the last moment Geresimos, who had been behaving in his outrageously lordly fashion, drew some coins which he kept in a leather purse next to his skin, begging the young farmer to accept them. He lost his lordly manner. He spoke about

Melos and Idumea, and how he adored the Greek island and the
Syrian province; he swore eternal brotherhood with the farmer,
promised to send one of the carts belonging to the theater to fetch
the young farmer for the performance of *Hercules in the Poisoned
Robe* and then whispered some outrageous nonsense in the farmer's ear; and when the farmer had vanished down the road Geresimos imitated all his gestures to perfection, his nervous simpering,
his silly smiles, and at the same time he conveyed the farmer's
honesty, his goodness and simple peasant courage.

The road to the theater lay through a grove of acacia trees not
five minutes walk from where they had feasted by the roadside.
Even now, though it was already an hour after sunrise, the highway was empty, the dust unspoiled, their long blue shadows
sweeping before them. It was very quiet in the acacia grove. There
were stone markers engraved with the emblem of Dionysus to
show the way. It was all shadowy here, and the place almost demanded that you walk sedately, but for some reason they found
themselves running. And there suddenly, at the end of the acacia
grove, directly in front of them was the immense white shimmering bowl of the theater, the circles of stone seats, the stage and the
semicircular dancing floor below and the painted palace which
served as the scenery with its three immense arching gateways.
The palace far below gleamed jewel-like in the mysterious shade
which hovered over the whole theater.

The short fierce race was too much for Geresimos, a man over
sixty who tired easily, though he gave an impression of terrifying
vigor.

When he caught up with them, he laughed: "I see that Yeshua
is in good shape. He is the least out of breath of all of us."

He threw his arms over Yeshua's shoulder and together they
peered down at this hollow in the earth, where the mysterious
blue shadows swirled, so that it was like looking down from a
cliff at a misty blue sea.

"I made you race on purpose," Geresimos said. "The first thing
an actor has to have is good lungs. After that he must have grace
of gesture, and after grace of gesture he must have presence."

"And what else?"

"If you are talking about great actors, and not the ordinary ones,
then he must have a sense of the divine, and then too a passionate
love for beauty—for the perfect beauty which the gods have re-

vealed only to those who are specially chosen; and perhaps if a
man loves beauty, then all the rest follows. Did not Socrates say
that beauty alone is lovely and visible at once, and it is through
beauty that the divine speaks to us?"

"Then you really intend to become an actor?" Atys interrupted.
"Geresimos is showing you more affection than he has shown anyone among all the actors he has trained."

"If I parade on the stage—" Yeshua began, and then was silent.
He was too dazzled by the quiet beauty of the theater, the tiers
of stone seats reminding him of the tiers of white stone houses in
the bowl of Nazareth, to understand what he was doing there. The
day before he had been a student in Ptolemais; more accurately,
he was a silent wanderer in the streets of the seaport, searching for
the truth which eluded him, sick of an obscure disease. Now it was
over. For a little while he would stay with them. He knew this
even before Atys said: "Are you ashamed to act with us? Even if
you were the Prince of the World you would be honored to act in
the plays of Sophocles? And surely you have read them?"

Yeshua nodded, for he had read many of them, perhaps twenty,
in the great library at Ptolemais, the scrolls kept in cupboards of
cedarwood, where little cups of spices reposed, so that the scrolls
remained fresh. And as they walked down the stone steps towards
the dancing floor, Yeshua had the curious feeling that he had been
here before: not in some other theater, but here, among these
curving stone benches, anemones growing in the cracks in the
stone, walking slowly to the bright pavilions below, in the misty
blue air.

It was like a ceremonial march, this slow descent, the empty
bowl of the theater rimming around them, so that they were lost
in its immensity, in the glitter and the whiteness. Geresimos was
silent. Yeshua was saying: "I have been here before, but I cannot
remember how many lives ago."

"Then you believe that the soul is reborn?" Atys said quickly,
his eyes darting.

"No!" Yeshua said solemnly. "I know only that I have the strangest feeling that I have been here before."

"And you were happy here?"

There was no answer.

"But if you remember it, then you must have been happy," Atys
insisted. "Besides I saw you smiling just now. Surely you were

smiling at the recollection? Plato says we all have an astonishing
memory of what we learned in previous lives, and this memory
comes when we least expect it. I think now you have opened the
doors of memory."

"For me," Yeshua answered gravely, "those doors are always
open."

He did not know why he was so moved. The beauty of the place
intoxicated him, as they drifted down the stone stairs between the
curving terraces. To Yeshua the place was so hallowed that it was
like entering a synagogue, only this synagogue was thrown open
to the blue air of morning. Far below he saw the small gilded
statue of Apollo in the center of the dancing floor. He heard some
birds calling, and then a faint rumble, and suddenly he saw
something he had never expected to see. Out of the air, it seemed,
an ox-wagon appeared. There was no ox-wagon a moment before.
Then he saw that the wagon came from behind the pavilions on
the stage. The oxen were enormous, pure white, with immense
horns shaped like lyres.

"Oh, they came from Egypt," Atys explained offhandedly. "They
were a present to us."

"Why do you need oxen?"

"Heavens, they are a present, Yeshua, as I told you! The ox-
wagon is for the actors, to bring supplies from Ptolemais—a hundred things. It is so simple. Menarchus drives the wagon. You will
like him. He is a superb actor—last year he was actually invited to
Greece."

Menarchus was a brown, solid-looking peasant with thick sun-
bleached curly hair. He was bringing wine and some much-
needed paint from Ptolemais. Menarchus and two other young
actors who had sprung out of nowhere began to roll the casks of
paint and wine off the ox-cart: then they stacked the casks on the
dancing floor. Some of the purple wine was spilling out, leaving a
trail like blood on the marble floor.

"But the important thing is that you should see everything and
really come to understand what we are doing. Do you believe in
devils?" Atys went on.

"What kind of devils?"

"Oh, it doesn't matter what kind. The important thing is that
they exist. There are devils in charge of everything in the theater
—something is always bound to go wrong! Do you agree?"

"I know nothing about devils."

"Of course, I should have known! But you know a good deal about angels?"

"I know only about God," Yeshua answered softly.

Atys was in no mood to discuss God, angels or devils. He took Yeshua by the arm and propelled him to the outer walls of the stage building. From a distance the stage building resembled a small and gleaming palace, but on closer acquaintance he saw that it was no more than a bare wall painted to represent a palace: the gilded marble columns were only paint. But the wall was solid: there were three doors cut into it: and they passed through one of the doors into the robing rooms, where huge masks hung on wooden pegs and great chests lay open, with sprawled vestments like enraged beasts leaping over the edges: scarlet, purple, crimson, blue, turquoise. It was dark in the robing rooms. Atys walked among the fantastic costumes like someone who could make his way in the dark.

Yeshua was murmuring to himself: "My God, my God, guide my footsteps, lest I fall into the path of iniquity."

But there was no iniquity in these costumes or in those staring masks, which looked in the dim light like the heads of bulls cut off and fixed to the wall. There was an overpowering smell of silk, linen and paint. Atys picked up one of the heavy scarlet robes and threw it over Yeshua's shoulders, afterwards making a mock reverence.

"A king already," he said, and because he was easily amused he burst out into wild laughter.

Then he insisted on showing Yeshua the long passageway immediately behind the painted façade. The passageway, about five foot wide, was filled with enormous earthenware jars, some of them fifteen foot high. Atys explained that the jars acted as resonance chambers, so helping the voices of the actors to reach the topmost tiers of the theater. He slapped one of the jars with the flat of his hand. Yeshua had expected to hear a single slapping sound: instead, all the jars echoed the sound. These hollow jars were brightly painted in black, ochre and white, and it was strange how they reinforced the voices of the actors, giving them a depth, a resonance, a richness they would not otherwise have possessed.

"And there are many other things you know nothing about," Atys said pleasantly, taking Yeshua by the arm and smiling one of his most piercing smiles. "Of course you will learn everything in time, but I assure you it is not easy! Geresimos says he is still learning, and he has been acting for more than forty years! They say he is the equal of the old tragic actors, but he is just as good in comedy. And now come and rest and meet the other actors, for by now most of them must have arrived from Ptolemais."

Atys led him to another room, a kind of tent, which lay against one of the wings of the stage building. Here the actors rested and took their ease between entrances: there were tables, chairs, cushions, a gilded statue of Dionysus, chests containing food and wine, and more chests filled with scrolls. But the room was empty, no actors had yet arrived, and so Atys insisted that they go in search of Geresimos. They went from one robing room to another, but there was no sign of him. At last Atys returned to the room they had originally entered. In the middle of the room an apparition ten feet tall glared at them.

Yeshua jumped. He had seen plays, but he had never been so close to a player. This player wore a heavy, embroidered robe of scarlet, yellow and blue, and on his head an enormous white mask was lolling. The mask had been carefully painted to resemble a man whose left eye has been torn out—an old man with long flowing gray hair and a thick gray beard. Wrinkles had been painted on the forehead; the cheeks were dead white. Out of the cavernous circle of the mouth a voice was saying:

> *What I have done is best done! Do not tell me*
> *There was some other way! Give me no counsels!*
> *For when I die and fall below the earth—*
> *Listen, my friends—how shall I gaze*
> *Eyeless upon my father, or on my mother?*
> *What I have done is done, deserving*
> *Worse punishment than hanging! And should I see*
> *The faces of my children, should I acquit myself*
> *With joy and gladness? Not with these broken eyes!*
> *These bloody sockets shall not look upon my city,*
> *The towers and holy places and the citadels*
> *Where the gods dwell in peace—all, all are gone from me!*
> *The crossroads, too, and all the holy woodlands,*
> *The oaks and secret pathways and the flowers*
> *That drank my father's blood!*

O marriage, marriage! There is bred in me
Out of the breeding of the marriage-bed,
Such agonies as brides and wives proclaim
The foulest evil ever known to man!

Then quite suddenly the mask was silent, as if the roaring voice
had been sucked into some hollow cave deep within it. Yeshua
had not recognized the voice: so heavy, so weighted with a terrible majesty, a voice that rose into paroxysms of passion and then
grew whispering-soft only to rise again. There was ferocity in it,
and a slow sustained poison of malice. A god was speaking, or perhaps some prince of the earth who had often communed with the
gods. When it reached the words "O marriage, marriage," the
voice had grown suddenly shrill, and at that moment a heavy
earthenware jar painted with red figures of actors had broken and
spilt its contents, and now in the silence the only sound came from
the trickling of wine on to the stone floor.

Yeshua stood by the door, his hair standing on end, gazing at the
mask like someone thunderstruck. Suddenly Geresimos whipped
the mask from his face, bellowed with happy laughter, made a low
bow, and said in an unusually soft voice: "That was from *Œdipus
the King* by Sophocles. But of course *Œdipus at Colonus* is infinitely better, as everyone knows. One day, when you are good
enough, Yeshua, I shall let you play the part of Œdipus when he
comes to Colonus and vanishes in a thunderclap. Will you play it?
Of course you will, dear boy. And don't look so alarmed." At that
moment, gazing idly at the painted leather mask he was holding in
his hands, he observed that there were red ribbons streaming
from only one of the eye-sockets. "You really must be more careful, Agathon," he shouted. "It is quite absurd to have blood streaming out of only one of my eyes! Please see that the ribbons are
attached to *both* eyes, dear boy!"

Atys smiled, reached out for the mask, examined it casually and
then tossed it to Yeshua, who caught it easily but immediately
began trembling. There was little light in the robing room. Even
when it rested in his hands, and even though there were red
streamers coming from only one of the eyes, the mask retained its
terrible splendor.

"And don't drop it, dear boy!" Geresimos said. "Please be care-

ful—these things are expensive." Then hearing the play-carts rolling in from Ptolemais, he said: "Put the mask away! I hear the
other actors are arriving, and it is time I introduced you to them!"

The Young Actors

Yeshua became an actor. He joined the company of actors for
many reasons, and not only out of affection for Atys. He had
watched the traveling players performing in the great theater at
Sepphoris, sitting high up among the shining marble benches, seeing the actors far below—flash of scarlet gowns and snow-white
masks, powerful voices booming across the immensity of the hollow bowl. Seeing these actors, he never felt he was losing his Jew-
ishness. It was simply that they were there, and he attended the
Greek dramas as he attended the other feasts in Sepphoris: and
had not Herod Antipas himself encouraged the people to attend
the plays, issuing proclamation upon proclamation in honor of the
players?

And there were other reasons, so many reasons that they were
past counting, and all these reasons came back to one reason:
Hellas, Greece, the clear skies over Athens, Plato, Sophocles, the
sweetness of their smiles, the clean-cut vigor of their minds. They
were not immersed in doctrinal problems; they were not everlast-
ingly talking about whether you might walk a mile or two miles
on the Sabbath; they did not wade knee-deep in the hot and smoking blood of lambs. The Greeks loved the simpler things of the
earth. They were always dancing and singing. They built splendidly, and they were aware of the fleetingness of life, and had no
hope of ever returning to Abraham's bosom or to the Father in
Heaven. When they awoke in the morning they threw a kiss to the
sun and in the evening they threw a kiss to the moon. So he was

happy with them, though he still attended the synagogue on the Sabbath and lived apart in his old lodgings, never living in the actors' community house in Ptolemais. Alone in his lodgings he wore the *talit*, the long-fringed scarf on which sentences from the Psalms were embroidered, and behaved like a Jew, eating Jewish food, performing all the Jewish rituals as he remembered them. Once outside his lodgings, he resembled a Greek—a red-haired, bronzed and barefoot Greek, who wore the Greek linen gown as though born to it. He was never aware of living a double life. He slipped easily from one to the other: so easily that he began to wonder whether there was so vast a difference after all between being a Greek and a Jew.

Geresimos and Atys took charge of his training. Not all the training took place at the theater. They wandered along the sea-shore, reciting Greek verses, shouting, roaring, hurling their voices above the crashing of the waves against the shore. He learned to shout even with a mouthful of pebbles, and to develop his chest and lungs he went swimming, and to acquire agility he learned to box and spar with staves, which were as thick as the shepherds' staves in Nazareth. He took lessons in dancing, the solemn cere-monial dancing which accompanies the Greek chorus on the stage. Geresimos made him learn by heart whole books of Homer, until his head swam with visions of the heroes of Troy in gold breast-plates and scarlet plumes. And when Atys said: "It is time you had a Greek name, for we cannot be always calling you Yeshua," Yeshua answered: "Then give me the name of Hector, for like him I am being dragged naked behind the chariot."

"Nay, we shall find you a better name," Atys laughed.

They never found a better name, but usually they called him "the red-haired one."

For Yeshua it was a strange world, and he never wholly accepted it. He was part of it, and at the same time he was outside of it. The players lived curiously self-contained lives: they were dedicated souls, dreaming and thinking only of their plays. Whenever they passed the statue of Dionysus on the dancing floor beyond the stage, they greeted it with the same expression as the priest in the Temple courtyard when he turned in the direction of the Holy of Holies: there was a terrible intensity in that brief gaze. At meals they talked of plays and players until Yeshua wanted to cry out against the violence of their obsession.

"There are more things than plays," he shouted once. "There is the sun in the heavens and the moon and girls and a million other things."

Menarchus jumped up and pointed to the marble bust of bearded Sophocles and said: "And it's all there—in his big brain! Only a fool wants to go further. Sophocles and Æschylus and a few others—it's the whole world, Yeshua!"

"It is all there save holiness alone," Yeshua muttered, and turned away to hide his confusion.

There were long peaceful days when the actors went off into the woods to gather berries or helped in the neighboring vineyards. Sometimes, when they had been working hard, Geresimos would order a sudden stop to the rehearsals and invite the actors to a feast in a nearby farmhouse. Usually he did not have to pay for the feast, since the farmers were delighted to have the actors among them. And once a year the theater carts were heaped with bright costumes and with wicker-baskets crammed with leather masks, and then the whole company went off to Sepphoris and then to Tiberias and twenty other places. Yeshua was a member of the company, but he had never acted in a play before a public audience. He was still an apprentice, still learning his roles. He understudied everyone in the company, but the players were so healthy that he was never called upon to act on the stage.

"In another five years you will be superb," Geresimos said. "Have patience! Have patience!"

One Sabbath, when Yeshua was quietly reading from the sacred scrolls in his own lodgings, Atys burst in. It was evening. The seven-branched candlestick was burning, throwing huge bat-like shadows across the wall.

Atys had never seen Yeshua wearing the *talit*, never observed before the peculiar rapt expression which he saw now on Yeshua's face. Yeshua was wholly absorbed. Atys had swung open the door, and all the candle flames were jumping, but Yeshua was wholly unaware of Atys's entrance. His lips were moving. There came a faint crackling sound as Yeshua turned the spindles of the scroll. It was astonishing that Yeshua should have no inkling of his presence. He coughed. Still there was no sign from Yeshua who resembled, except for the barely perceptible movement of his lips, a graven image. At last Yeshua turned slowly, fastened his eyes on Atys, murmured something which Atys completely failed to un-

derstand, and once again began reading from the scroll. Atys
waited for five minutes. He seemed to be rooted to the floor. He
tried to move away, but could not, only because he was completely
fascinated by the appearance of the silent youth bent over the
scrolls. At the end of five minutes he turned and began to make his
way through the doorway. He had almost reached the top of the
stairs when he heard Yeshua saying: "Please come in, Atys. It is
always good to see you."

Atys returned shamefacedly and closed the door softly. The
scroll had been put away, but Yeshua was still sitting over the
table with hunched shoulders.

"I am completely bewildered," Atys exclaimed. "I burst in—all
the candle flames were jumping about—there must have been a
draught from the stairway—and I swear you were not aware of
my presence."

He was not hurt. It was simply that he had never known such
powers of contemplation, so complete a withdrawal from the
world.

"Please forgive me," Yeshua said. "I was listening to the voice
of God."

"Then you didn't know I was here?"

"Yes, I knew."

There was a long silence. Atys gazed round the bare room: a
table, a bench, a mattress spread on the floor, a cupboard full of
scrolls and another with some clothes. Compared with the rooms
in the actors' community house, there was a stark barrenness about
this small room in the Jewish quarter.

Atys wanted to say: "You were listening to your god and you
were aware I was in the room. How can it be?" Instead he said:
"How strange! You are still a Jew. And I thought you were becoming more and more like a Greek!"

Yeshua laughed, putting the scrolls aside.

"Your god," Atys went on, "the god you are always talking
about—is he there in the scrolls?"

"Yes, He is there."

"And you talk to him?"

"No, I listen to Him."

"I understand," said Atys slowly, "he is a god who smiles rarely."

"My God is not like your god," Yeshua answered. "He is not
shaped like a man, and I do not believe He smiles. None have set

eyes on Him except Moses and the prophets. He is a God of terrible aspect, or so it seems to me." And then he added softly from the Book of Job: "Though He slay me, yet will I trust in Him, but I will maintain my own ways before Him."

Atys was sitting on the bench beside Yeshua. There was still a remoteness about Yeshua, a strange passivity, as though he were something written in the scrolls, not a man of flesh. His face was pale from too much reading.

"You live here alone?" Atys asked.

Yeshua made a little gesture of assent. It astonished him that Atys was so astonished.

"And you are happy?"

"Perfectly happy."

"And you read the scrolls all day when you are here?"

"Yes," Yeshua said, and he bowed his head over the scrolls. "I am a Jew. How else shall I live?"

There was a long silence. The candles were burning low, spluttering a little. Very solemnly Atys removed a green scarab ring from his finger and gave it to Yeshua.

"It's for you. It is from Geresimos. It is very valuable. He asked me to give it to you."

"Why?"

"Because, he says, you are performing so well. It is a present. He wants you to keep it. All the good actors wear the scarab."

"Why a scarab?" Yeshua said, gazing at the strange beetle, bright green, glassy. For some reason the ring terrified him, and he had to steel himself not to show his terror.

"Why a scarab?" Atys said, mocking. "Why not? It just happens that Geresimos chose a scarab ring. He might very well have chosen another kind of ring, but he happened to choose a scarab. I'm sure there is no mystery about it."

"You are quite sure?"

"No," Atys said. "I am sure of nothing. Have you ever thought that Geresimos looks a little like a scarab? And then of course everything comes from Egypt. All the Greeks go to Egypt to complete their education. Sophocles, Plato, even Homer went to Egypt. Plato studied at Heliopolis. They say that after Athens, the best Greek theater is shown there. Sometimes I truly believe that everything comes out of Egypt, and the Egyptians are the fathers of us all."

Atys spoke very seriously, even though he was smiling, and he still held the scarab ring, uncertain what to do with it, because Yeshua had made no movement to suggest he would accept it.

"Why not?" Atys said impatiently, holding the ring so that it shone in the light from the seven-branched candlestick. "What on earth makes you frightened? It is just a ring, and it will give Geresimos pleasure if you wear it."

Yeshua shrugged. His mind was still on the scrolls.

"Are you afraid of it?"

"Yes, a little."

"But the thing is dead, Yeshua. It is not a living beetle, and even if it were living— Why should you object to wearing a scarab if it pleases Geresimos?"

"The little dung-beetle is dead, but it is a sign of eternal life," Yeshua said very slowly, giving every word a terrible weight.

Atys was shocked. There was a strange haunted look on Yeshua's face, and the eyes seemed suddenly to have lost their life. To hide his confusion, Atys burst out laughing.

"What a monstrous fellow you are!" he exclaimed. "A little gift, and you make it a matter of vast importance! Everyone knows the Egyptians have an almost insane regard for dung-beetles. When they die their hearts are taken out, and a scarab takes its place. As you say, the scarab is the sign of immortal life. The Phœnix came to Heliopolis, burst into flame and one thousand years later the ashes sprang into life and became a Phœnix again. You don't have to believe everything the Egyptians say. For my part, I regard the scarab as an attractive ornament, and you must admit this little green one is exquisitely carved. I suppose you will tell me that because you are a Jew, you must not associate yourself with the sacred symbols of some other religion, and yet every day you associate yourself with the worship of Dionysus, who brought the theater to Greece. I have even seen you kissing the statue of Dionysus, and in this you behave like all the other actors, and surely Dionysus too is the symbol of a religion alien to you! So you are not in the least consistent! Why should a poor little dung-beetle terrify you?"

He waited in heavy silence, unable to take his eyes away from Yeshua's face, where a multitude of emotions were at war with one another. Triumph gleamed, then savage misery, then a look of hopeless pain. And all because of a dung-beetle!

"Then you believe only in your god?" Atys said at last, his voice rising into a tone of sharp annoyance. "And your god is so powerless he is afraid of a little dung-beetle."

"I believe only in my God," Yeshua said tonelessly.

"Then you have no right to take any part in the theater, which is after all an act of pure devotion to the god Dionysus."

"If I believed that Dionysus were a god," Yeshua said somberly, "then I would never have become an actor."

"So you are a pure believer? You believe that God is one, and beyond God there is nothing, isn't that so? And all the world, even Greece and Egypt, are in the power of that god you worship, who spoke through the lips of Moses. And perhaps all you say is true. Perhaps God spoke on Mount Sinai to the Jews, and to no one else. Perhaps the Jews are the chosen ones and the rest of us are cast into outer darkness. But I know that before there were Jews, there were Egyptians, and that the Jews themselves came out of Egypt. And if the Egyptians believe that a dung-beetle is a symbol of immortal life, then why should you deny them the joy of carving these delicate creatures? The truth is that the Jews do not believe in eternal life. They believe that when a man dies, he wanders among ghosts in Sheol and perhaps in some distant time there will come a Messiah to open their graves for them. For, you see, I have read all the works written by the Greeks and the Romans about the Jews. I am not so ignorant as you think. And that is why I think you are mortally afraid of a little dung-beetle."

"Yes, I am afraid," Yeshua said calmly, and it was as though by saying this, he had put his fears away.

"And you won't take it?"

"No, I won't take it.

"Even though it comes from Geresimos, who loves you?"

"Yes, even though it comes from him."

"Then let me tell you, you are behaving foolishly. It was Plato, I think, who said that all love partakes of the glory of sharing ourselves with others. Everything Geresimos knows, everything he has ever felt, he has shared with you. He has given himself to you. Every day he makes the sacrifice of himself for your sake. *He dies for you.* And that is love, and for the Greeks this is the most wonderful and the most terrible thing of all—to give everything to others, even oneself! And that is why we have no stiff-necked reserve, and no desire to impose ourselves upon others. We give all freely, and we regard those who refuse to give of themselves as barbarians. You refuse the ring, and that is a little thing. But you refuse the affection and trust of others, and that is a big thing. Have you ever loved anyone?"

"Yes, I have loved my God."

"I asked if you had ever known love for any person?"

"I have affection for people, but not love. I worship God. I cannot worship people. I cannot give myself to them, because I have given myself to God."

"It is a curious thing," Atys remarked quietly, "that those who give themselves to their god are those who suffer most from pride. By that sin fall the heroes. They are so beautiful, so good, so wholly devoted to their godlike divinity, but in the end they stumble. Beware thou dost not stumble, Yeshua!"

Saying this, Atys turned suddenly towards the doorway, his face contorted with rage, his eyes glaring, his mouth trembling. He had not thought that so small a thing as a scarab ring would make him so angry. As he turned, the candle flames jumped and the small room blazed with light, but immediately afterwards it was dark, and this pleased him. What was Yeshua but a mole burrowing in darkness? Groping blindly, hating himself, hating Yeshua, he stumbled towards the stairs. He was half-way down the stairs when he heard Yeshua hurrying after him.

"Please stop! Please stop!" Yeshua was saying. "Please give me the ring!"

"It will do no good!" Atys said cruelly. "Go your way! Refuse the gifts of the Greeks and the Egyptians!"

It was dark on the stairway. There was the peculiar sour smell which hovered over all Jewish tenements. The stairs creaked. They heard whispers from behind doors, and sometimes there came the sound of prayers being muttered in low voices. Atys remembered how he had to steel himself to enter this tenement building.

"Go your own way!" he shouted, and he began to run down the stairs, but he had run only a little way when he heard a shout like a cry of despair and a moment later something struck him. He was rolling down the stairs, and Yeshua was rolling with him. It passed through his mind that Yeshua must have leaped down ten stairs on top of him. It was dark on the landing where they wrestled. Doors opened. People were shouting. Yeshua's fist was battering him.

A candle gleamed. In the light of the candle he saw a streak of wet blood forming across Yeshua's pale cheeks, but it was not the blood which drew his attention so much as the wild, almost maniacal gleam in Yeshua's eyes. They were struggling as they had struggled on the platform of the temple of Serapis. People were trying to tear them apart, but they continued to fight, and there was nothing in the least decorous in their fighting. This was not the carefully ordered fight with staves which they practiced at the theater. They fought with elbows and finger-nails, and each was trying to get at the other's throat. An old wrinkled Jew, naked except for a loin-cloth, was screaming at the top of his voice. Atys felt a drop of hot candle grease falling on his face, but even if a hundred boiling drops of candle grease had fallen on him he would not have stopped fighting. It seemed to him that all the Jews in the tenement were on the landing. They were all cursing, and it was evident that they had more sympathy for Yeshua than for Atys. Yeshua was shouting: "Give me the ring! Give me the ring!" Atys had no desire to give him the ring. He was angry with Yeshua. He was weary of that secretive Jewish pride. Because it was the Sabbath, none of the Jews interfered with the fight. They simply watched and prayed that Yeshua would succeed in overcoming the youth who wore Greek clothes and was certainly not a Jew. But by this time, Atys was out of breath, there were scratches over his face and his long gown had been ripped from his shoulders. Dried spittle and dust from the landing covered the gown, which was now bunched around his waist. And still he fought blindly, though overwhelmed by the rage of Yeshua, not knowing which way to turn, deafened by the shouting of the people who were standing round and threatening him in a language he did not understand. He was glad neither of them had knives, otherwise they would have killed each other. He succeeded in rising from the floor and hurling himself full-length on Yeshua. Gasping, shouting incoherently, rolling among the feet of the people watching, they fought one another until neither had any strength left. Then, making grunting noises, their clothes ripped, their faces like red wounds, they lay sprawled out in a strange passivity, exhausted beyond all endurance, so that they seemed to be dead; and someone bringing a lantern to their faces announced that they were beyond help, until Yeshua said weakly: "Why do we fight one another? Why is there no peace between us?"

Atys tried to rise. He wanted to leave the evil-smelling tenement and never return. He tottered across the landing and then
leaned against the wall, breathing deeply. He knew the Jews hated
him, but now they were smiling at him, smiling at the bloody face
and the torn garments. Yeshua had risen to his feet and was
staggering across the landing towards him.

"Please come upstairs," Yeshua was saying. "You need to rest.
You can't go."

Atys ran his hand across his face, wiping away the tube of blood
which fell from his nostrils. There was blood in his hair, and
splatters of blood across his chest.

"We have fought twice," he gasped, "and I suppose you want to
fight a third time?"

"There will be no more fighting between us," Yeshua said, leaning close, shivering at the sight of so much blood. "I could not
have borne it if you went away. That is why I had to fight you.
Please give me the ring!"

Atys threw up his head, the sign of dissent.

"Why?" he asked miserably. "Why now? Why after all the
fighting?"

"Because I need it. I remember you said: 'To love is to die,' and
just when you were going down the stairs, the words came to me
and I knew they were true. I will wear it for your sake, and for the
sake of Geresimos, and for the sake of the scarab."

He smiled wryly. Atys was staring at him with a look of incom-
prehension.

"I had to make peace," Yeshua went on, "even if it meant hurling
myself on you."

"You must be insane! You threw yourself down a whole flight of
stairs. You could easily have killed yourself!"

"Yes, I could easily have killed myself," Yeshua said, and smiled.

Yeshua took Atys by the arm and led him through the crowd of
milling Jews to the foot of the stairs.

"Please come," he said. "Let me wash the wounds, and let there
be peace between us."

They climbed the stairs slowly and with difficulty. As soon as
they reached the small tenement room, Yeshua emptied a jug of
water into a bowl and washed Atys's wounds. Afterwards they
drank some wine. Yeshua's upper lip was trembling. The candles
had almost burnt out, and the small room was growing cold. There

was a long silence. At last Yeshua said: "Whatever happens to me, wherever I go, I shall remember the way you said: 'To love is to die.' You saved me from myself. It is so much clearer now—and the ring, too—everything is clearer." And then bracing himself, he said: "Everything I have is yours. Let us be friends to the end."

Yeshua had deliberately used the second person plural, because he was still unsure of himself. Suddenly Atys smiled, leaned forward and said: "Dost thou love me then?"

"Yea, to the very end."

Then they knew what they had only guessed before: they were forever bound to one another. They would never escape from one another, and never desire to. They would work together and play together and live under the same roof. Silently Atys gave Yeshua the scarab ring, and just as silently Yeshua threaded it on his finger. For half the night they discussed their plans. There was an empty room in the tenement, and Atys decided he would come and live there. He had no particular desire to live in the Jewish quarter, but he knew that Yeshua would never leave it while he remained at Ptolemais.

So for over two years they lived in the tenement at night and in the theater by day. They never touched, except by accident. They were inseparable, like David and Jonathan. And now simply because they were together, they no longer argued or fought. A ghostly affection bound them to one another, and this affection was so close, so all-pervading that it was not necessary for them to speak often: they were aware of one another's thoughts.

"If thou shouldst die, then shall I perish," Yeshua said once.

It was the only shadow that fell over their young lives. For the rest they lived joyously and gladly, and if one of them was even for a few hours separated from the other, they were aware of the shadow, but the joy remained.

Storm in Heaven

"A man in solitude, says Aristotle, is no man but a beast or a god," Atys said, looking up and frowning as they sat in the sunshine on the steps of the theater.

It was one of those clamorous blue days when the air is filled with bird-song and the rustling of the trees is like an echo of bird-song. Down below on the stage Geresimos, wearing a simple white peasant's cloak and some rags of black goatskins around his neck and shoulders (for he was afraid of draughts and always heaped skins around his throat) was declaiming the speeches of King Creon in *Antigone*. He strode up and down the stage; there were long pauses while he lost himself in thought; he would recite a line and then repeat it in another tone, and then repeat it again, until he was pleased with his performance. He always listened to himself, and while one part of his mind was engaged in roaring out the words, another part was watching, studying, minutely examining the timbre and pitch and expression of every word which came from his lips. It was perhaps the nine hundredth time he had rehearsed the part of King Creon, and he played it as though it were the first.

A flock of starlings winging their way across the amphitheater caught the sunlight, so that every bird came to resemble a winged golden arrow. Strange that golden arrows should darken the sky. Geresimos shook his fist at the starlings. Their sudden flight had attracted his attention in mid-sentence. He raged at them, and he was still staring at the sky long after they had vanished.

"Well," said Atys, turning to Yeshua, "don't you believe me—a god or a beast?"

"All actors are beasts," Yeshua laughed, "and Geresimos is the king of beasts!"

"Then you agree with me that he lives in a profound solitude?" Atys asked. "On the stage—and he is only really alive on the stage —he embraces solitude like a lover. Sometimes I have the feeling he is never aware of an audience, and would be perfectly content without an audience. After all, we are the only people sitting on the steps, and it is certain he is not acting for us."

Yeshua sat there with his hands clasping his knees, leaning forward, drinking in the scene—that scene in which Geresimos as King Creon berated the messenger for not bringing the message sooner. There were four other actors on the stage, but Geresimos was so immersed in his own role he paid no attention to them.

"Then if he is not acting for us," Yeshua asked, "whom is he acting for?"

"The ideal spectator—the absolute Platonic spectator who exists in heaven—the archetype of all spectators, or at least the intelligent ones," Atys answered with a note of bitterness. "It is my opinion that when Geresimos is acting, a part of him escapes from himself and watches himself. And in fact, this happens with all good actors; they actually see themselves at a distance of six or seven feet. I don't know how it happens, but I know it *does* happen. Isn't that the most extraordinary thing about acting?"

"No, the most extraordinary thing is that an actor can die on the stage and come to life again."

Atys said nothing. It was odd how Yeshua always brought the conversation round to death and resurrection. He seemed to feast on resurrection and to find comfort in resurrections wherever they occurred, whether in the Orphic mysteries, in the rites of Isis and Osiris or in the rituals of Adonis. But today Atys was in no mood to discuss such things. It had been a long lazy morning, and he hoped Geresimos would rehearse until mid-afternoon. Yeshua shared the same hope. He was perfectly content to spend the rest of the day there, allowing the rich Greek words to sink into him, happy to be in the sun. Here and there among the curving seats of the theater were flower-boxes filled with yellow daisies and red poppies swaying stiffly and gleaming in the hot sun.

"Enough about resurrection!" Atys said. "As for me, I shall descend in the shadows with no pleasure at all—everything in me cries out to live in the sunlight. But if it happened that I was somehow reborn in the flesh, then I should regard it as a trick played by the gods and refuse to believe it. And really there is nothing remarkable in an actor dying on the stage and then jumping up again. It would be remarkable if he didn't jump up again."

Atys smiled, pleased with his argument. Some butterflies were hovering over the stage, and it amused him to see them coming close to Geresimos. They danced around him. They brushed his face. They were completely impervious to the solemnity of the occasion and not in the least frightened by the astonishingly penetrating voice of the actor playing the role of the tyrant of Thebes. And because the butterflies delighted him, he leaned forward and clapped his hands vigorously, shouting: *"Authis! Authis!"* at the top of his lungs. "Bravo! Bravo! Please do it again!" He was not addressing Geresimos: he was addressing the butterflies.

Geresimos must have heard Atys applauding for he stepped towards the front of the stage and said: "So you liked what I was doing?"

"Geresimos, you excelled yourself!"

"So I did! It was a gem, a little gem!" Geresimos replied. "Did you observe how the rage was controlled?"

"Yes."

"And then I threw it away and picked it up again later just at the right moment."

"Yes, I saw that."

"You understand, it is much better than roaring full-throatedly. A real rage is never a roaring. There are hills and valleys. It is like a storm in the woods—tremendous crashes of thunder, but afterwards there is only the rain falling. I truly believe, Agathon, this is the first time I have done Creon's speech well. It shows you are very observant to have noticed it."

Yeshua was not sure whether Geresimos was talking ironically. His enormous forehead shone white in the sun. He looked old and strained, and the sweat was pouring down his cheeks, and there were black patches of sweat on his white cloak.

"Now I shall go through the part again, and if you like, Agathon, you may play the part of the Messenger."

A suggestion from Geresimos amounted to an order. Agathon climbed on to the stage, then ran to the wings. Then he shambled towards Geresimos, pretending to be fearful, turning his head quickly from side to side as if he were being followed. And then, after many pauses and feints, approaching Geresimos, in a strange, queer, twisted voice, he began:

My Lord, I'll not say I am out of breath from running.
That is hardly the truth. Indeed, there were times
When I stopped to think and loitered on the road,
Saying to myself: 'Why hurry to your doom, old fellow.'
And then I said to myself: 'You'd better, hurry—
You have to get the news to Creon, don't you,
And if you fail, well, there's no hope for you!'
So here I am! I've got some sense in my head!
But the story I have to tell makes no sense at all . . .

Geresimos, his lips pursed, his head to one side, listened atten-
tively. He rolled his eyes, but otherwise gave no indication of
displeasure.

"I doubt whether you could do it worse," he said.

"May I begin again?" Atys asked contritely.

"No, you may not! Ask Yeshua to come up!"

So Yeshua climbed on the stage and took the part of the Messenger. After two years of training and another year of touring,
he knew the plays by heart. He spoke the speech well, with the
proper stupidity and the proper pride. He showed abject fear
when Creon roared. But when the time came to relate in detail
what he had seen—how the body of the Prince had been quietly
removed—he concealed boldness under a mask of servitude:

There was nothing there.
No sign of a mattock, no spade scratch anywhere.
The ground was hard and dry, no trace of a wheel.
No one left any clues. The guard at the morning watch
Showed us an unfathomable mystery—the corpse had vanished.
Or rather it was hidden from sight by a sprinkle of dust
Put there perhaps by a kindly stranger. And no sign
Of any dog or animal having mauled the body.
Of course a thing like that makes a man angry:
So we shouted at one another, but it did no good . . .

Geresimos was pleased with the performance. Yeshua had
spoken the words coarsely, heavily, even menacingly, but always
with a servile attention to the King's pleasure. When the King
frowned, the Messenger was all misery. When the King smiled,
the Messenger's face lit up. Somehow, with a hundred little ges-

tures, little changes of expression, Yeshua had contrived to portray the wretched dust-stained Messenger to the life. There was no Yeshua: there was only the Messenger.

"An extraordinary performance," Geresimos exclaimed. "For a moment I thought you were on stage in mask and buskins. I really thought you were the Messenger."

Yeshua was pleased with himself, and he was exhausted, even though it was a short speech. He had put into it every art he had learned from his teacher.

"You whined well," Geresimos went on. "Tell me exactly where you came from."

"The body of the Prince was about a mile away."

"So you were travel-stained?"

"Yes. And breathless from running—making the journey twice, for when I was near the King's palace I ran back again."

"To make sure you had seen the body and the dust lying on it?"

"Yes."

"You did superlatively well, Yeshua. You thought it out to the last word and the last gesture, every pause deliberate. Agathon made him nothing more than a born fool. Now you can go back and lie in the lazy sun and suck your thumbs. One day I'll give you the Messenger's part in a proper performance. Does that please you?"

Yeshua smiled. He had sung and danced in the chorus, understudied nearly everybody, designed settings and furniture, but he had never been called upon to play an entire role in a play. He was giddy with happiness, even though the part was brief. It was an important part and set the tone of the play, for it came at the beginning and announced the theme. So he went back to his place on the stone steps beside Atys, who was pleased with his success and whispered: "I saw the light shine," a phrase from the poet Pindar which he used whenever he saw anything that particularly pleased him. And then he said: "I told you you would be a great actor. Geresimos has been watching you carefully and has been looking out for an opportunity for you." At that moment Yeshua realized that the incident had been deliberately contrived by Atys, who had underplayed his part out of affection for Yeshua.

"For you see," Atys went on, "the role is admirably suited to you. The Messenger is quite young—Menarchus always plays it as an old man, and that is wrong! You played it wonderfully!"

The butterflies soared over the stage, and the bees were droning. It was one of those calm spring days when the air is perfumed,
and the faint winds only made the perfumes sweeter. There were
no clouds. Suddenly, far away, Yeshua thought he heard thunder.

There was nothing unusual in spring thunder along the coast.
Twenty or thirty miles out to sea there might be a storm, and the
thunder would be heard clearly in Ptolemais. But this thunder was
like a sudden warning of storms to come, very clear and sharp, and
it was followed immediately by a whistling in the trees.

"Did you hear the thunder?" Yeshua said, turning to Atys.

"Yes, I heard it," Atys said, still gazing at the stage.

"It was very strange," Yeshua said quietly.

"How is it strange? Surely you have heard thunder before,
Yeshua! Good heavens, you are behaving just like the Greeks, who
believe that thunder and lightning are messages from the gods.
Are you really afraid of that little clap of thunder we heard just a
few moments ago?"

Yeshua could not have told why he was so affected by the
thunder. The bees were still droning among the flowers and the
butterflies were still hovering over the stage.

Atys burst out laughing.

"What are you laughing at?" Yeshua asked.

"It just occurred to me that when we depict rascals on the stage,
we give them red cheeks and red hair like yours," Atys said.

"And when we depict country bumpkins," Yeshua answered
tartly, "we make them sunburned like you."

He was out of temper. The air seemed to be growing thick
around him. It often happened on spring days that the air would
grow quiet in the bowl of the amphitheater. For some inexplicable
reason there would be no flow of wind down into the hollow, and
the actors, accustomed to the small winds blowing about their
faces, would find themselves for a brief moment unable to breathe.
But now the air was flowing free again: not so freely as before. It
was not the quietness of the air so much as the remembered
thunderclap which disturbed Yeshua.

"One thunderclap and you turn pale!" Atys exclaimed. "Well,
the truth is you have been studying too hard. You labor over Greek
and Hebrew all night, and you expect to be a good actor by day.
You are burning the candle at both ends."

Yeshua was gazing down at the green scarab ring he wore on his middle finger. In some mysterious way the ring bound him to the stage.

"Did the thunder really surprise you?" Atys went on insistently. "I never thought the Jews paid any attention to thunder."

"They do," Yeshua said quietly. "Sometimes the thunder is the voice of God."

"You really believe that?"

"I believe more than that. I believe that the Coming of the Messiah will be attended by thunder and lightning. There will be the ringing of bells and the sound of a ram's horn and great pillars of darkness and flame will appear over the earth, and the choirs of angels will attend His coming! It is all written in the books, and I believe it firmly, because there is no reason why I should not believe it."

"Behold, the great authority on the Messiah!" Atys said. "So just now you heard the footsteps of the Messiah?"

"No, I heard the thunder," Yeshua answered stubbornly. "I am sure this time it was not the Coming of the Messiah."

Atys was sucking at a thin, juicy blade of grass.

"Then tell me," he said, "isn't it true that even when you are rehearsing your roles with us, your most intimate thoughts are still concerned with the Messiah and with God?"

"Yes, it is true."

"And so whatever happens here, you are always coloring your roles with your Jewish beliefs?"

"I suppose it is true."

"And you could not escape from it, even if you wanted to?"

"No, I couldn't escape, but I am a good actor and I shall play my roles as long as I have any power to play them. Of course I believe the Messiah will come. I believe the world needs a Savior, who will put an end to all the wickedness and evil on earth. I cannot believe the world will go on forever. I believe there will be a thunderclap and the Messiah will come, and there will be signs before His coming—"

"Such as?"

"Oh, they will be secret signs, and perhaps only the Messiah will know them. Perhaps the priests in the temple at Jerusalem will know them. And the Messiah Himself will suffer baptism by fire and water, for so it is written."

"And the thunderclap—is it the same as the thunderclap in *Œdipus at Colonus?*"

"It may be," Yeshua answered. "God knows, there are some places where the beliefs of Jews and Greeks touch. There are times when I find myself believing that Œdipus must be the brother of Elijah. I see a play by Sophocles, and sometimes it seems to me I am seeing a play that might have been written by Job."

"You mean there is a marriage between the Jews and the Greeks?"

"I believe there will come in time a marriage between the Greek and Jewish beliefs, but how it will come about I do not know."

Then they were quiet again, watching the actors on the stage, while the long blue shadows tumbled over the stage.

It was an exhausting day. All afternoon and far into the evening Geresimos paraded his actors and put them through their paces. He had decided to offer the three plays of the Œdipus cycle— *Œdipus the King, Œdipus at Colonus* and *Antigone*—on the following feast day and then take the plays on tour. After spending the afternoon rehearsing *Antigone,* he asked the actors to go through *Œdipus at Colonus.* When it was growing dark pitch-pine torches were lit and stuck in iron brackets on the stage. The torches threw off great spluttering scarlet flames and thick black ribbons of smoke, and the huge shadows of the actors danced across the stage wall. The air smelt of resinous pine and charcoal. It was a hot evening, but Geresimos insisted that the actors perform in costume, wearing heavy flowing robes, painted masks and stout thick-soled boots. The effect was splendid. The leaping shadows added to the drama. Geresimos sat in the gilded chair of Dionysus at the foot of the immense cliff of seats, watching his actors, leaning forward a little, himself directing the play in which he would have the leading part, for it was unthinkable that anyone else except Geresimos would play the part of Œdipus, and all the time he was either growling to himself or barking out sharp orders. He barked especially at Menarchus, who temporarily assumed the role of Œdipus.

"Harder! Harder!" he kept shouting. "Is the man weak? Can a hero be weak? No simpering! Let him be like a rock even as he topples!"

The mosquitoes were buzzing, and fireflies flickered strangely. A wind came up. Great black shadows leaped into the air and fell

back again. Alone on his gilded chair, seeing the play unrolling
before him, Geresimos was completely content.

Suddenly he shouted: "Where's Yeshua?"

Atys, who was playing the role of Antigone leading the blind
Œdipus to Athens, stepped in front of the stage and said: "He is
sleeping in the robing-room, master."

"Then bring him here. It is nonsense that he should be allowed
to sleep!"

Atys was about to say something about Yeshua's long studies at
night in the tenement in Ptolemais, but observing the expression
on Geresimos's face, he darted round the stage wall, found Yeshua
sleeping on a straw mat and brought him to where Geresimos was
sitting.

"So you slept when you should be watching the play?" Geresimos
shouted.

Half-awake, Yeshua hung his head in shame.

"Slept when I am performing *Œdipus at Colonus* by torchlight!
Slept when Agathon was playing magnificently! Slept on a warm-
scented night when, if you were not watching the play, you should
at least be playing with a girl! All right! Sit by my side and
observe carefully!"

Yeshua had watched the play many times. He thought he knew
every gesture, every intonation of the actors by heart. But tonight
with the torches gleaming like scarlet and black banners, the
mosquitoes humming and the fireflies darting and exploding in
little blue fires, with no moon in the dark sky, it seemed more
poignant than ever, richer in meaning, gripping the heart. King
Œdipus, wandering forlornly across the stage, with his dark-
socketed eyes, taller and more dominating than the other actors,
was a sight to tear at the heart-strings even when he was portrayed
by an actor who had not one tenth of Geresimos's own power. It
was simply that Geresimos wanted to observe the movement of the
actors, the way they held themselves and grouped themselves
around Œdipus, seeing them from a distance as the audience
would see them. Above all he wanted to see how the actors "played
to Œdipus": there must be no movement or gesture which de-
tracted from the hero's fallen majesty. "Give him air and sunlight,
and stay in the shadows!" he would say, and if anyone objected,
he would roar out: "Remember the title—*Œdipus at Colonus*! The
important thing is Œdipus! Theseus and Polynices and Creon, God

help them, have no tragedy in them—they are the causes of tragedy; let them feed Œdipus—it is their only purpose!" It was a bad
argument, though an effective one: he could not have used it for
the third play in the cycle, *Antigone,* which is more about King
Creon than about the daughter of Œdipus.

Menarchus acted well, though his voice seemed muffled. Atys
was superb in the role of Antigone. When he said: "Father, father,
I would some god would give thee eyes to see!" or when he lifted
his hands towards the dark sockets and declared: "O father, O
dear father, now art thou shrouded in eternal darkness," or when
he begged: "Lean on my arm; it is I who love thee!" Yeshua felt
the hot, bitter tears streaming down his cheeks. The actors had
vanished. The god-like heroes stalked the stage.

Geresimos, too, was affected. He kept nodding his head in time
to the musical beat of the verses. He chewed on apples and drank
wine from time to time, leaning forward to reach for the apples
under the chair without taking his eyes from the stage, and even
when he lifted the wine beaker to his lips he held his head in such
a way that he had a full view of the performance. Once he was so
moved by the cries of Antigone that he gripped an apple so firmly
in his hand that he squashed it to pulp: a thing he had never done
before and never thought he had the strength to do.

The eerie light on the stage moved him profoundly. He saw
things he never expected to see: a sudden flood of greenish blue
light on the robes of King Œdipus, the strange swirling of the
transparent robes of the chorus. The smell of night was on the
play. The flute player, who provided the only instrumental music,
excelled himself. The flashing cut-and-thrust of the dialogue with
Theseus, the sudden burst of hot passion in the middle of the play,
the soaring of the chorus, all this delighted him. When Œdipus
said:

> *I come to offer you*
> *A gift—my tortured body—a woeful sight,*
> *Yet it has a more lasting grace than beauty.*

Geresimos could stand it no more, for Menarchus had imitated his
own precise intonation, and he leaped up and shouted: "Bravo,
bravo! The night is bewitched! Now we shall play it again for the
comfort of our hearts!" Soon afterwards he turned to Yeshua and
said: "Did I ask you to play the Messenger in *Antigone?*"

"You did, master."

"Very well, then, I shall make you the Messenger in *Œdipus at Colonus*! It is a fatter part, and may you perform well in it!"

Then Geresimos clambered on to the stage, scattering the actors as he passed, his face crimson in the light of the bubbling pitch flares. He spat out an apple core as he passed among them, to disappear into the robing-room. He had been no more than five minutes in the robing-room when he emerged carrying the mask in his hands, a more splendid mask than the one worn by Menarchus, with a crown like a band of gold flames.

Standing in the middle of the stage, his legs wide apart, arms akimbo, wearing the mask like a helmet, he shouted: "Where is the trumpeter?"

"We have no trumpeter tonight," Atys whispered.

"Then find the trumpet and blow a peal to the gods, to tell them we are about to play *Œdipus at Colonus* as no one has ever seen it played before!"

Atys scurried away in search of the trumpet, while Geresimos paced the stage. The actors slaked their parched throats with wine. Once Geresimos went up to one of the iron brackets nailed against the stage wall, those brackets which supported the long black torches, and he gripped it firmly, perhaps trying it for strength. High above the stage a smoky black cloud from the torches hung over them.

Atys blew on the trumpet—a long, bright, lingering note which echoed against the empty hills. Then with a graceful gesture he tossed the trumpet in the air and did not trouble to see who caught it. The play was on. King Œdipus, white-haired and blind, his crown awry, wearing a patched gown, leaning on his daughter's arm, came tottering on the stage: and then there were no more actors: only the great hero and his sorrowing daughter and the road to Colonus.

The torches spluttered and shot out little flaming sparks. It was not that Geresimos had vanished: it was simply impossible to believe that Geresimos had ever lived. He had become Œdipus, Prince of Corinth and King of Thebes, "the greatest of men," weighed down with grief—a grief so great it would have stricken any other man. The man he had slain on the road between Corinth and Thebes was his own father; the woman who had borne him two sons and two daughters was his own mother. So desiring only

to die, he made his way to Athens to plead for a quiet refuge only
to be tormented by his enemies who desired that he should indeed
die in Athens—his bones would bring honor and blessing on the
city, but they were preparing to use his presence there for their
own evil advantage. And in every gesture, every fold of the tattered
gown, every lift and thrust of the mask, Œdipus demonstrated his
faith in the goddesses of terrible aspect to whom he prayed and his
secret knowledge that he would find rest and consummation at last.
And yet seeing the play now, with the torchlight reddening the
face of the hero, shadows like wings sweeping around him, as he
bent towards Antigone or turned away or let his head fall on his
chest, he was so implacably a hero caught in the toils of his own
heroism that it was impossible to know how the consummation
would be brought about. When Œdipus appeared, there was expectancy in the air: every gesture fraught with futurity. And
though Yeshua knew the play well, he hung on the words of
Œdipus and could not conceive how the play would end.

The actor playing a tragic part does not himself know the end of
the play, even though he has learned by heart every word written
by the dramatist. If he knew the end, if he felt in his bones that the
play consisted only of a succession of movements and gestures
moving towards a preordained conclusion, then he would fail to
portray the role. For him every moment must be new, every word
must spring from him like a fountain, every gesture must be clean
and fresh as the morning dew. He must employ powers which are
godlike when he plays a god or hero, and he must summon out of
his immense reserves of inner strength still greater reserves, for the
puny strength of a human being is unworthy of a dramatist's
enterprise. Hero or god, he dominates not only the players on the
stage but the whole audience. He flashes fire. He summons the
forces of nature to his aid. He is larger, more elemental, more
complete than the people we see around us; and this is why the
Greeks gave actors the greatest honor, and regarded them as
priests and mediators between earth and heaven, and allowed them
the privilege denied to all others of passing across all boundaries
without let or hindrance even in times of war. An actor was the
sacred vessel of the almighty powers. As Geresimos moved about
the stage he was aware of these powers: he was summoning elemental forces to his aid. He knew also that he was playing for no

audience, and could not summon to his aid that strange prov-
idential strength which lies in the gift of an audience, dispensing
strength and weakness as it desires. In front of him lay the mysterious dark wall of the semicircle of stone, from where on occasion
his own voice came echoing back to him; and it seemed to him
as he played that this dark blue wall was a great beast which
would spring on him the moment he failed to give his best. He did
not notice that Yeshua, who would not be called upon to play his
part in the play until near the end, was sitting in the gilded chair
of Dionysus, chewing apples.

Sometimes, and always inexplicably, the light from the pine
torches failed. Instead of a soaring and rippling flame there would
be only a small ember glow from the torches until suddenly the
flames soared up again. The play was gathering its momentum.
Œdipus had announced his mysterious purpose. Time was awake.
The great wheel was turning. Suddenly there came a distant peal
of thunder and Œdipus stared up at the heavens, where there were
no clouds and the stars shone brilliantly, and after a long and
terrible pause he said: "God has thrown His voice across the
heavens to summon me to death!" It was a voice of wild joy and
also of utter amazement, for never before had thunder pealed in
the clear sky at the moment dictated by the play. The terrible
moment passed. When the thunder roared again the chorus was
singing:

> *Hear the pealing thunder sound,*
> *A holy clamor in the air*
> *Strikes upon the holy ground,*
> *And terror holds us by the hair.*
> *See the solemn lightning strike!*
> *Where the sacred gods have frowned,*
> *The thunder cracks the earth apart—*

Out of the darkness the terrified Theseus announces that this
was no ordinary storm, but a storm in heaven. Œdipus shouts
jubilantly. The time of his consummation is at hand! He is young
again, lifting his head high, all his burdens falling from his
shoulders. But what was strange above any earthly strangeness
was that lightning was streaking across the heavens and the
thunder was coming closer. Theseus, robed in purple, was shouting

above the sound of the storm: "What proof have you that your hour is come?" Œdipus roared from his brazen throat:

> *The proof is everywhere. Incessant thunder,*
> *Raging and roaring meteors, silver-dripping lightning*
> *Hurled from the armory of invincible God!*

And then there was silence, with only the low growling of the thunder out to sea, while Œdipus, standing a little in front of the stage, with the leaping flames of torches behind and beside him, explained how he had come at last to the place where he would die, and no one would know the place:

> *There shall come*
> *A holy mystery which no tongue may name.*
> *You shall then see and know, coming alone*
> *To the place appointed. None shall know it:*
> *Not my own children whom I love and cherish,*
> *Only you shall come to the place, and never reveal*
> *This sacred haunt to anyone but in your dying moment.*
> *Whispering to your heir, then you shall tell it.*
> *Then he in turn may teach it to his heir,*
> *And so across the centuries, and so forever*
> *The secret shall be told; and hallowed Athens*
> *By my arts shall be saved.*
> *So let us wander now towards the place*
> *Where I shall vanish. See, now I lead you*
> *As once in a former time you led the way.*
> *Come. Do not touch me. Leave me to find*
> *The holy place of the earth which is my shroud!*
> *O, Hermes, guide me! And you, dark angel,*
> *Beloved Persephone—*

All the heavens were alive with lightning: the white marble semicircle was like a blinding silver bowl. Dazzled, lifting his hands to his darkened eyes, Œdipus made his way into the shadows. And then at last, in the silence following his disappearance, the Messenger leaped on the stage, standing there, looking up at the heavens, lifting the folds of his sleeves dramatically, wearing crimson garments and a gold fillet round his hair, his face no more than a mask, but a mask which spoke with voice of quiet savagery,

as though rebuking the assembled kings and princes and princesses
while he declared the fate which overcame Œdipus:

O wonder of wonders! Our Lord has gone,
And you who saw him go know how he went
Along the steep untraveled places,
Beyond the hollow pear-tree and the marble tomb,
And there he rested, sat down and soon removed
His tattered garments, then called his daughters to him,
Begged water from a stream to pour libations
And watched them going to the Hill of Demeter,
The goddess of the springs. When they returned
He took the water eagerly, then drank and poured
An offering for the dead. Then he put on
His robe and waited till the thunder spoke
Far, far below. The women trembled.
They fell at their father's knees and beat their breasts—
The raging thunder tore their hearts asunder—
Yet he was quiet, embracing them.
"Have no fear," he said. "This day I go
Towards the end prepared for me. O hard it is
For children when they see their father's death.
But one word lifts us up. The name of love
Makes the task easy. None shall love you more,
Than I have loved you. Now live without me."
And so they wept and clung together madly,
And he too wept, and then the sobbing ceased.
Then silence, and in the silence suddenly
A voice of terror shouted: "Come, Œdipus!
Too long you have delayed." He heard the summons;
Then asked that Theseus should be brought to him.
"Beloved King," he said, "give me your right hand now
As pledge for my poor children. Treat them humbly.
So let them be about you, treated lovingly,
And give them what is best of a King's love."

Then we withdrew and left the King alone,
And when we had gone a little way we turned.
There was no sign of Œdipus, but Theseus stood
With hands before his eyes as though he saw

Some awful thing he dared not look upon,
Fearful and unendurable; then he bowed
Low to the earth and air with one short prayer.
And we—I say we know not how our Lord
Perished upon the road. Only Theseus knows.
It was no lightning lit by the hand of God,
Nor vast sea-wave engulfing him. I believe
An angel from the gods attended him, or else
Earth's foundations opened to receive him.
And this I know: there was no sigh or groan,
No moan, no lamentation and no agony.
So he died. And if it seems to you
Like some wild dream of fancy beyond belief,
I say it happened so, and his brief dying
Was marvelous beyond all marvels known.

In Yeshua's speaking of the part there was a terrible power of conviction. So Œdipus had died, and no one could have believed it otherwise. When Yeshua spoke of the earth's foundations opening, he threw his arms wide apart, so that the consummation of Œdipus seemed to be taking place before your eyes. When he recited the words of Œdipus's daughters, he spoke them in a woman's voice, and somehow he even imitated their weeping. But the strangest thing of all was that his voice seemed to be married with the intermittent roar of thunder, and to have the power of thunder, rolling triumphantly from earth towards the storm in heaven.

They played no more that night. Lightning flashed across the sky; and the actors caught in the silver glare were rooted to the stage, until a clap of thunder more violent than any of the others sent them hurrying to the safety of the robing-rooms.

"The thunder!" Atys shouted, throwing himself into Yeshua's arms.

His eyes were wild, he was laughing and the hot sweat was streaking down his face, for he had worn the mask of Antigone and in the heat of the mask he could hardly breathe.

Soon afterwards, while the thunder roared overhead and the lightning blazed, Yeshua went to sleep on some straw matting and slept soundlessly. When he awoke the air was fresh and pure, and there was no sign of the great storm except for the wild branches and broken boughs scattered and strewn upon the stage.

The Almond Trees

For three months Geresimos took his actors on tour. They performed in Sepphoris, in Cæsarea, in Jerusalem, and as far to the South as Petra. They traveled in ox-carts, all the oxen garlanded, and with gilded horns. They carried scenery and costumes in wicker-baskets and carried banners in which the name of the company was inscribed in Greek, Hebrew and Aramaic. There were seven carts, but the actors traveled in the two leading carts; and whenever they came in sight of a village or a town they blew on their silver trumpets.

It was autumn again when they returned to Ptolemais. Yeshua's face was deep-flushed by the sun. He had grown taller and stronger. He wore his red hair cut short like the Greeks, with a fillet around his head. He had a long straight nose and a jutting chin and enormous eyes. He carried himself easily, with instinctive grace, holding his head a little to one side: he had grown an inch during the three-month journey.

Though every day he looked more and more like a Greek, he remained a Jew. Returning to Ptolemais, he still lived in the tall tenement building in the Jewish quarter, walking out to the theater whenever he was needed for playing or for rehearsals. At night he studied the Jewish texts or pored over the Greek dramatists: more and more he came to see a similarity between them. It was as though the prophets of Greece and Judæa mirrored one another. He translated *Amos*, the *Song of Songs*, many Psalms and much of *Isaiah* into Greek. He worked quietly and swiftly. Atys lived with him, but they lived their own lives apart. Often Atys vanished on mysterious errands of his own, not to return for two or three days. Once Atys said: "I live with you because I love you, and because I have great fears that you will work yourself to death. Someone must watch over you." And Yeshua smiled, saying: "God watches over me." "Then you have no need of me?" Atys asked. "Yes, I have need of you," Yeshua answered. "To the very end I shall have

need of you." But he could not say in words why he needed Atys
so greatly. It was like the affection he bore for Yona, a thing
beyond human understanding and beyond the flesh. It was not
necessary that Atys should be there: it was only necessary that Atys
should know he was loved.

One morning towards the end of summer Yeshua was lying in
bed after a long night spent in studying the ancient texts. He was
awakened by someone thumping heavily on the door. The sunlight
was pouring through a small window. Atys was away. It flashed
through Yeshua's mind that Atys had returned after a night spent
in the cabarets at the port. There was a stout bar of oak across the
door to prevent anyone from entering. There was no voice, no way
of knowing who was there—only the thumping of a clenched fist on
the wooden door, terribly repetitive. Yeshua jumped out of bed,
swung the bar over and threw the door open. The door opened so
violently that Geresimos almost fell into the room.

"I greet the sun for you," Yeshua said, lifting his hands to his lips
in the Greek manner.

Geresimos said nothing. He simply stared round the small,
cluttered room: there were shelves full of colored tiles, old silver
coins, a pottery head of Apollo, Greek and Hebrew scrolls. Yeshua
had seen Geresimos two days before, but in the interval the man
had changed. There were black circles round his eyes. His cheeks
hung heavy. There was a strange sickly smell coming from his
robe, and at first Yeshua thought he was drunk. He came into the
room and looked around with a terrible, hopeless expression. He
was no longer the great tragic actor whose heaven-storming voice
sent the people of all the cities of Palestine into ecstasies.

"Have you seen Agathon?" Geresimos asked in a soft pleading
voice. "They tell me he lives with you."

"I saw him yesterday."

"Where?"

"In the market-place."

"But doesn't he live here, Yeshua? Please tell me the truth!
Doesn't he live here?"

"Yes, he lives with me, but sometimes—" Yeshua shrugged his
shoulders and smiled a quick happy smile.

Geresimos said nothing. He was no longer looking round the
room. He had withdrawn into himself. He made strange little
sucking noises and sometimes a faint smile flickered on his worn

features and sometimes he trembled. He gazed at Yeshua with a
veiled look, full of tenderness and compassion.

"Please tell me the truth," he said at last. "Are you sure you have
not seen him? I have looked everywhere! He was to come to the
rehearsal yesterday, but there was no sign of him. Of course we
have had arguments, terrible arguments! Everyone knows Agathon
is proud, and sometimes for his own sake, you understand, I have
to speak strongly to him."

Geresimos picked up one of the dusty scrolls lying on the shelf
and absent-mindedly began to unroll it, holding it upside down.

"Can you read Hebrew?"

"Yes."

"Well, I should have known. You are a Jew and you come from
Nazareth, I remember. Agathon tells me about you sometimes.
Are you sure you haven't seen him?"

"Quite sure. I saw him in the market-place yesterday afternoon
and since then—"

"Everyone tells me lies," Geresimos sighed. "I have been searching for him everywhere. I had a terrible dream during the night.
It's really too dark to be looking for him."

"It is not dark. It is bright sunlight."

There was a long pause, and then Geresimos gave one of his
small fleeting smiles and said: "For me it is night."

It occurred to Yeshua that Geresimos had gone mad. He looked
like a man who has run screaming through the streets and then
when he can scream no longer simply babbles in hoarse whispers.
His heavy beard was awry, his face swollen, his thick gray hair was
uncombed. Tall and powerful, his eyes unnaturally bright, his
huge hands hanging helpless at his side, he stood in the middle of
the room like someone who has forgotten why he has come.

"Yes, for me it is night," Geresimos repeated, and he lifted his
hand to hide the sunlight streaming into his eyes.

"I am sure he is somewhere quite near," Yeshua said. "You are
taking it too much to heart. He vanishes for two or three days on
end, but he always returns."

"You are sure he returns?"

"He has never failed."

Geresimos held his head a little to one side, imitating Yeshua.
Once again there was that terrible smile, and the quick diamond-
bright gleam in his eyes.

"Think," said Yeshua. "Surely there are places where he may be."

"I have looked everywhere," Geresimos answered. "Last night all the actors were searching for him. What is the use of looking?"

"Have you been to the theater?"

"Yes, dear boy, of course I have been to the theater."

"He may have returned there, Geresimos. If he knew you wanted him, he would return."

"You are quite sure?"

"Yes, I am quite sure."

Geresimos nodded. They walked down to the street, in silence. Then in silence they made their way across the city, past the forum and the baths, skirting the Syrian quarter, and then into the country. There was no sign of Atys at the theater. The stage was empty, so were the dressing-rooms, and on the stone seats there was no one —all the actors were evidently searching for Atys.

They wandered back to the city. First they went to the small house by the seashore where Geresimos lived, but there was no sign of Atys there. They went back to the center of the city. Geresimos went up to complete strangers and said: "Tell me, friend, have you seen Agathon?" If they asked which Agathon, for there were many Greeks in Ptolemais with the same name, Geresimos answered nothing at all, but simply bowed his head. Once when they were climbing the steps of the law courts—it occurred to Geresimos that Atys might be attending the trial of some pirates caught red-handed entering the harbor at Sidon—Geresimos said: "Why has he deserted me? Do you know what I will do when I find him? I will beat him until the blood comes out of his skin!"

There was such fierce passion in the old man's voice that Yeshua shuddered.

"No, it were better to kiss him," Yeshua murmured.

Geresimos glared angrily.

"And does it mean nothing that he has deserted me, and without warning?" Geresimos said. "Doesn't he know that I have need of him? Let be, let be!"

Saying this, Geresimos suddenly swung up the last steps to the law courts, and then turned to look down on the forum, leaning forward a little, unsteady on his feet, so that he was in danger of falling down the whole flight of steps, until Yeshua gripped his hand and pulled him to the safety of the portico; but in the law courts there was only the humming of voices and the rustle of the

heavy embroidered gowns worn by the advocates and there was
no sign of Atys.

They walked through the streets in silence, the glare of the white
marble buildings blinding them. Never before had Yeshua seen
such desperate loneliness, such misery, on the face of the old actor.
As the shadows lengthened the afternoon grew hotter, heavier and
more ominously silent.

They went to the baths and to the library; and in those two
places, where Geresimos was so frequent a visitor, people called
out his name, but he affected not to hear them. He followed
Yeshua, as a dog follows his master. Sometimes Yeshua saw him
shaping words on his lips: "Where are you, Agathon? Why have
you deserted me? Are you not ashamed?" A youth as handsome as
Atys, with the same kind of fair skin, the same mass of black curling hair, the same curiously aware look, emerged from the baths,
dripping silver with water, and shouted: "Ho, Geresimos, when
shall we act together?" Geresimos stared at the youth strangely.
The sunlight was beginning to fade, and the wind swept the scent
of oleanders among the columns. In this light the boy's body looked
like beaten gold on which quicksilver is playing.

"You are not Agathon," Geresimos said, shaking his head.

"Of course I am not Agathon," the boy laughed. "I am Apollo-
dorus, but I would act with Geresimos."

"Some other day," Geresimos murmured; and then taking
Yeshua's arm, he walked silently away.

Then it was evening, and the striped awnings in the market-
place were being taken down. The meat-shops were closing, and
soon only the silk-merchants and the dove-sellers were left in the
square. Women passed, scented and trailing the painted transparent veils which covered their faces. Geresimos did not see
them. He saw no one, not even the little dark-skinned Syrian boy
who led an enormous muzzled brown bear on a chain across the
market-place just a few steps in front of him. People stopped and
watched Geresimos and shook their heads. "Œdipus has become a
god," they whispered. "His eyes are sightless, but he is a god
nevertheless."

At last, wearying of their fruitless progress, Yeshua suggested
they should go to the seashore.

"Listen, Geresimos, we may find him by the sea. At least there is more light there, and we shall not have to walk through the infernal shadows."

Yeshua was quoting a line from Sophocles' play *The Labours of Hercules*. Suddenly the weight of misery seemed to lift from Geresimos. He smiled and said: "You quote well. Yes, you will be a good actor if you work hard enough. We will have to find some money and send you to Athens. Do you want to go to Athens?"

"Why Athens? I can learn everything here, master. You will teach me."

Geresimos shook his head sorrowfully from side to side.

"I shall not be a good teacher without Agathon," he said, weeping, "He is the son of my old age. Do you know what it means to have a son in old age? He was born of a Syrian mother, but he is a Greek, because he is my son!" And then while the tears trickled down his cheeks into his beard, he kept saying: "My son, my son, Agathon, the son of my old age!"

Yeshua had half guessed that his friend was the son of Geresimos, but had never dared to question Atys, never admitted to himself that he had suspected such a thing. He stole a glance at the old actor, the jutting forehead, the thick gray beard, the heavy lips, the enormous eyes. No, it was not an outward resemblance. Somewhere deep down, in some almost unapproachable place, there was a similarity between them. It was something unexpressed, no more than a hint, something in the slant of the eyes and the way the light gathered in the eyeballs, in the curve of their foreheads perhaps, for the curve of the forehead follows the mind's curve. Yeshua heard himself saying: "There is no greater love than the love between a father and a son. It goes beyond the love of women."

"Surely," said Geresimos, and once again he fell into a fit of weeping.

Along the seashore, beside the winding road, lay a grove of almond trees, and here they rested. The sticky white buds were bursting and filling the air with an overpowering fragrance. Geresimos leaned on his staff, staring out to sea and shading his eyes. Here, along the shore, the light was blinding. Fishing boats were bobbing up and down, close to the shore; some fishermen were bringing in their nets. The smell of fresh fish came with the wind, and the smell of the salt sea, and the smell of the almond grove, and somehow all these combined to produce a smell of quite unusual freshness and sweetness. The sun caught the small temple to Serapis on the cliff, which was all bronze now; and below the cliff lay a wattle-roofed fisherman's hut. One of the fishing boats, painted bright red with an enormous blue eye at the prow, was coming to shore close to the hut. Usually, when fishermen bring their catch to shore, they sing out raucously, shouting to the world how many fish they have caught in their nets; but this boat came silently.

Geresimos could not take his eyes from the boat. He gazed at it with a terrible intensity, his mouth open, his eyes bulging. Sweat trickled through his beard, and once he put his hand up to his mouth as though to stifle a groan. He watched the men as they dropped into the water and pulled the scarlet boat ashore. He watched every movement they made as they carried the fish in huge flat baskets on shore. Then quite suddenly a cloud shaped like a pearly fish covered the descending sun, and the great thumping heart of happiness which had uplifted Yeshua from the moment when he set eyes on the sea gave place to an inexplicable sense of warning. Geresimos flung his staff away, and began to run towards the scarlet boat. He ran like a madman, shouting at the top of his voice, his hair blowing wild, his elbows jerking. Yeshua ran after him, shouting that there was no hurry, they were only fishermen, why was he hurrying? The fishermen were carrying something off the boat. They made no sound. The nets of woven green rope hung limp along the sides of the boat; and there, lying in the shadow of the ship's prow, quite naked, lay a boy with a golden skin who seemed to be sleeping. He looked about sixteen years old, with a round dark sunburned face, and there were some pearls of water in his thick black hair, though there was no water on his body. He lay with his head bent a little to the shoulder, and one hand lay upon his chest. Lying there in the small shade, he gave the impression of someone enjoying the perfect laziness of summer; and there was a soft yellow smear of sand on one of his cheeks. He was dead. He had been dead for perhaps two hours, for the fishermen had caught him in their nets when they were still close to shore, and they said they had seen him swimming out to sea earlier in the afternoon.

Atys looked more beautiful in death than ever in his life. He was so calm and quiet in the sand, and every part of him so perfect, that Yeshua was more conscious of the boy's beauty than of his loss; and there was more admiration than sorrow in the brown faces of the fishermen. Atys lay there like someone still expecting the touch of the wind to awaken him from slumber; and when one of the young fishermen spoke of bringing a shroud, it seemed the highest indecency and the greatest wrong that he should not be given back to the sea whence he had come; and no one would have been in the least surprised if Atys had suddenly jumped up and flung himself upon the waves.

The fish were not dead yet. They were piled high in great silver piles; and as they tossed and threw themselves up in the air, shedding their scales, they rustled like leaves. As the sun sank, bonfires could be seen blazing along the coast.

The fishermen drew back when Geresimos forced his way among them. At first the old actor did not recognize his son; the face was fuller, the flesh so subtly swollen that it had assumed another countenance. Geresimos groaned. He started, and then turned slowly to meet the gaze of the other fishermen, and then bent his head, afraid of their compassion, the hurt in their eyes. He said softly: "Agathon, my son, where are you?" and then looked down at the body at his feet, surprised it was there. All the time his huge body was shaking, as if caught in a whirlwind.

When Yeshua recognized Atys, he screamed and shouted at the top of his voice: "Come back! Come back! Oh, Atys, come back to me!" He flung himself down beside the body, so strangely cold, and kissed the sleeping face, which shone with the dew of death. He huddled close to it, thinking he could warm it into life again, while the ragged fishermen nodded their heads and murmured prayers to the goddess Astarte. Lying at full length beside Atys, Yeshua began to repeat his friend's name over and over again, mournfully, in a voice from which all hope had been abstracted. Geresimos was kneeling beside him. The old man knelt there with his face averted, staring into space, seeing nothing but the changing shapes of despair.

"Yeshua, listen to me," Geresimos said helplessly. "You must be my son, do you understand? One son has been taken from me, and you have come to take his place. It is all simple—it is all written down somewhere. And now help me, Yeshua. I have heard that the flowering almond trees are the signs of resurrection. Oh, my son, let us take him there, so that he can rest through the night, and let us keep vigil."

"Then we shall all keep vigil with you," the fishermen said. "But tell us first who this boy is."

There was no answer from Geresimos. Soon, as darkness was descending, the fishermen helping them, Geresimos and Yeshua carried Atys to the grove of almond trees.

A City in the Sun

For days Yeshua wandered like someone in a daze. He was sick with grief, sick with fever. He haunted the places where he had wandered alone with Atys: the cliff with the blue statue of Serapis, the woodland behind the theater, the beach where they swam together. The days were dark and the rain fell, as he wandered along the shore, where the women hung up their frail fishing-nets, hoping the rains would cease. Sometimes he went into Ptolemais, gliding like a ghost in the dark alleyways, keeping close to the walls, never going near the baths or the places where the actors congregated, never going to his own lodgings because they were full of memories of Atys. He became gaunt and thin, slept in the open, in the rain, with only a sheepskin covering him. And sometimes out of hunger he would steal into the market-place, and buy a honeycomb or some other small thing, a handful of olives or some wheat-cakes, and then go on his way, a strange gaunt creature who belonged to the night and the shadows. Sometimes Geresimos or one of the other actors would catch a glimpse of him and run hurrying after him; then he would go running fleet as the wind with the actors in pursuit, to disappear in some hiding place. At night he stood by the seashore gazing enviously at the sea which had taken Atys from him.

He cursed the sea. He cursed the grove of almond trees, where the body of Atys lay on the night of his death. With the wind in his face and the tideless sea at his feet, he cursed himself for having given way to grief.

On his last night in Ptolemais he went up to the temple on the cliff. He went there only because it was a quiet place, sacred to him: sacred because of Atys, not because of Serapis. It was a wild night with black clouds scudding across the moon, all darkness and emptiness, with no ships at sea, and Ptolemais lost in the murk of darkness below. The statue of Serapis shone dimly with a greenish hue. Everything in the small temple was damp and chill. His teeth were chattering. He threw himself down in the wet straw at the foot of the statue, thinking to sleep, thinking to allay his grief, not knowing what else he would do there, or how long he would remain, in the loneliness of his grief, and sometimes he found himself murmuring some of the lines spoken by Atys, Atys in the role of Antigone: "Father, father, I would some god would give thee eyes to see!" Atys shouting in ringing tones: "O father, O dear father, now art thou shrouded in eternal darkness!" Always the young Atys stepping on to the stage, the terrible white mask bowed in grief, and the rich pure voice pouring out of painted lips!

"He is dead! He is dead!" Yeshua sobbed, as though just now, for the first time, the full realization of his friend's death had occurred to him.

"The old die, and this is a little thing, but when the young die—"

He lay on the straw like a spreadeagled bird, burying his face in the damp and the dirt, not knowing where he was, not caring. Fleetingly, there came to him the image of Yona. Beyond Atys was Yona; and he had known Yona only for a little while, before his father had torn him from Jerusalem. And he knew he would see Yona again, but not now, not for many years. He could not explain it to himself—this need, this knowledge, this grief, which was unending like the sea. To be alone: this he could bear and had borne: but to know that others have need of you— Even now Atys had need of him! Then where should he go? Should he follow Atys into the grave? And where then? And there was no answer to these questions: only the certainty that the answers would come at the appointed time. He told himself that the death of Atys was a punishment for his sins, for having turned his back on Jerusalem. Then he recoiled in horror. Not for this! Not for this! There was such innocence in Atys that the very heavens proclaimed it! Atys

had not died as a punishment for his sins! There was no reason for
his death. He had been swimming, perhaps after a heavy meal, and
suddenly suffering from cramps had lost all power of motion, had
simply surrendered to the power of the sea. And now was no
more. And now lay in a shallow grave beyond the almond trees, so
still, so quiet, that the offending rains must show their mercy to
him, leaving him untouched. And he knew it was untrue. Soon
there would be nothing: no bones, no flesh, nothing at all, for no
one buried on the sea coast survives in the flesh.

He turned, thinking he heard footsteps, but it was only the wind
in the dead flowers at the foot of the statue of Serapis. He tried to
sleep, but no sleep came. He was cold, and wrapped himself more
tightly in the sheepskin, waiting for the moonlight to strike the
temple, but when the moonlight was about to strike the columns,
another dark cloud scudded over.

"Lost, lost!" he said. "The beauty and the brightness—all lost!"

He did not know how long he stayed there. Suddenly, unexpectedly, while he was still lying among the dead flowers, the
offerings of peasant girls who climbed the cliff at dawn and sunset,
a sense of quietness came over him. He would go no further. He
would no longer torment himself. He told himself the dark ghost
who haunted Ptolemais would vanish—away, away, out of this
world! *Let your light shine upon men. Travel far. Learn—learn—* It
was his father's voice, and he knew there was no escape from it.
In the darkness, some hours before dawn, he rose, took up the stout
acacia staff which he carried at all times, and went down to the
harbor of Ptolemais. As always there were ships in the harbor. On
this windy night no one troubled to guard them. He slipped on
to the first ship he came to, climbed down in the deserted hold, and
went to sleep, telling himself he would go wherever the ship took
him.

When he awoke, the night's storm was over, the ship had already
put to sea and the sun was shining.

"Ho, there! Thou art like unto a dead donkey with thy bloated
head in the scuppers! And shall a dead donkey ride upon a lion,
eh?"

The old sailor had a skin of scarlet parchment wrinkled in a
million folds, and watery red eyes. He had the heavy hooked wide-
at-the-bridge nose of a Phoenician, and wore a greasy felt skull-

cap and trousers of coarse sailcloth. He smelled of wine, but on that morning everything smelled of wine, and the scuppers were swilling with it.

"Where am I?" Yeshua said, staring round the dark hold, where the smell of the sea and the smell of wine were overpowering. He was still half asleep.

"Thou art on a ship called the *Lion*, and thou art a donkey!" the old sailor said with rough kindness. "Thou wert near dead with wine, and if I had not found thee, thou wouldst have been drowned in it! Art thou a thief, then, for having escaped from Ptolemais?"

There was a stout stick in the old sailor's hands, and now he began to swing the stick lightly, and then he tossed it from one hand to the other.

"I asked whether thou wert a thief."

"Nay, not a thief—" Yeshua began, rising out of the scuppers, his long gown clinging to him.

The whole gown was dyed purple with the wine, and the wine had soaked into his hair, and there were stains of it on his face. It was so soaked with wine that he had difficulty in rising. The old sailor roared with laughter to see him so ungainly, and began to prod him with the stick.

"Atys is dead!" Yeshua said. "I came because Atys is dead!" He went on babbling about Atys, because the fumes of the wine intoxicated him and because he had been dreaming of Atys while he slept. He thought he was still dreaming. He tried to squeeze some of the wine out of his gown. He could not understand why he was drenched in it.

"Thou shalt have that smell about thee for everlasting." The old sailor laughed. "And who is Atys?"

"God has taken him," Yeshua answered, and turned his face away: there was such a look of blank horror there that the old sailor felt a pang of pity.

"Was he thy friend then?"

"He was more than friend, and yet not quite a friend," Yeshua answered, as though he were describing Atys to himself. "He died in the sea, as I would die."

"Then the fishes shall make a meal of thee," the old sailor laughed. "A pretty dish for fishes! Well, they say wine is a consolation, but I see thou hast imbibed enough consolation to last thee

a hundred dead friends! And good wine, too! That storm last night
stove in some twenty barrels. Didst thou sleep through it?"

Yeshua nodded. Through the hatchway he could see the mast
and the great yellow sails swinging against a perfectly blue sky;
seagulls were screaming at the mast-head; somewhere at the other
end of the ship some sailors were singing. Sweeter than their song
was the slapping of the sea against the strakes. The old sailor began to turn away. It was hot and close in the hold, and the wine
fumes were making his eyes water.

"Go clean thyself," the old sailor muttered, and he was half-way
up the ladder before it occurred to him that he knew nothing
about the youth who had spent the night sleeping through a storm,
with three or four hundred wine casks, unloosened from their
ropes, tumbling about him. He turned back to look at the boy. And
then seeing the silly expression on Yeshua's face, for he looked like
someone who had drunk heavily, he said: "The gods protect all
wine-bibbers, that's for sure! Well, what's thy name, boy?"

"Yeshua."

"A Jew, eh, and not seasick yet?" the old sailor laughed, remembering the few Jews who had traveled on the ship. "And where
from?"

"From Nazareth."

"And where's that?"

"In Galilee."

"A fisherman, eh? I have heard that all Galileans are fishermen
and liars."

"I was a shepherd, and shepherds are never liars."

"Well, there's some truth in that. A shepherd is as foolish as his
sheep."

"I was a good shepherd."

"So you say. I could give you some dolphins and see how you
shepherd them. You speak Greek well for a shepherd. Strip off
your clothes, boy, and dry them in the sun. I'll have work for you."
And then in a simpering voice, the old sailor went on: "But I see
thou art delicate-fleshed. Canst thou work a sail and climb the
yards?"

"I can, if others can."

"Then thou wilt make a good sailor, and if I am foolish I shall
apprentice thee."

And with that the old sailor, his face wrinkled with cunning laughter, so that he resembled Ulysses, climbed out of the hatch, leaving Yeshua behind to peel off his wine-drenched gown and climb out naked.

The smell of wine accompanied Yeshua to Egypt. Everything on the ship from the patched sails to the planking, and from the curving prow with the grotesque yellow eyes painted on it to the short, stubby stern-post decorated with a lion-head, smelt of wine; and this wine-smell came not only from the staved casks in the holds, but from the ancient wines of Lebanon which the old ship had brought long ago along these sea-lanes, so that sometimes standing on the poop or manning the oars Yeshua smelt an unfamiliar wine, vinegary, or very sweet, rising in a mysterious steam from the wood on which it had been spilt on previous voyages.

There were days when they were becalmed and all the sailors were forced to man the oars, and other days when they went whipping along with a following wind, the sea a deep blue and the seagulls of a startling whiteness overhead.

The old captain grew fond of Yeshua and spoke seriously of apprenticing him.

"I see thou hast good wits and can climb the yards easily, but thou hast a stubbornness in thee," he said, and he would look at Yeshua critically, as though he could see in front of him some flaw in the youth's character.

Yeshua had showed no signs of stubbornness. He had obeyed all orders at the instant.

"Then how am I stubborn?" he asked.

"I see it in thy eyes, which are the color of the sea. I shall not apprentice thee till I feel more sure of thee."

It was odd how the captain puzzled over Yeshua.

"And who is Atys?" the old sailor asked one evening when Yeshua was looking out to landward, seeing for the first time during this journey the green palms and yellow coast of Egypt.

Yeshua was frightened. It was the last thing he had expected the old sailor to say.

"When I found thee all soaking in wine, why, thou couldst think of nothing else to say but: 'Poor Atys, he is dead! I came because Atys is dead!' Thou wast a figure of grief! And now, after but five days journeying, thou hast health in thee! Well, Atys is dead and Yeshua is alive, and the gods be praised for it!" Then for some reason which was beyond all Yeshua's comprehension, the old

sailor began to talk of the theater and of the performances he had
seen and even mentioned a famous performance of Œdipus at
Colonus, but if he recognized Yeshua he gave no sign.

That night, when they sailed into the harbor of Alexandria,
Yeshua decided to slip away. He was tempted to remain with the
wine ship. At sea there are no responsibilities, no tragedies: a man
lives healthily with the sea wind in his face. He liked the old
captain, who hinted Yeshua might become a ship's master in time,
and he liked the crew, and he liked the sea, but he knew he must
go onward. So when the captain was sleeping and the crew were
on shore, he simply walked down the gangplank and made his way
to Alexandria.

For three months he wandered in the Delta along the banks of
the canals, sleeping in the fields, resting in the hot noon in the
shade of palm trees, begging for food. The sun burned him until
he was almost as dark as the slaves working in the fields. And
always he remembered Atys—not the Atys who paraded in mask
or scarlet gown across the stage, but the Atys who lived with him
in the Jewish quarter in Ptolemais, the Atys who lay dead under
the almond trees.

Once, haunted by grief and misery, wandering down a deserted
lane in the loneliness of evening, when the shadows were falling
around him like leaves, the memory of Atys oppressed him so
greatly that he fell on his knees and cried out: "O my Lord and
my God, if I think of Thee day and night, am I not in Thy hands?
Surely Thou canst protect me from grief?" And saying this, he
grew calmer than he had been for many weeks.

So he wandered in Egypt, and he knew that in time there would
be an end to his grief, but he did not know how it would end. He
was waiting for a sign. Perhaps there would come another youth
to share his loneliness. Perhaps it would be a woman. He did not
know. Indeed, he was content to walk alone, for he was never
alone: the Lord God was with him, and he blessed the Lord all
the days of his wandering.

He blessed the Lord even when he found himself in the desert,
feeling its furnace heat on his face, the gusts of hot desert wind
burning him. He blessed the Lord in his grief and when he was
ill, and when he was walking carefree in the shade. When he saw
the great barges with curving lotus prows and purple sails gliding
along the Nile, or the great stone pyramids flashing their white-

ness on the surrounding air, or the slender long-legged women
who carried baskets of fruit on their heads, he blessed the Lord
and uttered prayers for Egypt.

One evening, shortly after nightfall, when the moonlight was
turning the canal into a broad stream of shining metal, he saw a
white city in the distance and was filled with a strange feeling that
he had been there before. The high walls of the city were made of
a stone which glinted fiery blue-white in the moonlight, whereas
the pyramid which lay to the east on the other side of the canal
some four or five miles distant shone a duller white and further
away another pyramid glowed a shimmering gray. In the moonlight the city resembled a vast horn lantern lit with an intense blue
flame. Above the walls immense blue-white obelisks rose like
swords piercing the moonlit sky, and the humming noise of the
city was like the noise of Jerusalem on the days of Passover. When
he drew closer, the gleaming blue-white walls blinded him, so
that he had to shield his eyes with his hands.

"Strange city," he murmured, and closed his eyes, trying to
remember in darkness how he could have seen it before: he was
sure now he had walked along this pathway in some former time.

"I have seen those obelisks," he told himself. "I have seen these
dovecotes. I see myself—is it a nightmare?—walking along this very
road and holding my father's hand."

Soon the memories came crowding back to him, faint, indistinct,
always ghostly, memories full of shadows and torchlight: of long
nights spent huddled in secret corners; of going to sleep in a donkey's pannier; of his mother singing him to sleep, and then whispering to him to awake hurriedly, because there could be no rest
during these long night-rides: he must feed at her breast while she
still rode on the donkey. It was strange how these memories came
with the gleam of moonlight on the walls of a city. Then he said
aloud: "Beth-shamesh," and then the memories came crowding
more urgently, one memory flowing over another, until he was
overwhelmed by all this richness coming out of the past.

In all those months of wandering in Egypt he had been dimly
aware he would come to Beth-shamesh in the end. He had even
avoided the place deliberately, for fear he would reach it when he
was unprepared. He had been a small child when he came there
at the time of the proscriptions, still sucking at the breast, and yet
he remembered it. But it was not those early days he remembered

so well as the days when he was learning to walk—beside this canal he had first tottered into his mother's arms. So he said softly: "Blessed be Beth-shamesh," and thought of the day when his feet first touched the earth in the most sacred city of Egypt, for enclosed within its walls was the Great Hall of the Gods and here the Arabian Phœnix had died into immortality, its great nest being preserved in a basket of pure gold in one of the temples. Here the goddess Isis had spent the first of those long nights after her husband Osiris was slain, and here Joseph had married the daughter of Potiphera the High Priest. Here Plato had walked, for many Greeks lived there, and a whole section of the city was given over to the Jews, who took charge of all merchandise entering and leaving the city. Here, too, the Egyptians had founded the first university and scholars came here from all over the world. It had many names: the Egyptians called it Annumeht, which they sometimes shortened to An; the Greeks called it Heliopolis and the Jews called it Beth-shamesh, and both names meant the City of the Sun. And this city, older than Israel, shaped like a ship or a bird, with its hosts of obelisks where the storks nested, with its hundreds of temples, its thousands of white-robed priests, its great gardens and colonnaded streets, was still fanned by the Phœnix's wings and was still the most hallowed city in Egypt.

"How strange, beautiful and wonderful is the City of the Sun in the moonlight," he said, and all the time he was feasting upon the high walls in a kind of trance, seeing himself as a child, lost among the myriad pathways of his memories, remembering a garden somewhere and then a willow tree and his mother sitting on a stone bench below the willow, resting after the long journey, while high above him, almost blotting out the sun, rose an immense pointed obelisk; and then his mind went wandering along the dusty, cobbled streets of the city, while he rode on a donkey, riding in front of his father, a child of two and already able to ride, while the hot sun flashed from the porticoes of temples and streamed in fierce radiance from the obelisks plated with gold.

He was still nearly a mile from the city and weary after long wandering. Along the canal the barges had pulled up for the night, and he saw the small fires gleaming on the decks and heard the bargemen as they prepared to bed down for the night; and somewhere among the reeds the lovers were whispering. Beyond the long lanes of palm trees the cotton-fields glistened.

For Yeshua, it was pure benediction to be there: to be confronting his own childhood. He said: "Beth-shamesh" again, and the word was like a spell, putting an end to his griefs and all the fever of his wanderings. And he knew he would stay there, perhaps for many years. He would learn Egyptian, he would study in the schools, he would pay reverence to the golden basket where the Phœnix brought its ashes after raising itself to life. He remembered Atys saying: "The Egyptians are the fathers of us all." He remembered the Egyptians he had seen in Sepphoris and Ptolemais, fair of face and hawk-like, unlike the dark peasants in the Egyptian fields. And now as he wandered towards Beth-shamesh he was glad to leave the months of wandering behind and to enter a city again.

So he walked towards the gates, and when he came near them hundreds of bats swooped low over his head and once again he heard the vast murmur of the city. Once inside the walls, he saw white temples, groves of sycamores, springing fountains; from somewhere there came the voices of the priests chanting. And yet the city was quiet, and the men in long white robes who walked along the shadowy pathways moved silently, dream-like, strangely remote. No one paid any attention to him, and he remained in the shadows.

All night he wandered through the city. Towards morning he fell asleep in a grove of tamarisks beside one of the temples, near a lake crowded with lotuses. When he awoke it was noon. He drank some water from the lake and ate some dates, and then continued his wandering, coming out into the Jewish quarter, where many of the buildings had crumbled during the recent floods, and heaps of rubble lay everywhere: ditches, and ragged blue palms, and broken walls, and dust everywhere. A strange city, half in ruins: one half crumbling away and the other half gleaming with white marble. It had looked so new from outside, but there were places where he had to climb over pyramids of rubble and other places where the streets were too filthy to pass through. People lived in hovels or threw up matting against broken walls; and the air was loud with the black thunder of flies.

He wandered ghost-like, lost in himself, lost in his dreams. It was four hundred years since Plato had walked through these streets. A vague anger moved in him that the city should have seemed so beautiful, like a fruit with a rotten core. Near the gates the white temples and obelisks gleamed with a pure fire, but beyond the temples lay the ruins, where people walked listless in the heat. Once he stopped beside a drinking fountain set in the wall of a white tomb, where a native girl was drinking. She stood on tiptoe, her head thrown back, her lips pouted forward to meet the small basin; the lines of her body fell away, rigid from the strain, but perfect in grace and form; and the dull pink linen gown fell like Greek drapery. She drank her fill, descended from the steps, drew her shawl closer around her cheeks and then slid along the wall, vanishing at a turn of the road.

He came to the business quarter: the sound of hammering filled the air. Here were the tinsmiths' stalls white with vessels and big lamps and huge silver urns. Here were carpenters, tombstone-makers, pounders of spice and henna, harness-makers whose shops were brilliant with smooth yellow headstalls and saddlebags and leather trappings with colored tassels. Nearby lay the fruit market, the stalls piled deep with heavy-bosomed orange gourds, brown, white, dull red, russet and purple. Red apples, yellow oranges, sticks of garlic, green pears and silvery peaches, and everywhere the pretty dark-eyed girls, erect and graceful, wandering through the crowds, one hand steadying the jars on their heads. Here and there among the ruins corn-fields were ripening, and there were small orchards of plums, apricots and mulberries.

Towards evening, oppressed by the decay, he wandered out of the city. The sky was a white-gray, as though there were no sunset. Soon the sky turned to lead, and then to brown and smoky purple, and then at last, just before the night took full possession of the countryside, there was a sudden flare and in a moment the sky had turned blue as the enamel on the great copper vessels sold in the market-place. Before him lay the pyramids, and as the sun dropped down the light around the pyramids wavered, became for a moment intensely bright, and a huge reflection of the pyramids was painted on the sky. But this lasted only for a moment: soon there was only the dim sound of the city and the waving of the reeds and the lovers whispering.

He was about to sleep beside the canal when he saw a man in a black mantle over a flowing white garment coming out of the gathering dark towards him. The man was heavily built with an enormous shaven head, and carried a staff. His ears were fleshy and jutted out. There was about the heavy, rigid head something of the power which was in the face of Geresimos in repose: somber, but capable of flashing fire, like a closed lantern which could suddenly burst into flame.

Yeshua stepped to the side of the road to let the man pass. All his excitement had withered away—the excitement which accompanied him the previous night when he entered Beth-shamesh. He was lost again, shrunk into himself, and he was glad when the man in the black mantle seemed about to pass him by. All the sky was white with stars like a garden of lotuses.

Suddenly the man stepped forward, peered into Yeshua's face and said softly in Egyptian: "So you have come to us, and now you are departing."

Yeshua lifted up his chin and looked into the man's eyes, which were black as olives, very deep and glittering.

"I watched you wandering in the market-place," the man went on. "I saw the grief in your face, and the sickness which is like unto the sickness of death. I saw you watching a girl drinking water from a tomb. Did you not see me?"

"I saw no one—only the girl," Yeshua answered, and then a little later: "And some pariah dogs and some cats sidling along the wall. If you had been there—"

"I was in the shadows," the man said. "I was officiating in the temple when I heard a voice saying: 'Seek him, for he is there!' So I ran out of the temple shuddering, and the goddess must have guided my footsteps, for I knew not where to go. And so I was led by many small alleyways and dusty pathways to the tomb. I saw a man with a red beard and a face glistening with sweat, and I thought: 'Surely he is not the man—he is only a poor Jew wandering through the streets of Heliopolis, like so many other Jews.' So I went back to the temple of Isis, but the voice kept calling me. And all the afternoon I have been searching for you."

"And have you found me?" Yeshua asked, and he was about to slip away among the reeds when the man held him in a firm grip.

"Listen," the man said. "When the goddess calls, none dare oppose her, and certainly none dare oppose her in Heliopolis, which is sacred to her. I am a priest of Isis. Come with me. I will show you the way to peace and blessedness. Come to the fountains of Isis, where the healing waters are forever flowing. Come quickly, before you perish with grief!"

And then smiling, making a sign of blessing, the heavy, gaunt priest took Yeshua by the arm and led him along the pathway to the city.

They came to a white temple hidden among sycamores. It seemed small when they approached, but after they had entered the unguarded gates, Yeshua saw that one courtyard opened on to another, and all were of white gleaming marble. In shady corners almond trees were blossoming. Sometimes they came upon small processions of priests carrying lighted candles in one hand and shaking the sistrum with the other: and the tinkling of the sistrum was like a benediction on the night, a sound like flowing water, only even more mysterious. And everything in the temple, the processions, the paintings on the walls, the chained leopards, the fountains playing, the tonsured priests in their white robes, fingering their rosaries as they sat on stone benches in the courtyards, all these things gave an impression of utter peace and calm. The purple smoke of incense rose from bronze braziers. From the high dovecotes came the incessant cooing of doves. From far away there came the murmur of the city.

Once, as they moved through the courtyards, Yeshua held back.

"I am a Jew," he said, asserting himself. "I worship the Almighty God of the Jews."

He was standing beside a painted pillar. Strange animals were depicted on the pillar.

"I have not asked thee to worship Isis," the priest said, for the first time employing the familiar 'thee.' " "The goddess called thee to take rest in the temple. Thou art free to come and go at thy pleasure. None shall hinder thee. Take strength from her healing waters—she asks no more of thee."

Then he led Yeshua to a small whitewashed cell with a high window looking over a grove of tamarisks. In the cell there was only a small bed and a jug of fresh milk which must have been left there only a few minutes before. The jug lay beside the bed. It was warm milk, filling the air with its scent, and bubbles floated on the brim. Yeshua lay down, and supporting himself on an elbow drank down the whole jug of milk. When he looked up the strange priest was gone.

The Queen of the South

The stillness of the morning lay upon Beth-shamesh, the hot stillness which was only a single pulse-beat of the sun. The walled city shone like fire, and all through the long day there would be this shining. The river flowed, the winds played among the sycamores, the high dovecotes filled the air with a flutter of wings like the petals of oleanders, the naked children walked down the dusty road leading long-eared gray donkeys, and the black buffaloes wallowed in the mud-pools; and though everywhere there was sign of movement, yet all this movement was an illusion. There were days when time stood still, when time vanished. Time was a drop of water which had fallen on the sand: a little smoke rose: there was the faintest discoloration of the sand: and then the sand was exactly as it was before.

In the white temple the rituals succeeded one another according to laws established hundreds of generations ago. No one in Egypt could remember a time when there was no worship of Isis. The offerings laid at the foot of the altar, the morning and evening prayers, the daily pilgrimages to the shrine, the perpetual singing in the cloisters and the waving of incense, all this had been arranged according to the ancient books in minute detail; in the lives of the attendants and the priests every motion, every raising of the voice was calculated. There was a way of making genuflexions, a way of standing before the throne, a way of walking. There were long hours when the priests must stand silent in contemplation, with heads bowed and hands resting lightly across their breasts. Every day there were two sacrifices to be performed: not the sacrifices of living lambs or doves, but the sacrifices called "fire and water"—the lighting of the lamps before the shrine of the goddess and the sprinkling of the water.

During the long hot mornings, dazzled by the marble columns and the flashing courtyards, Yeshua wandered through the temple. Behind high walls lay vegetable gardens and orchards attended

by the priests. There was a vast columned hall, the walls inside
and outside covered with immense paintings depicting the story
of Isis and Osiris. There were kitchens and laundries and a scriptorium, and always he was meeting those small processions of
tonsured priests going about their affairs in silence, dark Nubians
in white robes, red-cheeked Greeks, Egyptians with hawk-like
faces. Twice a day, and usually when he was absent, a girl in a
long yellow robe darted swiftly into his cell, bearing a jug of milk
and a bowl of dates, cheese and apples. Then she vanished, as
silently and mysteriously as she came.

He rested, and his strength returned. He had been ill, and now
he was well. His cheeks, sunken before, filled out. It was strange
to him that the chanting of the priests and the soft rattling of the
sistrum helped to make him well, but it was so. For hours he
would wander through the courtyards, keeping close to the wall,
seeking the shelter of the colonnades: a ghost who was becoming
flesh again. He was alone with himself, very quiet and content,
observing everything as though he were looking through a small
brilliantly-lit window. A week passed before he saw the strange
priest again.

It was night. He stood in a corner of the cell, gazing through
the open doorway at the blue moonlight. The servant girl entered
with his evening meal. For the first time he caught a glimpse of
her: a long face with delicate bones and browned by the sun. Her
hair fell to her shoulders in thick clustered curls. She was full-
breasted and she walked barefoot, with little quick strides. She
stepped into his cell swiftly, bent down to place the milk and bowl
of fruit beside the bed, and she did not observe at first that he was
standing at the corner of the cell. For a moment their eyes met.
Then she was gone, hurrying across the courtyard like a young
and slender ghost. An hour later the priest entered the cell, standing a little in front of the doorway and blocking out the silver
light which flooded the whole courtyard. In the dim light, filling
the door, he gave an impression of extraordinary authority.

"So you have come to stay with the goddess?" he said. "I had not
thought you would stay."

Yeshua said nothing. He felt trapped in the dimly-lit cell. He
stood against the wall, smiling.

In the darkness the priest saw only the glitter of his teeth and
the faint gleam of his eyeballs.

"Did you understand what I said?" the priest went on.

"Yes, I understood."

"You know you are free to come and go as you please? There are no guards in the temples of Isis. All of us are free to come and go."

"It makes no difference," Yeshua said.

"What makes no difference?"

"Whether I come or go. I am resting here, and I am grateful for the rest, and soon I must go wandering again."

The priest stepped into the room. At once the room filled with reflected light from the courtyard. It was like an explosion of the blue moonlight.

"How long will you stay?" the priest asked gravely, and his deep-toned voice was like the booming of a drum.

"A week, two weeks—"

"Long enough," the priest answered, and for the first time a ghost of a smile appeared on his heavy face. "You are not healed yet. It is well that you are resting. You have eaten all the food that has been offered you and slept eight hours every night and for the first time tonight you showed an interest in those around you." And then because Yeshua looked blank, he said: "You watched the servant girl. You gazed at her. It means the sap is rising."

"So you know everything?" Yeshua said, making a little bow.

There was the faintest gleam of mockery in his smile.

"It is my business to know everything. I know you are well now, and will continue in good health as long as you stay here. They say the temple of Isis is like a hospital and all men are ill when they first come. But the goddess gives them health."

"Tell the goddess I am grateful," Yeshua said, and again there was the wall of reserve between them.

"She knows you are grateful," the priest answered. "It is not necessary for us to tell her. She has one favor to ask of you. Oh, I am not asking you to serve her and carry her sacred emblems—it is more than she could hope for. I am asking you simply to shave off your beard and hair, because it makes you too remarkable. To-morrow, if you agree, a monk will shave you."

"I agree."

"She asks one more favor. She begs you to wear a white robe, for your own is soiled."

"I washed it at the fountain."

"Still it is soiled. Is it the same robe you wore when you fell among the swillings of wine in the hold of the *Lion*?"

"Yes, it is the same."

"And you are not surprised that I know you were on the *Lion*?"

"No, I am not surprised," Yeshua answered wearily, shutting his eyes. "I am surprised at nothing—only by grief. I thought I had put grief away, but it comes whenever I am in darkness, whenever I see a shadow."

"So there will be no end to grief, for there will always be shadows," the priest said. "Yet there will come an end to grief. When a man dies, then there is an end to grief, and when he is reborn, no grief can ever touch him. Worship Isis, and all your grief shall perish!"

Yeshua stared into the shadows.

"I shall not worship her," he said after a pause. "I will shave my beard and hair, and wear a white robe, and do whatever else is demanded of me, but I am a Jew and shall not worship her."

"She does not ask you to worship her. She who is twice holy, being goddess and mother, asks only that you shall take shelter here, living in love and charity with all people. Sleep well, Yeshua."

Then the priest was gone, and there were only the shadows swirling in the dark cell and the purple-silver moonlight in the quiet courtyard outside. The doves moaned. A white-robed figure, a Nubian with a head of black marble, glided noiselessly across the courtyard, and somewhere nearby a priest was shaking the sistrum, summoning the goddess by name.

That night Yeshua was restless. He lay down on the bed, finished drinking the milk and stared out into the blinding purple-silvery courtyard, the altar heaped with flowers, the intense black shadows which cut the courtyard in two. A yellow kitten stalked across the brilliant, blinding space and was suddenly swallowed up in the darkness.

"Poor kitten," he murmured. "Now she has gone for ever."

He was surprised at himself, the terrible restlessness surging in him. The image of Atys rose before his eyes and would not be banished. Atys was laughing. Atys was running across the marble dancing floor at Ptolemais to leap upon the stage. Atys was wearing the painted mask of Antigone and suddenly he lifted up his arms, removed the mask and smiled broadly at the applauding

audience, the thousands of spectators in the great semicircular
theater, all cheering and standing up in their seats; and the sky
was streaked with yellow, and it was near the sunset.

"Poor kitten," he went on. "She went into the shadows, and will
never return. The kitten has gone into the kingdom of darkness!"

He smiled then, a sad smile of bewilderment, raising his hands
to hide his face from the intense glare of moonlight, and then he
heard a soft mewing and the kitten was gliding through the open
door. There were a few drops of milk left. He poured them into
the bowl and watched while the kitten was drinking, the long silky
pink tongue darting. Then he took the kitten in his arms and
stroked it, while little dancing blue flames of electricity rose from
the yellow fur. He sang a song to the kitten:

> Thou art a little tiger come from the kingdom of darkness:
> Thou hast come with a little red tongue to lick my face.
> Thou hast replenished me.
> Thou art my comforter.
> For there is the flame of the living God in thee!
>
> Go, little tiger, go seek thy milk elsewhere,
> And do not rend my garments,
> Do not draw blood from me.
>
> Thou art a little tiger come from the kingdom of darkness
> And shall enter into the greater kingdom of light,
> Where a thousand bowls of milk shall be prepared for thee.
> Go, little one, and when thou hast found the milk,
> Come and tell me!

The song pleased him and afterwards he was very quiet, holding the kitten in his arms, rocking it, while it licked his face. When
he fell asleep the kitten was still there, very warm against his
breast, and when he awoke in the bright morning it was lying like
a little pool of gold at the foot of his bed.

As usual Yeshua spent the morning wandering round the courtyards. Previously he had paid little attention to the white-robed
priests, only noting their existence, admiring their grace and dignity. They were wraith-like and walked silently. But this morning
he looked into their faces, looking deeply and profoundly, breaking through the mask. At first glance all these shaven and tonsured
priests looked alike. There was beauty in their gestures, and a
grave assurance. The fullness in their faces spoke of utter purity.

Most of all he admired the dignity of the dark-skinned Africans, whose white robes drawn close about their chests, leaving the arms and shaven head bare, only intensified the burnished blackness of their skins. So he followed them, or watched, leaning on a column at a corner of a marble courtyard, while they chanted psalms or gathered in quiet corners to discuss the sacred texts.

Strange priests! So quiet, so calm, so self-possessed. He could not understand their mysterious journeys and processions, their never-ending progress from one courtyard to another, but he understood their inner contentment, the profoundly reverent joy they showed at all hours of the day and night. He told himself he had never seen people more joyful. It was not the savage joy of the priests in the Temple at Jerusalem as they filled the silver bowls with the reeking blood of lambs and waded knee-deep in blood to the altar of holocausts. On the contrary it was a quiet joy: not tempest-ridden: more like the quiet lapping of the waves on a sandy shore on a sunlit afternoon. Strange that all this joy should come to them from adoring Isis, Mother and Goddess, as she holds the infant Horus in her arms! For them there were no mysteries; all secrets had been revealed to them; and so from day to day, and hour by hour, they walked in perfect assurance of the blessedness that came to them from Isis.

So he found himself increasingly drawn to them, and when later in the morning the priest came and asked whether he was ready to be shorn, he smiled and said: "I suppose you will offer my poor red beard to the goddess."

"So you guessed?"

"I guessed you would take something from me and lay it before her. I am not ashamed of my beard. I have seen it in a pool, and it is the color of blood, but it will do no harm to make this sacrifice."

His eyes were gleaming. The hot sun had darkened his cheeks, and the winds of health were blowing through him. Not since the day of Atys's death had he felt such strength in him. He ran his fingers through his ragged beard which grew in two long tufts from his chin and shook out the long red hair which fell to his shoulders, whispering a prayer of farewell to it, and then lifted up his chin in a manner which indicated: "Let it be done soon!"

The priest stepped back and looked at him searchingly.

"You are sure you are prepared to make this sacrifice?" he asked, and there was mockery in his eyes, the gentle mockery of a man who knows how other men are attached to trifles.

"It is a bloodless sacrifice," Yeshua answered. "I am weary of blood sacrifices. Yet I shall not deny my Jewish birthright," he added quickly.

"It is not asked of you."

"Oh, you are subtle, you Egyptians!" Yeshua exclaimed. "You ask nothing, and yet you ask everything! First you ask for the beard and hair, then I am robed in a white robe like your priests, and then no doubt I shall be studying the texts of the goddess!"

"You shall study them if it pleases you," the priest said, smiling.

"And if it doesn't please me?"

"Then the goddess will take no offense. Besides, they are written in Egyptian, and though you talk our language—Heaven knows, you are continually making mistakes—I doubt whether you can read the texts. Only, if you desire it, I shall place a secretary at your disposal."

"And if I refuse your secretary?" Yeshua asked.

"Then the goddess will wait. She desires no one to enter her mysteries except by his own will." And then after a pause, looking intently into the eyes of Yeshua which were still deep-sunken, though the flesh of his face was glowing with health: "My goddess conquered death through love, she gathered the broken pieces of the body of Osiris and made them whole. Shall she not do the same to thee?"

It was hot in the courtyard. A steamy mist coming from the Nile made everything sparkle. It was on the tip of Yeshua's tongue to say: "I am not broken! Why do you thrust this thing at me?" He would have gone on to say something of less weight, but at that moment the servant girl darted out of deep shadow, slipped hurriedly into his cell, laid the milk and fresh fruit and cheese beside his bed, and fled away. Yeshua could not help following her with his eyes. She came with such a birdlike rush and flutter of her soft yellow robe, and there was something so beautiful in her coming, that he turned away from the priest and for a moment was lost in admiration. Then she was gone, silent on sandaled feet, hurrying round the corner, and so to some other courtyard; and it occurred to him that whenever she came, she chose a different direction for her coming, and always she brought with her an un-expected scent: today it was honey, yesterday violets.

When Yeshua turned to say something to the priest after follow-ing the quick birdlike movements of the girl, he was surprised to see the priest's face reddening with anger. It was no more than a spark, a small explosion that soon burned out, but it was fright-ening. On that grave, heavy, impassive face any emotion was disturbing.

"Should I not have gazed upon her?" Yeshua asked with sudden effrontery.

"Better to be at peace," the priest answered. "And now it is time you were shorn and wore a white robe."

Saying this, the priest led Yeshua through three courtyards and across an open space to a garden where a fountain was playing and there was a pond full of pink lotuses and beside the pond a small green summerhouse painted with garden scenes. There were windows in each wall and fruit trees all round.

Yeshua was bidden to sit down on a stone seat in front of the summerhouse.

"Rest here," the priest said, then walked away, disappearing be-yond a clump of sycamores behind the summerhouse.

An hour later he returned with an acolyte, a fresh-faced, ton-sured boy of about twelve years, who carried a white robe over one arm and a heavy brass bowl.

Without a word the boy began to snip off Yeshua's beard, catch-ing the red hair and solemnly depositing it in the brass bowl. He did the same with the hair. Afterwards he rubbed a sweet-smell-ing ointment over the whole of Yeshua's head and over his chin, and shaved him. All the time the boy was humming a little tune to himself.

Once the boy looked up at the priest and said: "Does he speak Egyptian?"

"Yes."

The boy seemed satisfied. A few moments later he said: "Is he a Jew?"

"Yes, little one, and now ask no more questions."

The boy went on humming merrily to himself. He was an expert barber, very deft with the razor, but he had no intention of keep-ing silent. Holding the razor high above his head, he said: "Can he write Egyptian?"

The priest was almost out of patience—once more there was the reddening in the cheeks and the little blaze of anger in his eyes, but he said in a level voice: "No, he cannot! You are a better barber than he is, and you know how to write Egyptian!"

Yeshua smiled. It occurred to him that in a community of tonsured priests the barber held a rank almost as great as that of the ruling priest.

The boy continued humming. The yellow birds were flitting among the fruit trees. It was very quiet in the garden. Here and there among the rows of trees beyond the fountain Yeshua thought he saw some white-robed priests half-hidden in the foliage. Probably they were gardeners pruning the trees, but they resembled ghosts.

The priest said: "Would you like to learn Egyptian?"

Yeshua was gazing at the fountain, and at first he did not hear the question.

"Would you like to learn Egyptian?" the priest repeated.

"Yes," answered Yeshua, but he was on his mettle. He had known since earlier in the morning that the priest wanted him to read the sacred texts.

There was a sprinkling of sand near the stone seat. With his staff the priest wrote out a name in Egyptian:

"Can you read that?" he asked. "I see you cannot. It is the name of this city, which you call Beth-shamesh, but which we call Annumeht. The symbol at the left represents the shape of the city seen from afar. The symbols at the top represent the bread and the wine. Then there are the lotuses springing from the Nile. Below there are crosses, whose meaning is lost in antiquity. Shall I explain the meanings again?"

"No, there is no need," Yeshua said, and he began to draw in the air the Egyptian name for Beth-shamesh, smiling to himself, for he liked this language where the bread and the wine and the appearance of cities was drawn so cleanly.

The shaving was over, the boy standing back and admiring his handiwork. The two forks of beard and the long tresses lay in the brass bowl. It was time for Yeshua to remove his gown. So he turned away, facing the summerhouse, and disrobed, and the boy came near and offered him the white robe. There was a secret malice in the priest's eyes as he watched the robing.

"For shame!" he said. "Dost thou hide thy body? Is there something there thou wouldst hide?"

Once again the black eyes of the priest gleamed with a quiet malice.

"The face of the goddess is not hidden," he went on. "She lives behind a veil, but three times a day the veil is removed. Surely she is not hidden when we see her with our eyes." And then a little later: "Wouldst thou look upon her face?"

"I would look upon her face for the beauty of it," Yeshua answered.

"For the beauty or for the holiness?" the priest sighed.

"For the beauty alone," Yeshua answered, and added: "Surely the beauty is a holiness!"

The priest was pleased with the reply and took him by the hand, leading him across the sunlit gardens and through a maze of courts until they came to a large painted temple with a gilded roof supported on lotus columns and surrounded by a high wall.

In this vast cavernous temple with painted beams and immense spreading frescoes on the walls, they walked silently, the boy going a little ahead, holding up the bronze basin which contained Yeshua's hair. Far away, at the very end, lay the shrine of the goddess, concealed by a filmy white curtain. There were many small shrines in the courtyards, but this was the shrine of Isis Triumphant, Isis in the joy of discovery after finding the broken body of Osiris, and therefore the most sacred of all.

In this darkness the white curtain was like an eye gazing upon them. As the wind disturbed the curtain, the eye seemed to grow brighter. When they drew closer, Yeshua thought he could distinguish the shape of the goddess behind the curtain. The priest was murmuring prayers. It was very quiet. The boy was kneeling, offering up the bronze bowl to the invisible goddess behind the curtain. And then one by one, springing into flame, the oil-lamps at her feet and on the wall behind her dazzled them, and at the moment when the lamps were ignited the veil was drawn aside by invisible hands.

The goddess stood on a plinth of blue rock above them. She

wore the diadem of Isis and the golden vulture crown, and carried
the child Horus cradled on her arm. Her long thick hair fell in
curls on her lovely neck, and the crescent moon shone on her forehead. She stood erect, one leg a little forward, and her many-
colored robe fell to her ankles and left her feet bare. The colors
of the robe were blue and saffron and bright orange and fierce
scarlet, and all were shimmering, and the shape of the young body
below the robe could be seen beneath the translucent cloth. She
wore a girdle round her waist adorned with two golden crocodile
heads, and between her breasts a strange and complicated knot
gathered the two folds of the robe together. But it was the face
which held his attention. She seemed to breathe. The fire of life
seemed to glow in those dark heavily-lidded eyes and in those
flushed rosy cheeks. She was not made of stone. If she was made of
wood, then she was made by a master-craftsman.

"She is the Queen of the South," the priest was murmuring. "All
things obey her. The stars wheel in the heavens for her sake, and
the young lambs skip for her, and the Nile flows for her."

Saying this, he lifted one of the oil-lamps at her feet and pointed
it in the four directions, and afterwards he sprinkled water over
himself, then over the boy, and then over Yeshua, saying: "All
things may be made pure in Isis by fire and water." Then he took
the bronze bowl and lifted it high above his head, offering the red
hair to the goddess, and said a prayer.

Yeshua was dazzled. He was dazzled not only by the youthful
beauty of the goddess but by the wealth of flashing jewels which
shone from her. Rubies and emeralds glittered from her pectoral,
and there were amethysts in her hair. Though she held the infant
Horus in her arms, one hand held a jeweled sistrum while the
other held a small cross. Her sandals were of gold that glittered
redly like fire.

So she stood there, smiling her faint smile of triumph, goddess
and mother, very calm and gentle in the flickering oil-lamps, gazing
upon the world in affectionate tenderness. The Egyptians called
her the Queen of the South, and of the dead, and of immortals,
sovereign of all things spiritual and all earthly things, of the stars
and of every grain of wheat, every seed. She was formed in the
shape of a young girl with a child in her arms. This was the mystery, and before that mystery he bowed his head, unable to look
on her splendor any more.

Then he heard a sound like a great rushing wind and suddenly all the lamps went out. In the darkness the priest was still murmuring prayers.

The White Ibis

"Thou canst worship Almighty God, who is the God of the Jews and of the universe, but none can prevent thee from worshiping Isis," the priest was saying. "For surely the divine goddess and mother is an aspect of God's tenderness?"

"God's tenderness," Yeshua repeated suddenly, and he wondered why the words sounded strange on his ears.

"Surely He is tender," the priest went on. "They have said God is a stone on a high mountain or a piece of flint or a wind blowing through the Ark of the Covenant, but we say He has the aspect of a young girl, and wilt thou accuse us of idolatry? Thou seest how worshipful we are. We come from an ancient race and have long meditated on the mysteries. Surely thou canst worship her?"

The priest, whose name was Khefre, meaning "the Master of the Courts," went on to speak about the mysteries and of how after many years of preparation, many trials of the flesh and of the spirit, the novice was led in the depths of night into a *cella* where the goddess revealed herself in a blinding light. He would put out his hands and touch her and be blessed by her, and because she had touched him and blessed him, he would become a god. Before this time it was necessary for the novice to progress by slow degrees in the arts of initiation. He must prove himself by offering himself wholly to her service. He must make the vow of chastity and learn her hymns by heart: he must die and be buried in the earth for four days and arise again like Osiris: he must grieve with her and be made whole by her. He would suffer baptism, death and rebirth; he would descend into Hell and be transfigured in the Sun: and all this was written in the mysteries of Isis. As he listened to Khefre, Yeshua felt he had heard it all before, it was all familiar to him, it was not even necessary to read the books because he could guess what was written there. Sometimes, because he was free to leave the temple whenever he desired, he would wander down to the Nile and lie among the reeds, looking out over the slow, wide yellow river with the large clumsy red-sailed boats and barges moving up and down; and there, with the reeds waving over him, lying naked in the sun, his body half-immersed in the river, he would lose himself in long contemplative silences, thinking of the goddess, only the goddess.

"Surely she is beautiful among all things," Yeshua told himself. "Surely she heals the wounds of the flesh."

The black panther was dying in him: all the things of the world were slowly dying away. The blessing of Isis was on him, and so he sang:

All things are alive in the goddess, all things are dying away.
They enter her, and become her, and softly she changes them.
Her benediction touches my eyelids and caresses me.
She is the sun dancing at the bottom of the wine-jar.
She is the starlight on the waving reeds
And the soft, soft flowing of the Nile.

Sweetly she arises from the river attended by scorpions,
And her jewels flash in the hot sunlight.
I name the black god with a slow breath.
I say to the god: "Thou shalt be gone and be buried,
And thou shalt rise again by the blessing of Isis.
For she is merciful."

Osiris, Isis, Horus! O holy family!
Like the seeds of the pomegranate, surely they are brought together
For the pleasure of the worshipers:
And the little kitten creeps in the moonlit courtyard
To attend the worshipers.
Osiris, the dark god with the face of gold,
Unknown and unseen, only to be imagined,
Whose limbs were cast to the four corners of the earth,
Mysteriously art thou gathered together
By the blessing of the goddess.

The mystery is upon me!
Shall I worship the girl who comes walking towards me
With softly flowing raiment, with a child in her arms,
Or shall I wander alone through the dark pathways
Over deserts and mountains and the shores of a dead lake,
There to receive baptism by fire and water:
Though fire and water are enclosed in the river beside me.
The flash of fire! The sweetness of living water!

Now among the feathery reeds I lie in the sun,
I am gathered together like a beautiful hawk of gold,
I enter the Pool of Flame which is the Field of Fire:
I am become a flame, I am become water.
O holy fire of Egypt, rain down on me!
O holy waters of Egypt, bathe me!

Sweet it is to contemplate the goddess by the river:
For the voice of the river is the voice of the goddess,
And the sighing of the feathery reeds is her sighing,
And the sun shouts her praises.
And every dead leaf floating on the river
Is only the body of Osiris,
And every cloud
Is the breath of the dying god.
Sweet it is to contemplate the goddess by the river
And to drown in her waters.

Now the black panther is dead within me:
The fire from his nostrils is utterly quenched,
And the strength of his loins has withered away.
I have nailed to the cross
The mangy skin of the panther:
And now I am free of him!

I am free and exultant! I shout her praises!
I enter the sunlit courtyards! I have found my home!
And I shall rest by the living waters in the sun
In the House of Eternity to the end of my days!

But though he sang the song to the priests of Isis, he was not
always exultant. There were times especially at night when he was
sunk in melancholy, and when the memory of Jehovah's curses
upon the gods of Egypt returned to him. He remembered Jeremiah,
speaking with the voice of Jehovah: *I will kindle a fire in the houses
of the gods of Egypt, and he shall burn them, and carry them away
captives; and he shall array himself with the land of Egypt, as a
shepherd putteth on his garment; and he shall go forth from thence*

in peace. Yet he knew that if he left the temple, he would not go
forth in peace, but on the contrary he would go forth in trepidation
and sorrow, in fear and trembling. So during the long nights he
wrestled with himself.

One night when he was lying on his bed in the summerhouse,
which Khefre had given him so that he could continue his meditations far from the courtyards where the priests were incessantly
wandering, he was awakened by the soft rustle of a linen gown.
There was no moonlight. Only a few stars were shining. He lay on
a bed near the open window. He was aware that there was someone else in the summerhouse, but he could not see clearly. Half-
asleep, remembering the torments which had plagued him during
the evening, frightened by the soft rustling sound, he cried out:
"Who is there? Art thou my God?"

He did not know what he was saying. There was a cold sweat
of fear pouring down his cheeks.

He rose, strode blindly across the room and almost stumbled
over a low chair. There was no strength in him. He regained his
balance and blundered against a wall. Some forgotten nightmare
was continuing within him.

"Who is it?" he shouted, and then fell silent, listening intently.

He heard breathing. It was very soft, very low, very gentle. He
put out his hand, and instantly recoiled, for he had touched flesh.

"It is I—I—your handmaiden," a voice said, and he knew someone was cowering in the darkness against the wall.

He said nothing, staring into the darkness. She came out, and
by the faint starlight he observed that she was wearing a blue gown
curiously knotted between the breasts and there was a diadem
binding her hair across her brows. He recognized the girl who was
accustomed to coming secretly into his cell in the courtyard, with
milk and bread and dates. At first he thought she was afraid, but
there was no fear in her when she stood in the middle of the
summerhouse, smiling at him.

"Who are you?" he repeated.

"I am your handmaiden, surely you recognize me? I came to see
you, for it is the will of the goddess that I should watch over you."

There was something in her voice which suggested that she had
entered the summerhouse many times, and always at night.

"So you came often, to spy on me?"

"For the sake of the goddess," the girl answered, lifting her chin.

"To see me sleeping?"

"Yes, to see you sleeping, and because you cry out so often in your dreams. I came to see your dreams."

"My dreams?" he asked. "What are my dreams to thee?"

"The goddess knows," the girl answered, and said nothing more for a while.

Her fingers moved about the knot at her breast, and he saw her large dark eyes were fixed on him. He had never seen eyes like that, so dark, so soft, so melting, except in his mother's face. So he smiled, and made a curious gesture with his hands, blessing her.

She led him to the window. The scent of the garden came flocking round them. Her body was very warm under the thin linen gown. She could not have been more than eighteen or nineteen.

"So thou rememberest me?"

"Yea, I remember that thou broughtest me honeycombs and sweet dates and many bowls of milk, which I shared with a kitten."

"The goddess was pleased."

"So the goddess knew?"

"She knows everything," the girl said, and she gave a low tinkling laugh. "I told her thy dreams, as well as I remembered them, and also many other things."

"What things?"

"Thy torments, thy rages, thy songs—and more still, for I told her how thou hast gone bathing thy body on the shores of the Nile, and the sun did not harm thee. And nearly every night I came to see thy dreams."

"And thou art my handmaiden!" he exclaimed softly, and wondered.

As his eyes grew accustomed to the starlight, he saw something he had never expected to see: the girl's face lit by the silver stars, and it was the face of the goddess in the temple. In the temple she had carried the infant Horus in her arms and was robed in jeweled garments, but it was the same face, the same modeling of the chin, the same curve of cheek-bones. Surely the goddess in the temple was modeled on this girl! And then seeing the diadem which bound her hair across the bow, he knew she was a priestess of Isis.

"Thou art not angry with me?" the girl whispered.

"Not angry," he answered, "nor shall I ever be angry. Now I know thou art a priestess of Isis, and a handmaiden—"

"It is good to be a handmaiden," she answered.

"And a priestess?" he asked insistently.

"That, too," she smiled, and again there was the soft tinkling laugh which was like the whisper of the feathery reeds.

She took his hands.

"Come," she whispered. "I shall take thee to my house. It is small and comfortable, and we shall drink wine together."

Keeping to the shadows she led him silently across many courtyards until they came to a small white palace set among pomegranate trees. A nest of ibises crowned the roof of the palace. She put her fingers to her lips and pointed to the white birds sleeping on the roof.

"They are sacred to Osiris," she said. "While they are there, no harm can come to me."

He followed her into the palace. It was simply furnished, and yet there was luxury in this simplicity. Water flowed under the cool marble tiles. She lay on a lion-headed couch, while he sat at her feet, drinking the wine she poured for him, and she told him about the mysteries—about the Holy Vigil and the Judgment of Osiris and how the soul at the moment of initiation becomes changed into the soul of Isis. Painted on the walls all round him, in full flight or perched on roof-tops or skimming low over the Nile, were white ibises. So many ibises, such a flutter and splendor of wings!

"And those mysteries which are secret shall be revealed to thee, to the number thou desirest," the priestess was saying. "Nothing shall be withheld from thee, for truly Isis loves thee."

And so, until the dawn came up, she spoke of the mysteries and the blessings that flowed from them and how all things were made known to those who followed the pathways of the goddess, and at the first coming of the sun she put a finger to her lips and bade him return to the summerhouse.

One day three weeks later, Khefre told him he had been invited to attend the Mystery of the Ship. He was asked to disguise himself by wearing a goat-mask.

The sun was striking their faces, when the procession formed in the temple. He had never seen so motley a procession. Everyone was disguised. There were priests wearing the uniform of Roman soldiers, waving swords. Others were dressed as huntsmen and carried swords at their waists. Some wore wigs and silk garments and the gilded sandals of women. One wore the heavy iron boots and copper shield of a gladiator, and another wore the purple robe of a magistrate. There was a philosopher with cloak, staff, clogs and trailing white beard, and a bird-catcher who waved a long feathery reed dipped in lime. One priest, disguised as a she-bear, rode in a gilded sedan chair, and another disguised as an ape wore a straw hat and a saffron-colored Phrygian cloak and held a gilded cup between his paws. Then there was an ass with wings glued to its shoulders and an old man doddering on its rump. There were all manner of clowns and acrobats. There were musicians playing on pipes and flutes, and choir-boys singing psalms to the goddess. At the head of the procession walked the priests and priestesses of Isis in glistening white linen garments, waving sistrums, and some of them were hidden by soft filmy white veils which covered their faces and fell to their feet.

Khefre walked near the head of the procession, holding a sacred lamp which rose from his cupped hands: a lamp shaped like a golden boat with a tongue of flame issuing from it. Another priest carried the Pot of Sacrifice shaped like a wine glass, only larger, and made of glass of many colors. A third carried a palm tree with gilded leaves and a fourth carried an enormous metal hand with the fingers stretched out. The fifth carried a golden vessel shaped like a woman's breast from which there issued a thin stream of milk. And there were others carrying winnowing-fans and sacrificial wine jars.

Then there were priests disguised as the gods of Egypt: the dog-faced god, the Serpent, the Crocodile, the Cat, the Vulture. These came at the end of the procession, to signify perhaps that the goddess Isis had assumed power over all the former gods. And so all morning and all afternoon the strange procession wound through the temple, singing hymns to Isis, performing strange dances, never still. Late in the afternoon all these priests gathered in the great hall and made offerings to the goddess, whose statue was revealed to them exactly as it had been revealed to Yeshua: they entered the hall in darkness, there was a blaze of lights and suddenly they were in the presence of the goddess. And at nightfall the procession made its way to the Nile.

Yeshua was strangely excited by the gaudy costumes, the revelry, the way in which all the partakers of the ceremony seemed to be perfectly at ease. Everything had meaning: every gesture was fraught with consequence. It was hot under the goat-mask. He looked for the priestess, but he did not find her and it occurred to him that she was perhaps disguised as one of the animal-headed gods. But at midnight, when they came to the shores of the Nile, he observed that quite suddenly a golden litter had been elevated among the crowd of worshipers, and on this litter, wearing a jeweled costume exactly like the costume worn by the statue, was the priestess. On her lap she held a gilded ship.

Priests in white vestments gathered round her, singing her praises. Everybody was waiting, waiting. The Nile mirrored the lamps and torches, and the reeds rustled, and they were all waiting for the moment when she would descend from the litter and offer the ship to the water. And he knew there was a mystery in this which explained many things, which could not be put into words: the goddess with a ship on her lap. And sitting there in the litter she seemed of stone, so motionless she was, so much like the goddess, at once so delicate and so powerful. He whispered her name—the name she had told him to use—and for a long time he kept repeating it. "Meri, Meri, Meri." It was like an incantation. All the time he rejoiced that she should be there, shining among the torches.

And then at last, after the priests had purified the ship and swung censers over it and held it high so that all the worshipers could see it glinting in the flame-light, it was returned into the hands of the priestess who waded out through the reeds until the water came to a level with her breast and then she set the ship on the water. A little nest of flame glowed on the ship, and everyone watched it until it sailed out of sight—a small ship, perhaps two feet long, with white ghostly sails and a prow shaped like the neck of an ibis, sacred to Isis. And then it was very quiet, with no hymns playing, only the rustling of the reeds and the memory of the ship which had disappeared into the darkness.

The next day Yeshua went down to the river. He wanted to meditate upon the ship launched at night, becoming ghostly, no more than smoke. Why had he been asked to wear the goat-mask? Why the ape wearing a straw hat and a Phrygian cloak? And yet in some mysterious way this charade seemed perfectly appropriate, and the singing of the hymns was appropriate, and so was the long wandering amid the courtyards. It was Isis, preparing for the long journey of discovery, Isis rejoicing in the coming of spring, Isis offering her gift upon the waters.

It was midday. He lay among the reeds, naked, lost in thought. He was glad to be away from the summerhouse, glad to be alone and rejoicing in the pure air of the Nile. Suddenly he heard a voice calling him, and the snapping of reeds underfoot. He rose and turned in the direction of the voice. It was the priestess of Isis, and she was no more than a few yards away.

He stood there, raging, while the air trembled with heat and the blue flashing of the river nearly blinded him. In the wind from the desert the reeds were rustling.

She was still staring at him, looking him up and down, admiring the bronze torso, the heavy shoulders, the ripples of muscles along the brown arms. Drops of water, all silver, glistened on his dark skin.

Time stood still. He could not have told how much time had passed. He knew only that she was feasting on him, her wide-open eyes like little tongues licking him. He was trembling in the agony of it, the agony of those soft feasting eyes, her young body thrown forward a little, her lips parted.

She said softly: "Come! Come! There is no need to hide! No one shall ever see us!" And saying this, she put her hand over the strangely woven knot at her breast and moved a little closer, until he could feel the warmth of her body across the blue space of the reeds.

"I know that knot," he whispered, and tried to look away, but her eyes held him. He could see her long fingers working at the knot. A little pulse was moving in the cup of her throat, and her cheeks were flushed. And suddenly, seeing the wind pressing the silken raiment against her skin, seeing the uplifted face, the lips so curiously parted, the whole face transformed into a strange dead mask of desire, so that she was like a skull, though beautiful, no longer in possession of herself, he cried out: "Shall the virgin destroy herself? Shall the gold hawk fall from the sky?" But she only gave a little moan and stumbled a little closer to him, while the blue raiment swirled around her.

The heat came out of the sky, remorseless, unrelenting. The sun was a blue ball in the heavens of hammered bronze. And there was no sound, only the pulsating rhythm of the sun like the rhythm of heart-beats. And he felt weak in this furnace heat, watching her

hands, the fingers busy at the intricate little knot, which was sacred
to her, and her knees pushing up through the long blue gown, as
she swayed there, with that dreadful dead mask of passion engraved on her face, and far behind her the unmoving green palms
and the white marble temples.

"Thou art Osiris," she said, and a shiver ran through her young
untouched body. "Truly thou art Osiris. Truly thou hast been
given to me."

"Am I hawk-headed?" he asked.

"Thou art hawk-headed, and hast the golden body of a hawk, and
the far-ranging eyes of a hawk, and thou art come to me to be my
Osiris."

"I have not come to thee," he said, and it was like the tone of a
commander. "Not yet, not ever. I shall not fall from the sky. I
shall not wear the green feathers, nor wear the crown. I shall go
about my business, wearing the tonsure and bearing the sistrum, till
I weary of it, and then I shall go in my own time to some other
place."

"And leave me?"

She said the words in a dead voice, not comprehending what she
was saying.

"I shall go away from thee, and from all men and all women," he
said softly, and he knew she understood nothing he was saying, for
still, with invisible tender creeping movements of her feet, she
came towards him, so close that he could feel her scented breath on
his face, and see the white flesh, sweet as lotus blossoms, beneath
the blue gown.

There was nothing he could do to keep her away from him: he
had no strength, no desire to hold her at arm's length, and no
desire for her: only that there should be a space between them.
She was more beautiful among the reeds than she had ever been
when she tended the altar flames or sent the ship floating on the
Nile or stood supremely holy with the child Horus in her arms
behind the white veil. Her eyes startled him: they had become
enormous, and glistened strangely. Her lips were curved in an
unchanging smile. The blue veins at her temples were pulsating,
and the hot blood rushed to her cheeks and fell away again, and all
the time she was trembling. She was beautiful with a terrible dead
beauty, with a terrible clear singing wantonness, for her voice had
become richer and quieter, yet it was a dead voice, the voice of

one of the ghostly presences who haunted the temple, the voice of
the shadows that lingered in the blue moonlight among the lotus
columns. And as she came towards him, her bare feet rustling
among the pure white stems of the reeds, crushing them, so that
sometimes a reed stem cracked with the sound of an explosion,
there was in her expression, in the way she held herself, the long
fingers still clutched around the sacred knot, something of the
appearance of a sleep-walker, and therefore it was impossible not
to have pity for her; and it was only when she was very close to
him, when she was only a few inches away and the heat from her
young body was more burning than the heat of the sun, that he was
aware of being in terrible danger.

She was very close to him when she pulled at the knot at her
breast—the sacred knot of the Priestess of Isis. Her hand flashed
down. The little silken ends of the knot whirled up, brushing her
cheek, as the gown slipped from her, falling from her shoulders,
hanging for a moment on her breasts, then sliding away from her,
caught on the spikes of the reeds as she ran forward, her face
uplifted, her white shoulders catching the sun, her young body
gleaming like salt, very white and strangely pure and untouched.
The clamor of the breaking reeds as she ran forward was deafening.
She fell against him. The blue gown floated away, billowed and
then sank out of sight. She was very warm, pressing herself against
him, her lips parted, her eyes wild with expectancy.

"Come, come," she murmured. "Thou shalt be my Osiris! See, I
have come to thee!"

She swayed there, nestling against him, the hot red body of the
man and the white young body of the priestess. Then, seeing that
he was weakening, she pulled him down into a bed of cool waters
of the Nile, with curtains of reeds all round them, and all the time
she was moaning softly: it was like the moaning of doves. The river
washed over them, lapping them, and now there was no longer the
loud clamor of the snapping reeds, only the silence as she lay close
to him, a little ashamed now, covering her soft proud breasts with
her hands, gazing at him, lying back against a pillow of reeds,
amazed to see herself stretched out at full length with the water
lapping her breasts, only her head and shoulders rising above the
green water.

It was strange to her that she had descended among the reeds,
into this green world of lapping waters. She had thought it would

happen in some other way, not this descent into the river, into this coolness. She desired him, and she knew she had awakened him, but he was reserved from her, only barely touching her. There was a strange silver film over his eyes, so that his shaven head rising above the water resembled a mask. When she pressed herself closer to him, he said: "Touch me not! Rest quietly in the sun! This is the best!" And she gave a little moan, flung her arm across his chest and buried her head on his shoulder, saying over and over again: "Thou art my Osiris! Come to me! Touch me! I am a virgin, and I have brought my virginhood to thee, to be taken by thee!" And he held himself away from her, though lying close to her, so still and supine in the water that he was like one of the statues which have toppled into the Nile, while the little tender flame of life agitated him and sometimes he turned slowly towards her and smiled caressingly, but it was the smile of someone who has withdrawn and says farewell.

"I shall go soon," he said, and he was gazing into the endless blue spaces of the sky where the kites were wheeling.

"Shall I become carrion, and shall they descend upon me?" he murmured, and he thought of himself lying dead, his body turned purple, bloated and festering, and the sharp beaks of the kites and carrion eagles tearing at his flesh.

He smiled at her again and let her rich black hair pour through his fingers.

"Soon I shall go," he said again, for she had not heard him.

"And leave me?" she answered, and there was no strength in her words: she seemed to be speaking mechanically, reciting something she had learned long ago. "If thou leavest me now, I shall perish, Osiris."

He closed his eyes, weary of the beating of the sun and the lapping of the waters among the reeds.

"Nay, thou shalt not perish," he answered tenderly. "Thou shalt search for thy Osiris and thou shalt find him, but he is not I!"

"I know thou art he. I have seen the signs upon thee. Thou hast the face of a god, and beyond this I cannot go, only I know thou wast made for me. Am I not beautiful? Am I not worthy of thee?"

"Yea, thou art worthy," he said, caressing her body with his eyes, the proud full face the color of honey, the white shoulders, the full breasts with their pink nipples and blue veins like delicate tracery and the long white body submerged in the green river; and she was all dappled and young and green like the young stem of a lotus rising from the river.

And he turned away from the young lotus to the blue immensity of heaven, and said slowly: "I have been to the Temple and walked in the blood of the lamb. I have been to Ptolemais and worn the mask of the Messenger and heard the thunder. I have been to the seashore and seen my brother lying dead. All these were sacrifices, and shall I take this last sacrifice unto me?" Soon he turned to her and said softly: "Soon I shall go from here. I shall go into the desert and see the face of God. But not here, not among these reeds!"

She did not hear him: perhaps she had no desire to hear him. She lay with her head on his shoulder, smiling blissfully, and sometimes stroking him. Once she murmured: "I am the image of all things. All things take my form. None shall escape from me!"

"I shall escape from thee," Yeshua said gently, but his voice was so low that she heard it only as a whisper among the reeds.

"Thou art my Osiris," she said again, and she began to stroke him more feverishly. "Thou art the risen Osiris! I have seen on thy shoulder and on thy thigh the mark left by the falcon on thee!"

She was swooning. Her eyes were closed. As her hands moved over him, the green water rippled and sighed, that little bay of water among the reeds which was like a covering to their bodies. And the reeds were like a tent. Strange that they should be lying in the water, clothed and tented!

"Thou shalt wear the helmet of Osiris and sit on the throne by my side," she went on. "Thou shalt have power over all the priests of Egypt! All things shall come to thee! The Sun shall shine for thee and the Moon shall be raised up for thee! Look, touch me here! Thou shalt give me a child, who shall be called Horus, the sun of a new day, and all this is given to thee because thou lovest me!"

He shivered and looked down at the long lean body lying in the soft swirling waters of the Nile. The sun was still beating down relentlessly, sparkling off the reeds. He saw the waving reddish-gold hairs of his sex washed by the rippling Nile, and the proud knees which jutted up a little like mountains of bronze, and the long golden-green torso in the dappled sun. And he knew he could never give her what she wanted.

She was moaning: "Thou art Osiris, and I am thy sister and thy wife, and thou shalt die in me, and I shall make thee whole!"

"It is all finished!" he said.

"What is finished?"

"There will be no child, no love-making! The seed shall not go from me to thee!"

His voice had gathered strength, and rang out fierce and terrible.

She clung to him, buried her head on his shoulder, kissed his cheek and his forehead and tried to hurl herself on him. With all his remaining strength he pushed her away, rose to his feet and began to walk through the reeds until there was only the green river flowing in front of him.

As he swam along the edge of the river, he heard her moaning: "Osiris! Osiris, come back to me!"

Then there was silence, and thinking something terrible had happened he half rose among the reeds to spy on her. She was gathering her blue robe about her and with bent head returning in the direction of the temple. Soon she became a shadow against the early evening blue, and was lost from sight.

He waited until it was dark before returning to the summerhouse. He could not have told why he returned. The stars glittered overhead. He passed the night thinking of her. He thought of her asleep, he thought of her waking. It was like a fever, but not a fever of love. A terrible beauty came from her. She had never been so beautiful as when she lay there beside him, in the cool lapping waters of the Nile, her limbs so white in the shade of the reeds, the full breasts pushing up, the smile of derision and pride and tenderness on her lips.

"Tenderness," he murmured. "Shall I surrender to tenderness? Shall the softness of the flesh overcome me?"

He heard chanting far away in the temple.

He remembered how he had sprung out of the green reeds and hurled himself upon the swift-flowing river, and the smell of the river was still in his nostrils.

"My God, what a terror it is!" he exclaimed. "Works of love without love, works of light without light! Why did I return? Have mercy upon me, O God!"

He shuddered and tried to lie still, but the waves of blood were breaking over his body. The heat, the fierce heat of the Egyptian night, was pouring through him. He told himself he would slip

away from the temple at dawn, but there was no strength in him.
He tried to sleep. He would be drowning into sleep when the
word "tenderness" would rise to his lips and awaken him.

"Let her go from me," he prayed. "Let her tenderness flower,
but nevertheless let her go from me! Let me worship my God! Let
me put grief and love behind me! Let me go alone along the holy
pathways!"

Long after he had fallen asleep he was awakened by a sharp
cry. Awake, he knew the priestess was in the summerhouse. In the
moonlight he saw her gliding towards his bed wearing the lotus-
blue garment with the knot of Isis at the breasts. She walked like
a sleep-walker, her hands outstretched. In one hand she held an
immense purplish-red pomegranate, in the other a knife.

He thought it was a nightmare. There was a terrible inhuman
look in her eyes. In the moonlight her face was marble-white and
the red lips, parted a little, seemed to have been smeared with
blood.

"Meri!" he shouted.

There was no answer. She came steadily forward. He heard the
rustle of her gown. She laid the pomegranate beside his bed and
placed the knife beside it. Then she lifted a sleeve to hide her face
and murmured: "Shall we eat together for the last time?"

"If it pleases thee," he said, and at once the sleeve dropped away
and she gazed upon him smiling.

"For this is the body of Osiris," she exclaimed. "Shall we eat of
the body of Osiris?"

"Thou hast no regrets, no sorrow?"

"None," she answered, "but let us eat the pomegranate together
for the sake of the love that flowed between us."

"There was no love," he said softly.

"Nevertheless there was love, for it flowed from me and went
to you and then returned to me, and so there was a chain binding
us together."

She crouched over the pomegranate. She was very pale, shivering.

"I knew thou wouldst return to the summerhouse," she said, and
there was a note of triumph in her voice. "Was it for my sake thou
hast returned?"

He shook his head slowly from side to side. There was something ghostly about her as she hovered there. Very solemnly she

handed him the knife. It was like a dagger, straight and slender, with a sharp point gleaming silver.

"Cut well," she said, and watched him closely as he lifted himself on one elbow and leaned over to cut the pomegranate. "Cut hard, Yeshua! Cut deep!"

It was the first time she had ever spoken his name.

Pressing firmly with the knife, Yeshua sliced the pomegranate into four quarters. The red juice spurted out and spattered her gown. She laughed softly, no longer afraid, no longer quivering, all the ghostliness gone from her. She lifted the slice of pomegranate to her lips. She was like a young girl, kneeling there beside the bed, while the full blue Egyptian moonlight flooded through the window. Here there was only calm and peace, and anyone observing them would have said they were lovers sharing a meal in the moonlight. Her eyes gleamed, and sometimes she closed them in weariness and pain, but a moment later she was laughing again.

"Who art thou?" she asked once, and he replied: "I am a shepherd, searching for my sheep."

"A good shepherd?"

"Truly a good shepherd," he said, and then she began to ask him how he cared for his sheep, and where, and how he cured them of sickness and protected them from wild beasts, and as he spoke about the sheep, he held her hand in his own. The touch of his hand was light and cool and deeply comforting.

Once she whispered: "I could have killed thee with the knife!"

"To what purpose?"

"For the pleasure of killing thee and for all the harm thou hast done to me! I have loved thee since I set eyes on thee!"

"It is better to be alone," he answered slowly. "Better not to love! Better not to enter that nest of flame!"

"But the Phœnix is reborn: shall there be no Phœnix from our ashes, Yeshua?"

"The Phœnix is dead," he said, "and shall not rise again."

For a little while longer they talked in whispers, then she kissed him solemnly and slipped away into the moonlight, leaving the green rinds of the pomegranate on the floor.

He slept fitfully. There were quick nightmares, flashes of terror lighting up the dark skies. When he awoke the sunlight was pouring into the room, and Khefre was standing there, shouting at the top of his voice: "Where is the priestess? Have you seen her? They say you were lying with her among the reeds?"

"Who said so?"

"The priests say it! They say she came from the Nile with her hair dishevelled, and some time later you came from the same bed of reeds!"

"And they believe it?"

"They are wild with grief and anger! They will kill you! Go quickly! Leave the temple! Hurry!"

Yeshua looked on the floor. The hard rinds of the pomegranates were still there, but there was no sign of the knife. He leapt from the bed, took Khefre's arm and shouted in a voice of agony: "Her palace! She is in her palace!"

The small white palace lay quiet in the sun, with the flaming pomegranate trees surrounding it and the nest of ibises on the roof. The priests were searching for her through the temple: none had yet come to the palace. In terrible fear they ran up to the palace, shouting her name. Already, before they came to the walled-up entrance, Khefre's mouth was twisted in agony. The palace was a closed tomb. They smashed through the bricks and hurried inside. The priestess lay crumpled at the foot of the bed. She wore the same blue gown she had worn when she came to the summer-house, spattered with blood and stains of pomegranate juice. On her head she wore the golden diadem of Isis with the vulture crown, and there was a wreath of blue flowers round her neck. She had stabbed herself with the long slender dagger-like knife.

Because she was warm, and there was still some life in her, they carried her out into the sun. At the moment when the sunlight touched her white waxen face, the ibises rose from the roof with a loud clatter of wings and flew away.

"The white ibises," Yeshua sobbed, watching them as with slow flapping of their wings they flew into the sun.

The Yellow Flower

The sun like a sword hung in the asphalt-blue heavens. It was mid-day and the dust rose in devil-whirls, while the kites circled aimlessly overhead. It was the hour when the people of Beth-shamesh hide in the coolness of their houses and only the swarms of black flies or an occasional mangy donkey, tethered to a house post and frisking its ears, give any sign of life.

Yeshua walked down the dusty street, more ghost-like and silent than ever, keeping close to the wall, lost in himself, not knowing where his feet were taking him. He was alive, and not alive. His eyes were red-rimmed from sun-glare, and his face was ashen white with grief, and as he walked with curious shuffling strides the dust blew in clouds around his feet. If anyone had observed him as he walked down the desolate street, they would have said he did not belong to this world and had emerged from a tomb. And so he had; and the scent of the tomb hung over him.

So he walked slowly and listlessly in the heat of the sun. Once he bent down, picked up a pebble and put it in his mouth, perhaps to relieve his thirst. Afterwards he walked straight forward, hardly seeing where he was going, until he came to the place where five years before he had watched a girl drinking at a fountain set in the wall of a white tomb. The tomb had not changed save for the flaking of the plaster which left some of the red bricks bare. A trickle of water still flowed from the spout into the stone basin, but there was no sign of the girl. Almost he had expected to find her there.

"She has gone," he said, and the words sounded like a requiem.

A great weariness overcame him. It was beyond anything he had known: that terrible separateness of inertia which welled in him. He did not desire to die, nor to live. There are things which happen to a man which break into his most secret heart and burst the covering of the heart, and yet the heart lives on. There are things that make the life of man as thin as a spider web, and still he continues to go on living. For a long time he gazed at the trickle of water issuing from the fountain, and then he turned his face to the wall and wept.

The long noon hour in Beth-shamesh was coming to an end. The city was stirring. A string of donkeys passed, turquoise beads hanging from their necks. They were led by a blind boy with a small wizened face and a thick cluster of black curls reaching to his shoulders. Women and girls passed, coming to the well. They were very erect, very graceful. They carried jars, baskets and trays on their heads, while babies sat straddlewise on their shoulders. Their limbs were lithe and assured, and they carried themselves like queens.

Some, when they came to the well, kilted their long robes up to their knees and splashed their feet in the water dripping off the basin, revealing round brown legs. The sun was a glare of white, and the whitewashed houses glittered unbearably. Swarms of black flies, after their long siesta, gathered around the tomb, while the women talked in whispers. No men passed: only the blind boy with eyes like blue pebbles and his string of donkeys.

As he stood there by the wall, deep in the shadow, he could not have told what he was waiting for. After he had seen the priestess lying at the foot of her bed, he had returned to the summerhouse without knowing where he was going or what he was doing. Then he wandered out of the temple into the white morning, alone and barefoot, without a staff. He had no feeling that he was escaping the vengeance of the priests. He felt only that the place where the priestess had died was in some strange and terrible manner defiled. So he wandered through Beth-shamesh, keeping close to the walls, sunk in torpor, enclosed within himself, until he came to that ancient tomb where long ago Khefre had observed him.

As the shadows lengthened, this winding lane beside the tomb grew crowded. Donkeys, mules, an occasional camel came through the dust. The smell of hollyhocks and pinks and pomegranates came to his nostrils. It was hard to come back to life, the women walking in the sunlight, the panniers of fruit buzzing with flies, the quick smiles, the soft eyes of the girls. He had abandoned this world and never desired to return to it, and it surged around him like a fierce wave and he was caught up in it, and yet he was separate and apart, standing there in the shelter of the wall.

When it was evening a few lanterns burned in the street, and he was still there. It was almost dark when a boy came sidling up to him. The boy was about twelve, dark-skinned, with a small delicate-pointed face, a little wizened, like so many of the children who inhabited the Jewish quarter of Beth-shamesh. The boy wore a long white kilt which reached to his ankles, and there was a yellow flower tucked behind his ear. He curled his small warm fingers round Yeshua's hand and whispered: "Come with me." And Yeshua went with him, because he had no will of his own.

The boy led him to a little hovel. The place was no more than a matshed tent erected against a wall in a deserted lane, sour-smelling. A clay oil-lamp gleamed in the darkness. There was a smell of mangoes and dead fish. An old man, naked except for a greasy loincloth, lay on some heaped cushions at the back of the shed. The boy smiled, leading Yeshua right up to the man, making little clucking noises to attract attention. The man was monstrously fat and bloated, and his face was pockmarked, and the eyes that turned towards Yeshua were covered with a thick white glittering film like dried spittle. There were flies everywhere, and it was very hot.

Yeshua was so horrified by the sight of the man sprawling there, his bloated skin purple in the light of the oil-lamp, that he held back.

"There is nothing to fear," the boy murmured, and the old man lifted up his head and gazed sightlessly at the boy.

"Who is it?" the man asked in a surprisingly shrill voice.

"A priest from the temple of Isis."

The man nodded.

"Is it the priest you were speaking about?"

"The very same," the boy said, kneeling beside the man. "He was at the fountain since early morning."

Yeshua shivered. Though the hut somehow concentrated the heat of the night, he felt cold.

"Is he afraid?" the man went on.

"No, he is not afraid."

"Describe him to me."

The boy described Yeshua briefly, saying that he was tonsured and wore a white robe and sandals and there was a little green scarab ring on the third finger of his left hand.

"A keepsake?"

"Shall I ask him?"

"There is no need. Tell him to come closer."

Yeshua knelt down beside the man. The smell of rotten fruit and dead fish was overwhelming. The man's horny hands reached up in the air and suddenly descended upon Yeshua, gripping him by the shoulders; then they moved over his face and over his chest and along the length of his arms.

"It is the same," the man said contentedly. "I see he is a Jew."

"As I told you," the boy said, and he was still making the curious clucking sounds. "If they find him tomorrow, they will kill him! They will trample him to death in the dust! Did I not tell you?"

The man's head jerked up. Long strands of lifeless gray hair fell to his shoulders.

"Then he must go with the slaves and you must go with him," the man said. "Has he any weapons on him?"

"He has no weapons."

The man began to fumble among the cushions with his horny hands. From some hidden place he produced a thing Yeshua had not expected to see—a dagger in a wooden sheath. The handle of the dagger was thickly encrusted with rubies.

"It is for you," the boy said, lifting it up and smiling at Yeshua.

"Why for me?"

"To defend yourself. The slaves are always quarreling among themselves, and besides you will need it."

"To what mines are you sending me?" Yeshua asked, thinking perhaps the old man was an agent in charge of sending slaves to the mines and quarries or to man the Roman cornships.

"Not to the mines," the old man said. "I see you know something of our ways. There are caravans for Beersheba and Hebron leaving nearly every week. They need slaves for their camels, and they pay for the slaves—"

The old man began to laugh, throwing back his head and shaking his shoulders.

"It is a hard journey," he said. "May God give you blessing on the journey." Then he turned to the boy: "Tell him he can sleep here—it is better; no one will find him. In the morning take him to the west gate. Keep an eye on him. Make him sign a receipt. The money will be paid to me." The old man leaned back, sighing contentedly.

Early the next morning, before the sun rose, the boy led Yeshua out of the matshed along the road to the west gate. There the camels were waiting, tethered to rope-stalls, black against the sunrise, resembling as they rested on the ground huge tortoises with long necks. On some camels emerald-green cushions were being strapped. These were evidently for the women who would accompany the merchants to Hebron. The boy stood there smiling. There was a fresh yellow flower tucked over his ear. An hour later, joining the slaves, they were riding towards the desert and the sunrise. Soon Beth-shamesh was no more than a small glittering nest of obelisks in the distance.

On the third day, when they were resting at noon and the tents were being put up, a sandstorm arose. Suddenly the air, which had been sweet with the winds of the desert, grew heavy and unbreathable. The cooking fires died down, the thorn-bushes were scattered away, and the tent coverings flew up in the air. The sky darkened. For an hour, for two hours they were deafened with the rattle of sand blowing against them. The sky became leaden, invisible, and the neighing of the camels filled the air. All the rich panoply, the bright carpets, the beautiful copper vessels, the veiled women—all disappeared in the torrential vapor-like sand which whirled round them and pummeled and obliterated them. The slaves roped themselves together. The merchants and their wives, wrapped in blankets, huddled together, praying at the top of their voices and sometimes interrupting their prayers to bark out orders to the slaves; but neither the prayers nor the orders could be heard. The fine sand caked their skins like powder and filled their mouths. With bloodshot eyes, stumbling and cursing, the slaves huddled together until it occurred to them there was more safety in lying flat on the sand; then the slave who was underneath the quivering sand-blown huddle of slaves accounted himself the most fortunate. He could hardly breathe, but at least he was protected from the thin spears of whirling sand which choked him and tore into his skin like knives.

These inexplicable sandstorms arise often in the desert and rarely last more than a few hours. There had been clear blue skies in the morning. In the afternoon there were clear blue skies again. An hour after the storm they continued their journey.

At first it seemed that nothing had changed—not even their tempers. The slaves sang softly as they rode, the camels plunged and rocked and lurched as they had done since they left Beth-shamesh. There were more arguments and the laughter was louder. But these things could have been expected. What could not have been expected was the sudden note of panic which entered their voices a little later, when the sun began to sink over the desert.

That night, when the tents were put up, the whips cracked, the merchants screamed at the slaves and there was pandemonium. The women could be heard wailing in their tents. It was an unusually calm evening with soft winds blowing from the sea. Far to the west the sun sank in immense jets of golden flame.

The boy called Abraham, who brought Yeshua to the camel-train, came sidling up to him. Yeshua was leaning against a tent-pole and gazing at the sunset.

"They are all out of their minds," the boy said, his little wizened face lighting up with a smile. "They talk of nothing else but the djinns in the sandstorm."

The sun sank at last. Now in the afterglow a solitary palm tree stood out on the horizon.

"The last palm tree," Abraham said. "There will be no more until we have crossed the desert. There will be no more villages. And no water. Only scorpions and snakes and vultures."

He smiled, saying this, his teeth glinting, and the wind rippled his thick black hair. He clutched Yeshua's arm and said: "Do you like the desert, Yeshua?"

"I like it," Yeshua answered, hardly aware of the boy's existence, lost in contemplation of the desert.

Now it was as though thousands of dark veils were falling softly from the heavens. The stars were coming out, white and lustrous, large as apples, but they were still veiled with the coming of the night. Soon all the dark veils would be falling to the earth and the stars would be revealed in their perfect nakedness.

Abraham tugged at Yeshua's sleeve again.

"Why do you like it, Yeshua?" he asked, and almost without thinking Yeshua answered: "It is like the sun, it is pitiless like the sun."

There was a long pause. A slave came by to say the evening meal was prepared. As he walked, he carried a bowl of oil in his hands and dipped bread in it.

Abraham was peering up into Yeshua's face.

"Were you a priest of Isis?" he said.

"No, I was never a priest."

"Or of Serapis?"

"No, why should you think I was a priest?"

"They say you were," Abraham answered, pulling again at Yeshua's sleeve. "They say you were a priest of Isis and killed the priestess, and that is why you are running away. They say there is a curse on you and a price on your head. Of course I never believe the things they say."

Yeshua smiled. The last of the black veils had floated to earth, and high above him the stars shone with wintry splendor, glittering and winking. The black roofs of the tents cut against the sky. Little blue flames rose from the burning thorn-bushes, and there came the smell of lamb. Most beautiful of all were the little flurries of blue smoke which drifted away from the thorn-bush fires, drifted and vanished like steam. He was losing himself in the night, becoming one with it, no longer afraid of shadows as he had been at Beth-shamesh. "I am the night," he murmured, gazing deeper and deeper into the immensity of starlit darkness around him until he seemed to himself to be sucked into the night's tide, into the swirling black waves which would softly lap the desert until the run rose.

"Strange that I should be so at peace with myself," he murmured. "If I gaze deeper, shall I be entirely consumed by the dark fires of the night?"

Abraham was saying: "Take heed, Yeshua. They are murmuring against you."

"Why are they murmuring?" Yeshua said as if from a long way away.

"They say you brought on the sandstorm. The slaves say it, and the rich ones listen to them. Could you bring on a sandstorm?"

"Why do you ask me these things?"

"I asked whether you could bring on a sandstorm. They say the priests of Isis can do anything they please. They can conjure demons out of the air and swallow fire and turn snakes into sticks like Aaron."

"And you believe it?"

"I believe whatever you say, Yeshua. You can trust me. I shall lie awake while you sleep, so that no harm comes to you."

Yeshua felt the youth's warm hand slipping into his own.

"I shall lie awake when you sleep," Abraham went on. "I shall stand guard over you."

"For what purpose?" Yeshua asked. "The night protects me."

"You do not know the slaves," the boy said in a hushed voice. "They say that when the storm came, you raised your arms to heaven and summoned the djinns. And some say you wanted to take all the treasure on the caravan, and let us all die. So they said, but I believe none of it. And they say you have great wealth."

Yeshua laughed. It was a small dry laugh from somewhere deep down in his throat.

"I have no wealth," he said. "Only the dagger."

"And the ring on your finger?"

"Yes, the ring on my finger. It was given to me long ago in Ptolemais."

"And is it worth anything?"

"It is worth nothing," Yeshua answered, and he wondered why so many of the slaves were coming close to him. "There are thousands of scarab rings like this."

"Can I see it, Yeshua?"

"Yes, you can see it."

Then Yeshua removed the ring and handed it gently to the boy, who quickly slipped it on his own finger. More and more slaves were taking long, slow walks past the tent. Yeshua was not afraid. If they tried to kill him, he would protect himself with his dagger: and if he was killed, then it was because God willed it: so he remained in thoughtful silence, resigned, resembling the night and remembering the priestess with her crown of flowers. A little later he took the boy by the hand, and they went to the cooking fires for their evening meal.

The flames from the thorn-bushes shone on the boy's face as he crouched beside the fire. This was the supreme contentment of the desert night: the crackling flames, the ruddy glare of the fire and the darkness outside. No wind was blowing. They put their hands in the meat and ate in silence, and from time to time the boy would look up at Yeshua and smile consolingly.

A little later everyone in the camp lay down to sleep, wrapping themselves in blankets.

Yeshua was asleep when the boy came to his side and whispered: "Yeshua, awake!"

"What is it?"

"They are whispering about you."

"Let them whisper."

"And there is another thing."

"Yes?"

"I forgot to give you your ring."

Half asleep, Yeshua saw the boy threading the scarab ring on his finger. The boy kissed him. Then, lying there, Yeshua watched for a little while as the boy stood guard, standing like a young warrior with a yellow flower tucked behind his ear and his black hair glinting in the moonlight, for this tent was open to the winds of the desert: there was only a roof of cloth supported on tent-poles.

The dawn was a ruby fire blazing over the desert. They had come to the rocky wasteland, naked and barren under the Arabian sun, with only a few wild *sarba* trees in the shade of the rocks, all bent and withered from the flaming desert winds. There were no more wells, no palm trees, no flowers growing in the crevices of rock. The ruby flame gave way to dark purple and then to gold, and then the full dawn came up: the heat was breath-taking. It would grow worse by noon, but the first shock of it in the early morning was always stupefying. This naked heat seemed to drive straight out of the heavens on a man's face, blistering his eyes, blazing on his cheeks and drying up his lips. Every day, during the journey across the desert, it would be the same.

They rode off shortly after dawn in a strange silence. There were no murmurs from the veiled women on their emerald-green cushions, and the only sound came from the footsteps of the camels and the slow dirge of the camel bells. Yeshua rode beside Abraham. At midday they paused, flung up the tents, ate dates and camel meat (for a camel had gone lame during the morning and had to be killed) and prepared to continue the journey.

Yeshua was standing beside his camel, arranging the saddle-bags when he heard shouts. He paid no attention to them. He threw one leg over the camel, prodded it, felt the movement of its legs as it half rose. The rump rises first, and the rider has to pull his weight backwards to counterbalance the lurch of the camel as it rises to its feet. The shouts were growing louder. Twenty slaves came running towards Yeshua with clenched fists, shouting at the top of their lungs. At the head of them was Abraham. The boy was smiling and waving his arms, as though to say: "Please stop! We have something important to tell you." Yeshua jerked on the camel rope and slipped down to the ground. The boy's face was streaming with sweat which glistened in the sunlight. He still wore the yellow flower in his ear. The slaves were coming nearer, like a great wall. They were jabbering and shouting, but it was impossible to understand what they were saying.

"They are asking you not to bring on any sandstorms," Abraham said, smiling and running up to Yeshua.

"Tell them to have no fear," Yeshua answered, and all the time he was looking at the boy.

Abraham put his arm round Yeshua's waist. It was a protective gesture, done with grace and charm. Yeshua did not realize the purpose of the gesture until he saw that Abraham had seized the jeweled dagger, removing it from the scabbard. As Yeshua half-turned, the boy raised his arm, the jewels flashed, and the smile faded on the boy's face. Suddenly Yeshua felt the whole earth leaping up to him and there was a terrible, excruciating pain in the middle of his back.

As he lay there in the sand, he heard the laughter of the slaves and the neighing of camels. He could not move. The pain was too sharp. When he opened his eyes he saw only some naked feet trampling on a yellow flower.

"Will they leave me here? Will I die?" he asked himself.

A long time passed. He was aware of the trampling feet and the yellow light pouring down like molten tin. He heard the sound of mattocks scratching against rock, a dull rhythmical sound. He thought he was dreaming, because the agony was so great. The sound was insistent and repetitive. He knew they were digging a shallow grave in the desert. Then they dropped the mattocks with a loud clatter, and began to shout, but he could not understand what they were saying. He heard the rattle of dice, and knew they were throwing dice for his possessions: the clean white robe, his drawers, sandals, jewel-hilted dagger. He could feel their hot breath on his face, but he could not lift himself, there was no strength left in him, too much blood had flowed out of his wound. He was glad they were standing round him, protecting him from the sun.

Then he knew he was being lifted into the shallow grave, lifted hurriedly and quickly. They were all cursing him and joking. They smelt of garlic. He was terribly afraid, but he could not show his fear even when they began to heap small rocks and stones

all round him, and after a while they lifted a heavy slab of smooth
rock across his chest, pressing down on him. He heard Abraham's
high-pitched voice. There were so many rocks, and all of them
were cutting into him. They heaped small square rocks over his
face and filled the interstices with pebbles, so that he could hardly
breathe. The shallow grave was perhaps two feet deep. He was
lying there, at the bottom of the grave, and they had heaped rocks
and pebbles all over him, and he could see nothing. And now it was
dark, dark, deep under the rocks and the stones and the hot wind
of the desert, and he was no more than a little jelly quivering there,
protected from the wolves and the panthers. Terrified, he lay
there very still, only barely able to breathe, gasping for breath, the
veins standing out on his forehead, his eyes bleeding, gashed by
the rock.

"I shall die here," he whispered, and for a long time he prayed
silently, and when the prayer was finished he heard the camels
moving away.

The sound of their footsteps across the desert was like the booming of a drum.

A Death in the Desert

When he awoke it was dark and there were no more sounds of
footsteps. A terrible silence gripped him, a silence beyond silence.
Over all the red and broken desert the sun lay hot, and the dead
heat gathered on the shelves of rock. He knew it was evening, and
soon the sun would go down, and then there would be another
emptiness, a greater silence.

It was dark in the grave, and yet the air poured down upon him.
A thin fountain of air offered itself to him, pouring down through
the crevices between the stones and rocks piled over him. Though

there was barely enough air to keep the small flame of his life
burning, yet it was enough. He thought: "Even though I perish, I
shall praise my God."

There came a time when he wanted to sleep, but he dared not.
It was strange how quiet and calm he felt, alone in the grave. He
had no fear, no suffering, no regrets, no griefs: only a sense of
separateness, of being withdrawn from the world. Again and again
he praised the name of the Lord. Sometimes he thought of Khefre
and the long white processions through the temple and the smile of
the priestess as she came to him through the reeds, but these things
happened long ago and he dared not think of them for long. "I
must think of my death," he murmured, and he would have wept if
there had been any strength left in him.

There was a metallic taste like copper in his mouth. The night
was descending, and it was growing cold. He knew his wound had
opened. The blood was pouring out and soaking the earth. He had
expected his blood to be warm, but it was ice-cold as it trickled
out of the wound. He had expected to die, but instead he was
being held in the ice-cold grip of the darkness. It occurred to him
that perhaps the caravan had come to a halt nearby, and soon they
would come and lift him out of his grave, for it often happened that
travelers in the desert returned to a former camp to look for
something they had forgotten. But he knew there was no hope: he
would lie there forever, and the camel trains would come and
step over his grave, without knowing or suspecting he was there.
And so he whispered: "Out of the depths have I cried unto Thee,
O Lord." And then he shuddered, caught up in some terrible
paroxysm, remembering Atys, who was dead, and the dead priestess of Isis whose service he had attended, worshiping her according to a strange worship of his own, and suddenly there came
from deep down in the grave a terror-stricken cry, the same cry
which was torn from the lips of Isaiah: "I, only I, am left!" And
then there were no more cries, only silence, and the body wasting
away.

He slept fitfully, but it was not real sleep: there was always a
small thin flame of consciousness burning. He did not know how
much time passed. He was aware that it was day, and then night,
and then day again. And still there was that little brush of flame
burning deep down below the heaped rocks and stones. "So I am
following her," he whispered, and it seemed right and proper that

he should die close after her death. He slept again and when he awoke he whispered: "There was always too much death. Death is the angel we must wrestle with. Surely we must put an end to death!"

When morning came he was still lying there, breathing in those huge shallow breaths, very slowly, not knowing where he was, suffocating and yet breathing, in the warm darkness of the earth. And as he breathed, there came to him the faint slithering sound of the rocks and stones as they rose and fell with every movement of his chest. It was a sound that reminded him of scree falling down the side of a cliff.

He murmured: "I am in my grave, in the darkness of my grave, and there is no way for a man to rise from the grave."

He lay there very quiet, very still, numbed, without feeling in his legs or arms: only in his face was there feeling. He had no knowledge of how long he had been there, cooped up in this desert tomb, with the sharp stones pressing on him. He knew only he had been there many days and nights, and there were times when the wind howled overhead and other times when he was aware of the burning sun coming down through the stones; there were moments of agony followed by a strange peacefulness, his body like a seed below the earth, naked like a seed, and hardly breathing. And there was no strength left in him. He could not move these stones and pebbles and the trickling dust; he could not lift an arm or a finger. Sometimes he remembered the shapes of the Arab caravan, the tasseled carpets, the women perched on emerald-green cushions: and beyond this he dared not go, for he had no desire to go beyond recent events, no desire to remember his childhood, no desire to remember flowers or any growing things. So he whispered: "How much longer, O Lord? Shall the seed remain in the earth and never come to flower?"

Ever since consciousness came to him in the shallow grave, he had thought of himself as coming alive. No colors penetrated his tomb: in this hushed world even at high noon the sun was hidden, though sometimes a strange pearly grayness seemed to flicker and then vanish, to return many hours later. He knew heat and cold, but he could not have said how he knew them. And now on the third day, as the sun rose, he was aware of other sounds: not the scurry of loose stones only, but the sounds made by his own body, the listless blood, the heavy sap, the straining sinews, as they held

up and supported the crushing weight of stone. This sound seemed
to come from the region of his heart; and when he heard this, he
knew he would not die.

When it came to him that he was still alive, that he was not
wandering amid the dark fumes of Gehenna, then a wild and
intoxicating hope sprang in him. "God has been merciful," he
murmured. "The Lord is my shepherd, I shall not want. He
maketh me to lie down in green pastures: He leadeth me beside the
still waters. He restoreth my soul: He leadeth me to the paths of
righteousness for His name's sake. Yea, though I walk through the
valley of the shadow of death I will fear no evil: for Thou art with
me, Thy rod and Thy staff at my side."

Soon afterwards he slept, but even in sleep he could feel the
burning heat of the sun pouring over the stones, and he was aware
of a little filament of life, like a green thread burning in the dark:
and if this light should go out, then he knew he would die. But he
knew, too, that this little green thread of life would remain burning through all the darkness of his sleep, and while he slept the
strength would come into him.

It was noon when he awoke, and he could hardly breathe. The
air seemed to have become heavy with doom, not porous any more,
nor sweet. His heart was like fire in his chest. He breathed with
difficulty, suffocating and choking. Gasping for breath, he lay quiet
and rigid in a strange trance, unable to understand any more what
had happened to him except that he seemed to be falling deeper
and deeper towards the center of the earth. Yet all the time the
life was stirring in him, and there was a roaring in his blood, and
he knew that if he waited a little while longer, then this terrible
weight would be lifted from him.

"I shall not die," he murmured. "They have pressed stones upon
me, and I am alive! I can hear the blood pounding through the
chambers of my heart, and I am still whole, still untouched!"

Once again he heard the creaking sound as his muscles prepared
themselves to thrust up through the ground. Gradually he began to
gain strength again. He felt like a seed pushing upward through
the earth. It was like a convulsion, like a volcano exploding. He
pushed with all his strength, but now his strength did not decrease.
When he thought he had exhausted every available atom of
strength, then in some mysterious way it was replenished. He was
pushing up, higher and higher, and all the stones upon him were

making a sound like a rending, like the cracking of a great roof-beam. So very patiently, resting for long intervals, he exerted his new-found strength. A long time afterwards, while he was resting after the immense labor of forcing two sharp-pointed stones off his neck, he heard scratching sounds; and these sounds, coming from a long way away, he recognized instantly. It was the scratching of the vultures' claws as they stood in a ring round his grave.

As the sun rose higher, the heat of the day warmed his slow blood and the ice of the long night's coldness crept away. He was still forcing himself up, pushing with all his strength against the overwhelming weight of stone. For a whole hour, he waited: there was only this waiting, for the heavy slab of rock over his chest pinned him down and he had not strength enough to hurl himself upward against it. Then, collecting all his energy, straining against the slab, tormenting himself, heaving and lifting himself, he pushed more fiercely than ever before. The slab did not move. It fell back against his chest when his strength failed. But this tremendous effort produced a miracle. Though the slab remained on his chest, yet some of the pebbles which covered his face slipped away, and he thought he saw a little gap of blue light; and when he saw the light there came a ringing in his ears.

Now he breathed more easily, no longer in terrible slow spasms. All the unimpeded air of the heavens seemed to be rushing towards him. Strength came. He began to lift and heave and pull himself out of the tomb. It took a whole minute, more than a minute, to dislodge a single pebble. He could not get his hands out from under the close embrace of the slab across his chest, but he could use his shoulders, which became shovels, and he could push up slowly with his forehead, pressing up with all his force, till the pin-point of crystal-blue light became a blue flood; and the touch of the welcome air on his face, when he came out at last into the sunlight, stung him and made him cry out, but he did not for a moment stop the slow rhythmic rolling of his shoulders, at once soft and power-ful, gentle and violent. Hours passed before he could move the heavy stone across his chest. His body was bathed in sweat, though his lips were parched. He strained against the heavy weight which pinioned him to the earth, and when at last the stone fell away, he lay limp and exhausted, breathless, without any desire to move, grateful for the freedom which had come to him at the moment when he heaved the heavy rock away, staring at the sky.

So he lay very quietly in the little hollow of the desert, lying limp and exhausted, breathing the soft sweet air of Arabia, in the utter stillness of the afternoon.

"Oh, how wonderful life is!" he murmured. "Even now it is wonderful! It is here in all its majesty, a gift, a treasure, though I am lying in my grave and the sun is burning me and the vultures are coming nearer."

The vultures were standing in a circle round him, blue-necked and hideous, with heavy leathery wings.

"So you have come for me," he whispered, and a strange smile appeared on his blackened lips.

He lifted his head a little, turning it slowly from side to side, gazing at the vultures blankly, not understanding. They did not move. They were terrible in their remoteness, in their unpitying silence.

He did not gaze for long at the vultures, for the heat came out of the sky like a sword, blinding him, glaring off the bright sand and the honey-colored boulders all round him. There was nothing but the swimming, waving heat, shaking him and stabbing him, almost worse than the darkness and the stones. The heat sucked the moisture from his body. And so he found himself doing a thing he never thought he would do: he began to dig feebly into his own shallow grave, to make it deeper, so that he could lie down in the shade. So he rested, lying there in the grave, turning his face away from the sun, waiting for evening, and sometimes the blue-necked vultures came closer, making little scratching sounds with their claws on the rocky ground; and there were no other birds, only the vultures.

With the dusk came the cool evening winds, and a great freshness. He breathed deeply and easily, lying in the quietness of the grave. The dusk grew and flowed like the breath of some powerful and beneficent living thing, the desert no longer swept by the flaming winds. Night came, comforting like all desert nights, and the blinding stars softened the bitterness of his despair. Now for the first time he had strength enough to lift himself entirely from the grave.

At first he was perplexed by the brilliance of the stars and the glitter of the low-lying desert. He opened his eyes wide, those eyes which were scarred and bruised and swollen by so many sharp rocks. He had not strength enough to stand, so he crouched,

shivering with cold, staring at the glimmering rocks, the silver
meadow of the earth, all dead, but strangely beautiful in starlight,
with no living creatures in sight; and seeing the earth so calm, he
broke out into little babbling songs of praise, saying over and over
again: "Praised be the Lord! Praised be the Lord!" Like a fisherman who throws out his net, he threw out his overwhelming love
for the world, which always delighted him and never once failed
to please him, so admirably was it made and so wonderfully was
it preserved.

"How wonderful and gracious is the world Thou hast made, O
Lord!" he murmured, and then fell into a long silence, thinking of
the time when he had wandered with his sheep, the rams and the
ewes, on the cliffs of Nazareth; but that was long ago, and he dared
not think of what had happened in the world since then. Where
was Geresimos? Where was Atys? Where was Yona? All these
had perished, were no more than the taste of ashes in the mouth,
and the priestess was walled up in the temple of Isis, and that too
was beyond anything he expected; but he could not remember
these things clearly, and the blood was trickling over his naked
body, and the cold was biting into his wounds.

He had been gazing across the plain for perhaps half an hour
when he heard the heavy beating of leathery wings and the scratching of claws on the earth. He turned sharply, and screamed. The
vultures were behind him, gathered in a half-circle, the starlight
shining on their curving beaks and hooded eyes; and slowly, very
heavily, lifting their wings, bringing the evil carrion smell of death
with them, their bald heads like little skulls, they began hopping
towards him.

"Begone!" he shouted, his voice coming hoarse in the wind.
"Devils, begone!"

But they were not devils: they were five vultures crowded
together, their glistening beaks like sickles in the moonlight, and
the sound of their heavy wings as they made little hops towards
him was like the flapping of bellows.

He half lifted himself and threw a stone at them. It made a
sound like a pebble plopping in water.

He screamed again, but they knew he was dying and so they
came nearer, smelling the blood on him.

"Not now, O Lord," he whispered, and he stared at the dark
leathery bald-headed vultures, dark against the starlight, like

someone bewitched. "I have raised myself with my own hands from the tomb, but not for this."

There was no strength left in him. He fell back in the shallow grave and lay still, waiting, listening, staring at the star-flood in the heavens, his teeth chattering with cold. He heard the scratching sound again, but the vultures had stopped: they, too, were waiting. They were waiting for the moment when, with a great groan, he would give up the ghost. So he remained in his grave, in the pure quiet of himself, gathering his strength again. Towards morning he rose and began to crawl slowly on hands and knees towards the north, away from Egypt. When he looked back, the five vultures were still standing there.

He awoke with the dawn to find himself in the shelter of a great rock. The sun struck him, huge and overwhelming. He began to cry out. There were small patches of hard yellow grass close by, but when he pulled at the roots there was no sap in them; and when a golden-skinned lizard scuttled over his feet, he cried out in anguish at the pain—the touch of the lizard on his inflamed feet was like a drop of poison. And then, standing on the plain, he threw out his arms and whispered in a hoarse voice: "Lord, help me now in my adversity!" But when, in answer, he heard only the thundering silence of the vast desert, he buried his face in his hands and sobbed and huddled in the shelter of the great rock, until a little strength came back to him, and then in desperation he began to walk, crouching low, towards the ragged blue hills he saw in the north.

From the desert a mist arose, dancing and shimmering, conceal-ing the glare of sand and the gray boulders. The flame of the morning mist was unwavering: only mist and the dead sand underfoot and nowhere any hoof-marks left by camels. The mist was blinding, and sometimes the sun burst through, and the hot glare fell on his cheeks. He told himself he was too weary to walk, but he went on, his body burned black by the sun. Underneath the mist the dead land stretched away: there was the glint of cattle bones and blue rock. He would walk for a little while, and then feel himself, looking down at the torn flesh of his arms and chest, calling on the name of Jehovah and then of Isis, and always in delirium. His mouth was wide open, and the blackened tongue which had swollen seemed to have rolled back to the pit of his throat, choking him. Sometimes he flailed this arms wildly, and

often he would stand very still, glaring at the hot white misty world
around him. By mid-afternoon he had staggered nearly three miles
from the grave.

It was then, in the heat of the afternoon, that he came upon a
flowering acacia tree with little yellowish flower-tufts, full of
moaning bees of the desert, and casting a weak perfume. It was
like the perfume of old wine, but very faint. One by one he
plucked the flower-tufts and put them in his mouth, sucking the
petals. It was his first drink in four days.

How good it was to drink! But the weakness remained, and the
silence, the horrible silence of the desert without the breath of any
living being! As the day was slowly passing he thought: "If only
something living would come here, bird, gazelle, delicate lizard,
even a beast of prey!" But nothing came except the fire of the
descending sun and a hot wind which sent the dust whirling up in
his face. He staggered on, hungry and footsore, treading carefully
because every pebble, every grain of sand hurt him; but now there
was only sand and gray boulders; sand, and yet more sand; sand
clinging between his toes, sand in his wounds, sand on his swollen
tongue. He walked like a blind man with his hands outstretched
towards the sun. And just before nightfall he found himself once
more where he had begun: at the open grave.

He had spent the day walking in a huge circle, though at every
moment of the day he had told himself he must walk due north.
The grave was as he had left it, and the vultures were still there.

The night passed in cold and misery, his strength draining away.
There were moments of remarkable lucidity, but there were long
hours when he fell into a lethargy. He thought he was in Jerusalem,
looking down from the pinnacle of the Temple at the crowded
courts, Yona by his side.

"It is written that the Messiah shall die like a common felon and
be born again on the third day," Yona was saying.

Yona was holding in his arms a red doll which he must have
found in Meriamne's room.

Then Yona vanished, and the dream of Jerusalem gave way to a
high green cliff above Nazareth, the sheepfold and the black
panther springing out of nowhere; and seeing the eyes of the black
panther, he woke up and cried out in agony. Above him the pure
white stars were shining, and the ice-cold wind was blowing over
his grave.

The next morning he awoke to grayness, gray low sky, and the air very still. There was no hot sun sucking the water out of his skin. Once again he began to crawl away from the grave on hands and knees. Towards midday he found some brackish water under a rock and rolled his body in it, crying out in delight. The water was oily, only a few inches deep, thick with sand, and he knew animals had come there, for there were jackal droppings nearby; but he had no fear of animals now. He knew he was suffering from fever and hallucinations. He heard birds singing, but he knew there were no birds. He heard the shouting of muleteers, but there were no mules or caravans in sight: no asses, no camels, no boys running beside donkeys. The only moving thing was a green scorpion scuttering among the dead grasses near the trickle of brackish water. Then another scorpion appeared, very small and delicate and almost transparent, and its little spear was uncoiling. Because the sun was coming out, he drew into the shade of the rock, panting like a dog which has been running for a long while, soaking in the cool air under the rock, running his hands over the wounded flesh which seemed to be coming back to life now that it had absorbed the water from the pool.

Squatting there, gazing at the bright-green scorpions, he was aware of voices he had not heard for many years. His imagination peopled the desolate desert air around him. Figures moved, came to him, beckoned. He closed his eyes, and when he opened them he saw, far to the left, a huge lake of clear and rippling water, with rows of terebinths growing on its banks. Some Arabs were riding along the shores of the lake on sleek ponies, and their shadows, lengthened by the sunlight, fell upon the surface of the lake: and while some dismounted and entered their black tents, others went on, until they had reached the end of the lake and then they vanished. He knew it was a mirage. He knew the lake was no more than tremulous vapor and all those rows of terebinths were no more than stunted shrubs. He knew that if he walked up to the lake it would disappear when he was very close to it, and therefore there was no reason to walk towards it. The lake was floating a little above the level of the desert and there was a strange wavering in the appearance of the Arabs: they were not of this earth. He even knew how these things come about, for he had observed the transparent mist which arises when you hold a flame between the eye and the bright sunlight.

He slumbered for a while, and when he awoke he bathed in the brackish pool again. Now the lake and the Arabs had gone. Instead there were white temples and flower gardens moving out of the silver mist towards him. The domes of the temples dazzled, they crowded one another, they were arranged in tiers. Huge staircases of glistening marble led from one temple to another, and in some of the temples there were gardens, in others fountains, and all were peopled with silent worshipers who thronged before the altars; and above the temples, never still, always burning with incandescent flames, lay a wavering blue sky crowded with angels.

"Where now?" he whispered. "To what end? How shall the promise be fulfilled? Is it not written that I shall die in Jerusalem? Or shall I die here in the shadow of a gray rock?"

He knelt down by the water and began to drink like someone who has never drunk before, splashing it over his face, pouring it all over himself, and not caring when it soaked into the sand. A wild feeling of dizziness came over him. He reeled, fell forward into the little pool, and lay still. He was conscious of no pain, only of a great peace and a great weariness. So, waking and dozing, his head lying in the water, he spent the hottest hours of the afternoon, and sometimes a green scorpion would gaze at the sprawled figure lying there, but none stung him.

In the evening he awoke like someone refreshed. His mind was clear, clearer than it had ever been. The shadows were lengthening and the mists were gone, but the white temples hovered near and the angels sang, dancing across his vision like motes of sunlit dust, and still the throngs of worshipers marched up the marble stairs. "If this is Paradise," he said, "it has a bitter taste." Then he moved into the shelter of the rock, away from the brackish pool, and wondered how he could spend another night in the freezing cold.

The night passed, and another day, and another night. He found some wild grasses, pulled them up by the roots and ate the thin white succulent flesh of the grass. He planned to kill a scorpion by crushing it with a stone, and to eat it, but he had no strength for it. He began to walk towards the north again, but on the eighth morning after he had risen from the grave the sun burst over him with fiery breath, and all his strength left him. He wept, and then he slept.

He was awakened an hour later by the sound of camel bells. He looked up. Something was moving in the colored mirage before his eyes. It moved very softly, bright yellow at the edges, throwing out great streamers of yellow silk, altering its shape, becoming translucent. He heard a faint sound like the plucking of a harp string, very brittle and high-pitched, and this sound came insistently and could be heard above the ringing of the camel bells. He knew there were people there, far beyond his reach or the sound of his voice. When the mist veils drifted away from his eyes, he saw a man riding slowly past on a camel. The man was a weather-beaten old Arab, with gray beard and sunken cheeks, his head wrapped in a bright-colored headcloth, wearing a sheepskin loosely thrown across his shoulders; and behind him came other Arabs, younger, with the same hawk-nose, the same sharp features. And seeing these riders, he knew that the sound of these harpstrings was in reality the high-pitched chanting of bedouins on the march in rhythm with the camels' tread; and now the chanting was growing fainter.

Out of the shelter of the rock Yeshua flung himself, screaming wide-mouthed at the top of his thin hoarse voice, scuttling across the sand and the loose stones with desperate awakened strength, body low to the ground, arms and legs working maniacally, so that he resembled a huge black crab.

A spear with a heavy oak shaft whistled close to his shoulder, then fell in the sand and quivered there.

He expected another spear, but there was none. He lay spread-eagled in the sand. Now at last all the strength which he had guarded carefully even in moments of delirium was gone from him. He turned over on his back, and lay panting, staring at the sky.

Afterwards he remembered a hand coming between himself and the sky, but he could not understand what the hand was doing there. He remembered the gray-bearded Arab bending over him, pressing a dirty moist rag to his mouth. He remembered two or three young men in bright headcloths, wearing long trailing costumes, as they grunted in their throats: *"Kha, kha, kha!"* and then the answering groans of the camels as they twisted their long necks and swung forward and crumpled on their fore-knees. The old man was pouring water from a pigskin bladder over Yeshua's blackened body, and from time to time he dipped the moist rag in the water and pressed a few drops on his lips. Yeshua tried to rise, but they held him down to the ground. The water burned him.

He locked his teeth, to prevent the water from scalding his throat, but they pried his teeth open. A smell of fats and perfume came from the young sons of the Arab, but from the old man there came only the scent of the desert.

"Hast thou come from the dead?" the old man asked tenderly. "Praise be to God we have found thee! We thought thou wast some treacherous crawling thing, a leopard or worse, sent by the djinns to afflict weary travelers!"

"A leopard," Yeshua murmured, and wearily closed his eyes, thankful for the cool water from the pigskin bladder.

"Aye, that is why we struck at thee, not knowing thou wert a man. But thou art truly a man, with that dagger-wound to prove thy manhood! See, he has a wound as deep as a forearm," the old man went on, turning towards his ringleted sons. "Wash the blood cleanly, for I can see there is a waking in him, and all poor wanderers of the desert are blessed by God!"

He said this because the task of cleansing the dried blood was distasteful to his sons.

"Be thankful, Ahab, thou didst not kill him with thy spear," the old man clucked, his eyes brimming with light and pleasure as the blood and sweat were washed away. "Thou wert always too quick to take offense of men, even the poorest of them! Didst thou think he was a tiger?"

"Not a tiger, but a foul serpent by the way he crawled! I thought only to put him out of his misery!"

"Nay, but the hand of God protected him, for I have never known thee to miss with thy spear! So bathe his wounds with thy young hands, for does not God protect poor wanderers in the desert even to the uttermost, and did not God lead us to him?"

In a low voice the young man said: "It would have been a mercy—" but he did not go on. Instead of arguing, he did as his father commanded. He bathed the wounds, wrapped white cloth over them, and according to the fashion of the time, he poured unguents over the white cloth, and he did all this pitilessly, with a clear, hard and chaste look. There was something almost malevolent in his queer, senseless efficiency. His beard was dyed with henna, he had high cheek-bones and large brown eyes, which were like brown glass. His brother was younger, less finely built, with no will of his own. Only the old man seemed to possess a quick comprehension: the two sons were mindless, belonging to the

desert, with no more compassion in them than the scorpions which
hid in the shelter of the rocks.

"The scorpions," Yeshua whispered, and turned his face away,
thinking how the desert had swallowed him and now once again he
was to be given over to the people of the desert.

The man who had been addressed as Ahab looked searchingly at
Yeshua.

"How art thou?"

"Better, by thy mercy."

The man paused.

"It is no mercy," he whispered, and for the first time there was a
little flicker of life in his glassy brown eyes. "Thou wert so close to
death it would have been easier to make the journey, but this
coming back— How didst thou come here? Didst thou fall from a
caravan, or wert thou waylaid by robbers?"

"Nay, I was stabbed and then buried and spent four days in my
grave, but God was merciful, for He brought thee to me."

Overhead the gray vultures were circling, waiting for his death.

"So the vultures are following me?" he whispered, and smiled at
the youth with the henna'd beard.

"Should they not follow thee when thou wert so close to dying?"
the youth said, and once again there was that sharp, efficient,
merciless smile.

And then very quietly Yeshua whispered: "I have been born
again. I shall not die."

He closed his eyes, and even with his eyes closed he saw all
round him the color of tranquility—the desert in the sun: not the
flashing, but the deep yellow of pollen, all the sand transformed
into a soft yellow dust, the uncurling of a yellow flower. And
above the expanse of yellow lay the dead burnt-out blue of the sky.
Only this: the yellow and the blue, himself like a thin blade of
light separating them.

Afterwards he did not know where he was: only he was aware of
a secret life streaming into him. He knew voices. There were
glimpses of tumbled rocks and thorn-scrub, of terrible desolate
purple-red buttocks of rock hemming them in. He knew the creak
of the leather thongs which held him to the side of the camel, and
he remembered being sick into the wool blankets they wrapped
him in, but there was so much strength pouring into him that he
began to enjoy the journey. He was being carried as they some-

times carried sick lambs and goats, but he knew that life was
returning. The vivid flame of life, almost extinguished in the grave,
was soaring again, soaring and shaking him, making him drunk
with the joy of being alive. And so at the next meal, when the
camel lurched down on its forelegs, he crawled out of the wool
blankets and tottered towards the tent stretched over low posts
where the merchants were sheltering from the sun.

The dried flesh of a goat was being roasted over burning thorn-
bushes. They were all gathered over the fire, oblivious of his coming. And then in a strange broken voice Yeshua asked for permission to ride one of the camels, for there were many tethered and
riderless camels accompanying the merchants.

The man with the henna'd beard laughed when he saw Yeshua
standing there.

"The dead one has come to life!" he exclaimed, throwing back
his head.

"Yes, he has come to life," Yeshua murmured, and the smell of
the roasting goat-flesh came to his nostrils.

"And he wishes to eat with us?"

"Yea, indeed, if thou wilt give me this mercy. And out of thy
mercy give me a camel to ride, for I am strong enough!"

The man with the henna'd beard leaped up and with the lightest
of pushes sent Yeshua sprawling to the ground.

"See, he is strong!" the man with the henna'd beard bawled at
the top of his voice, and then fell into a fit of laughing.

Suddenly the old man, who had been resting among cushions,
leaned forward and said: "Ahab, thou shalt help him to his feet, for
are not all wanderers in the desert our brothers?"

"Thou hast spoken truly," Ahab said, and he drew his hand along
his henna'd beard and groaned and went to help Yeshua, who was
covered with sand and twigs of thorn-bush.

Yeshua stood there, leaning against the tent-post, tottering. His
hands felt unnaturally large and his head felt heavy and awkward.
His wound had opened again, and he could feel the gnawing agony
of it.

"And he shall feast with us," the old man said, leaning forward,
"and he shall ride on thy camel, Ahab, and thou shalt attend him
all the length of the journey."

The man with the henna'd beard made a sign of obeisance to his
father. His anger rose in him, but he was powerless to express his

anger. So Yeshua feasted on a little goat-flesh, and in the afternoon
he was mounted on Ahab's camel after his wounds were bandaged.
Then, riding beside the old man, he continued on his journey.

That day they saw only tumbled rocks and great stretches of
sand: never a bush, nor a blade of grass, nor a stone; only the rocks
and the sand. But on the next day, late in the evening, they saw
palm trees, and two days later, riding at a leisurely pace, they came
to Beersheba. There they exchanged camels and set out for Hebron. They rode along the worn-out gullies of dead rivers. Here
and there on the slopes the farmers were reaping the stunted yellow barley. Seeing Yeshua sunk in contemplation, the old man
asked gently: "What thinkest thou, Yeshua?"

"I was thinking that every blade of grass is holy," Yeshua answered.

"And beyond that?"

"That God has been good to me."

"And He has been especially good to thee this day," the old man
said, smiling and pointing to the north-east. "Soon thou shalt be
among friends in Hebron."

Faintly, far away still, a wisp of dust hung against the blue hills
indicating the citadel of the sacred city.

The Ferry-House

The evening breeze was blowing very faintly on the vineyards, and
already the fat grapes were swollen and purple. The sunset came
like a gash of gold in the heavens and smoke rose from the cooking
fires. As the camels came into the market-place, past the synagogue, Yeshua held his head high the better to breathe the scent
of the place: the rich smell of vines, of fruit, of people surging
through the dusty streets. Northward lay the vineyards and

orchards in bright splashes of green against the rolling hills, but the color of the leaves was as nothing compared with the rich carpets hanging from balconies and the riot of colors in the market-place: saddlecloths, turbans, heaps of fruit. After the long journey through barren country he was dazzled by the splendor of the place.

"And so thou shalt rest here, and make thy home with me," the old man said, smiling, and he too was pleased to have returned alive after the journey across the desert. "I have a house and many slaves," he went on, "and all things I possess are for thy pleasure. Only beware of my son Ahab. He shall not touch thee if I am by thy side."

And then whispering, taking Yeshua by the hand, the old man walked towards a large pink house overlooking the market-place and bade the slaves prepare a meal of barley-cakes and young lambs and put the best guest-room in the house at his disposal, saying there was no greater honor than to serve a stranger within his gates. "For thou art come from the dead, and behold I, even I, have taken thee up. And let all things be done according to thy desires."

That night Yeshua slept on a silken bed with silken hangings in a large room overlooking a courtyard where a fountain played. In the evening a doctor was called in to examine his wound, which was smeared with ointment and carefully bandaged. Jugs of scented water with rose petals floating on the surface were brought to him to bathe in, and he was given a gown of silk from the old merchant's wardrobe. An armed slave kept guard at his door while he slept.

Within a week he was well again. He slept peacefully, for the old man had put drugs in his wine which made sleeping easier. Ahab had been sent away to investigate a copper mine which had been opened up on the edge of the desert. Yeshua wandered in the gardens, rested quietly and for the first time since leaving Ptolemais he read from the sacred scrolls. Gradually he forgot the death of the priestess of Isis and the long journey in the desert; he forgot the vultures around his grave and the scorpions and the yellow sky over the desert. All these things had entered into him and been absorbed by him, as food is absorbed. There was only the garden, the old man and the birds singing in the pomegranate trees.

One day the old man summoned Yeshua and said: "If it pleases thee I shall make thee my son, for my youngest son no longer has merit in my eyes."

Yeshua knelt at the old man's feet.

"I am no man's son," he said. "It is better for me if I am alone, without encumbrances. Thou hast rescued me from the desert, but it is better for me to wander in the desert than to live amid wealth. So let me be at peace, let me wander."

"I have great wealth," the old man said wistfully, "and none to give it to. Think, Yeshua. Stay with me a little while longer."

"I will stay a week," Yeshua said.

Together they went on pilgrimages. They rode to the oak of Mamre a few miles north of Hebron, where Abraham had pitched his tent. On another day they went to the Cave of Machpelah which was within the walls of the city and let themselves down by ropes until they were standing in the darkness beside Abraham's tomb. Spellbound, they threw themselves upon the tomb and prayed fiercely, their voices echoing back strangely in the great underground cave. Cobwebs floated down from the roof. All was dark, menacing, yet curiously comforting. It was as though power came streaming from the black marble tomb and those smaller tombs which contained the bones of Isaac, Jacob, Sara, Leah and Rebecca. Even in the dark no one could mistake the tomb of Abraham. And the darkness glittered. Though there was no light at all, and no gleams of light, yet they were perfectly aware of the outline of the tomb and could not doubt that the bones of Abraham reposed there.

"Old father, old patriarch of my race," Yeshua prayed, "forgive me if I have wandered far from thee. Thou didst sacrifice the ram and spare thy beloved son, and didst lead us out of darkness by performing the sacrifice. Have mercy on me now! Forgive my trespasses now and in the future! And let Almighty God give rest to thy bones!"

One day when Yeshua was walking about the market-place in Hebron, he saw a man in a white robe carrying a flowering staff. The white of the robe had faded, and his sandals were no more than thin wafers of leather. He wore a long black beard and carried himself straight and was well-muscled. He paid no attention to the stall-keepers, but kept looking out for children, smiling at them and asking them whether they would like to live among "the Companions of the Palm-trees." Women, seeing him, clutched their children to their skirts and hurried away, making the sign against the evil eye. Yet there was nothing intimidating in the man's appearance. He spoke gently and smiled readily, flashing his teeth, and he walked among the crowds in the market-place like a young prince.

A red-faced meat-vendor with a flabby belly and pendulous purple cheeks was shaking his fists at the man in the faded robe.

"Thief! Betrayer of children!" he was shouting. "Sodomite! Torturer! Refuser of sacrifices!"

The meat-vendor was choking with rage and almost bursting through his own skin.

"Be at peace!" Yeshua murmured.

The meat-vendor turned on Yeshua savagely.

"You ask me to be at peace? Ask the sodomite! Ha, watch him talking to children! Impale him on a sharp stake, that's the best for him! Scoundrel! Son of Belial! Is there to be no end to this child stealing?"

The sun glared in the market-place. The heaps of ripe fruit, mauve, purple, brown, brilliant yellow, seemed to tremble in the heat haze. The man in the faded robe was walking towards Yeshua, two young children clutching at the skirts of his gown.

"*Shalom*," Yeshua said, and made a little bow of greeting.

"May God's blessing be upon thee," the man in the faded robe replied, and would have passed on, but something in Yeshua's expression held him.

He paused, looked into Yeshua's face and said softly: "Hast thou wandered far?"

"Far enough," Yeshua answered. "But I am no child. Thou canst not take me among the Companions of the Palm-trees. I shall not clutch at thy skirts."

"There is peace among the Companions," the man said. "It is the peace that flows from God. Come to Engaddi, and thou shalt see a land of milk and honey in the sunlight of God."

The purple veins on the neck of the meat-vendor were swelling. He was beyond anger, beyond speech, shaking his fists uncontrollably.

"They say we take their children," the man went on. "It is true. We take all the children who come to us, and in this way we continue God's work. We live without women and without money, and shall we be blamed for it?"

Then the man smiled and made a sign of blessing and disap-

peared through the crowd, with the two children still hanging on
the skirts of his gown.

During the following days Yeshua made enquiries about the
Companions of the Palm-trees. He learned they were a group of
Essenes living on the slopes of the hills of Engaddi overlooking the
Dead Sea, a three days journey from Hebron. Though they were
Jews and obeyed the Jewish laws, they refused to perform blood-
sacrifices at the Temple. In the morning they turned towards the
sun and blew a kiss to it in the Greek way, but they did not worship
the sun: it was simply that they believed God spoke out of the
heavens, and the sun reigned supreme in the heavens. They lived in
perfect purity, possessed all things in common and refused to make
implements of war, though they were excellent craftsmen in metal
and wood. They went to work before the sun rose and did not
cease working until after sunset. Each man had his appointed place
in the community and everything he earned was given over to a
steward. But the most surprising thing about them was that they
possessed the gifts of prophecy and second-sight and of healing,
and whenever a Companion appeared in Hebron or in any of the
surrounding villages, the sick were brought to him. Only their
habit of disappearing with children infuriated the people of Hebron.

One day at dusk Yeshua slipped out of the house of the wealthy
merchant and riding an ass bought in the market-place made his
way to Engaddi.

The community house lay against the hills, the white marble
columns gleaming in the afternoon light.

The moment he saw the place Yeshua knew he would stay there.
In the very design of the columns, in the way the house nestled
under the hills, in the quietness and peace which settled over the
rolling valley there was a strange tenderness which went to his
heart. He saw white-robed men walking among the palm trees.
There were little flocks of sheep on the hills. Somewhere a wooden
bell was tolling. Here men lived, as the priests of Isis lived, in
quiet beauty and solemn ceremonial, but not in cloisters and
artificial gardens. The salt winds of the Dead Sea blew over these
fields. It was a wild place, but the priests had cleverly tamed it,
planting trees where there were only granite rocks, building a great
columned house at the foot of the hills, scoring and scratching
white criss-cross pathways up the slopes—strange pathways, glisten-

ing like snail-tracks in the evening light. And somehow—and this
was beyond all explanation—all the land the companions had
carved out for themselves seemed to glow with a faint translucence,
so that even when the sun fell at last this valley of palm trees
glimmered and shone faintly, asserted itself against the night, even
though only a few lanterns were moving among the trees.

The smell of mule-dung and fresh milk came to his nostrils.
He passed a small barn hidden among the trees where the ewes
were being milked and another where the mules were being
bedded down for the night. And then going further towards the
steps leading to the columned house, he heard the booming of
the wooden bell again and this was followed by the voices of
children singing psalms. He tethered the ass to a palm tree and
walked up the long low steps onto the columned terrace. Behind
the columns lights were flickering, and he saw that the temple had
been carved out of the living rock. The children were singing:

> We thank Thee, O Lord,
> For thou hast lifted us out of the pit.
> Thou hast brought us among the Companions of the Palm-trees
> Into a cool place where we may rest,
> And where no fires of the world may touch us.
> Here we are at peace.

> We thank Thee, O Lord,
> For Thou hast given us the savor of good food,
> And the breath of holiness is upon our nostrils.
> In the cave of light, the holy dwelling-place,
> We observe Thy holy commandments.
> Here we are at peace.

And watching the white-robed children in the huge cave lit by
flickering oil-lamps hanging from the cave roof, Yeshua murmured:
"I have come to my own place, among my own people. Surely
from the beginning it was intended that I should live among the
Essenes!"

A small fire of thorn-bushes glowed on the floor of the cave; the
children stood behind the thorn-bushes; fierce flames lit their faces.
All round the walls of the cave the companions were standing
quietly. Strange cave, which had seemed a temple from outside!
Strange children, who lived in these hills without the companion-
ship of women!

The singing came to an end and slowly the children shuffled away, past the blazing thorn-bushes and so to the columned terrace. They were red-faced, healthy, but there was a curious look of reserve on those young faces: almost they were priests and priestesses already. There were young girls among them, but the girls were out-numbered by the boys.

"Where are they going?" Yeshua asked, for the children were being swallowed up in the night.

"They live in the caves, Yeshua," someone whispered at his side.

He turned sharply. It was the lean man in the faded robe who had walked through the market-place in Hebron.

"So you have come, Yeshua," the man said. "I knew you would come."

He took Yeshua by the arm and led him towards an old man robed in white with a gold chain hanging over his breast. At the end of the chain hung a ruby like a drop of blood.

"He is Manahem, the Master of Righteousness," the man whispered.

Yeshua fell to his knees and kissed the hem of the Master's robe. The Master lifted him up. An old face, very ruddy, with sparkling blue eyes, a heavy nose and thick lips pursed together: an air of quiet authority, with no fat on him.

"Thou hast come to the eternal dwelling place where the children of light make war on the children of darkness," Manahem said softly, speaking in the dialect of Galilee, and then taking Yeshua's hand led him to an alcove formed from the living rock and immediately began to ask questions: where had Yeshua come from, what had led him to the cave, was he prepared to work and surrender all his earnings to the steward of the Ferry-house?

"The Ferry-house?" Yeshua repeated, remembering that he had seen no ferry-house on the shores of the sea.

"We call this place the Ferry-house," Manahem explained. "From here we send the bright ships into the sea of God."

The cave was emptying. Fresh rushes were being strewn on the floor. A file of white-robed men passed close to Manahem, and to each he raised a hand in blessing. Yeshua's head was whirling. He had not eaten since the middle of the day. He was close to fainting.

"Give him some bread and a little wine," Manahem said, and then lifting his hand in blessing, followed by three or four children who were especially close to him, he moved towards the columns.

Later that evening Yeshua was taken to a cave high up on the hillside.

There was no moon. The journey up the hill was a nightmare. He kept falling in rushes of scree, while his companion was sure-footed, holding a clay lamp in his hand and somehow protecting it from the gathering winds. Inside the cave a linen shirt and a woolen tunic, wrapped in a bundle, were given to him. Except for a small spade, which was to be used for turning the earth before excreting, there was nothing else in the cave. That night he dreamed he was once more in the desert and the blue-necked vultures were slowly circling round.

For a year Yeshua became a novice among the Companions of the Palm-trees. He worked in the carpenter's shop—another cave. He tended the fruit trees and sometimes accompanied the doctors in the hospital, which was a cave hidden by a grove of palm trees. He learned the Essene hymns by heart and listened to Manahem commenting on the Essene scriptures, which included all the books of the Jewish sacred texts and contained in addition many others, many of them written by Manahem himself. He was not allowed to speak to the children: permission to speak with the children and to work with them was given only after the three years of the novitiate. A cruel simplicity ruled the lives of the Companions. In their white robes, their lips pursed together, rarely showing signs of emotion, strangely calm, they lived on earth as though they were already inhabitants of heaven. There was fire in their eyes, but it was the fire of fever and obedience: there was no gaiety in them. When they spoke of themselves as the children of light they lifted their heads high, proud of being so close to the angels.

During his second year, when he had grown thin as a reed and spent all his time in the hospital, making simples from herbs gathered in the mountains, Yeshua acquired the gift of perfect obedience. By day he lived. By night, alone in a clammy cave, he felt his life ebbing away. And one day, braving the old patriarch's wrath, Yeshua asked to be allowed to shepherd some of the sheep belonging to the community.

"What shalt thou gain by being a shepherd?" Manahem asked gently.

"I shall gain my God," Yeshua answered, and he fell at Manahem's knees, sobbing uncontrollably.

He was given twelve sheep and ordered to pasture them on the uplands facing the Dead Sea. No longer did he need to sleep in a cave. Instead he slept at the gate of the sheepfold, under the stars, alone, remote from the community.

One evening an hour before sunset, while Yeshua was tending the sheep, calling them by name and speaking with them, he saw a dark figure marching towards him from the shores of the Dead Sea. He paid no attention to the figure except to observe that he was not coming in the direction of the Ferry-house, but straight towards the sheepfold. Yeshua could see long distances, and it occurred to him that the man was a mendicant like so many others who came along these shores, spent a night in the hospitable guest houses of the community and then went on their way. He was not sure, but he thought the man was about twenty-eight, young and vigorous, with a sharp narrow face, very sunburned, long hair flowing to his shoulders, wearing patched camel skins. After that glance, he paid no more attention to the man striding towards him.

He was gathering the sheep around him, making deep noises in his throat. "Abeydah!" he called to a small black sheep with tufts of white in its thick coat, and to a heavy sheep white as ice on the mountains, he called: "Hinoon," meaning "the one who gives milk easily." He had names for them all, and when he was weary of calling their names he played on his reed pipe. The sun was beginning to set behind the hills. In that golden light the fleeces gleamed like bronze.

For a while he remained with them, holding them back, for they were eager to make the journey to the fold, and it amused him to watch their eagerness, the quivering of the beautiful bony heads, the startled look in their eyes, the way they crowded together and turned expectantly towards the fold. He ran his fingers through their fleece and stroked them, and moved among them, crouching over them as he always did and sometimes looking up to make sure there were no wolves or jackals on the crags. All the time he was listening intently for the creaking sounds that accompany the coming of night, and the whirring of the wings of eagles.

"Oh my sheep, my sheep," he murmured. "Blessed be Thou, O Lord, who hast created the angels and the lambs! Blessed be Thou who hast created the grass on which my lambs pasture! Be merciful unto them, O Lord! Let them sleep peacefully in the night! Let them utter forth Thy praises and sing Thy blessings! Holy, Holy,

Holy is the Lord Sabaoth, for heaven and earth are filled with Thy glory!"

The sun sinking behind the high crags turned the Dead Sea into a lake of blood. The wind was rising and the thorn-bushes near the coast were making the peculiar crackling they always make in the wind. Yeshua glanced up. The man was within hailing distance, but was making no sign to attract attention. He came straight forward with huge strides—a thief perhaps, but what would a thief be doing in these desolate valleys? The night was welling up round him. Already the Dead Sea was streaked with the leaden blue color which comes when the sun has dropped behind the hills, yet here and there it was brilliant scarlet.

"Come," he murmured, and he was about to steel himself to move towards the fold when the stranger came right up to him.

Yeshua glanced up again, raising his head slowly, shuddering. The stars were beginning to come out in the sky.

Far away he heard the barking of a hyena.

"So thou hast come," he murmured, and he did not know why he said these words.

The wind, the breath of God, was pouring down the mountains, and the man who stood there, with long black beard and dark staring eyes, seemed too frail to stand up against the wind. This man with the fiery red sunburned cheeks was lean and long-boned, taller than Yeshua, and the thick hair falling to his shoulders was tangled and stringy, and there was a smear of salt on the stranger's lips. Yeshua stood among the sheep, and the man stood just outside the circle of sheep.

"Art thou the shepherd?" the stranger said.

"Yea, I am the shepherd," Yeshua answered sorrowfully, "and so I shall be to the end of my days."

"And thou lovest thy sheep?"

"Truly I love them."

"More than thou lovest men?"

There was a long silence. They were like two men measuring their strength.

Because Yeshua made no answer, the stranger went on: "And thou goest to the sheepfold to sleep beside thy sheep?"

A terrible power streamed from the stranger's face. The salt smear gave his face the impression of a mask. As it grew darker, the sheep began to rumble. The sky was growing black above the hills, and already there were lanterns moving about the Ferry-house.

"Shalt thou sleep forever?" the stranger said. "But thou wast not sleeping when I knew thee in Jerusalem."

"Yona!" Yeshua cried out. "Is it Yona?"

Then he shouted and made his way through the sheep and they fell into one another's arms, and at that moment the lightning, playing on the distant shore of the Dead Sea, illuminated Yona's face, so that it shone like silver. The sweat dripped down the lean face and the burning eyes were like sparks glowing among embers. But Yeshua did not see his cousin's face. He stood there with his head on his cousin's shoulder, sobbing, saying: "Yona, Yona, thou hast come back to me!" again and again.

All the years of his wandering he had known he would see Yona at the end of the journey, but he had not known it would be in this way—on a barren upland on the shores of the Dead Sea, at sunset, among the sheep, the evening star shining and the wind blowing among the thorn-bushes.

For a long time they stood there, breast to breast, knee to knee, while the sheep grazed peacefully.

At last Yeshua said: "Stay with me tonight. We shall both sleep beside the fold. The stars shall bless our meeting."

"The stars?" Yona said with a hint of the old mockery.

"The stars and the firmament," Yeshua went on. "Surely they shall bless us, and God also."

So in the darkness, the sheep pattering beside them, they made their way to the fold. As usual Yeshua stood just inside the gate, counting them and summoning them by name. He knew where each sheep would rest, the stronger and fatter ones taking up their places close to the stone wall, the weaker ones in the center. In the starlight the sheep gleamed like mist. Only when the sheep were all on their knees did Yeshua leave the fold and lift into place the heavy thorn gate. He stood for a while listening to the sounds coming out of the night; the hyena was still barking, but it was a long way away.

They talked all night in whispers, lying side by side near the thorn gate. Yona told how he had studied in the Temple after Elizabeth's death. As she lay dying, his mother had begged him to assume the role of Sacrificer, though every fiber of his being spoke against the sacrifices. At the age of twenty, when he was about to

wear the blue garments of the Sacrificer for the first time, he had
suddenly returned to Ain Karem, sold his possessions and gone into
hiding. In the Temple it was believed that he had been murdered.
Then, for many years he had lived in a Ferry-house along the
northern shores of the Dead Sea. At last, unable to bear their calm
and gentle life any more and suspecting them of a secret sympathy
for the Zealots who followed the orders of the surviving sons of
Yudah of Galilee, he had departed from them to wander restlessly.
A month ago he had heard that Yeshua was tending sheep near
Hebron. He had been amazed. He knew about the years in Ptolemais and Beth-shamesh, though he knew these things indistinctly
and often inaccurately. He had not believed everything he heard.
Especially he refused to believe that Yeshua had become a priest
of Isis.

"And didst thou serve in their temples?" Yona asked.

"Not as a priest, but as an acolyte," Yeshua said, and he began to
tell Yona about the virgin goddess who rocked the child Horus in
her arms and gathered together the dead body of Osiris and
breathed life in him, and how her bounty was shed on the priests
who served her.

"There were no sacrifices," Yeshua said. "No reeking altar of
holocausts. Only quiet and compassion and endless meditation
before the statue of the goddess. The worship of the goddess and of
dark Osiris and of Horus, the god of the new day—all this was
beautiful beyond any earthly beauty. It was all perfect and beautiful except for the most important thing. I read the scriptures of Isis
and adored the goddess, and I found they have everything except
God, and I know my God liveth. So I became a shepherd again, for
among the sheep I am left alone to worship my God. But now I
know it cannot be. I know thou hast come to torment me. I know
thou wast sent to me by God, that the words of the Prophets may
be fulfilled. I know I am in the hands of God and a stranger shall
guide me."

"Am I then a stranger?" Yona asked.

"Yea, thou art come as a stranger unto me," Yeshua answered
softly, and he looked away towards the sheep, thinking he heard a
movement among them, but they were sleeping peacefully. And
then a little later Yeshua said: "Thou hast come to torment me,
truly. Thou shalt lead me to the Place of Fire and the Place of
Water, where I shall be burned and drowned. And thou knowest I

am weak and unworthy of the sacrifice. I would be happier if I were left among my sheep."

As he lay there in the starlight by the thorn gate, he looked haggard and gaunt.

Once he said: "Thou knowest, thou knowest—"

"What do I know?"

"Thou knowest I am unworthy, for there is no sacrifice greater than being burned in the flame of the living God and being drowned in the eternal fountains of God. Three times I shall die, according to the Prophets. Have mercy on me, Yona! Have mercy!"

Then he shuddered and the sweat pricked out on his face and he went a little way apart to pray. He prayed that the burden should be lifted from him. He begged forgiveness for his sins. He asked that the cup should be taken from him. And when he returned to Yona, he whispered: "The last days are at hand! *Hosanna b'harom!* Hosanna to the highest!"

"And am I still a stranger?" Yona asked.

"Nay, thou art closer to me than mother or father, and thou shalt stand at my right hand!"

Soon afterwards they slept, and early the next morning Yeshua made his way to the Ferry-house and asked to see Manahem.

"I must leave the Ferry-house," he said, "and another must look after the sheep."

"What madness is this!" Manahem cried.

"It is not madness, father. God has given me my own sheep to care for. Let another look after the sheep belonging to the Ferry-house. Let me go, father! Let me go in peace and with thy blessing!"

"Thou wast the best of my sons," Manahem said. "Stay with us, Yeshua. Thou hast found thy place. Stay with our sheep and be good to them. They have grown fat under thy staff."

"I must go, father, and God knows where I shall wander, but I know that God summons me to be purified in the flame and cleansed in the living water. A stranger came to me, and though I wrestled with him, I know I am summoned. And have pity on me, father!"

"Then I have lost my best shepherd," Manahem exclaimed, and he smiled sadly. "So much wandering, Yeshua! There was Ptolemais, I remember, and Egypt, and many other places, and now must thou wander again? But if it is God's will, I shall not hinder thee! Go in peace, and may God's blessing be upon thee!"

Manahem sent another shepherd to look after the sheep. All morning Yona and Yeshua wandered along the shores of the Dead Sea. Towards noon they came to a long valley and because the sun was hot on their faces they turned inland, following the flight of some rock pigeons which came winging across the sea.

The Holy Fire

All through the afternoon they wandered through the hot valley, not knowing where they were going nor where they would spend the night, content to be together, in the closeness of one another. The dark red rock glowed savagely. Coarse thorn grass whistled in the wind, and lizards crept in the empty gullies. Half of the valley lay in the blue shadows. Here and there, withered by the salt winds, were clumps of stunted terebinths. Afar off, the very end of the valley glowed with a feverish yellow light.

So they walked, listening to the cry of the eagles overhead, very grave, full of one another, speaking in whispers, and sometimes they would pause and stare at each other in silence, as though they could not believe this meeting had taken place. Once Yeshua said: "I could not have lived if I had known we would never see each other face to face." And then a little later: "It is all mystery. To come back from the dead is a mystery, and to be born is a mystery, and to meet those you love—this is the greatest mystery. And God has blessed our meeting. Surely there is a trembling in the air!"

He shuddered and buried his face in his hands, and suddenly looked up, as though he thought there would be a sign in the heavens to bless this meeting with Yona. But there was no sign: only the perfect emptiness in the heavens.

They walked on in silence, the sound of their footfalls echoing in the valley.

"There have been so many signs," Yeshua said a little later. "The black panther was a sign, and the trembling of my hand when I killed the lamb in the Temple—that, too, was a sign; and in Egypt and in the desert—more signs than I could understand, and so many they were past counting. I was like a man who walks blindfold along the edge of the abyss and wherever I put my feet, God guided me. But when you came to the Ferry-house, then I knew this was the greatest of all signs. They shall say afterwards that no sign was greater than your coming. And truly I believe God will speak to me this night."

He shuddered again, for he was aware of the power and glory coming closer. He could not have said how he was aware. It did not come from the heavens or from the earth, but that it was already coming, this was something he was certain of, more certain of this thing than of anything that had ever happened. In that moment when his eyes met the eyes of Yona, then all things were determined: all things save the blessing, all things save the voice of God. For was not Yona the Sacrificer, and was he not the Victim? And now they had confronted one another, and there remained only the blessing of God. And all this might have happened long ago in the past, but God must first show the way and lead them to man's estate. If he had spoken on the steps of the Temple, he could have destroyed the Temple: but the moment passed, he had slain the lamb and walked away to eat the Passover meal, in grief at the sacrifice. And so he whispered: "The days of mourning are coming to an end."

"And when shall we see the sign?"

"Soon, Yona, for at the moment of our meeting, I knew this sign would be given to us." And a little later Yeshua said: "A pillar of cloud by day and a pillar of fire by night. I know I must be baptized in fire and water. I know He will speak to me. But this other thing, this knowing deep in the heart that we are together and shall always be together—perhaps this is the sign, and no other is needed. I knew you would come, but I never hoped for it, never dared to hope for it."

Towards evening they rested in a grove of stunted terebinths

and broke bread and ate some wild figs. As the sun sank a dry
wind rustled the reeds in the gullies. The red hills glowed purple.
The first stars were coming out.

"Shall we sleep now?" Yona said. "Then if we sleep, God may
reveal Himself in our dreams."

As the sun fell behind the mountains, the air turned bronze and
the shadows wheeled. Now the hills were bluish, and here and
there they glittered like damascened swords, with ripples of yellow light along the blades; and there were no more birds. Silence
gathered for the night, the long silence of the crumbling valleys.

The faint look of annoyance on Yeshua's eyes did not vanish; his
eyes gleamed in the dark.

"No, not in dreams!" he said. "Not that! God spoke to many in
dreams, but now I know he speaks through the clear skies! Do not
ask me how I know! We must be as Moses was, standing before
His face, even if the face is veiled! It must be in the light!"

"Then we shall pray here and wait?"

"No, not in prayer and not by waiting," Yeshua said, and he
walked a little way away, until he was outside the grove of terebinths, the cool of the evening wind on his face.

The night had gone still, very dark, the shadows creeping
stealthily. He could see the wavy ridges of the mountains, the
sharp points of the highest, and sometimes in the hollows of the
mountains he saw the faint light of the reflected stars. All the
valley was hushed and still, caught up in the terrible stillness
which precedes a storm.

He stood there, lost in thought, looking down the dark valley,
shivering a little in the evening breeze. The air quivered. He was
not thinking of the coming storm. It was enough to be there with
Yona in the terebinth grove, with no thought of what the morrow
would bring, no care for food or sleep; alone there, in the neigh-
borliness of love, which was also detachment. He whispered: "Tonight I shall fall into the hands of God." Then he went back to the
terebinth grove.

A few moments later the first drops of rain fell, striking against
the terebinth leaves like shattering glass, and almost instantane-
ously the wind sprang fierce along the valley. The rain beat down
on their backs. Suddenly the night darkness was very thick, brooding, immense; and the stinging rain came like whips. The wind
blew, shaking the terebinths: far away, as the hurricane increased

in fury, they heard the rocks plunging down the slopes, loosened by the sudden rain.

It was dark, pitch dark, and shivering cold. In the rainy season, in these valleys south of Engaddi, the nights can be very bitter: men have died of exposure when the storm overtakes them in the late evening, though there were no clouds at sunset and none at dawn. At such times the wanderers in these valleys try to make for the caves, where they lie numb and prostrate with cold, quaking before the enormity of the storm, the thunder rolling over them, the flash floods streaming down the valley. A whole caravan can be lost on such a night, the tents staked, the donkeys and camels sleeping, the merchants lying on quilted silks: and in the morning only some shreds of tent cloth, and a dead camel curled round a rock.

Yona took Yeshua by the hand and shouted: "Hurry!" All the waters of the sky were being emptied out on them. Stumbling, shouting, blinded by darkness and rain, they ran towards the sloping hillside where, half-concealed behind boulders, Yona had seen a cave earlier in the afternoon. It was one of those caves where in former ages the anchorites of the desert had lived. Long crested lightnings, silver and purple, shot across the valley. By this light Yona thought he could make out the cave behind the boulders. The smell of the rain, the smell of the newly-awakened earth, stung their nostrils and the rain tore at them. It was ice-cold rain and it was merciless. For a long time there was no more lightning. They stumbled, fell, groped blindly, shouted and heard their voices echoing from the rocks; and when the lightning came, long flashes of purple and blue and silver darting down in double chains, there was no thunder: only the pure lightning, the ghostly blue rocks, looming thorn-bushes, no cave in sight.

It was a night of terror, of pure blinding terror and endless groping. For after leaving the terebinth grove, they groped their way along the hillslope, searching for the cave which was perhaps no more than a shadow thrown by the afternoon sun. And when at last they found a cave, it was further down the valley, and higher up, a thing seen for a moment in the smoke of the purple lightning.

They threw themselves down on the cold, steaming floor of the cave, gasping for breath. It smelt of animal fur, animal dung, bones and the empty shells of scorpions. Half-naked, exhausted, their hair matted, bruised, drenched with rain, they lay there panting, while the wind tore at the clump of thorn-bushes just outside the cave, smacking them from side to side, tearing off little sticks of branches and throwing them into the night. The food in Yona's satchel was sodden. In the spasms of purple lightning the cave would light up, every ghostly crevice and knob of rock filling with light, so that the whole cave and everything it contained, the broken water jars, the little heaps of dried dung, the scorched places where long-dead fires had burned, all these assumed a startling clarity. Yona's dark face, the long awkward beard, the arched brows, the slanting black eyes, the delicately carved mouth —these, too, assumed the purple color of the lightning, glowed and went black, sucked into the surrounding darkness of the night.

So while the wind blew they huddled on the edge of the cave, staring out at the valley where the flood-waters were pouring in spate; and sometimes when the lightning lit the heavens, they looked at one another exhausted, standing back, clinging to the rock, overwhelmed by the blazing terror of the night, the deep rumbling which came out of the hills. Somewhere a wolf howled, and there was the sound of scree slithering down the bare rocky slopes, but more terrible than anything else were the sudden cracks of thunder which broke the strange silence of the place.

Stumbling, they made their way to the back of the cave, where the lightning flashed less piercingly than at the mouth. High above their heads were strange inscriptions in the ancient letters of Aramaic. Yona was shaking. The fever of the night had gripped him: his lips were drawn back in a grimace. In the fierce gaze of his eyes there was a terrible hurt, a terrible savagery. He was hurt for his cousin's sake, not for himself.

"Truly He is a jealous God," Yona said. "Truly He is more powerful than all the creatures. He maketh the mountains to flow like water."

"Hast thou lived in caves?" Yeshua asked, gazing at the damp and smoking walls of the cave by the flicker of the lightning far away.

"For ten years I have lived in caves," Yona answered. "So merciful is God to provide caves for shelter."

In the voice there was a hint of irony, and a savage adoration of God's splendor. Strange that Yona could simultaneously possess towards God such irony and such love. And then in a gentler voice Yona said: "Is not a house a cave?"

"Surely."

"And the body, too, is a cave in which we hide. We have a little lamp burning in our cave, but the winds of God blow it out. And when we hide at night from God's elements, we are no more than a cave within a cave."

The thunder was coming closer. The whole hill was quaking. Through the open mouth of the cave they saw the valley and the flood-water lit by almost continuous lightning.

"I have been further than I ever thought I would go," Yeshua said. "I did not think it would end in a cave."

"Why are you sure it will end here?" Yona asked, and there was tenderness in his dark, fiery eyes.

"I am sure this is the end," Yeshua answered quietly. "There will be a revelation, and this will be the end."

"And there will be no beginning?"

"Yes, there will be a beginning, but whether I shall see it, only my Father knows. I know I shall be tried and tested in the fire. I know He is close to me. I know I must wait upon Him. But I had not thought the end would be in this cave."

For a while Yeshua stared round the cave as though at last he recognized the place: the little heaps of dung, the shells of scorpions, the strange carved inscriptions over his head, almost out of reach. The cave was like a great sounding board, the thunder exploding up and down the length of it. Yona was leaning against the damp wall, his eyes closed, the terrible straggling beard falling over his chest, strings of hair falling over his forehead. And shivering, hardly able to stand, never taking his eyes off his cousin, deafened by the vast roar of the approaching thunder, Yeshua said: "I shall die again, and I do not know whether God will have mercy on me. There have been too many dead."

"Too many?"

"Those who are closest to me have died, and I have died, and shall die again. There is no end to death, Yona. If I am one of the chosen ones, I must put an end to death. Only I know there is no more lonely road."

There was a long silence between them. Yeshua spoke with difficulty. There were moments when Yona had to guess wildly at the words, for here and there Yeshua used words in Greek and even in Egyptian. His eyes were ghostly, and sometimes he turned away, muttering to himself.

Once Yona heard him saying: "Where are the waters of resurrection? Where are the fountains of life?" And then again, more softly: "The road is lonely."

"I, too, have known loneliness," Yona said, remembering the long years he had spent in caves with only the wild beasts as his companions. "There is no end to it, unless you walk hand in hand with God, and then there is no beginning to it. God withholds loneliness from the chosen ones, and surely thou art chosen!"

"I know not what I am," Yeshua answered. "I have seen the signs and the wonders. I have known God's holiness. I have seen the glory with my eyes, and known the suffering, and wrestled with black panthers, but whether I am one of the chosen ones I do not know, and perhaps I shall never know." And then becoming calm, he said: "The loneliness remains. Where shall I turn so that the loneliness is taken from me?"

"Into the heart," Yona said, and smiled, wondering why Yeshua asked such simple questions.

"And then?"

"Beyond the heart."

"Yes, that too. I have been there. I know the place. You come to the end, and then at that very place, where it is impossible to go further, still you go on. It is the last loneliness of all. God tempts you. You walk unaided, and God is far away, and still you know He is there. I have been there before, and would prefer not to go again, not into that loneliness. Have you been to that place, Yona? You cry out with all your strength, out of the depths you cry out to God, and there is no answer, no echo, only that terrible silence, which is greater than I can bear." He went on a little later: "If only there was someone to go with me. Not a woman—I have no love for women. I have love for men, for brothers. It is time I returned to men, but how shall I return?"

There was a strange fire in Yeshua's words. He looked curiously withdrawn, as though he were wrestling with an unaccountable melancholy, and at the same time he looked expectant and watchful. Cold rushes of air blew on them. The storm gathered, unceasing. There were moments when Yeshua would look around in confusion, as if to find answers in the shadows. "I do not recognize him," Yona murmured. "I did not expect him to be the same after so many years have passed, but he is altogether changed. He is afraid, and I have never seen him afraid. He talks so quickly, and there is so little strength in him. And if he should give himself up entirely to God, if he should wander in these deserts, I am sure he would die!"

"I shall not die!" Yeshua said, as though he could read Yona's thoughts. "This I know! I know I am chosen, as Elijah was chosen! I have lain in the snares of the Queen of the South, but I escaped from them! I have seen the signs; only the last of them has not been vouchsafed to me!"

"There will be many signs," Yona said, and once again he looked away, not daring to contemplate the face of Yeshua, which gleamed blue in the lightning.

"I shall go among men," Yeshua said. "I shall find the signs there."

"You talk of men, but not of women."

"Who are women, that I should talk of them? Ah, but tenderness! Let there be tenderness between men and women. Let it not break. Let it be a soft thing, as soft as water. But it is the other thing I speak of, that men should be brothers. This I know. For four days and four nights I lay in my grave, and even then I saw the glory. I knew my blood was streaming within me, and my blood was singing a song of love, and even afterwards when I escaped from the tomb, when with my own strength I had pushed the heavy stone away from me, when I was crawling over the earth like an animal in the hot sun, when I was starving and closer than ever to death and the vultures were watching, then I knew there must be an end to sacrifices, and there is no sacrifice greater than love. Can you understand that?"

"Yes," said Yona, "I understand that when a man comes back from the dead, he rejoices."

Yeshua shook his head. There was so much he wanted to explain, so many things he wanted to convey, and there were no words to explain this thing. Perhaps it would be better if he simply looked at Yona as they crouched together in the cave, where the fur and bristles of animals stuck to the damp walls, seeing one another in the flicker of the terrible lightning, in the blue breathless moments of illumination, and then in silence they would say what needed to be said. And there were other reasons why he could not speak the thing close to his heart: he was afraid. He did not know why he was afraid. He knew only that fear was coming out of the night, coming towards him. Outside in the valley, in the

darkness between the high rocks, there, near a terebinth grove and
not far from Engaddi, a dark wave was lifting. It had shape and
form and color, and a terrible power lay concealed within it. It
would rise and thoroughly engulf him. It was something like a
tangled, heaving knot of ropes, and it was growing larger, and
more and more ropes were being gathered to it: only it was not
rope: it was power, a terrible breathing knot of power, huge and
silent, gathering there in the dark, a power that could burn the
rocks away, melt Palestine to a cinder, tumble the Pyramids until
they were no more than a few grains of powder. And this power,
relentless, unalterable, glowing in the dark, was coming towards
him. He knew it was there, but there was no name for this power.
He knew it would come and in some strange way destroy him, and
he knew he would be unable to resist it; and he had no desire to
resist it. And so he waited, but he could not take his eyes from the
entrance to the cave, and when he replied to Yona's questions, he
was talking like someone bewitched, hardly knowing what he was
saying, so overcome was he by the presence of the strange glowing
knot of power in the valley beyond.

He said softly: "When a man comes from the dead, he rejoices.
Yes, that is true, and perhaps it is the only thing that matters, the
rejoicing. But it is more than that. The blood sings aloud. God
knows, never have I felt so alive, so wonderfully alive, as when I
came back from the dead. My blood sang with love, and nothing
else. It said: 'Go out into the world, tell them to love, for you have
come from the grave. Will they ever believe I have come from
the grave, Yona?' And then I tell myself it is not enough that men
should love, or that I should be a messenger of love. I know that I
must be an example of love to the very end, and that I must die of
love, and there is only love. Beyond love it is impossible to go.
And I know there must be an end to all sacrifices. There have been
too many sacrifices. The earth is red with the blood of my lambs.
And there must be an end to it. And I cannot see clearly the pur-
poses of God, but I know that He, my Heavenly Father, has set
His face against blood sacrifices, and the Temple shall be destroyed, and perhaps there will be an earthquake, and perhaps it
is now."

Yeshua said these words softly, and then made a strange sign in
the air like a cross. His lips were pursed. All the time he was gazing at the mouth of the cave. Yona saw a look of intense suffering

pass over his face: it was the look of a man whose body stiffens and recoils. And now Yeshua was saying: "I have come from the dead, Yona, and I know this: even the dead are encompassed by God's mercy. But the living must love one another."

Afterwards they were silent, listening to the storm. Now the thunder came still closer; it seemed to come from the living rock, and the roots of the rock. There were shattering peals of thunder followed immediately by flames of purple lightning. Scurries of hail flew along the valley, and the flood-waters were roaring. Somewhere on the rocky heights the jackals were howling, as though they were intent to drown the noise of rolling thunder echoing against the cliffs, the sound whipping from one side of the valley to the other, then whipping back, or cracking against the flood-waters. Yona knew these storms well, but he had never known one so violent as this. They came suddenly; they ended suddenly. Always the temperature dropped, and the ice-cold wind blew, and there was no snow, only the scurry of hail and the harsh rain, and then the blue darkness settled: in the darkness the sky was lit with trickles of silver lightning. But this storm was unlike any storm Yona had known. Shivering, his lips pursed in an extraordinary smile, he heard himself saying: "Come deeper in the cave, Yeshua! Come deeper!" There was no answer from Yeshua, who was walking towards the mouth of the cave.

There was a long silence, a burning hot silence, in the cave. Beyond the fierce eye of the storm a deeper storm was brewing. The whole cave, the whole mountain began to shake in the violence of the storm.

"Come back, Yeshua!" Yona sobbed. "For the sake of the living God, the Father of Abraham, come back to me!"

A thunderbolt struck the rock near the mouth of the cave: a dazzling, shimmering silver light exploded, and threw the shadow of Yeshua along the whole length of the cave: and still he went on, walking slowly, seeming hardly to be walking at all, moving closer to the cave mouth with his arms wide apart, his eyes closed. Yona was stricken with fear. He shouted and sobbed, crouching in the deep recess of the cave, staring after Yeshua, murmuring prayers, not knowing what he was murmuring, his spirit broken, dank hair matted over his face, saliva flowing from the corners of his lips, his eyes shining with a glassy stare.

"Where art thou?" he murmured. "Oh, my beloved, where art

thou? Come back to me! Do not go into the storm! Do not go
from me!"

An extraordinary thing was happening. Yeshua stood now at the
very lip of the cave, his hands stretched out towards some invisible thing hovering in the storm, and all the time his head was
lifted up and he was speaking, and now the lightning seemed to
be gathered all round him, and the air crackled, and there was the
smell of burning. The little scraps of dark fur on the cave walls
burst into little flames until all were ignited, and all the animal
bones on the floor were glowing blue, as though lamps were burning inside them. Blue veils of hissing fire hung over the entrance of
the cave, and in these veils Yeshua was still standing with his arms
outstretched, and his head was turned a little to one side, so that
Yona could see him clearly, the face uplifted, the lips opening and
closing, but no sound came from him. And now there was no thunder and no lightning: only the still blue fire, the little tongues of
blue flame, blue upon blue, and the whole cave was filled with
the fire.

"What magic is this?" Yona whispered, staring into the blue
fire. "It is something he has learned in Egypt? He stands there,
summoning the heavenly powers. Surely when a man summons
the fire, there is only evil!"

Yeshua was groaning. His face, his whole body was white, transfigured in the blue blaze. The blue fire was beating against him,
fanning him, lifting him up, curling along the outstretched arms,
a blueness so intense it was like daylight, and in this soft effulgent
blueness, in this stillness like the stillness of a summer afternoon,
Yeshua stood with arms uplifted towards the heavenly powers,
speaking in a strange voice, humbled, enclosed in the splendor of
blue fire as in a tent. And then there was only stillness, and the
little wavering of the blue flames.

In his own time Yona had performed miracles. He had lived for
a month on a single crust of honey, he had healed the sick, spoken
with the dead, wandered barefoot and naked through storm and
tempest, wandering as people wander through the summer corn-
fields, his spirit never failing him; but he had never known the
caves to be filled with blue flames, never known the silence at the
heart of the storm, never seen a man standing on the lip of a cave,
rejoicing in the flames, standing there with arms uplifted as though
attending upon a ceremony, never seen a man turned to whiteness

and transparency. While the blue flames lapped around him, brightest at his face and finger-tips, the body of Yeshua seemed to melt in silver: there was no body, only a transparent whiteness, a shining ghostliness: and then it seemed to Yona that Yeshua had become a vessel into which all these flames were being poured, and he could feel the movement of the air around him, the flames rushing about the cave, all pouring into Yeshua, flowing into him, so that every moment he became brighter, more dazzling, more terrible.

"Now is he become the Son of God," Yona whispered, sinking to his knees.

He hung his head. He could not bear to look for long at the blinding whiteness, the terrible transfiguration. He could not have told how long the naked blue flames streamed through the cave. He remembered afterwards that an eternity seemed to pass: an eternity of brightness, of rushing winds, of whirling snow, of soft lambent flames. And he must have fallen unconscious, for when he looked up again Yeshua was standing over him, a face no longer young, but terrible with age, and gleaming with a brightness, which was not the brightness of the flames, and somewhere in the heart of this face Yona thought he saw a strange pitying smile; and it was the smile which held him. He did not know what Yeshua was saying, though the lips moved. He knew only that Yeshua had become someone else, a stranger to him, a glowing mask, and the eyes were hollow and dead like ashes as they had been on the day when, wandering round the walls of Jerusalem, Yeshua had suddenly fainted and leaned against the walls of a grave. And it was this face which Yona saw now, here in the deep recesses of the cave, a white, a terrifying face, hollow eyes, the faintest suggestion of a pitying smile.

"The Anointed One," he whispered, and put his hand to his eyes to shield them from the streaming radiance.

Afterwards he was silent for a long while, not daring to speak. He must watch to the end, uncertain whether he was dreaming or the victim of hallucinations, while the storm increased in fury outside the cave, and all the time Yeshua was standing over him. He had thought that if Yeshua was the Anointed One, the King of the Jews, the Son of God, then he would announce himself in the Temple. He had not thought that Yeshua would appear in glory in some obscure storm-lit cave on the shores of the Dead Sea. Not

in a cave, not among broken potsherds and the excrement of wild
beasts would the Son of God show Himself first to man! And yet
it was so. He did not know how it had happened, and he would
never know. He knew only that the terrible face was there, and
the flames were licking the walls and all the cave was full of these
rushing flames which assumed the faces of angels, but the faces
were continually changing, and all of them were singing hosannas. And Yeshua stood there, summoning the flames to himself,
standing very still, so that the folds of his garment hung straight
to the ground, and he seemed higher than the mountains as he
stood there. And then quite suddenly Yona understood that all
these things were taking place according to the ancient prophe-
cies, for men had known long ago that the Son of God would be
born in a cave, and surely He was being born again! And was it
not written that His coming would be attended by fire, flame,
darkness and cloud, the ringing of bells and the clash of thunder,
and the sound of a ram's horn, and the trembling, and the Presence, and the choirs of angels?

So it had happened, and Yona steadied himself to observe a
thing he had never expected to see, and he did not feel faint, but
on the contrary the more he looked, the more the strength poured
into him. Once he cried out: *"Hosanna b'harom!* Hosanna in
the highest! Blessed is He who is born of the Fire!" And at that
moment he thought the pitying smile on the face of Yeshua
changed into a smile of the most perfect triumph, but it was not
this smile which attracted his attention so much as the sight of the
white doves like spurts of flame, with yellow beaks and incandescent wings, circling high above Yeshua's head, and it was
strange how the wings fanned him. Strange, too, how the cave had
vanished, now there was only the warm blue sky above, and all the
rushing blue flames had melted in the blue air, and Yeshua seemed
to be standing amid summer flowers on some hillside. It seemed
that he stood there for an eternity, but it may only have been a
moment. Gradually the light faded from the summer sky; once
more he was in the cave, and there were no more blue flames licking the damp, scored walls. Now he could see the stars glimmering at the mouth of the cave and Yeshua was standing close to
him, whispering some words he failed to understand because he
was so surprised to see the starlit sky. Darkness and damp and the
wind in the thorn-bushes and the storm moving away!

And not knowing what he was saying, Yona whispered: "Shall the glory never be seen again?"

"The light thou hast seen," Yeshua answered, "is nothing compared with the greater light thou shalt see at the appointed time. I have been baptized by fire. There shall come a time when I am baptized in living water, for this I heard from the lips of my Father in heaven. But who shall baptize me, or what waters shall receive me, all this is unknown to me." And a little while later he said: "Let us sleep now, Yona."

So they slept, and in the morning when the sun rose over the dark waters of the Dead Sea, they were still asleep on the floor of the cave.

Behold the Lamb

As he knelt beside the sleeping Yona, Yeshua said: "Surely this cave is a temple where the spirit of God moves, and surely its priest is Yona. Therefore is he blessed above all men. Already is he become the Sacrificer. So let him sleep in peace." Saying this, he blessed Yona, and kissed him, and stole out of the cave into the morning. The sun was singing in the valley. In the gullies the storm-waters flashed, and on the hillsides the rain had awakened the buried seeds of the anemones.

Everything sparkled, and the rain-washed air was utterly transparent, pure, touched with flame. A warm wind blew along the valley. On the clumps of reddish rock beside the gullies there were frail anemones, no more than small scatterings, the buds still unopened, and all these were mysteriously born of the rain and the lightning of the previous night: almost they were gossamer, little shimmering veils of color clinging to the rocks. And so all down the length of the valley there was greenness and hot patches of

color. Green lizards basked on the rocks, their little lungs beating
wildly. A golden-red serpent glided through the fresh grasses.
Birds sang. And walking down the valley he breathed lightly and
easily until he saw that his gown was still damp and clinging to
him, and he removed it and laid it on a rock to dry and bathed in
the white stream flowing down the gully. Afterwards, feeling hungry, he searched for honey. In the wildest and most deserted
places the bees fill hollow trees and the crevices in the rocks with
their waxy combs. He found a hollow pear tree in the shelter of
some rocks and broke off a piece of the brown wax and then
prayed, glorifying the Lord and blessing the pear tree and the
bees who provided the honey. Then, because he had left his staff
behind in the cave, he cut down the branch of a fig tree and set
out along the valley in the hot sunshine.

Towards evening he came in sight of the Ferry-house. Standing
in the shadows on the hillside, he saw the brothers walking in the
fields, their white robes trailing, with sometimes a child walking
gravely by their sides. They were all moving towards the great
white temple set in the cliffside, and the setting sun touched them
with unearthly gold. He thought he could recognize some of them.
Was that not old Abadiah, limping a little, the long white beard
like thistledown, and Moshe too, who could not walk gravely, but
made hurried skipping movements? And it was all behind him.
Never again would he enter their gardens or serve in the dispen-
sary or work in the scriptorium: all past, all done with. The Ferry-
house now was as distant as the temple of Serapis on the cliff
above Ptolemais, as far away as the temple at Beth-shamesh, where
the nest of the Phœnix glowed on the darkest night. All gone, all
past, and yet there were curious gossamer chains which bound
him to the place, so that he watched until the last of the white-
robed figures had disappeared in the temple, and smiled to himself. He heard the trilling of a flute, and soon the voices of the
choristers came welling out of the darkening temple:

> We give praise, O Lord, because Thou hast placed us
> Among the flowing streams in a dry land,
> A spring of water flowing from the rock.
> The trees shall put forth sweetness,
> And they shall send their roots down among the streams,
> And the bud of the branch shall be touched with living water.
> O praise the Lord, who has fashioned the branch.

All the beasts of the field shall feed upon it,
Every winged bird shall alight on it,
This branch endureth for ever:
For thou, O God, has blessed this branch for ever,
Thou hast put a hedge about its fruits,
For the mystery of mighty men of valor and holy spirits,
And the flame of fire turning every way.
O Lord, we praise the flame and the holy branch.
Praised be Thy name for ever.

It was dark when the last note of the thanksgiving psalm died away, and then there was only the murmur of whispered prayers coming across the valley. Leaning on his staff, Yeshua waited until the last light had faded from the sky. And still gazing in the direction of the Ferry-house, he said: "I am the branch, I am the fire which turneth every way, I am the first and the last, I am the root and the offspring of David, the bright, the morning star." And a little later he said: "I am the mystery. I am the one clothed in darkness who hurries through the night. I am the brother of Yona and the son of Meriam. I am the flame which will set the world alight!" And then he walked alone in the darkness along the shores of the Dead Sea.

For more than two years he wandered alone, mostly on the north shore which is barren and treeless, with marshlands stretching up to the strangely-shaped rocks, a wild land, strewn with boulders, and here and there you would come across dead palm trees, brought down by the flooded Jordan, thickly encrusted with salt, gleaming white, dazzling in the sun; and sometimes great masses of palm leaves rose like hills of salt, from a distance appearing like mounds but when you came close to them, you saw every frond of every leaf. But there was little vegetation, only some reeds gleaming out of the leaden-blue water. He lived in caves, in shelters of the cliffs, in the lea of boulders. He was alone with himself, very quiet, in a forbidding land. He had been baptized by fire, and soon he would be baptized by water, and he did not know how it would happen: he knew only that God would give a sign.

Sometimes he wandered into the towns and small villages on the shores of the Dead Sea. They saw him standing at the crossroads, muttering, stretching out his hands in blessing. And no one would have recognized him as the Son of God. His cheeks were hollow, his eyes sunk deep and inflamed, his ankles and wrists

were swollen, his fingers raw, cracked and bleeding. He wore the
remnant of the cloak he had worn when he left the Ferry-house,
with palm-leaf sandals on his scored feet. His hair was matted and
thick with salt, so that sometimes he gave the appearance of an old
man, white-bearded and bent with sorrow, though there was nothing sorrowful in the words of blessing he used when he stood at
the crossroads. Sometimes they placed food in his hands, but fearfully, half afraid of this man whose beard was rimed with salt and
whose eyes were so deep and penetrating. Soon he would wander
away, back to the shores of the Dead Sea, where the great white
sand-storms rose in the howling winds. On these shores the lean
jackals barked, hyenas howled and the eagles sailed high over
the sea.

There came a day when he vanished from the shores of the
Dead Sea: people thought him dead. In some abandoned crevice
in the rocks, along some boulder-strewn shore, they thought his
bones lay. Often they had seen him communing with God on
those lonely stretches below the cliffs and watched him as he stood
at the crossroads. And because he was gone and there was no
sign of him they tried to remember the things he had said, the
words of blessing, but all they could remember was that he spoke
of the flame of fire turning every way.

One day when Meriam was attending the oil press, she looked
up to see a strange gaunt creature standing there in the courtyard.
His cloak was in rags. His bare arms were like bones, his cheeks
were sunken and he seemed to have no eyes, only two terrible
black hollows. His beard, once red, was gray, wiry, ill-kempt and
straggling. Meriam gave a little scream, put her hand to her mouth
and then looked distractedly round the courtyard to see whether
one of the servants was present, but there was no one there. The
gaunt man did not move. He was like an apparition. There was a
terrible solemnity in his gaze. Standing there, he seemed to be
reproving her. It was a hot day, with the sunlight flashing across
the courtyard, which was filled with great wicker-baskets heaped
with olives and flowering plants. Somewhere along the steep
white road outside the house a shepherd boy was playing on a
flute and there came the quick patter of the sheep on the stones.
And then there was silence: the sheep had gone, and there was no
more flute-playing.

Somewhere deep in the folds of her blue gown lay a leather

wallet. Thinking this man was a beggar, she began to search for
the wallet, intending to give him a few coins and send him on his
way. She was terrified. Her hands shook. She was afraid the man
might die, standing there in her courtyard. She wore a blue hood,
and along the hem of the hood, over the forehead, hung little
golden coins, and these gave a little tinkling sound as she searched
hurriedly for the coins.

Suddenly there came from the man a cry like the cry of an animal in pain.

She paused, stopped searching for the wallet and made a step
towards him, and while she was still moving towards him, he said
in a dead, broken voice: "Dost thou not know who I am?"

"Nay," she began, and then she searched his face, for something
in his voice was familiar to her.

He towered above her, terrible in his power, in his weakness, in
the blankness of his reproving gaze. His face was the color of deep
flame, the skin stretched tight over the bones, deep lines of suffering etched into the rounded forehead. The wiry gray hair hung to
his shoulders, with here and there some strands of orange.

"Yeshua!" she moaned, and with her hands outstretched she
tottered towards him, not seeing him, because she was blinded by
her love for him, and when she reached him, she fell in a little
heap at his feet.

Then he lifted her up and together they entered the House of
the Oil Press.

The days passed, the long winter days when the hills of Nazareth are white with snow and the shepherds huddle in the caves,
lighting fires of thorn-branches to keep them warm. On those days
the sound of someone walking in the steep streets came sharp and
clear a mile away, and the sound of the frost-coated camels coming from a long way away could be heard as though they were
already in the town. Then the rains came, and the farmers went
out on the flooded fields to plant the seeds of barley and wheat to
be reaped in the spring.

In those early days of winter there were clear blue skies, and
icy cold winds raged across the Plain of Esdraelon. The walls of
Sepphoris gleamed with frost and ice. As far as Mount Hermon
in the north and Mount Carmel in the west the winter earth
stretched like a white lake under the winter sun.

Yeshua lay on a bed of cushions in the small room he had occupied when a boy. It was in this room that he had recovered from
the mauling by a black panther. A fire of juniper wood burned
there. On the floor beside the bed were pots filled with winter
flowers, and others filled with ointments and medicaments. He
lay on the bed, listening to the rain, which turned into ice when
it reached the courtyard. He lay there very quiet, very still, removed from the world, for hours staring fixedly into space, silent
as in a grave. When a servant entered the room, he was not aware
of her presence, did not turn towards her and showed by no sign
that he was conscious of her attentions. He spoke rarely, and then
only to Meriam. Once she heard him say: "Shall the flame consume the branch?" Another time he said: "The seed is in me." One
afternoon she heard him shouting in Greek some lines from a play,
and a little while later he began to talk about the Queen of the
South. At night, standing outside the door, she heard him intoning
psalms, but they were not the Psalms of David, and indeed he
never spoke of the sacred scrolls. Though he wore clean clothes
and his hair had lost its deathly whiteness and the eyes were not
quite so sunken, he had hardly changed since the day when he
entered unannounced the courtyard of the House of the Oil Press.

For Meriam in those days the most painful agony was his remoteness. He seemed to have gone away from her. For a moment
he had been given to her, but immediately afterwards he was
snatched from her. He had entered some far, remote and terrible
landscape, where he wandered like a lost soul. And he was not
himself: there was so little of him she could recognize. It was
seventeen years since she last saw him. He was fourteen when he
left her, and now he was nearly thirty, a gaunt hollow-cheeked
stranger in her own house, who spoke rarely, demanded nothing,
slept by day, prayed earnestly at night, and sometimes gazed upon
her with a look of fierce dismay, as though he had expected her to
be someone else. Herself, she had changed hardly at all. There was
the same calm moon-face, the same youthfulness, the same grave
and casual demeanor. She brought him rich foods, but he drank
only a little wine and ate only dry figs and some thin slices of dry
bread.

One day towards the end of winter, when she stole into his room
and watched him lying there, she decided she had reached the end
of her strength. She must know more. She could not help him un-

less he told her more. Her heart was being destroyed by her knowledge that there was nothing she could do. He was filling out. All
his sores had healed. Occasionally in those sunken eyes she thought
she had detected a momentary gleam of tenderness. But the horror
remained, the horror of his remoteness. It was as though, living in
the House of the Oil Press, he had brought with him the terror of
the lonely, barren mountains where the spirits of darkness dwell. It
was as though, there, lying on that bed, was a man who had absorbed into himself the coldness of winter nights and the silence of
the heavens.

She knelt by the bed, took his head in her hands and murmured:
"Where art thou?"

It was evening, and a small oil-lamp was burning beside the bed.

"I am in your hands," he whispered, and for the first time there
was a hint of a smile on the gaunt features. "And in the House of
the Oil Press," he added a little later.

"Come closer to me," she whispered, but he shook his head
gently and kept his distance.

Time passed. She could hear the water-clock in the courtyard,
the sudden swinging back of the wheel. His heavily-lidded eyes
were closed. Deep, deep down a mysterious new life was stirring
in him. He groaned once and said hoarsely: "I am waiting for the
blessing of the water."

"The water?" she asked anxiously.

"The water of eternal life."

"And where shalt thou find it?"

"In holiness and the remission of sins," he said, and then he
turned away from her, facing the wall.

Then there was silence again, the long silence of separation, the
knowledge that he was gone from her, that he was traveling in
some barren uplands where none could follow him. She threw
herself upon him and clung to him, and at that very moment she
remembered how they had brought him on a sort of stretcher into
the courtyard on the day when he was mauled. Not knowing
what she was doing, insane with grief, she screamed: "The black
panther!"

At once he turned to her tenderly. Light flooded his eyes. For
the first time since he returned, there was an expression of compassion on his face.

"Nay, it was no black panther," he said. "But wandering and torment and the flames of the living God!"

She thought he was becoming delirious again and clutched him.

"Come to me," she said helplessly.

"How shall I come to thee, who art a woman? I am not come for the sake of any woman or any man, but to bring the tidings of a new covenant."

"Thou art hard."

"And shall be harder. Let me be! Let me worship in silence! Let me not be touched by thee!"

It was terrible how he came close to her and then departed from her. She was beside herself with grief, with the agony of knowing she would never be able to reach out to him. She could think only of her loneliness and her grief, the long empty years she had spent without Yusuf in the House of the Oil Press. She had loved Yusuf, and he had been taken from her. She had loved Yeshua, and he had been taken from her. She said: "Since thy father has gone from me—"

"He has not gone," Yeshua answered quietly. "Knowest thou not he is with our Father in Heaven?"

"Yea, I know that."

"Then weep not, for he is with thee." Then he said: "And I also am with thee."

"Nay, thou art gone from me."

He smiled, lifted her chin and looked into her eyes.

"How am I gone, my dearest mother? I am with thee, surely! See, I kiss thee. Is not a kiss being with thee? And thou art trembling! Why shouldst thou tremble when I am with thee?"

"Because thou hast been so far from me," she answered, and fondled him, drawing her fingers over his face, watching the light as it poured into his eyes.

He sat up among the cushions, no longer strained, smiling at her, and sometimes whispering blessings over her. Seeing some apples on a dish at the foot of the bed, she went to them and brought them to him.

"Thou shouldst eat, my son, and take care of thyself."

"Should I care for myself," he answered, "when my Father in Heaven takes care of me?"

But he bit into the apple, and suddenly remembering Yoachim, he found himself staring into space, lost in memories of Sepphoris:

on the edge of tears. It was many years since he had thought of
Yoachim and the apple, and many more years since he had thought
of Sepphoris burning. The past was dead, like a burnt-out wick.
"Yoachim," he murmured, and then was silent.

"He was my father," Meriam said.

"Yea, truly, and for being thy father he is with our Father in
Heaven."

Meriam bowed her head.

"Thou hast no need for grief," he said sharply. "Have I not told
thee he is with the Father in Heaven?"

She smiled and took his hands, and seeing the strength coming
back to him, she began to tell him about all the things that had
happened in his absence: Anna was married, the sawmills were
sold, the synagogue had been struck by lightning and a new one
was being built. For a long time she spoke about events in Nazareth, and at last she said: "Now I have told thee about Nazareth,
thou must tell me about the places where thou hast been."

He did not answer.

"I asked thee, Yeshua, where thou hast been," she said insistently, dreading this sudden silence.

"I have been beyond all beginning and all ending," he said. "I
have been where there is no beyond."

She looked puzzled.

"Didst thou go to Jerusalem?"

"Nay, not once."

"Then where?"

"To Ptolemais, mother, and then Egypt, and then by the shores
of the Dead Sea."

Meriam was puzzled, surprised and hurt. So he had never been
very far from her! She had thought that he must have traveled at
least as far as Rome to be absent for so long.

"And wast thou among friends?"

"Nay, among strangers," he said, adding quickly: "All save one,
who was not a stranger to me."

"And who was it?"

"Yona."

At the mention of Yona she gave a little cry.

"Didst thou know he was with me?" he asked.

"Nay, I knew not that thou hadst been with him, but I have
heard that thy cousin is wandering abroad. Thou knowest he re-

fused to become Sacrificer? And now they say he is baptizing
sinners in the Jordan and lives in caves. When he was young, I
had not thought he would become a beggar and a hermit. Aye,
and they say he wears the mantle of Elisha and there are some
who whisper he is the Messiah."

These last words were uttered in a low voice, shamefacedly.
She did not, she could not believe the tall and handsome youth
she had met at Bethphage was the Chosen One.

"Shalt thou be baptized by him?" Yeshua asked.

"If it will give thee pleasure," Meriam answered, and once
again there was a long silence.

From that moment Yeshua lost his reserve. While the strength
came back to him, they talked often. They were like children, chattering together. They went about Nazareth together. Yeshua even
had her carried up the hills on a litter, so that she could see the
places where he had herded sheep when he was a child. He took
her to the cave where he had killed the black panther. There, just
outside the cave, she knelt down and kissed the grass, and when
she rose, it seemed that a great weight had been lifted from her. It
was the end of winter and there was no more ice on the hills.

Two weeks later they rode away in search of Yona. Wherever
they went, they heard reports of him. In every town and village
were people who had been blessed or baptized by him. His fame
had spread like wildfire. At first people thought he was mad; then
they said: "Is he not Yona Ben-Zechariah, the Sacrificer?" Some
believed that at one and the same time he was serving in the
Temple and baptizing sinners in the Jordan. They said he had a
hoarse croaking voice and was shaggy like a lion, wearing a shaggy
cloak of camel hair which hardly reached to his knees. He had
many names. He was called "the wild one," "the accursed one,"
"the grasshopper," "the forerunner." They called him "the grasshopper" because he resembled one of those huge gray Arabian
grasshoppers which have immense claw-like legs. And everyone
spoke of his great matted beard which reached to his chest and his
fierce burning eyes.

Yeshua and Meriam traveled in litters with silken curtains.
Yeshua had wanted to travel on a white ass, but Meriam begged
him to travel in comfort for the sake of his health. To humor her,
he gave way to her.

It was ten days before they set eyes on Yona. A shepherd told them he was to be found at Bethabara, but when they reached the place, they heard he was in Ainon by Selim, where the Jordan, weary of its long wandering progress, widens out between oleanders and tamarisk hedges into a great lake clear as a mirror. The river was in flood, and the roaring of the yellow, turbulent waters could be heard far off in the hills.

The sun was shining in a clear sky, and the blue dome of the heavens was filled with the scribbling of millions of wildfowl. A faint bluish haze lay over the river: all the fields were aglow with scarlet anemones, yellow marigolds and thistles with gorgeous purple blossoms. Here and there were small lakes where the river had overflowed its banks, and along the whole length of the river were clumps of willows and wild oaks. In the distance, perched on high basalt cliffs, lay the fortress of Machaerus, where Herod Antipas now held his court. Beyond the fortress, amid the lilac-colored mountains of Moab, the rugged summit of Mount Nebo shone clear against the sky, streamers of light dancing on the horns of the mountain where Moses had died in mystery, looking out upon the Promised Land.

It was halfway through the morning, and still the blue mist swirled over the grasses. The air was full of liquid light and the sun fell strong on the silken curtains of the two litters as they breasted the hills. Down below, people were gathering in haste from all directions in a grove of willows. Very faintly they could hear the voice of Yona summoning them to repentance.

Yeshua lay in the litter with his eyes closed. As they came closer to the willow grove, the murmur of the crowd rose like the buzzing of bees. Above this murmur came the solemn, powerful voice of Yona—a voice like a trumpet-blast, piercing-sweet, but yet with a terrible weight and force. And just as Yona in his youth simultaneously resembled a savage and a young nobleman, so his voice resembled in some curious way both the thin, clear notes of a flute and a lion's roar. He stood on a heap of stones in the middle of the willow grove, while not far from him some woodmen were beginning to cut down a lightning-blasted willow.

"Repent! Repent!" Yona was saying, his eyes flashing over the heads of the small multitude gathered round him. "Woe unto you, ye rich men! Woe unto you, ye that are surfeited, for ye shall learn what it is to hunger! Woe unto you, ye that are laughing today, for ye shall learn weeping and mourning on the morrow. The King is knocking at the gates; He shall demand that your cities be burned to the ground! He shall show you no mercy."

All round him people were clamoring to be baptized. They adored him and feared him and wished an end to his solemn denunciations.

"How shall we be saved unless we are baptized?" they cried. "Come down from thy little heap of stones and baptize us!"

He paid no attention to them. He seemed unaware of their interruptions.

"O generation of vipers, who hath warned you to flee from the wrath to come? Bring forth therefore fruits worthy of repentance, and begin not to say within yourselves, 'We have Abraham for our father,' for I say unto you that God is able of these stones to raise up children unto Abraham!" And then he paused, and pointed in the direction of the woodmen who were cutting down the blasted willow. "Woe unto you, for now is the ax laid unto the root of every tree, and every tree which shall not bring forth good fruit will be hewn down and cast into the fire!"

By this time Yeshua and Meriam had left the litters and were standing on the edge of the crowd.

The people were all shouting: "Baptize us! Lead us into the waters of life! What must we do that we shall be saved from the wrath to come?"

"You know what to do!" Yona shot back at them. "Have ye not heard it a thousand times? Give to the poor! If you have two coats, give to the man who has none! He that hath meat, let him do likewise! Walk quietly and chastely in the pathways of the Lord! Ah, but ye do none of these things! Hypocrites, vipers! Ye pretend to worship the Lord, and shall not God see the pretense?"

And then he began to chant in a voice like thunder:

> *I am the voice of one crying in the wilderness,*
> *Make ye ready the way of the Lord,*
> *Make His paths straight.*
> *Every valley shall be filled,*
> *And every mountain and hill shall be brought low,*
> *And the crooked shall be made straight,*
> *And the rough ways smooth,*
> *And all flesh shall see the salvation of God.*

Women were weeping. Some were beating their breasts and others were reaching out to touch his cloak of camel hair. They wanted to be baptized; they did not want to listen to this chanting. Was not Yona a holy man? Would not his touch heal their wounds? He stood on his little hill of stones uttering threats and imprecations, his wild eyes darting, searching them out, always accusing them.

"We have committed no crimes that you accuse us of," someone sang out. "Lead us to baptism! Lead us to the living waters! They say you have only to touch us."

He only answered: "Repent ye! Repent ye! The Kingdom of Heaven is at hand!" or else he chanted:

> *I shall baptize you with water for repentance,*
> *But He who cometh after me is mightier,*
> *The laces of whose sandals I am not worthy to unloose.*
> *He shall baptize you with the Holy Spirit and with Fire.*
> *His winnowing fan is in His hand.*
> *He will thoroughly clean out His threshing-floor.*
> *His wheat He will gather into the garner,*
> *But the chaff He will burn with the unquenchable Fire.*

There was a path from the willow-grove to the river bank, and about midday a hush fell on the gathering, for it was seen that Yona had bowed his head in prayer. The wind played with the long strings of hair that fell to his shoulders. He was in a trance, utterly unaware of those around him, and so they waited, in a sort of dumb patience, which was partly indifference, for while he communed with his God he was beyond their reach. If only he would open his eyes and lead them to the waters of baptism! If only he would hurry! Had he not promised there would be a day of endless lightning followed by a night of earthquakes? The Kingdom of Heaven was at their very doors! The Messiah, the Chosen One, the Son of God, was He not already stalking the land like a wild beast? Crowned with the crown of David, holding the three-bladed sword of righteousness, surely the Messiah had come to punish sinners! So Yona had painted Him, a ferocious King, robed in golden robes, helmeted with glory, and almost they could see him, that giant who would put Goliath to shame, breasting the hills overlooking the Jordan, striding with ten-league boots across the shivering earth. And none of them would have recognized that ferocious King in the quiet man, whose red beard was streaked with gray, standing on the edge of the crowd. If they had seen him, this man in the white seamless *sudar*, they would have said he was some rich merchant's son, or perhaps a young lawyer, or even a tax-gatherer, for everyone knew the tax-gatherers wore good clothes and carried themselves with an air of quiet ease.

They began to shout again: "Baptize us! Baptize us!"

Yona's eyes opened wide. Standing there on that little heap of stones, he seemed at that moment to tower above them: the mere opening of his eyes was a command for silence. And when he spoke, it was the voice of a man who speaks after prayer, a voice so low and muted it seemed to come from somewhere below, from some deep pit in the earth, not from the throat of a man.

"I told you yesterday," he said, "when we were at Bethabara beyond Jordan that One shall come after me who came before me! He shall come in glory who came in glory before the beginning of the world! He shall be called the Lamb of God, and to Him all the angels shall bow the knee!" And then more softly he said: "*Hosanna b'harom!* Hosanna to the highest! Blessed is He, who is born of the Fire!*"

Suddenly Yona began to groan in a loud voice and sweat ran down his face. It was the sign that the hour of baptism had come, and there was a sudden rush towards the river. Everyone was shouting: "He is coming now! Prepare yourselves for baptism!" They were all gathered by the river bank, shouting and embracing one another, for had not Yona come to baptize them for remission of sins? Had he not promised they would be free of guilt and mortal error once he had taken them in his arms and suffered them to drown in the water, and then those same arms would lift them out of drowning into a world reborn?

"He is coming! The prophet is coming!" they cried, for they saw shadows moving among the willows.

In the quietness of the willow grove no leaf, no blade of grass stirred: only the dappled sun seemed to move gently on the little heap of stones.

Yona sighed, his head bent on his chest. When he looked up, Yeshua was standing before him.

"Dost thou not know me?" Yeshua asked.

"Nay, I know thee not," Yona answered, a smile hovering on the corners of his lips. And then a little later: "Art thou the same who abandoned me in the cave?"

"Yea, the same," Yeshua answered, and he took Yona's hands in his own. "And shalt thou baptize me now, as thou hast baptized so many against my coming?"

Yona groaned and looked away, not daring to speak. The silence was deepening. Far away he could hear the roaring of the flooded river and the cries of the people demanding baptism. He bent his head and said sorrowfully: "I have need to be baptized of thee? Why comest thou to me?"

"For the sake of the glory," Yeshua answered. "Suffer it to be now, that the ripeness may be made known."

And while Meriam remained among the willows, Yona and Yeshua walked along the river bank away from the people waiting on the shore. Soon the crowd began to run after them, shouting: "Our prophet is taking a stranger to be baptized in the river! Has he not promised that we shall be first to enter the Kingdom of Heaven? Then why does he go from us?"

Hand in hand, Yona and Yeshua walked past the tamarisks and the pear tree till they came to the reeds, and then slipped down into the roaring water. The reeds parted. They moved effortlessly and lightly into the river, all yellow now, flashing in the sun. Neither was aware of the crowd threatening them from the bank. People were rushing up to their knees in the water and shouting: "Come back! Do we deserve to be forgotten? Surely thou rememberest what thou hast promised us!"

So they walked into the cool waters, and when they were twenty paces from the shore, Yona threw his arms wide apart and turned his face to the heavens and said: "Almighty God, Father of Fathers, make me worthy of this sacrifice. For generations Thou hast made my forebears Sacrificers. Thou gavest them the strength to fashion holocausts according to Thy law. But now are all things changed according to Thy will. Thy temple has become a flowing river, and Thy knife of steel is become a knife of water. Come down to me, O God, that with Thy help I may perform this sacrifice!"

Then he smiled and took Yeshua in his arms and rocked him as he would a child, before letting him sink into the river. Yeshua sank like a stone. He fell into the coolness of the living waters, where no fire could penetrate except the fire of God, into the

silence and holiness of the Jordan, deep, deep down, beyond the
reach of man, into a place of utter coolness, anointed by the fountains of the deep as once before, in a remote cave on the shores
of the Dead Sea, he had been anointed with the living flames, the
glory and the heavenly fire of God. And beyond this he could not
go. Beyond this lay vacuity and nothingness and the march of
error across the face of the earth. But in these swirling waters
there was freshness and peace, and gentleness, and a strange
sweetness. He was no more than a seed or a dead leaf caught up in
the raging flood; he was like some lost and abandoned thing, without flesh or breath, forever descending into the pure waters which
would germinate the seed or bring life to the dead leaf. Here there
were no flames of glory to light the way: only darkness: but in this
darkness he was aware as never before of the presence of God.

Yona was in terror. It seemed that Yeshua had vanished forever
under the water, would never rise again.

"Come to me!" he shouted hoarsely. "Come from the waters of
baptism! Come out from thy grave!"

In the shuddering silence, as the face of Yeshua appeared on the
waters, the livid lightning flames flashed in the heavens, scarlet
and purple and blue, thickening above the place where Yona
stood, arms uplifted to the heavens. There was a clap of thunder.
The wind roared. A flame of perfect whiteness touched the water.
Flames hurled themselves from one end of the sky to the other,
abandoned, joyful, leaping up and then bending down to touch
the earth, and all the time the thunder pealed. The crowd on the
shore staggered and reeled in the ghostly incandescence of
the flames, which turned the willow groves and tamarisks along the
shore into a transparent whiteness. A scream rose from the crowd.
Petrified with fear, they huddled together, cowered, bent their
heads and threw their hands over their eyes. The wind whistled
in the willow groves. The huge roar of the rushing river was
drowned by the tumult of the heavens. All things were flowing:
not only the river, but all the world gave the appearance of streaming away, hurtling past, lit by the savage flames which flung themselves now more and more upon the place where Yona stood with
arms uplifted to the roaring heavens. Blinded, the people on the
shore choked back their sobs and shouted: "The Messiah has
come! Yona is the Messiah! Pardon our sins, and lead us into the
paths of righteousness!"

Yona was coming out of the water, leading Yeshua by the hand and saying: "Behold the Lamb of God which taketh away the sins of the world! Rejoice in Him! Unto us this grace is given! The Lord walks in our midst! Rejoice in the Lamb! Rejoice! Rejoice!"

When they came to the shore, the sun was shining in a clear sky and there was no more thunder.

The Beginning

When it was evening and the first stars were coming out, Yeshua made his way along the river bank until he found a place where he could rest and meditate. It was one of those clear spring evenings when the fresh wind comes from the desert, a wind bearing with it the scent of immense spaces, pure as the purest water. A few clouds were swimming across the heavens, but they did nothing to fill the emptiness of space. Now there was only space and the crackling of the tamarisks and the papyrus leaves growing out of the rushing waters—only the vastness of the coming night and the splendor of the coming moon and the river whirling at his feet.

So he rested there, lying on the grasses by the river's edge, and sometimes he would take a fallen leaf in his hands and set it adrift on the river, watching it until it vanished in the darkness, himself no more than a leaf flung into the dark waters of baptism, at the mercy of every current. It pleased him that he had given himself over wholly into God's hands, and that he possessed no will of his own. There was no more Yeshua, no longer would he wander across so many unavailing deserts. No more would the shepherd tend his flocks of sheep; no more would he haunt his mother's house, or take refuge in caves, or in the hospitable houses of the Essenes; no more would he wrestle with the black panthers. At long last, after many weary years, knowing himself to be the descendant of kings, he had found his royal place, and nothing had ever happened as he expected it to happen. From fire and water and the voice of thunder he had received his kingship; and no one else, not even Elijah, had received his badge of authority in this manner.

For a long time he remained by the bank, wrapped in a thin cloak, gazing at the waters and sometimes gazing up at the stars which he knew by their Greek names—the Dragon, the Belt of Hercules, the Great Serpent. And as he watched the river flowing tumultuously towards the Dead Sea, all the ages seemed to pass before him. There was no past, no present, no future. There was only the eternal stream of God, lit by the fiery starlight, following the unalterable course laid down at the beginning of creation; and as he lay there, sometimes idly waving a dead branch in the waters, he was aware of a strange lucidity, a brightness in the mind he had never possessed before. How bright everything was! The water rushing over the dead branch and breaking against the dead leaves seemed to be alive with a thousand lights, and the river itself was a living thing, and the stars were brighter than he had ever seen them before; and from all the spaces of the heavens voices were rushing towards him, so many that they were past counting, and yet all were clear and he heard each one and they were all rejoicing, all singing *Hosanna b'harom!* The angels sang, but the reeds were also singing, and he could not tell one from the other, for in the silence of night all nature was rejoicing.

In all this there was nothing in the least strange, nothing he had not expected. There was the mark of the *aleph* and the *tav* on him, and he had known since childhood that he was the chosen one, but how he would be chosen and what would be the manner of his ministry on earth, all this was unknown to him. And even now he did not know what was expected of him, only that he had become the creature of God to lead men into glory, but whether that glory was to be found in heaven or on earth, this too was unknown to him. But he knew that everything would begin afresh, and this night was unlike any other night, for it was the beginning of the new creation.

In the brightness of the heavens the stars were like flaming meteors, and the silver reeds on the river's edge shone with the brightness of stars. Everything glowed with the light of baptism; in all things the element of water was uppermost. And seeing his reflection in water by starlight, Yeshua reflected how he himself had become like water, forever flowing through creation, untouchable, intangible, assuming the shape of the world, yielding and unyielding, soft and hard, bright as water in sunlight and dark as the water in caves, silent as a mountain pool, thunderous as water falling over rocks; for the Jordan flowed through him.

Not from Jerusalem but from Jordan came the sign. Now all things were made fresh as the cool river flowing in the starlight.

So he mused, while the heavens wheeled round him and the river rushed past him—a river that was more like a waterfall or a series of cascades than any ordinary river, tumultuous and free, bearing with it the snows of Mount Hermon and the waters of Gennesareth, a river which seemed to belong more to heaven than to earth, more to starlight than the steady light of day, more to the wandering clouds than to the reed-bordered banks. There was no river in the world like this river, and he knew that wherever he wandered, he would never be far from it. Even when he wandered in the desert, the coolness of the river would comfort him. Never again would he be able to free himself from the river; nor would he ever want to.

It did not seem strange to him that he belonged to the river, and that it was touched with divinity. What seemed strange, after so many torments, was the sense of illimitable peace and blessedness which came to him from the river, and this was all the more strange because the river itself was not in the least peaceful, but raged unceasingly, throwing up great waves and carrying along

its surface many dead branches and whole trees plucked from its
banks. There were whirlpools in the middle of the river. If you
threw a branch into the river, it might remain for a few moments
where it fell, turning rapidly, until at last it was drawn beneath
the surface, to reappear perhaps a hundred yards away. All kinds
of mysterious properties were ascribed to the river. It cured sickness; it changed color before every change of the weather; and
people said that no one had ever drowned in it. But none of these
things was as mysterious as the property it possessed after Yona
the Sacrificer led men down into the torrents and baptized them.

And sometimes as he gazed at the river he dipped his hand into
the water and watched the spray curling round his fingers, trickling upwards, climbing along his hand, reaching as far as his wrist;
and it pleased him that the water should fling itself upward so
gaily and impudently. He was still playing with the water when
the moon came up, blinding him so that he had to shade his eyes.
The river, which had been silvery gray, became molten silver, and
all the tamarisks were silver, and all the earth was silver, hot and
feverish in the growing moonlight. The moon rose slowly. Everything was hushed. The tamarisks no longer made their clamoring
sound; the cicadas were silent; even the river seemed to be flowing noiselessly. Blue and golden haloes shimmered around the
moon which filled all the reaches of the heavens with its dazzling
radiance.

All through the night he had been aware of the presence of God,
but in the raging moonlight God appeared to be closer than ever.

"All the heavens and all the earth are penetrated with thy
mercy," he murmured. "Thou knowest I am thy Son. Therefore
let me be a sacrifice for thy sake! Let me be like the shepherd
who sacrifices his life for his sheep, and let me come soon into my
kingdom!"

He knew he had only to wait and God would speak to him out
of the radiance of the heavens.

He slept, but even in sleep he was aware of the sound of the
river rushing beneath him and the brightness of the night sky,
and he was aware of God's presence. He slept dreamlessly until
shortly before dawn, and then he was shaken by nightmares, one
nightmare following quickly upon another. They were the most
terrible nightmares he had ever known. Rivers of blood, thick as
jelly, were pouring over the Altar of Sacrifice, and the reek of it

came to his nostrils. He saw the white sheep without blemish skipping up the marble steps, and suddenly a curved knife was drawn across their throats, touching the bone. There passed in front of him an endless procession of faces—the sick, the maimed and the blind, crying out to be cured, making strange jerking movements with their arms. Long ago in his childhood he had seen crucifixes standing above Nazareth, and now he saw them again; and the bodies of the crucified were black and green, and falling apart, and their mouths were open as they prayed for deliverance. He saw the world bathed in tears: the endless suffering, the agony and the torment. He saw himself being carried to his tomb while the blood dripped from his wounds. There was no end to the torture inflicted by men on men. He saw three trees standing on a hill, and a helmet flashed in the sun, and there were five soldiers throwing dice into the helmet. He saw human eyes being burned out, and mouths that opened to reveal running sores; and when he could bear it no longer he cried out in the midst of the nightmare against the horrors he had seen, and still the nightmare went on.

When he awoke at last, he was shuddering and the sweat of fear rolled down his cheeks. Then he saw that the dawn was coming up, and the river was the same deep blue as the sky, and the earth lay peaceful under the sun.

"I shall bring peace to men," he said, "for all this warfare must cease! I shall make men whole! I shall cure the lame, the maimed and the blind! I shall show men the paths of righteousness and peace, and for all this I offer myself as a sacrifice!"

For a little while longer he stayed where he had rested during the night, and when the sun rose higher he made his way along the river bank to Galilee.